PRAISE FOR THE NOVELS OF ~~DONNA FLETCHER~~

Magical Memories

"A passionate tale . . . [Fletcher] is one of those gifted writers who makes the unbelievable believable."
—*Rendezvous*

"Ms. Fletcher places her fans under a magical spell of enjoyment." —Harriet Klausner

"A heartwarming story." —*The Romance Reader*

"Ms. Fletcher's world . . . is a fascinating and enriching place to visit." —*Romantic Times*

"Enchanting! Ms. Fletcher's many fans will be pleased with this tale." —*Old Book Barn Gazette*

The Irish Devil

"A richly textured medieval romance."
—*Historical Romance Reviews* (four stars)

"This . . . story will endear itself to readers longing for a richly textured medieval romance." —*Romantic Times*

"[Ms. Fletcher's] talents are unfathomable and I expect nothing but the best from her." —*Rendezvous*

"A fresh medieval romance . . . Charming."
—Harriet Klausner

Magical Moments

"A refreshing romance with classic elements, sure to cast a spell on a wide and appreciative audience."

—*The Romance Reader*

Wedding Spell

"Light, bright, and entertaining . . . I flew through the pages."

—*Rendezvous*

The Buccaneer

"The witty characterizations, unique situations and swash-buckling action combine to make a terrific fast-paced romance that is thrilling to the very last word. This sensuous romance is a delight—right down to the very last sigh."

—*Affaire de Coeur*

"*The Buccaneer* is a grand adventure and a . . . romp on the high seas. Fast-paced and well-written, it sizzles!"

—*The Paperback Forum*

Whispers on the Wind

"[This] ghostly romance is a treat. Lively, passionate . . . a fine adventure."

—*Affaire de Coeur*

"An exquisite mixture of suspense, fantasy, and blazing passion. The plot is fresh and the characters are remarkable. This is a magnificent book that is worth another read."

—*Rendezvous*

ISLE
OF LIES

DONNA FLETCHER

J
JOVE BOOKS, NEW YORK

ISLE OF LIES

A Jove Book / published by arrangement with
the author

PRINTING HISTORY
Jove edition / March 2002

Visit our website at
www.penguinputnam.com

ISBN: 0-515-13263-2

A JOVE BOOK®
Jove Books are published by The Berkley Publishing Group,
a division of Penguin Putnam Inc.,
375 Hudson Street, New York, New York 10014.
JOVE and the "J" design
are trademarks belonging to Penguin Putnam Inc.

PRINTED IN THE UNITED STATES OF AMERICA

10 9 8 7 6 5 4 3 2 1

*This book is dedicated to my two best friends,
Helen Cavanagh and Marie Tracy.*

*They have been there for me through the laughter
and the tears. They are my soul sisters and
I am forever grateful for them.*

*This one is for you, Helen and Marie—and remember,
"We'll always have Ireland!"*

❧ one

SCOTLAND 1513

The incessant pounding shattered the peacefulness of the quiet night. A candle flickered in a lone window of the convent and soon a succession of flickering lights followed in the other windows. Hushed whispers echoed through the stone halls, doors creaked open, and bare feet were heard padding along the stone floor.

The endless pounding continued.

Most of the nuns, twenty in all, who resided at the convent knew full well to remain abed; if needed they would be summoned. Mother Superior would see to the impatient arrival, and several laughing smiles were followed by prayers for the unfortunate person. Mother Superior did not take kindly to the convent being disturbed in the dead of night; therefore, candles continued to burn and ears remained alert.

The thick wooden door sounded about to splinter when Mother Superior, fully attired and fully annoyed by this untimely intrusion, took anxious steps along with Sisters Elizabeth and Anne across the courtyard.

The autumn night held more than a mere chill. The wind swirled in gusts around them, sweeping up the leaves on the ground and sending them twirling through the darkness. The playful wind and the unexpected drop in temperature caused a shiver to race through the three women, who grasped their white shawls tightly around them in hopes of warding off the cold that seeped into their bones as they hurried to bring a halt to the persistent pounding.

The door trembled against the weight of the mighty fist that refused to cease its steady and annoying rhythm. The unidentified person presumably was intent on entering the convent by any means, and with the convent grounds being fortified by a surrounding six-foot stone wall, the door— along with Mother Superior's approval—was the only way to gain admittance.

"Cease, or I will refuse you entrance," Mother Superior shouted. Her strong deep voice carried her demand with force and timbre and the pounding abruptly stopped and blessed silence once again reigned.

Pleased with the obedient response Mother Superior continued. "Who bids entrance to the convent at such a rude hour?"

The reply was immediate and strongly male. "I bring an urgent message for Moira Maclean from her father, Angus Maclean."

Mother Superior grew alarmed. Moira Maclean had been placed in the convent when she was but ten and two with direct orders she was to take no vows but to wait on her father's word. Since that time, ten and seven years ago, the only message from her father was the yearly stipend he paid the convent for her care. After all these years of neglect and disinterest, why had he sent an urgent message in the middle of the night?

With concern for Moira, and having no other choice, Mother Superior reluctantly signaled Sister Anne to open the door. No sooner than the bolt was released, did the door burst open, and it was not only a sole messenger who entered but what appeared to be a whole clan. The courtyard was soon filled with men who seemed to have come straight from a battlefield.

Their faces and clothes bore the signs of a hard-fought battle and one that looked to have been less than victorious. Streaks of blood covered flesh and clothing, and dirt clung to them as tenaciously as the sweat-drenched garments. Though the clansmen looked too weary to remain afoot, they all stood with pride and dignity and respectfully bowed their heads to Mother Superior as they passed by her.

Their manners won her respect.

The man who first stepped through the door differed from many of the men in height and form. While the dark night, heavy smudges of dirt, and streaks of dried blood masked his features, there was no denying his unique size. Most of the men were average in height and weight, possessing stocky, solid forms. Not so the man who spoke for the group. He towered over them by at least two heads. He was lean in build yet solid in muscle. At first glance one might mistake his slim form, but a keen eye would catch the hard definition of muscle in his arms and the veins that bulged with his life's blood. He was a force to be taken seriously and one better yet to avoid.

"I must speak to Moira Maclean."

Mother Superior caught the wide-eyed looks of Sisters Elizabeth and Anne and was not surprised by them. The strange man's voice belied his ragged appearance. He spoke in a fine articulate tongue, but it was the soothing lilt of charm in which his words were delivered that caught their attention. It coerced, cajoled, and captured.

Mother Superior was well aware of the consequences of such a charmed tongue on innocent women. She silently prayed he did not possess a face to match or at least that his face remained dirt ridden and he smelly while at the convent. She wanted none of her innocent, naive nuns tempted by this devil's charm.

"This message is so important that you disturb our sleep?" Mother Superior demanded. She crossed her arms, fixed her most stern expression on him, and stood straight, and still she had to tilt her head back to look him in the eye. And she was no small size herself. She stood a good head over the average woman.

His manner was polite, as was his apology. "Please forgive this untimely and unavoidable intrusion. Moira's father sent me along with fellow clansmen for her protection. I must speak with her privately."

Mother Superior wagged a finger in his startled face. "I will not permit you to speak with Moira alone. 'Tis not fitting nor proper."

The man acknowledged her remark with a respectful nod. "Forgive my ill manners. The message I have for her is urgent and of the utmost importance. I was told to repeat Angus Maclean's *dying* words only to his daughter."

Sisters Elizabeth and Anne gasped and Mother Superior grew alarmed. "Dying? Why did you not say this immediately?" She gave him no chance to respond. "Come, I will summon Moira to my quarters and I will remain in attendance, but do not worry—I will repeat none of what I hear, on that you have my solemn word."

The man gave a brief nod, whispered quietly to the man directly at his side, and walked over to stand beside Mother Superior.

"Sister Elizabeth, wake the other sisters and see to providing these men with food and drink," Mother Superior instructed firmly. She then turned to Sister Anne. "Go wake Moira. Tell her to hurry to my quarters."

Both sisters nodded and immediately did her bidding.

"My deepest appreciation for your generosity," the man said.

"It is not generosity, it is the right thing to do," Mother

Superior stated and waved a hand for him to follow, and he did.

"Moira, wake up, wake up." Sister Anne nudged the soundly sleeping woman several times before receiving a response.

"Go away," Moira snapped irritably. "The sun has yet to rise."

Sister Anne reluctantly continued to nudge her. All at the convent knew it was not wise to wake Moira. Unless allowed to wake on her own, which was always with the first light of dawn, she was irritable and snappish, but Mother Superior had specifically instructed her to do so and it was an emergency.

"An urgent message from your father has arrived."

Moira shot out of bed, her wide brown eyes rounder than usual if that were possible. The nuns all gossiped about how Moira's quick wit and sharp intelligence came from the fact that her eyes were so large and round that they enabled her to see everything and therefore know everything. The truth behind her well-honed intelligence was a secret only she and Mother Superior shared.

"What of this message?" Moira asked, pushing her long straight dark hair out of her face and rubbing the last remnants of sleep from her eyes.

"A man awaits your presence in Mother Superior's quarters to deliver it to you. You must hurry." Sister Anne reached for the familiar white wool shawl that all the nuns wore and that lay on the back of the single chair in the small room. Though Moira had never taken the vows, she wore attire similar to the nuns' garments and lived as they did, sleeping in a cell-like room that contained a single bed, a chest, a chair and small table.

Moira wrapped the wool garment around her shoulders, the heavy chill of the autumn night already beginning to seep through her plain white wool sleeping gown. The hem barely reached above her ankles, the sleeves fell to her wrists, and a white ribbon drew the garment together at her neck. Her feet remained bare and grew chilled, sending further shivers through her body as she hurried along the stone corridor to Mother Superior's quarters.

Her heart beat a frantic rhythm in her chest. Why after all these years would her father send a message to her and in the middle of the night? It did not bode well. It couldn't.

When her father sent her here to the convent at age ten and two she was angry and lonely. Lonely for a father who ignored her or raised an angry voice to her, not to mention a hand on occasion. She missed her brother Boyd, who was four years younger than herself. They had spent much time together riding and fishing and getting into all sorts of trouble. Those were happy times. Then her mother died giving birth to her youngest brother, Aidan, and life changed. Her father grew solemn and argumentative and barely spoke to her. Five years later he announced his decision to send her to the convent near Loch Lomond, where she was ordered to live and learn how to become a proper wife. When he arranged a beneficial marriage for her he would send word. But no word ever came; the only acknowledgment of her existence was the annual stipend he sent to the convent for seeing to her care. As the years passed she assumed that her father was too ashamed of her to offer her in marriage to anyone. She was aware she had not inherited her mother's beauty. She was plain, with large eyes and thin lips and a body that was better concealed by nun's garments.

And now, ten and seven years later, it was too late for any such marriage proposal. She was twenty and nine, far past marriageable age and more importantly far past childbearing age. No one would want her and she was much too accustomed to her independence to want a husband. So what did her father want from her?

Sister Anne left her at Mother Superior's door after gently knocking. When the strong familiar voice bid her entrance her legs grew weak, her stomach churned, and her heart took flight, but with a deceptive calm and confidence she entered the room.

Her eyes immediately sought Mother Superior, ignoring the man who stood by the window. This tall, dignified woman, who showed barely a trace of wrinkles for all her sixty and two years, was like a mother to her. She had never forgotten how the woman had helped her adjust to her arrival at the convent those many years ago or how she had held her in her arms that first night when she had cried for a father who did not want her. And she was here yet again to help her through another ordeal. Only this time Moira had her own courage and strength to rely on, but she still felt safer with Mother Superior close by.

"A message has been received from your father," Mother Superior said, wasting no time, and turned to look at the man standing in the shadows of the room.

Moira turned her full attention on him as he stepped forward. His battle-worn appearance would have startled, even frightened, most women, but Moira was not interested in the man, only the message from her father.

"Moira Maclean?" he asked as if doubting her claim to the name.

"Aye, that is me," she said and waited, her wide, intent glare steady on him.

He gave a simple nod accepting her claim and proceeded to deliver the much awaited message. "Your father has sent me for you. A battle has broken out between several clans."

Moira shook her head and frowned. Word had been received that since the death of King James IV at Flodden six weeks ago the Highlands had once again turned chaotic. What now would become of a land where men seemed to think of nothing other than war and destruction? And why would her father worry about her now, when surely his mind was on saving his vast holdings?

The man continued. "Your father's message is simple

and he begs you to heed it and obey him without question. On his deathbed—"

Moira gasped. "My father is dead."

His answer was to step forward, take her cold, trembling hand, and place something in it. When she looked down and saw the object that lay in her palm she knew the truth of his words. A single tear trickled down her cheek as she looked upon the gold brooch that had been in the Maclean family for over two hundred years. She had listened over and over when she was just a little girl to the tale of how the gold brooch had been crafted by a Viking for laird William of the clan Maclean and had been passed down to every eldest son ever since. Angus Maclean boasted of how not even in death would an enemy be able to pry the brooch from his dying hands, for it would pass on to his eldest son, Boyd.

"My brother Boyd?" she asked, her lips trembling.

His silence confirmed her suspicions.

"I have little time," the man said anxiously. "Your father's edict was for you to marry immediately, the marriage protecting all the Maclean holdings."

"Aidan?" Moira asked hopefully, not believing her whole family was lost to her.

"Your father would not issue this dictate if he thought there was another way."

The man's voice soothed even in this troubled time and he chose his words carefully so as not to hurt her. He never once spoke of her father's or brothers' deaths but in a kind way made her understand no Maclean but her remained to save her father's lands.

"What clan wars with the Macleans?"

The man appeared reluctant to answer, perhaps wishing to spare her even more anguish and pain, but she insisted. "I must know. Who brings this tragedy to my family?"

This time he spoke without hesitation. "The clan Cameron of Glencoe."

Moira was startled. "But the Macleans rule on the Isles

of Mull and Jura, my father making his home on Mull. Both are a distance away. What is it they want from us?"

He shook his head at her questions and attempted to offer a hasty explanation. "King James's death brought turmoil to the Highlands. With no ruling hand to keep control of the clans, chaos reigns. The new king is but two years old and there is talk that John, duke of Albany, will act as governor until James V is of age to take the throne. Until that time no one knows for sure the future of Scotland, and the Highland clans are taking full advantage of it."

"Fools," she whispered and, surprisingly, received a smile from the stranger.

"It would be better for them to band together, for in numbers there is strength, but the Highlanders are a stubborn lot and they will have their way no matter the consequences. Your father wishes to protect what is his and with you his only heir, marriage is the only solution."

"But will it stop the bloodshed?"

"Aye, lass, that I can promise you it will," he said confidently. "The union will guarantee a strong enough force to bring the fighting to an end."

Uncertain if her father's decision was wise or born out of desperation, she asked the one question that troubled her the most. "Who is it my father wishes me to wed?"

The man took another step toward her and softly answered, "Me."

Startled, Moira simply stared at the strange man who claimed to be the man her father wished her to wed. His face was much too dirt ridden to determine his features. His long dark brown hair was matted with sweat and blood, as were his garments, and he smelled none too appealing. Her own height reached only to below his chin and he looked to be in fine physical shape. He did have nice green eyes, or were they blue? The shade was hard to confirm by candlelight. But then did his features or form really matter? Her father ordered her to marry him to save the Maclean lands. What choice did she have? And why was she apprehensive about the message?

"Did my father speak of my age to you?"

He nodded. "Twenty and nine."

"And your age?"

He offered it without delay. "Twenty and five."

"My age does not offend you?"

He spoke firmly though with a charm that captured her attention. "This marriage will save lives and bring peace."

Again he answered without answering and the thought troubled her. Her own doubts and wisdom warned that she proceed with caution. "When does my father request this marriage take place?"

"Now."

Mother Superior gasped right along with Moira.

"You cannot be serious," Moira said with a shake of her head.

"Aye, that I am." And with those words said he took another step toward her, bringing him to stand directly in front of her. "Listen carefully for I have wasted precious time in delivering this troubling and startling news. The enemy is on my trail. I am certain they will arrive by first light. By then we must be married—" he paused and gently delivered even more disturbing news. "—and the marriage consummated. I can take no chance of our hasty marriage being claimed null for lack of consummation. We must speak our vows and seal them the way the church dictates and we have little time to assure that it is accomplished before dawn."

"This is much too sudden," Moira protested, stepping away from him and his shocking suggestion.

He pursued her, remaining close by her side. "I wish there was a different way to settle this matter. I wish there was time for us to come to know one another. But there is no time. You must do as I say. You must trust me."

"I know you not," she said softly. "How do I put my

trust in a stranger? How do I know what you tell me is true?"

He reached for her fisted hand that held her father's brooch and firmly wrapped his hand around hers. "I would never hurt you, Moira Maclean. I do what must be done. What is best for all. Of that you have my solemn word."

Her father's brooch dug into her palm from the strength of his clasped hand around hers. She felt he spoke the truth but yet again not a clear truth. What was she to do?

He seemed to make the decision for her. "Mother Superior, if you would please send word to the priest we brought along with us that we need him, we will begin."

"I am not dressed," Moira said anxiously.

"There is no time," he said and turned to Mother Superior. "Please, we must not waste another moment."

Mother Superior looked at Moira. "It is your father's dying wish; you must obey."

With a shred of reluctance she nodded her consent. She would be a good daughter and obey her father. He had told her to wait on his word and now he had sent it and she would do her duty. She only wished she felt more comfortable with her decision.

The priest appeared out of nowhere, as did Sister Anne and a man who appeared as battle worn as the stranger. Mother Superior stood to the side of the priest, Sister Anne stood to Moira's left, and the man stood to the stranger's right. All was ready for the exchange of vows.

The ceremony was quick and painless since Moira barely listened to the words and only responded when spoken to. Her thoughts were in turmoil. When young she had dreams like any other young girl of one day marrying and having a family. She had created an image of her wedding in her head. Her gown she would stitch herself. Her few childhood friends would be in attendance. And the man she would call her husband she would certainly love. Her dreams had faded with the passing years and she was no longer that young, naive girl, but a woman full grown who no longer dreamed such a childish fantasy.

Yet here she stood in a bed gown and shawl, her feet bare, her hair uncombed, exchanging vows with a stranger covered in sweat, dirt, and blood. If her youthful thoughts were dreams, this was a nightmare and she prayed she would wake.

A distant rumble of thunder caught her attention and brought her out of her musings. She was surprised to learn that the ceremony was near done and in a moment she would be a wife to the man who stood beside her.

"It is done," the priest said solemnly, closing his book.

"Your name?" Moira asked of her new husband, suddenly realizing she had failed to learn his name before wedding him.

"Ian," he said hastily and turned to the man beside him to speak in a Gaelic unfamiliar to Moira. He then turned back to her and took her hand, which he had released only moments before, after having slipped the plain gold band on her finger. "Show me to your room."

She froze, realizing his intentions.

He leaned down close to whisper in her ear. "I wish I had time to properly make you my wife, but that distant thunder you hear is our enemies' rapid approach. They ride hard and they ride fast. In a short time they will arrive at the convent and unless you wish bloodshed we must consummate our vows."

She pushed her fearful thoughts away. She had committed herself to honoring her father's dying words. And Ian had given his word that their marriage would bring an end to the senseless slaughter. All she had to do was her wifely duty and it would be done.

She shivered, blaming the reaction on her cold feet, and said, "This way."

She avoided looking at Mother Superior and Sister Anne as Ian followed her out the door.

"We must hurry," he urged and she hastened her steps.

Three candles glowed on the table in her room and a bowl and pitcher of water sat nearby. Her blue wool blanket had been neatly folded at the foot of her narrow bed and her bed coverings had been changed. The thought that the sisters had taken the care to make her room welcoming and comfortable for her wedding night brought a tear to her eye.

Her husband came up behind her after closing the door. He took her shawl from her shoulders and tossed it on the chair, then he slipped his arm around her waist, holding her firm against him. "Know if there were time I would make this night special for you and know I do this of free choice."

She had no time to wonder over his words; he turned her in his arms and all but lifted her from the floor as he walked her to the bed. He followed her down on the straw-filled mattress and his hands immediately went to her night shift.

Her body responded to the intimate invasion of his warm hand slipping up her thigh by growing as taut as a bowstring.

He placed his cheek next to hers and whispered gently, "Do not fear that which is natural."

She wanted him to understand that this was foreign to her. She had never experienced an intimate touch or a simple kiss, and she was frightened by the unknown. "I have never—"

He stopped her with a brush of his lips across hers. "Aye, lass, I know. That is why I wish—"

The rumbling thunder caught both their attention. The riders drew near, very near, and little time was left to them.

Ian looked at her with regretful eyes. "I am sorry."

With that sincere apology whispered in her ear he raised himself over her, pushed her shift up, and plunged into her. She screamed out from the pain of his forceful entrance and even his gentle words and the soft brush of his lips over hers did little to alleviate her discomfort as he drove in and out of her in rapid strokes.

She braced herself against the lingering pain and the steady, intimate pounding of her body. And she could not help but feel disappointed in an act that was supposedly conceived of love.

She was relieved when he finally ceased all movement and lay completely still on top of her. She wiped away the tears she had spilled, not wanting him to judge her as weak. She had always prided herself on her strength and that was how she wished her new husband to come to know her.

Raised voices, shouts, and scuffling could be heard in the courtyard, a short distance from Moira's room.

Ian raised his head to listen for a moment before he asked, "Are you all right?"

Her pride would let her answer only one way. "Aye."

He looked about to say something when screaming voices pierced the night. Ian was off her in a flash and she hastily pulled her garment down over her legs and hurried off the bed.

"I must dress," she said, bending down by the chest near her bed.

Ian grabbed her arm and yanked her up beside him. "There is no time."

The brilliant green of his eyes alarmed her. She had thought them a soft blue when she had gazed into them when he had kissed her. But this color was harsh and filled with the cry of battle and she shivered.

He grabbed her wrists and pulled her up against him. "I will allow no harm to come to you, on that you have my word."

She nodded, unable to speak. The strength of his grip and the determined glare in his eyes warned her that he was not one to give his word lightly. He would protect her with his life if necessary.

"Come, it is time," he said and released her wrists to tightly grasp her hand.

She followed him out the door, though she had little choice. His firm grip cautioned that he intended to keep her close beside him. He hurried down the corridor toward the shouting voices that sounded as though they were in a direct collision path with them.

Moira hurried her steps, her bare feet ignoring the chill of the cold stones. She wished she had had time to dress. She preferred to meet her enemy fully attired, but she understood her husband's intentions. By seeing her improperly clothed, her enemies would know their vows were sealed.

A deep, angry—and familiar—voice sounded from around the corridor and Moira froze, though it did little good—her husband dragged her alongside him with fierce determination and she had all she could do to keep up with him.

The voice sounded again and it was her name that was called out. "Moira!"

"Father?" she whispered as she tugged to free herself from her husband, who refused to look at her or to release his sturdy grip. He just kept walking.

They turned the corridor and halted abruptly as they came face-to-face with Angus Maclean, his two sons, and the man who had stood beside Ian when their vows had been exchanged.

They were a fierce sight, her father and two brothers, as bloody and battle worn as Ian and his men. And a large lot, the three of them all standing almost a full head over the man beside them, though none equaled Ian's height. She wondered if there was any who matched his height. Her father had grown heavier than when last she had seen him, though it was hard muscle the extra weight held. And her brothers were handsomer than she remembered, both having grown into men of impressive size.

It was with much relief Moira uttered, "You are not dead."

"A miracle," Ian said with amusement that brought a wide-eyed, incredulous stare from his wife.

"What have you done, daughter?" Angus shouted.

Fear gripped Moira's stomach and unconsciously she gripped her husband's hand as she answered, "What you asked of me?"

Angus grew red with fury and stepped toward Moira, who was about to retreat when her husband stepped directly in front of her.

"This senselessness had to end," Ian said, standing right up in Angus's face.

"You soiled her," Angus said in rage.

"I consummated our wedding vows," Ian corrected, his voice calm and controlled.

Angus grumbled loudly and pointed an accusing finger in his face. "You had no right."

"I gave you a choice," Ian said, releasing her hand and taking a step toward Angus.

Angus shook a fist at him. "I refused your offer."

"An unwise choice," Ian said emphatically and smacked the shaking fist out of his face.

All hands went to the hilts of their swords.

"No battle will be fought in God's house." The sharp, furious voice of Mother Superior echoed off the stone walls of the corridor and the men parted, allowing her to pass.

Moira stepped forward, her body trembling, her eyes brimming with tears she fought hard to control. "You sent no message." It was not a question; her mind had grasped the implications.

"You fool," Angus snarled at his daughter. "Do you know who you exchanged vows with and who you welcomed between your legs?" He pointed at the stain of her virgin blood on her night shift.

All color drained from her face, but she refused to hang

her head in shame. She kept her chin up and her eyes on her father and waited. Waited for her suspicions to be confirmed.

Disgust for her foolish mistake was heard in Angus's harsh response. "You wed my fiercest enemy, Ian Cameron, laird of the clan Cameron of Glencoe."

❧ *two*

TWO MONTHS LATER

Moira added the long column of numbers for the second time, confirming her previous calculations before closing the leather-bound ledger. She favored her work at the convent. It challenged her intelligence, keeping her mind sharp. She never made a mistake when calculating numbers. Their components were clear and understandable and never failed to provide an answer or a solution to any given problem.

With numbers there were no errors; life however was a different matter. She had badly miscalculated and made a terrible mistake though it had produced a startling result.

Moira stood with a slow stretch, easing out the ache in her lower back. She had tallied over the ledger since early morning and it was near to midday. She required a reprieve from her tedious work, perhaps a brisk walk in the fresh winter air.

This room she worked in day after day was small, cell-like, and much too confining. A plain wood table supported all her needs; stacks of ledgers, candles in pewter holders, and an inkpot and quill. A single, sturdy, and most uncomfortable bench was her only seat and a fireplace barely big enough to hold a single piece of peat heated the stone-walled room. One window, narrow and drafty, provided her with a view of the front courtyard.

Two steps brought her to the window and with her hand rubbing the curve of her back she looked out on the dormant garden beds that from spring to fall burst to life with a glorious profusion of color and produced a bountiful harvest.

Her life at the convent might appear restrictive to some but to Moira it was a blessing. Strangely enough it was here she felt free. Here she was able to pursue her interests and here was where she was given an unexpected opportunity to learn.

The midday meal bell sounded, calling all to nourishment. Moira draped her white shawl around her neck and over her shoulder. Her pale blue wool underdress and tunic kept her sufficiently warm but with the recent winter frost sending a steady cold wind to batter the old stone walls, the rooms had taken on a constant chill that could seep through to the bone.

Her stomach rumbled as she hurried along the corridors to the main hall where all the sisters gathered for meals or meetings. Already she could smell the roasted mutton and she was certain wild onions scented the meat. And if she was not mistaken, that was a whiff of fresh apple tarts that teased her nostrils.

She smiled as she rushed her steps and gave thanks for her presence here. Each day since her wedding, two months before, she gave daily thanks. She had thought that night would end in bloodshed and tears. And while no blood was shed—her tears were spilled.

She had been so very foolish and trusting, believing all

she had been told—all the lies—and she had paid dearly for her hasty and unwise decision.

That night remained clear in her mind and lingered like a bad nightmare one prayed to forget. She had been ordered to return to her room by her father. He had screamed at her and shaken his mighty fist in her face while she stood her ground. Her husband would hear none of his bellowing tirade and with his own booming voice informed her father that it was now Moira's duty to obey her husband. Their marriage was valid, sanctioned by a priest and consummated, there was nothing Angus Maclean could do to change that. And in the end it was her husband who instructed her to return to and remain in her quarters until he sent for her.

It was with an angry heart and bitter disappointment in herself that she obeyed her husband. She refused to meet his eyes, to look at him at all, for she was certain if she did she would lose control and curse him until his dying day for making a fool of her.

Upon her return to her room Moira had dressed and braided her long dark hair and spent the rest of the time pacing the floor, concerned, angry, and fearful for her future. How could she ever trust a husband who deceived her? She had ripped the bedcovers off the narrow bed, completely distraught that she had submitted to him as only a dutiful wife could. She had thought his words kind and gentle and yet they had been lies. There was not a word of truth in the words he spoke to her. He'd deceived her and she would never forgive him.

Her father and husband had talked until past dawn when finally her husband summoned her.

She had been escorted to the main hall by Sister Anne and the man who had stood beside her husband when they had exchanged their vows. She paid him little mind; her thoughts were for her own fate.

The main hall had always appeared large to her but filled with the sheer number of men whose height and width dominated the abundant space it suddenly felt tiny and lacked sufficient air.

Regardless of her suffocating surroundings Moira had stood with pride before her father and husband and it was her father who delivered her fate with a smug grin. He informed her that she would remain at the convent, loudly claiming that she was too old and barren to satisfy her young husband's needs. He would recognize their marriage and in so doing their union would unite the two clans in strength and holdings.

Angus Maclean bellowed with pride when he delivered the next news. He told her that the agreed marriage arrangements called for the clan lands to remain their own, with both clans offering protection to the other when needed, and if—here he laughed, and it grew deeper and more hardy—if Moira should bear her husband a child he would see that Ian Cameron received a substantial portion of the Isle of Mull to be passed on to the child.

Then he had turned angry words on her, calling her a foolish, weak, and stupid woman and he was glad he would not have to lay eyes on her again. And with a jerk of his hand he had ordered her out of his sight.

Ian Cameron had stood beside her father; she had felt his eyes on her but had refused to meet them. But with her father's staunch edict she had turned her husband's way and with one sharp look her dark eyes had made her hatred of him known, for he recoiled as if she had slapped his face and she thought for a brief instant she had seen a flash of regret. But she did not care what Ian Cameron thought or what he felt. He was a man she could not trust and she would never forget or forgive his deceitfulness.

Her husband rode off that night without a word spoken between them and she was relieved, so very relieved, it was over and that she would never see him again. Her life was once again hers and she intended never, ever to forfeit her trust to any man.

The main hall was only a few steps away and the enticing scent that filled the air made her mouth salivate in anticipation. With her hunger occupying her thoughts and her feet making haste she did not pay attention as she turned the corner, and she collided with Sister Anne. Both women held fast to each other and while Moira thought the incident amusing, Sister Anne did not wear a smile.

"What is wrong?" Moira asked with alarm.

"Mother Superior wants to see you. You have a visitor."

Moira shook her head and took a step back. "I never have visitors."

Sister Anne spoke with reluctance. "This one returns."

A violent shiver raced through Moira and though Sister Anne was only a wisp of a young girl, standing not more than an inch or two over five feet, she closed a firm and steady arm around Moira.

"Do you feel well?" she asked of Moira anxiously.

"Startled. Do you know—"

Sister Anne shook her head before Moira could finish. "I was only told to escort you."

"Then how—"

Sister Anne was astute, especially with Moira; it was as if they understood each other, often finishing the other's words: "—do I know he is here?"

Moira nodded.

"I recognized the man who stood beside your husband when you exchanged vows. He calls him Blair and I think they are close friends."

Moira appreciated the information. Like a row of numbers waiting to be summed up, the more information provided, the better accuracy in calculating the correct answer. And though concern furrowed her brow, determination raced through her blood. But what worried her the most was his reason for being here. What did he want?

There was only one way to find out. "Let's not keep him waiting," she said to Sister Anne with a courage that brought a smile to the young novice's pretty face.

"I knew you had the strength to face him."

"Did anyone think otherwise?"

"From what Mother Superior implied, your husband thought you might deny his request to meet with you."

That stiffened her spine. "My husband thinks me too much of a coward to face him?"

Sister Anne grinned. "Not so Mother Superior. She directed me to bring you to her quarters; there was not a doubt in her mind you would come."

"Then let us go and settle this so we may send these intruders on their way and I can enjoy that roasted mutton that smells so heavenly."

"And apple tarts," Sister Anne said with a sigh. "Sister Mary bakes the best apple tarts."

The two women walked to Mother Superior's quarters discussing Sister Mary's divine talents with food and it was with a light rap on the door by Sister Anne that they signaled their arrival. Moira was told to enter.

Cautious steps brought her into the room and she looked to Mother Superior before her glance settled on the man near the lone window. She kept her silence, her dark eyes steady on him, showing no emotion though his appearance did startle her. Without the stains of blood and grime she was able to clearly see the man she had married.

He was as tall and lean as she recalled, a wall of solid muscle and fierce determination. His red and green plaid cloth was wound smartly around a pale yellow linen shirt, and thick leather sandals hugged his feet with leather thongs crisscrossing up his thick calves. His dark auburn hair fell down over his shoulders with two thins braids running down each side. And his face?

She refused to acknowledge his good looks, a reaction she was almost certain he was accustomed to from women. She imagined women's eyes turned wide and their mouths fell agape. Some probably giggled and favored him with generous, not to mention inviting smiles. But what woman wouldn't look with desire at his arresting features? He possessed a strong jaw line, sharp cheekbones, a narrow nose that amazingly looked to have never been broken, long auburn lashes, and perfectly shaped auburn eyebrows that framed blue green eyes that could easily melt a woman's will in one suggestive glance.

He was much too handsome and much too young; not a single line, crease, or scar marred his clear complexion. The cold weather had even managed to favor his high cheekbones with a faint touch of windburn, giving him a hint of color that heightened his compelling features.

He smiled at her then, slow and lazy, and with much too much confidence, and she silently cursed him.

He waited in silence and she knew he was giving her the chance to speak first and giving himself the opportunity to weigh her reaction to his return. She refused to give him the advantage and held her silence.

The room grew heavy with silence; not even a worried breath could be heard and Moira continued to keep her gaze steady. She would not turn away, she would not show him doubt or fear though she felt both. Her worst fear being that he intended to take her from the convent.

He finally surrendered, his eyes and senses sharp enough to realize that she would not capitulate. His timbre was calm though firm. "I have come for you."

She responded with a sharp tongue. "I will go nowhere with you."

He retained his calm composure, his charming smile remained wide on his face, but his tone warned he would have his way. "I am your husband and you will obey me."

Her temper slipped from her tenuous grasp. "I hate you."

"A common affliction amongst husband and wives."

She thought to scream out her refusal and all the reasons she wished to see him rot in hell but she held her hasty and unwise words behind tight lips. He remained calm and in control, his tone tinged with a hint of humor. It would do her little good to act foolishly. She had mistakenly done that the last time and she would not fall into his trap again.

"What do you want of me? And the truth, please, if you can tell it," she said, her tone considerably calmer.

His smile quickly vanished and he advanced on her with rapid steps. "It is bad manners to call your *husband* a liar."

His sudden closeness intimidated and she fought to quell her nervous tremors. "You spoke no truth to me that night."

He lowered his voice for her ears alone. "I spoke many truths that night."

She attempted to argue but he refused to allow her to speak. "Enough. This matter is private and is better left for another time. My only concern at the moment is that you will be joining me when I leave here within the hour."

His sudden return did not make sense and she wanted a clear answer. "Why? Why now do you come for me?"

"You wound my heart, wife," he said with a teasing smile and a hand to his chest.

His charming antics annoyed her. "You think me foolish enough to fall for foolish words."

His smile slowly faded. "I think you wise enough to know when to obey your husband."

"I will obey if you give me a good enough reason."

He laughed at her and shook his head in disbelief. "You have courage, lass, but reason or not, you will come with me."

"And if I refuse?" she asked with an obstinate glare.

He reached out, took her long dark braid, which lay over her shoulder past her breast, and wrapped it slowly around his hand, drawing her toward him with each twisting motion. When she stood almost firm up against him he spoke. "Then I will tie you up, dump you over my horse, and ride off with you."

Mother Superior gasped but he paid her no mind.

"Do I make myself clear?" he asked her, his eyes fixed directly on hers.

Green, she thought. Now his eyes were green and heated with anger. And she understood without a doubt that he would do as he warned. But her own stubbornness would not allow her to capitulate so easily. "I cannot be ready in an hour."

"Two hours," he said and released her braid to walk away from her.

"Tomorrow morning," she bartered.

He turned around near the door, his humor once again evident and once again irritating. "You bargain with your husband?"

She meant her words to sting. "I only speak the *truth*. I cannot ready myself in that short of a time."

Clearly her barb did not penetrate his thick skin; his smile merely grew more generous. "My men could use a good meal and a good night's sleep out of the elements. We will leave at dawn." He opened the door and walked out without a backward glance.

Moira contained her annoyance and hurried over to close the door, wishing there was a lock on it. Wanting nothing more than to lock him out of her life forever. Then she made a hasty return to Mother Superior's side and asked the one question that had worried her. "Did you tell him?"

Mother Superior whispered her answer, fearful of being heard. "No, my child, I would never betray your secret."

"Then what is he doing here?" Moira paced the floor. "What does he want from me?"

Mother Superior attempted to comfort her. "Perhaps he does wish for you to be his wife."

Moira laughed at the ridiculous thought and stopped her anxious pacing. "No disrespect, Mother, but did you take a good look at the man? I doubt he ever lacked for female companionship."

Mother Superior placed her hand on Moira's shoulder.

"Does his reason matter? He is your husband and you have no choice, you must obey him."

Moira looked with teary eyes at the woman who had cared for her like a mother. "This is my home; I do not want to leave here."

The older woman spoke calmly and with the wisdom of age. "My dear child, you were never meant to live your whole life here at the convent. It has come time for you to leave, to live your life and to fulfill your duties as a wife."

"We do not love each other and I do not trust him. How then can we live as husband and wife?"

"Love and trust are earned and come with time."

Moira walked over to the window and stared out at the grounds so familiar and so comforting to her. This was her sanctuary. She felt safe and loved here. How could she surrender warmth and security for life with a complete stranger?

"What of my work?" she asked with concern.

Again Mother Superior's voice turned to a whisper. "You know that you can tell no one of your skills in mathematics and science or how you came by them. It is a secret that we promised to keep and we must always honor that promise."

Moira shook her head. "But I love my work and wish to continue it. Look what it has done for the convent."

Mother Superior smiled with pride. "Bishop Roderick still cannot understand why we are so prosperous. We are the only convent that depends on no stipend from the church but survives strictly on our own. I tell him that we sell our harvest and wares at market, but he cannot understand how that can sustain us."

Moira smiled herself, pleased by the strides the convent had made over the last few years. They had continued to reap a generous harvest, enough to feed the convent, help the needy, and sell the remainder at market. The sisters spun such a fine and colorful wool cloth that there was a waiting list to purchase it. And the pottery they produced was much in demand by merchants who claimed the pieces sold as fast as they received them.

"We prosper because of you, Moira," Mother Superior said with a grateful heart. "You taught us much."

"I learned—"

Mother Superior placed her finger to her own lips in warning and spoke softly. "Do not speak of it. I fear anyone discovering the secret."

"How will I ever continue to make use of my knowledge or continue my work?"

"I have an idea that will not only serve you well but will solve a problem that I am having."

Moira huddled close to Mother Superior to hear the whispered suggestion. "Sister Anne is not suited for convent life. She is much too curious and not at all obedient. She has nowhere to go and while she could remain here, I do not think it is where she belongs. I think it would be wise for you to take her along with you. She would serve you well and above all you can trust her. She listens well and hears more than most think, and she would help guard you from prying eyes."

"Which means with her assistance there may be a way for me to continue my work."

"And perhaps teach others how they can prosper as you did for us." Mother Superior paused and said gently, "Besides, you will need a caring friend when your time comes."

Sorrow along with tears filled Moira's eyes. "I had so wanted to have my . . ." She wiped her falling tears away. "What do I do?"

Mother Superior closed a tight arm around her. "Tell your husband the truth. You have no choice and he has a right to know."

Moira shivered at the mere thought of confronting her husband with her secret. "I do not know if I can."

"You fear his reaction?"

"I do not think he will believe me," Moira said.

"Why?"

"If you recall, on my wedding night my father made it clear that I was too old and barren for my young husband." Moira paused and placed a protective hand over her stomach. "How now do I tell my husband that his seed fell on fertile soil and in the summer I will bear his child?"

Mother Superior cupped Moira's chin in her hand. "With pride, Moira, hold your head up and tell him with pride."

❧ *three*

"*Your thoughts rob your appetite,*" *Blair said with a* nudge of his elbow to Ian.

Ian gazed down at the trencher of mutton in a sauce flavored with wild onions and shrugged. He then gave a quick, cursory glance around the large room where his men had anxiously gathered for the midday meal. The sisters had been generous and his men grateful for the tasty fare, and their courteous manners demonstrated their appreciation, which made the sisters all the more generous. He was relieved that they would not be leaving until morning. His men would probably be too stuffed to mount their horses if they left now.

"The meeting did not go well?" Blair asked, refilling his tankard with warm cider from the large pitcher on the table.

"Not entirely as I expected," he admitted easily to his friend. Blair and he had grown up together and shared a brotherlike bond. They both claimed it was due to the fact that Ian had but one younger sister and no brothers and

Blair had three older sisters who ordered him about. They had no alternative but to band together against females. Of course, that was when they were young. When they matured they found females quite to their liking. And then there were their charming tongues, which could talk a woman into almost anything. Their looks helped, of course, Ian being handsome with his defined features and Blair being roughly attractive with a nose that had been broken twice, dark eyes that seemed to entice with every glance, and full lips that captured the attention not to mention the imagination. They were a devil of a pair and had a devil of a good time growing up. And Blair had steadfastly remained by Ian's side, being there for him when his friendship was needed the most. When Ian was ten and his mother had died of fever, Blair had told him that they could share his mother. And they had; Blair's mother had fed, threatened, and loved him as if he were her own son.

They had celebrated many of life's adventures, including Ian's marriage to Kathleen when he was ten and nine, and Blair had grieved along with him when a year later Kathleen died in childbirth along with their stillborn son.

Then maturity had reared more of its unruly head and with the death of Ian's father four years ago he was faced with the prospect of leading his clan, and Blair was his cohort in leadership. They had made a comparable pair and the Cameron clan had survived; now Ian wanted the clan to thrive and grow.

"So tell me about her," Blair urged, as only a close friend could.

Ian rubbed at his chin. "My wife is stubborn."

Blair laughed. "What woman is not?"

Ian smiled and nodded. "I suppose you are right and yet . . ."

Blair waited, knowing his friend had yet to finish.

"She seems different in her stubbornness, and then there is her anger."

"That was expected," Blair said. "You deceived her."

Ian winced at the painful word. "I despise deception."

"There was no other way. Too many would have died a senseless death if you had not taken matters in hand."

"I remind myself of that daily, but it is of little comfort when I recall how easily she surrendered to me."

"Ahh," Blair said with a grin. "There lies your problem. You have never deceived a woman into bed before and it does not sit well with you."

Ian grew annoyed. "I did not deceive her *in* bed. I spoke true words to her that night and meant every one. I wish that I could have made it different for her. There was no time."

"You have time now."

Ian shook his head. "She not only openly speaks of her hatred for me but I see it in her eyes. She does not trust me."

Blair smiled when his glance caught the tray of apple tarts that the sisters carried into the room. "Then you must win her trust."

"Easier said than done."

Blair slapped him on the back. "A challenge, my friend, and the good Lord knows you have never avoided a challenge."

"She is not what I expected in a wife and yet . . ."

"She haunts your thoughts."

Ian looked at Blair with surprise.

Blair leaned in close so their words were private. "I have seen the way you have been the last two months. Your interest in women has waned and you are often deep in thought as if far away. Your wife has left her mark on you."

"And I do not understand why. She is not a beauty though she is fair to look upon. Her wide dark eyes betray her every emotion and leave her vulnerable and yet she stands tall and proud regardless of the circumstances."

"A challenge," Blair reminded in a whisper.

"Perhaps," Ian admitted and grew silent. What was it about the dark-haired, dark-eyed woman that had haunted his thoughts since consummating his vows with her? Their intimate time together had been brief and yet he could not forget that night. He could not forget the feel of her soft cool skin or the way she quivered in his arms or the courage with which she accepted her fate.

She had surrendered willingly, trusting him, submitting to him and accepting him as her husband. And he had enjoyed her surrender. His loins had grown hard with passion for her, so hard he was afraid he would hurt her in his haste. But she had held fast to him and taken him inside her without hesitation. And he could not forget the feel of her, soft and vulnerable and yet willing. Innocent and inexperienced, she had lain beneath him in surrender.

He had spoken the truth to her that night in that little room. He had wanted to make it special for her. He had wanted the time to quiet her trembling, soothe her apprehension, and touch and taste her until her body quivered with desire. But he had no such time and his hands had run over her flesh in haste and he had entered her like a youth eager to spill his seed. And spill it he did, her passage was so tight, barely moist, barely accepting of him, engorging his own flesh to stronger life and speeding his climax to a full explosion.

This was what he could not forget. This woman who was almost five years past his age, this woman who had never intimately known a man, whose body was barren, who made him explode in a fiery climax that stole his senses and haunted his mind and made him wonder if it would always be that way with her.

And while he had debated this tormenting issue, rumors had reached his ears that had forced his return to the convent. Rumors regarding Moira's safety.

Ian spoke his thoughts. "I cannot understand why Moira's life should be in danger."

Blair kept a steady eye on the young novice who approached them with a serving tray full of apple tarts. "Unfortunately, I have not been successful in discovering where the rumor originated."

Sister Anne smiled pleasantly at the two men as she placed the tray on the table and served them each a freshly baked tart.

"My wife is to be watched at all times, make certain of this," Ian ordered and Blair nodded in response. "I want to know her every move. Where she is at all times."

Sister Anne refilled the men's tankards with cider and continued smiling.

Both men ignored her lingering.

"The men have their orders," Blair informed Ian. "They will not fail you—Moira will have all eyes on her. They are surprised, though, that she returns with you to your home."

Ian sensed his friend had more to say. "You have never failed to speak the truth to me, Blair. Why hesitate now?"

Blair spoke low. "This wife is old and barren. She can never bear you the son you have always wanted. Why take her back to your home to live as your wife?"

"I have a duty to her as a husband. She is my responsibility. That is all anyone needs to know."

Sister Anne hoisted the tray from the table and with her fixed smile made a hasty exit.

Blair watched her scurry off and with a grin turned to Ian. "That one has a much too tempting sway to her hips to devote her life to the convent."

"Your thoughts are better kept to matters at hand," Ian warned. "I want none of the men getting ideas tonight."

Blair attempted to hide a laugh. "And where is it you will be sleeping this night?"

Ian stood, his tall, lean, hard body casting a shadow over Blair. "Wherever I choose."

"Responsibility?" Moira repeated angrily upon hearing Sister Anne's words. "I do not need the likes of him being responsible for me. I can take care of myself." She set the

three wooden bowls in the basket atop the table, placing a protective cloth over them before adding two leather flasks.

"He says you are to be watched at all times." Sister Anne related all she had heard while helping Moira to pack the contents of her private workshop where no one but Mother Superior and Sister Anne were permitted. There was always something bubbling over the fire in the hearth or being mixed in a bowl or drying out on a cloth. It was a fascinating place and Sister Anne loved being part of the mystery.

"At least I know why two of his burly men were trailing after me. I thought they were up to no good so I made certain to lose them in the winding corridors. Then another one pops up outside my quarters and it took me almost an hour to lose him."

"But you did?" Sister Anne asked with a laugh.

Moira managed a smile. "It is rather simple to lose a simpleton."

Both women laughed.

Sister Anne grew serious. "I will miss you."

"My goodness!" Moira said suddenly. "I forgot to tell you. Mother Superior feels that convent life might not suit you and she suggested you accompany me to my new home and remain with me; that is, if the suggestion is to your liking."

Sister Anne's response was instant. "Mother Superior is perceptive and I am grateful for her suggestion. I would love to go with you."

"And of course you will continue to help me with my work," Moira said, "though I must warn you that it will be necessary to proceed with caution and keep our activities secret."

Sister Anne grew excited. "I am very good at keeping a secret—and *learning* secrets."

Moira's own excitement grew. "A spy. How perfect for us. You will join me then?"

Sister Anne nodded her head so vigorously it looked about to fall off. "Aye, I am most pleased to join you."

"Good," Moira said, handing her a stack of ledgers. "Safely secure the remaining items in this room in the baskets while I go gather the convent ledgers to take to Mother Superior."

"I will see that everything is packed and ready for our journey."

Moira smiled her satisfaction and left the room, wrapping her white shawl around her and tossing one end over her shoulder. She hurried along the twisting corridors and as she took one corner with haste she almost bumped into one of two brawny men who looked to be lost though pleased to see her.

She simply shook her head at them and turned in the opposite direction. It took her but a few minutes to lose them, only to meet up with two more men who looked just as perplexed as the last two. They were soon on her heels but once again it took her a short time to free herself from them trailing after her. By the time the third pair of men with wide stunned eyes nearly ran into her she had had enough and with a sharp tongue she ordered them to take her to Ian Cameron immediately.

With his men dispensed to their duties, Ian and Blair sat at a table in the large, empty hall discussing their return journey. It was with a startled jump they both stood as the door was flung open and in marched Moira followed by two of his men.

She did not pause for pleasantries; she walked straight over to Ian and made her demand clear. "Why are your men following me?"

Ian could not hide a smile. She looked to be in a snit and her flaring temper appealed to him. Her cheeks were blushed red, her round dark eyes sparkled with a watery brilliance, and he noticed that her silky dark hair he had thought a simple brown shined with honey-colored strands in its tightly fashioned braid.

He crossed his arms over his chest and regarded her in an arrogant stance, as only the laird of a clan could do. "They follow you because I ordered them to."

"Whatever for?"

Blair and the two men glared at her as if she were daft. No one spoke to Ian in such a demanding manner. Absolutely no one, and least of all his wife.

But Ian seemed to take no affront to her forward manner and answered her with his usual charm. "Because, sweet wife, I command it."

"I am not your *sweet wife,*" Moira nearly shouted at him, her display of anger managing to get a chuckle out of him and irritate her all the more.

"Nay, lass," Ian said with a soft laugh. "Sweet you are not."

Moira tossed her chin up. "I will not be watched over like a child. I will do and go where I please. And *you* will keep your men away from me."

Ian's smile did not fade but his tone took on a dire warning. "My men do as I dictate, as you will, *my sweet wife.*"

Moira's fist came down hard on the table, causing all but Ian to flinch. "Do not call me *sweet wife.*"

With huge grins moving across their faces his men took several steps back and Blair hid a chuckle beneath his breath as he inched away from the warring couple, all three men confident in who would be the victor.

Ian placed his hands gently on the table, bringing his face to rest within inches of hers. His words were a strong warning for her to take heed. "While your tongue is far from *sweet,* I will call you what I wish."

Moira was about to tell him exactly what she wished to call him when a wave of dizziness washed over her, causing her to grow pale and weave to the side, her hand reaching out in desperation to balance herself.

Ian did not waste a moment. He vaulted the table and

had her up in his arms in seconds. Her head fell against his chest and her eyes fluttered closed.

"Get Mother Superior," he ordered his men. They rushed from the room.

Blair stood looking completely helpless. "I do not know the first thing to do for an ill woman."

"I am not ill," came her muffled yet willful voice. "Put me down."

Blair laughed, Ian smiled, and both men shook their heads.

"Do you hear what I say? Put me down," Moira demanded, but her head continued to rest against her husband's sturdy chest.

"When you are well enough to stand I will put you down," Ian said firmly. "Until then you will remain in my arms. Now tell me what ails you."

Moira answered quickly enough. "A husband who makes unfair demands of me."

"And you are not up to these demands?"

That brought her head up quickly though she regretted her unwise action. The dizziness assaulted her once again and she quickly returned her head to her husband's comforting chest. She attempted an excuse, any excuse but the truth. "I have had little sleep of late. I am but tired."

"Older women need more sleep," Blair said as if explaining her ailment.

Moira turned her head and was about to tell him that young men were fools when she realized he had provided her with a perfect excuse and one that men would foolishly believe. She almost choked on her own words when she said, "You are a wise and understanding man."

Blair smiled, basking in her compliment.

Ian hoisted her up further in his arms, causing her to hastily wrap her arms around his neck as he walked over to a bench and sat down, holding her firmly in his embrace.

She thought to protest but kept her silence, wanting him to believe his friend's ridiculous reasoning that she was old and tired; maybe then he would change his mind about removing her from the convent. After all, what would a young, virile man like him want with an older, ailing woman?

And she had to admit he was virile. She could feel the strength of his muscles through his clothes. His chest was hard, his arms solid, and there was a scent about him that tingled her senses. It was not an odor she was familiar with or could describe; she only knew that it pleased her. It made her feel warm and comfortable and it enticed her to bury her face in his chest and breath deeply of his rich scent.

"Moira!"

Moira jumped at the sound of Mother Superior's sharp voice as she entered the room and, realizing how intimate she had been with her husband and how comfortable she felt in his arms, she grew irritated with her own foolish actions and attempted to slip from his embrace.

Ian had other ideas. He tightened his hold on her and looked to Mother Superior. "Moira explained how she has not been sleeping well lately. I think it would be wise for her to rest."

Mother Superior agreed with a nod. "A good idea. I will take her to her quarters."

Ian stood with his wife in his arms, her added weight causing him no problem. "I prefer to carry her and make certain she is tucked soundly in her bed."

"That is not necessary," Moira said, squirming to break free.

Ian yanked her hard against him. "I say it is."

Moira realized wiser action was called for and she quietly surrendered, knowing she would rid herself of him faster if she appeared to capitulate. To her surprise and annoyance he did not need to be told the way to her room. He entered with a shove of his shoulder against the partially open door and gave the door a soft shove with his foot when they entered. The soft click of the closing door sent a rush of goose flesh over her warm skin.

Ian carefully deposited her on the narrow bed, tucking the blue wool blanket up to her neck, then he squatted down on his haunches beside the bed. "I intend to have one of my men guard your door, in case you require anything. I expect you to rest for at least a full hour."

"Is that an order?" she asked, moving her arms from beneath the blanket.

Ian's smile was much too pleasing. "It is a suggestion." He tucked the soft wool blanket over her arms once again.

A battle of wills, she thought, and charged full speed ahead into the melee. "I am feeling much better." Out came her arms.

"Regardless, you will rest." With a jerk of the blanket he replaced it over her arms.

"I have much to do before we leave tomorrow," she insisted and freed her arms yet again.

He stood and leaned over her, moving the blanket very slowly up and over her arms. "A caution, sweet wife, I am a husband who expects obedience." He tucked the blanket firmly around and beneath her shoulders.

Moira was about to candidly tell him that she would be far from an obedient wife, when he leaned down and stole a faint kiss from her open mouth, only to quickly return his lips to hers and shock her by invading her mouth with his determined tongue.

Her own tongue warred with his in an attempt to chase him away, but their feverish dueling startled her senses and when finally he ceased his attack she felt a faint hint of regret.

His hand softly brushed a few stray strands of hair from her face and he seemed about to speak when he shook his head, stood straight, and walked to the door.

Moira was already wiggling herself free from the blanket.

"Do not dare move from beneath that blanket," he

warned, turning to face her as his hand locked on the metal latch. "Or else, *sweet wife,* I will join you in that bed."

Moira grew as rigid as a stone statue.

Regret was evident in his face and he hastily left the room.

Moira was up at dawn. Her short rest the previous day had renewed her energy and she and Anne had completed all the necessary packing that evening. All that was left this morning was to see to the removal of a few plants she wished to take for replanting in her new home and, of course, to say her good-byes.

The day was blustery, with a sharp bite to the winter air and gray skies promising a touch of cold rain or perhaps snow. It was not a day for travel and not a day to be digging in the cold, hard ground.

But early morning found Moira on her hands and knees, a worn brown cloak wrapped around her, digging in the garden with Anne at her side as Ian and Blair approached them.

"What are you doing?" Ian demanded with none of his usual charm.

Her voice held a forcefulness of its own. "Digging up plants to take with me."

"I will have two of my men see to the task for you," Ian said and held his hand out to her.

Moira shook her head, her hands remaining busy at her chore. "Nay, their hands are large and clumsy. Anne and I will see to the task."

Ian wasted no time with words; he reached down, grabbed her by the arm, and yanked her to her feet. "My men will see to the chore or the plants remain behind."

Moira took note of the way his gentle blue eyes were turning a potent green and she wisely nodded her consent. "Anne will direct your men so that the plants do not suffer any injury."

"We leave within the hour whether you are ready or

not," Ian informed her brusquely and released her arm to walk away.

Blair remained and knelt beside Anne, asking how he could be of help.

Moira was about to join them when Ian's voice rang out in the courtyard. "Do not dare let me turn and find you on your knees."

Moira stumbled to keep herself standing and mumbled, "Stubborn Highlander."

Blair offered a steadying hand from where he knelt and she wisely accepted it. "That he is, and that he must be if he is to lead his clan, and *you* are now part of his clan."

Moira made no comment, but she did give his words thought. She had always been proud of being a Maclean and these past two months she had not thought of herself as a Cameron, and yet she was now wife to Ian, laird of the Camerons of Glencoe. And she carried the future heir of the Cameron clan.

Her free hand protectively covered her flat stomach.

"Do you feel ill?" Blair asked with concern and stood.

Moira shook her head with a smile. "No, I but thought of the good-byes I must say."

He nodded his understanding.

"And since you will be helping Anne with the plants, I think it is a good time for me to see to those good-byes." She turned and hurried off.

"She is just as stubborn as the Highlander," Anne said with pride as Blair knelt by her side.

He turned a charming smile on the young, pretty woman. "Then their match should prove to be an interesting one."

Anne's own smile could be just as disarming and Blair dug in the dirt beside her with the enthusiasm of a young boy at play.

•   •   •

Moira had but a short time left. The men and horses were gathered in the courtyard impatiently waiting to depart, but she had yet to make her final good-bye to the person who mattered most to her, Mother Superior.

She entered her quarters after rapping lightly on the door and hearing her familiar voice bid her to enter. She stood staring at the woman who had raised her, who had encouraged her intelligence, who had been the only source of love for a desperate, lonely young girl.

Mother Superior extended open arms to her and Moira gratefully ran into her welcoming embrace. They hugged, shared tears, promised to visit though both knew that would be near to impossible, and when there was nothing more for either of them to do but say their good-byes Moira kissed her cheek and whispered, "I love you, Mother."

A soft knock on the door parted them and Anne peeked her head in. "Your husband grows impatient."

Mother Superior hurried her out the door. "You must not keep him waiting and I have a few questions concerning the ledgers. We will discuss the matter as we walk."

Mother Superior was not the only one in the convent that had more questions for Moira. Before she reached the courtyard several sisters approached her with various concerns ranging from the dye used in the wool they weaved to their pottery that demanded hefty prices at market.

Ian paced the courtyard, his men mumbling and growing more impatient with each passing minute. And his annoyance escalated even further when Moira made her entrance surrounded by a dozen sisters all chattering away at once. He thought she would dismiss them when his eyes met hers and he made it known with a scowl that his patience had ended.

She, however, seemed to ignore his silent warning and continued to talk with each woman, looking as if she were settling major problems, since one by one they left her side with a smile of relief.

Two sisters remained and while he much preferred to dismiss them with a shout he chose to remain impatiently patient. He braced his arms across his chest, angled his head, and focused glowing green eyes on his wife. It was a potent stance and glare that never failed to make his men take heed.

His wife, however, was a different matter.

An audible sigh of relief was heard through the men when finally only one sister remained chattering with Moira, but it was followed by a groan of frustration when six more sisters hurried into the courtyard to surround her.

Ian's patience snapped. He strode straight for his wife, the chattering women growing silent and moving out of the way of his determined strides.

One look in his blazing green eyes and Moira knew she was in trouble. She took a few steps back but little good the distance did her. Ian swooped down on her with the speed and agility of an avenging warrior. He scooped her up, tossing her over his shoulder, and marched toward the horse that had been prepared specially for her.

Moira was mortified and she paled from the embarrassment of his actions and the intimate display of his arm under her backside. She looked with worried eyes at the sisters, who stood in stunned silence, their own eyes round with disbelief.

"Blair," Ian shouted, "step around to the other side of the horse just in case I miss when I throw my wife across her mount."

His men laughed and with a smirk Blair did as ordered.

Moira tensed. He could not possibly be so thoughtless and worse yet she had the well-being of the babe to consider. She was about to tell him she could mount her horse herself when Anne's frantic voice ripped through the chilled air.

"Put her down, you imbecile, or you will harm the babe she carries."

❧ four

The only sound in the large courtyard was the winter wind whipping in and around the startled men. Most stood with their mouths agape, others stared with wide eyes, while the nuns simply shook their heads in silence.

A quick hand had gone to Anne's mouth but too late. The secret had spilled from her lips and there was no re- canting it, no way to make amends for her hasty and fool- ish tongue, only regrets for her impetuous action.

Ian carefully lowered Moira to the ground, keeping his strong hands locked firmly on her shoulders. He would take no chance of her fleeing; he would have an explana- tion and he would have it now.

He asked the one question he had never thought he would have reason to ask of his wife; she was after all older than him and her advanced age led him to believe her barren. So he felt odd asking, "Do you carry my child?"

Moira held her head up with pride and placed a protec- tive hand to her stomach as she answered, "Aye, I carry your child."

Gasps and hushed whispers raced around them but were brought to an abrupt end when Ian raised one hand commanding his men to silence; even the nuns obeyed and ceased their chatter.

"Blair," Ian said and the man immediately moved to his side. "Our departure will be delayed for a short while. See that the men remain ready and I will hear no complaints from them."

"Aye," Blair said and turned, his booming voice issuing orders that the men sought quickly to obey.

Ian turned his attention to Mother Superior though he kept one firm hand on Moira's shoulder. "A private place where I may speak with my wife."

Mother Superior took them to the closest place of privacy, the small chapel, and closed the door quietly behind them.

Moira did not wait for him to take command and demand answers. She felt safe and protected in the confines of this holy dwelling and she spoke with confidence. "I know you and my father thought me old and barren." Her hand once again sought to protect the tiny babe. "And I do not in the least regret disappointing either of you. Your babe nestles comfortably within me and I will see him delivered safely."

Ian maintained a calm composure though inwardly he was fueled with worry. He had lost one wife and child to childbirth; he did not wish to helplessly watch another die. And his first wife had been young and healthy; Moira was older and birthing would surely be difficult if not impossible for her, though the thought that disturbed him the most was that she had not made her condition known to him. Had she ever intended to tell him?

He voiced his concern. "When had you planned on informing me of the child?"

She defiantly remained silent.

He understood and grew angry. "What right have you to keep this from me?"

She defended herself. "What right had you to lie to me?"

"Senseless bloodshed needed ending," he said in hopes she would understand his reasons.

"And I mattered not?" She raised her chin a notch.

"You mattered more than I."

She laughed, though it sounded more like a cry. "I mattered so much that my husband discarded me on my wedding day."

"This bickering does us no good," he said, his own guilt at hurting her that day weighing heavily on his mind. "We are husband and wife and we have a duty to each other."

As much as she wanted not to agree with him, she could not find fault with his words. They were wed and according to the church their duty was clear. She, however, wanted him to clearly understand how she felt about her forced circumstances.

"You are right."

He smiled triumphantly, assuming he had emerged the victor in their skirmish.

"We do have a duty, and I will honor my vows." She hesitated only a moment then added, "Though they were spoken with deceit."

His smile vanished in an instant and with two quick strides he was near on top of her.

She showed no fear of him and felt none. The truth was on her side and Mother Superior had taught her that the truth always prevailed.

Ian hesitated when he caught the stubborn glare in her wide, expressive eyes. They were deep brown and fringed with the longest curled lashes he had ever seen. He could almost feel the intensity of her determination through her intriguing eyes.

He placed his face a mere breath away from hers. "I did what was necessary, as did you."

She attempted to dispute his remark.

He stopped her with a finger to her lips. "Another time

we will discuss this matter. Right now I wish to know if you are well enough to travel." His finger lingered a moment on her lips before he removed it so she could answer.

"Why would I not be?" she asked indignantly, annoyed that she had suddenly become answerable to a husband.

"You did not feel well yesterday," he reminded her.

"I feel fine and fit enough for travel," she insisted and momentarily regretted her hasty words. She probably could have convinced him that she required a few days of rest, allowing her to remain at the convent. But then it would be a brief reprieve; her departure was inevitable. Why should she prolong it?

Her answer came easily to her. The convent had been her home, her sanctuary, a place she felt protected and loved. Now she was going off with a strange man, to a home that was foreign to her with no one but Anne to truly care for her.

She was feeling vulnerable but would let no one know it.

Ian looked her over in silence. She appeared healthy. Her cheeks glowed red, her skin was smooth and creamy white, and deep dark red streaks ran through her dark brown hair, which was braided and lay down her back to rest just above her bottom.

He would have never thought her to be with child. But she had almost fainted and he had to consider her age. She was his wife and he intended to protect her not only from possible physical harm, but from her stubborn self.

"I will have the wagon prepared for you."

"Whatever for?"

"So your journey may be more comfortable."

"I am comfortable on a horse," she said, having learned at a young age to ride and having continued to do so while at the convent.

"The wagon will allow you to rest when necessary. The horse will not." Surely she would realize the wisdom of his words and capitulate.

"I require no special consideration for this journey. I will ride like everyone else."

She truly was a stubborn one and he did admire her tenacity, but he was responsible for her and the child.

Child.

He was to be a father. The thought struck him suddenly as if he only now realized the fact. He had wanted children, many children, and when he first married he thought it not a problem. His wife was young and healthy, her mother having delivered five fine children of her own. But it was not to be and when he wed Moira he had assumed no child would come of their union. Now this child would probably be the only one she would give him.

He had to protect her and keep her safe so that she would have a chance to give the child life and that she herself would live to watch the babe grow.

"You will ride in the wagon," he said adamantly.

Her response was delivered with defiance. "I will not."

He held his tongue and his temper, wanting to tell her that she needed to learn obedience, but he knew they would be unwise words. And he had learned that words, at times, could settle differences more easily than a rising temper or swinging fists.

"I think of your comfort and the babe."

The truth of his words surprised her though she made no show of it. She, herself, chose tact, understanding full well that it was necessary she learn to deal with her husband. It would not do well for her to be at constant odds with him. She wished to establish a relationship with him that would be comfortable for them both. After all, he did not love her nor she him so a mutual understanding would be best established early between them.

"I appreciate your concern, but I do enjoy riding and see no reason not to begin my journey on horseback."

He admired her tact. She was not completely unwilling to submit to his demand, though she made it known to him she would have her way first. He chose to allow her her way. In time she would learn to accept him as her husband, though he doubted she would ever submit willingly to his orders. But then he was not certain he wished her to. Weak-willed women never appealed to him. It was the woman who stood with pride and courage that interested him. And Moira possessed both, which he assumed was the reason she remained on his mind since the day he had wed her.

"You will let me know if you grow tired?"

"Aye, I heed well the babe's wishes, for I want him to grow strong within me."

Ian smiled with pride he did not realize was evident. "Do you think you carry a son?"

Her hand splayed over her barely rounded stomach and she could not say why she felt as she did but she was eager to share her thoughts with him. "Aye, it is a son I carry, I know it."

He believed her, though he knew not why, perhaps it was because he wished a son to carry on his name. Concern once again reared up to worry him and he had to reassure himself. "You do feel well?"

She eased his concern with her confident words. "I am strong and stubborn, though not foolish. I would do nothing to place the babe at risk."

He nodded and sought to reassure her. "I think we will do well together."

Moira hoped they would, for she knew she had no other choice and that was what made her doubtful. "We shall see."

"You are stubborn," he said with a smile and stepped close to kiss her.

She recoiled from him, sending him a deadly stare.

He said nothing. He honestly understood her reaction and knew it would take time for her to learn to trust him. He would be patient, but eventually she would respond to him. She was his wife and he intended they live as such.

He held his hand out to her.

Moira knew he extended her a peace offering, a start for

them to begin anew. It would be rude of her not to accept it. And while she wished to refuse him, she also wished for him to realize that she could never be intimate with him again. He had deceived her, made a fool of her, and try as she might it was a hurtful memory she could not forget or forgive.

She could however be civil and courteous and with that thought in mind she took his hand.

They entered the courtyard hand in hand, to the surprise of all.

"We depart," Ian announced with a firm command that left no doubt he was a leader of men.

The men cheered.

Tears filled the nuns' eyes.

In minutes hasty farewells were exchanged for a second time and with Ian's help Moira mounted her horse. He saw that she was settled comfortably and safely, examining her mount with a careful eye.

"You will ride beside me."

She did not argue though she would have preferred to ride alongside Anne. Soon enough he would grow tired of her company and dismiss her. She would be patient.

She held the reins tightly when the convent gates opened and they proceeded out. She took a deep breath. This was her final farewell. She would never again set eyes on this place she had called home for the last ten and seven years. This part of her life was over and she was about to begin a new life with a total stranger.

Fear nagged in the pit of her stomach and she placed her hand there to rub it away.

"You feel ill?" Ian asked anxiously, having kept a watchful eye on her.

"Nay, I am fine." Her voice lacked its usual confidence.

He studied her a moment and seeing that her color remained healthy he decided she was truthful with him. She did feel fine, but he was astute enough to understand that something disturbed her.

"This departure is difficult for you."

"Aye, it is," she admitted with a nod. "I have spent many good years here."

"Then you have good memories to take with you."

She smiled. "Many good memories."

He reached out to place his hand on her hand that held the reins. "And you, I, and the babe will make many more good memories together."

For a brief moment she believed his words and then recalled his deceit and wondered. Did he speak the truth to her or did he lie?

"We shall see," she said and turned to see Anne's whereabouts.

Ian removed his hand from hers. "Sister Anne rides four rows down. She is well protected."

"Thank you for seeing to her care. And she is no longer a sister," Moira explained. "She actually had never taken her final vows and now that she has chosen to join me she never will."

"Why did you never take the vows?"

She would only tell him so much about herself and this question she did not mind answering. "My father gave specific instructions that I was never to take the vows. I was to wait on his word."

"Did you wish to take vows?"

She realized he probed and she would allow him to go only so far. "I was content as I was."

She had not answered his question, but he was persistent and given time he would have his answers. "What occupied your time?"

She did not want him to know the extent of her knowledge and chose to tell him what he would find most acceptable. "I worked in the garden and with the pottery. I tried weaving but my hands were not as nimble as others'."

"I hear that the sisters weave a fine cloth, that none better can be found."

Moira smiled, her pride obvious. "The sisters weave the

softest and finest cloth in all of Scotland. It is much in demand."

"I hear tell the pottery is just as fine."

"Artistic hands," Moira said and thought it best to change the subject before he asked questions she did not wish to answer. "Tell me of your home."

Ian realized the subject change was intentional and while he wondered why she would not wish to discuss the abbey's success in producing such fine craftsmanship he chose not to question her. In time she would willingly discuss things with him.

He spoke with pride of his home. "My castle cannot be seen in early daylight or when the weather turns gray for it sits on a hillside where the mist protectively lingers over it. From the battlements I can view the area for miles and worry not about surprise attacks. Its safety is secured."

And that castle was where he wished his wife to be, for within the walls of the keep he could afford her the best protection. This journey there would take a couple of weeks and traveling the open road left them much too vulnerable to surprise attacks, though he had come with a strong contingent of men. Still he knew not what he was up against or even the why of it. He simply could not understand why someone would wish to harm his wife, but he intended to find out.

Moira watched him drift into deep thought and did not disturb him. She waited patiently to see if he would continue and he did, shaking himself out of his musings.

"The keep has recently been completed, and though not large it is comfortable in size. A thriving village surrounds it and our harvest this year was plentiful. It will be a warm and bountiful winter we share."

"And what of your family?" she asked, curious as to who she would have to contend with.

"My mother passed on when I was young, my father only a few years ago. I have one sister, Brianna," he said with a smile. "She is married and lives not far though re-

mains on Cameron land, her husband Arran joining our
clan when they wed. Blair, who you have met, is like a
brother to me, his mother having helped raise me and his
father seeing to my care as much as my own did. They are
good people."

He hesitated a moment as if he debated telling her more
and she watched him war with himself.

His decision was made quick enough. He had wondered
whether to speak of his first wife to her. He was not obli-
gated to do so but he felt if he was to win her trust he must
speak honestly with her. She had to understand he did not
wish to keep secrets from her and while he did not inform
her of a possible threat to her life, it was done out of consideration, for he did not wish her to worry.

"There is something I wish you to know about me."

She looked with intent interest to him.

"I was wed before you." He paused, waiting for her reaction, and when she simply remained silent he continued.
"Her name was Kathleen and I loved her dearly. I lost her
and my daughter in childbirth. It was a difficult loss for me
but one I have come to accept."

She could not help but feel for him. Her mother's passing when she was seven years had torn at her heart. And
now that she carried a child she understood the maternal
need to protect. She could only imagine his helplessness
when there was nothing he could do to save those he loved.
She had experienced the same when her mother had died
birthing her brother Aidan. Her life had simply slipped
away before her eyes.

"I am sorry for your loss and understand. My mother
passed on giving birth to my youngest brother." She realized too late her words.

"Your mother passed birthing a babe?" he asked anxiously.

"Her third child," Moira said in an attempt to allay his
concern.

"We will have no more than one," he said as though reassuring himself of her safety.

Moira had no intention of ever being intimate with her husband again so his words rang true. "Aye, we will have but one child."

Ian seemed to require more reassurance and spoke his concerns aloud. "This child is a special gift bestowed upon us. With your age you will never be able to conceive again so there is no need for concern."

She grew indignant. "I will never conceive again because there will be no intimacy between us."

That brought a sharp snap of his head toward her and the soft blue of his eyes turned a glowing green. "You are my wife and according to our vows you have a duty."

"Aye," she answered calmly. "And I have performed it. I will deliver you a child and since you feel that afterwards I will be barren there is no reason for us to be intimate. Intimacy is only necessary when conception is desired."

He cringed at the thought. "There is much more to intimacy than conception."

"It does not seem that way to me."

He cringed again, recalling their one time together and how the hasty act must have left bitter memories. "You will learn differently."

"I think not," she said with a certainty that irritated him.

"You deny me my husbandly rights?" he said and attempted to charm her with a smile and ease the mounting tension.

Her stubbornness prevailed. "You have the right to pleasure and may take it with whomever you choose, but it will not be with me."

"And if I say otherwise?"

She looked at him oddly. "Why would you want to bed a woman that does not wish to bed you?"

Her words stung his ego. "You are my wife and have a duty."

"And do you not have a duty to me? Should I not be

able to trust the man I wed to speak truthfully to me? Your deceit has left a heavy burden on my heart and I speak the truth when I say I do not wish to share the marriage bed with you."

She spoke with conviction and a determination that would be difficult to penetrate, but he had every intention of penetrating her self-imposed armor. "In time you will see things differently."

"I know how I feel and that will not change."

"We have yet to come to know each other."

"I know enough," she insisted.

"You know nothing of me."

"I know all I need to."

His hand shot out to grab hers. "You know nothing, but I intend that you learn everything and that includes the pleasures of the marriage bed."

She intended to retaliate but he stopped her.

"Nay, say nothing, for if you do it will be tonight I begin your lessons."

✄ *five*

Ian helped his wife off her horse and could almost feel her
fatigue. He silently cursed himself for traveling as far as
they did this day, but for safety's sake it was necessary. The
area they chose to make camp was a secure place where a
surprise attack was unlikely.

He kept a firm hand on her as he summoned Anne.

The young woman came immediately, slipping off her
horse without Blair's assistance. She was a wisp of a
woman barely standing an inch or more over five feet. Her
curly dark hair framed a pretty face that drew many a
man's eye and her small size belied her energetic nature.

"See that my wife rests while camp is set up."

Anne nodded and spoke her mind, which was her way.

" 'Tis too long a day for one in her condition."

Blair stood behind the woman and smirked at Ian.

Ian did not feel the need to explain and did not understand why he did. "Safety reasons brought us this far."

She seemed to accept his reasoning and asked, "Could
a fire be started immediately? The night is cold and it is

best if Moira remains warm. I can brew a drink that will help keep the chill from her."

"I will see to it," Blair said without waiting for a command from Ian.

"I think over there"—Anne pointed to a secluded spot shadowed by bushes and saplings—"would be a good and private place for us."

Blair smirked again.

The women in the abbey seemed accustomed to giving orders. Anne made it clear that they would have their own fire and sleeping palette. Did she too assume Ian and Moira would not live as husband and wife?

"I agree," Ian said with a firm nod. "A private spot for my wife and me."

His remark brought the desired results—both women stared at him in surprise.

"See to it, Blair," Ian ordered before he walked off and called over his back. "And lift not a thing, Moira, or you will answer to me."

Moira made no comment though the thought that she was now answerable to a husband rankled her.

Anne placed a fur hide on the ground after they both availed themselves of the privacy of the bushes; she insisted that Moira rest while she saw to helping Blair collect wood for the fire.

Moira relaxed back against the small tree and smiled. Anne was a sociable one, finding it easy to converse with people, which was why convent life was so difficult for her. She chattered incessantly and would constantly be reprimanded by Mother Superior. A restricted life did not at all suit her spirited nature and in all honesty Moira was pleased Anne had chosen to join her. Her presence made her feel less lonely.

Anne returned more quickly than Moira had expected though the glow on her pretty face informed Moira that she had discovered interesting information.

Anne dropped the bundle of sticks she cradled in her

arms on the ground. "Mumbles and whispers are prevalent in the camp."

Moira leaned forward so that their whispers would not echo in the silent night. "What have you heard?"

"Their laird is concerned for your safety."

This news was not new to her. "Aye, he worries over the babe."

"Nay," Anne said, with a brief shake of her head. "Your safety was his concern before his arrival at the convent."

Moira furrowed her brow, confused. "Why should my safety have been a concern to him? I was in no danger at the convent."

"It seems otherwise to him, which means he knows something that we do not."

"Which also explains the reason for his return. He is my husband and it is his obligation to protect me." Why she felt a twinge of disappointment she could not say. She supposed there was that womanly side of her that had hoped he returned because she had touched some deeper emotion in him. Not even love but perhaps regret and guilt for having treated her so badly.

"The question is, protect you from whom or what?" Anne asked curiously.

"Like any equation, it is necessary to have all the numbers. We seem to be missing several numbers, therefore the equation fails to add up or make any sense. We must find the missing numbers so we may determine the sum of it all."

Anne grew excited. "I so enjoy solving mysteries."

"This may be a difficult one," Moira advised. "I do not think my husband wishes me to know anything of this matter and he will make certain I do not learn of it."

Anne's faint laughter was for their ears alone. "I am certain that within one day's time I will know this secret he keeps from you."

"With that confidence I cannot see how you can fail."

"I will not fail you, Moira, I will always seek to help you."

Moira grasped hold of Anne's hand. "I am glad you are my friend and that you chose to join me."

"It is I who am grateful to have you," Anne said with relief. "I do not know how I would have survived convent life. I am thankful to Mother Superior for taking me into the convent that fateful day I collapsed at her door, otherwise I would have perished being on my own. But I knew in my heart that I was not fit to devote my life to the Lord. And when I learned of your remarkable skills—"

"Shhh," Moira warned with a finger to her lips. "No one must know of my unique education. I made a promise and he warned me it was for my own good that I did."

"We will continue your work though, will we not?"

"We must," Moira said on a soft whisper. "There is much to learn and improve on. Knowledge is for the betterment of all, though many think that knowledge is only for a chosen few."

Anne hesitated before asking, "Will you teach me? I so want to be knowledgeable like you and when I watch you work I hunger to understand."

"I will teach you, for it is only fair that knowledge be passed on. But we must be cautious and trust no one until we learn who we can trust, and that will take time."

"I will be patient and learn all I can about those around us," Anne assured her.

"As will I," Moira said and they gripped hands as if sealing a pact.

Anne turned, hearing someone approach. "It is about time. She will be chilled to the bone by the time you start a fire."

Blair stared at Anne's pretty face and smiled. "You have a sharp tongue on you for one so young and small."

That brought Anne to her feet in a flash. "I am twenty and two and can hold my own even against the likes of one as fat as you."

Blair dropped his sticks to the pile on the ground and looked himself over, squeezing his forearms and knocking on his hard stomach with his fist. "Nay, not fat, all muscle."

Anne boldly chose to see for herself and fisted her hand to jab at his stomach. It was rock solid and, more alarmingly, the touch of him sent a tingle racing up her arm. She would not, however, admit her mistake. "Your bulk slows you down. The fire should already have been started."

Blair laughed. "You are a bold one."

"Aye, I say what I think and I do my share." She bent down to gather the sticks to make the fire. She looked up at Blair. "Do not just stand there, help me."

He laughed again and followed her order.

Moira watched the dueling pair. They were verbal combatants and yet their sparring seemed to spark a passion in them. They laughed and teased and shared the work in friendly camaraderie and a good, strong fire was soon going.

Moira eagerly stretched her hands out to the welcoming flames. "Thank you, Blair, the night chill seeps through me."

Her words concerned him. "Does the fire offer you enough warmth?"

"It will warm me sufficiently and Anne will brew me a drink that will help and we have extra blankets yet to fetch," she assured him.

He did not look convinced, though he nodded. "The men prepare the game they caught."

"Already they have found game?" Anne asked.

"Ian makes certain the hunt is seen to just before we camp for the night so that the meal may be prepared as the camp is set up. The men complain less when they smell roasting meat."

Moira listened and took in all she heard. She wished to learn all she could about her new husband. Like an equation, all numbers must be present to reach an accurate conclusion, and until she possessed sufficient knowledge of Ian she would never truly know his character.

Anne, however, made her own opinion known. "He is wise and considerate of his men."

"Aye," Blair agreed with a nod. "Ian is a good leader. He protects the clan wisely and makes difficult decisions when necessary and he is a fierce warrior of immense skill. The clan respects and admires him."

Difficult decisions.

Moira thought on those words. Had his decision to wed her been one of those difficult but necessary decisions?

Difficult.

Necessary.

Those two words were the reason she was wed and the thought did not sit well with her. While she could respect his skill as a leader, she could not condone his deception, not when he had hurt her so badly.

"Ian is a good man," Blair repeated as if attempting to convince her.

Moira, however, would determine that for herself.

Anne once again took charge. "Show me where the men prepare the meal. I have herbs that will make the game more succulent and tasty."

Blair licked his lips. "I and the men will forever be indebted to you if you can improve on our meal."

"Then you are in my debt," Anne said and turned to address Moira. "I will brew a blend of herbs for you and return with added blankets."

"Do not rush. I am fine," Moira insisted though a chill chose to rush over her at that moment and she shivered.

Anne and Blair made no mention of it though they exchanged knowing glances before hurrying off.

Moira enjoyed the peace of her temporary solitude. Though camp activity went on around her she was able to bask in the relative quietness of the chilled night. She had spent much time alone in her studies. The more she learned the more she wished to learn. She was forever writing in her journals or calculating in her ledgers. And then there were her experiments, where she would delve into the variants of agricultural growth; the substance of clay and the properties by which to make it stronger; and the numbers, always the numbers, which would teach her so much, from the movement of the stars to the cycles of the moon, which could produce a more bountiful harvest when followed properly.

There was much for her yet to learn and discover and she ached to proceed with her studies. How she would do that at her new home she was not certain, but with Anne's help she did not think it would be a difficult task. She and Anne would find a way to keep her activities secret from her husband.

She yawned, feeling tired but in a way refreshed, for this journey was an adventure for her. She had been confined to the convent much too long and while she felt safe and secure within its walls, her ability to continue learning was hampered. Now there was a chance for her to expand her knowledge and that excited her.

She yawned again, her hand covering her mouth.

"You are tired."

Moira jumped, not having heard Ian approach.

He covered her lap with a warm fur wrap and then draped a soft blanket around her shoulders. The warmth of the soft wool seeped immediately into her body and she pulled the blanket more tightly around her.

Ian sat down behind her, stretching his legs out around her. He placed his hands on her shoulders and ran them down her arms and then up again. He continued rubbing warmth into her chilled body and she began to relax.

"Blair told you I was chilled," she said, as if offering to herself an explanation for his presence.

"He mentioned your discomfort."

"And as my husband it is your duty to see to my care."

He leaned in closer to her, his body moving up against hers. "I care for and protect what is mine."

"And I am yours." It was a fact she could not deny though she would have preferred to.

"Aye, Moira," he said on a whisper. "You are mine."

His lips drifted far too close to her neck and his breath faintly brushed her sensitive skin. She tried not to react, tried to ignore the shiver that raced through her, tried to pretend that it did not affect her.

Tried but failed.

She leaned back against him and he wrapped strong arms around her. His body heat slowly seeped into her and he drew his legs more closely against her, encasing her in the warmth of him.

"Warm enough?" he asked, though her answer was not necessary. Her body told him everything even though he was certain she did not understand her own response.

She nodded, drifting in the comfort of his embrace. She thought to question her actions but she was too tired and he much too comfortable. She yawned and settled herself against him.

He crossed his arms over her chest, hugging her to him, and he was not surprised when she did not resist. She was too tired to object to his actions or debate her own reaction. He hoped this was the beginning of a trust between them; though a tenuous one, he was sure it was at least a start.

There was no attempt at discussion and he did not feel it necessary to converse with her. He thought it more important that they establish a physical comfort between them. He did not wish for her to recoil at his touch or from the mere nearness of him. He wished for a strong intimacy to develop between them.

Why?

His silent question made him give pause. He was attracted to his wife though he could not state the reason. She did not possess a beauty that would turn a man's head, yet there was something intriguing about her. Her wide, dark eyes had a way of captivating the attention and drawing a person into their depths. Once captured, escape seemed impossible—or was it that escape was not desirable?

Then there was that brief moment of intimacy they had shared and that haunted him. He would recall the littlest detail, the fresh scent of her soft skin, or the tense feel of her supple body, or the courage with which she submitted to him. And guilt would raise up to torment him.

His decision had not been easy, but it was a necessary one.

Her head fell gently to rest on his chest and from her even breathing he knew she was asleep. He rested his cheek on the top of her head, shutting his own eyes and savoring the sweet scent of her silky soft hair.

He knew this forced change in her life would not be easy for her and that she resented his deception. But he wondered if the deception was truly the reason for her resentment. She had not once questioned him as to why he had not taken her from the convent the night they had wed. In essence he had abandoned her upon their wedding and yet she made no mention of it.

His careless actions had to have hurt her and he doubted that she would ever understand the reasons for his decision. He would make no mention of it. He would simply attempt to make amends in his own way.

Regardless of what she thought of him or felt, she was his wife and she would obey him. He smiled at his own foolish words. Since his return she had demonstrated an independence that surprised him. Their first meeting he had thought her more of a meek, agreeable woman.

Not so.

Moira possessed a distinct personality. Obviously her independent nature came from growing up in surroundings that had allowed her a sense of freedom. There was no male authority to dictate to her, only women of strength and character. She had developed a strong sense of herself from her environment and he admired that in her.

She stirred and he relaxed his hold on her so that she

could settle herself more comfortably against him. When she finally grew still his embrace grew firm.

His sense of protection toward her overwhelmed him. No one would hurt her. He would not allow it. He would protect her and the babe with his life.

When he had first learned of a possible threat to her life he had grown alarmed and then angry. To think that anyone would dare to hurt someone under his protection was an affront to his leadership. And to think that someone would target his wife caused a fury to rage in him.

No one dared hurt or destroy what was his and think that they would not feel his wrath. His fairness was well known, his warrior skills legendary. A fool would only tempt his temper. So, therefore, he believed he dealt with a fool . . . and a fool could be dangerous.

He wished to get Moira home and in the safety of his clan. No one there would harm her and he would then have time to discover who was the threat to her. He preferred she remained unaware of the problem. The news would only cause her distress and needless worry. She had enough to concern herself with at the moment and he wanted no more worries heaped upon her.

There was after all the child to consider.

His hand drifted down to rest over her stomach. It was flat, he felt not even a slight roundness, but then it had only been two months' time. The child would begin to grow soon enough and make his presence obvious.

He smiled with pride and satisfaction.

He was to be a father and the thought delighted him. When he had wed and bed Moira he had never thought his seed would take root. He had not even given it consideration. Her age had led him to believe she was long past her fertile period.

How very wrong he had been.

And glad of it.

The thought startled him. He actually was pleased that she carried his child and, though concerned for her well-being, he somehow firmly believed Moira would, out of sheer determination, deliver a healthy babe.

She stirred once again in his arms and whispered. "Safe."

"Always," he whispered back and kissed her cheek softly.

❧ six

The next day Moira once again traveled alongside her husband. She was quiet, her thoughts on the previous evening. She had woken in his arms to the smell of roasting meat, her stomach letting her know of her hunger. No mention was made of their intimate embrace. She simply sat up, stretched, and announced she was hungry.

He had told her the meal was near ready and he had allowed her and Anne to eat alone. He had joined his men and she had wondered when he would return, having made known the sleeping palette was for him and his wife.

But she laid her head down alone on the comfortable bedding and wondered what kept him away. She did, however, wake the next morning in his arms. When he had joined her, she could not say, nor could she remember turning into his arms and settling into his powerful embrace.

There was no time to comment on their intimate position. The men were up and eager to be off, breaking camp with enthusiasm. A light meal was taken as everyone prepared to depart and Moira soon found herself once again riding next to her husband as they began their day's journey.

She could not understand how she rested so comfortably beside him. She had been accustomed to sleeping alone, her narrow bed sufficient for one and her solitude gratifying. Why then did she accept his presence beside her so easily?

"Did you rest well?" Ian asked with a smile, since he knew the answer. She had cuddled against him throughout the night without the least bit of difficulty. And when he stirred she drew nearer as if in fear he would leave her side.

"Aye, I did," she admitted, but made no comment of their night together, although she wondered if he would continue to expect her to share his bed. She did not know and did not intend to ask. Not just yet.

Ian thought to ask her if she was comfortable and then thought that he had plagued her enough with his worries. He decided to remain silent and see where it took them.

He had no chance to discover her intention. Blair rode up to him in haste.

Ian did not wait; he reined his horse away from her.

Several men immediately moved in around her.

She knew the roads could be dangerous and her concern grew. She kept steady eyes on Ian until he disappeared over a rise. He sat his stallion with confidence and determination and looked to be a mighty warrior ready for battle.

She glanced around her and saw that all the men appeared alert, some with a hand on the hilt of their swords. She also noticed that their pace had slowed considerably.

Moira felt a sudden chill and wrapped her green wool cloak more tightly around her. She glanced up at the gray sky and the faint mist that capped the hills in the distance. The weather did not look promising and would only serve to make their journey more difficult.

Her mind began calculating possibilities and the best approach to each. It would do them well to push forward and attempt to make it to the foot of the hills by nightfall. The hills would provide a certain amount of shelter from any severe storm.

A sudden gust of cold wind whipped around the slow-moving group and she shivered from the chilled wind that seeped through her.

One of the men drifted away from her and rode ahead at a forceful gait. The other three closed in around her.

Ian certainly made sure she was well protected—or was he fearful of her attempting to take her leave of him without notice?

Moira turned to see if she could spy Anne. She had hoped to ride alongside her during part of the day's journey so they would have time and privacy to talk. Anne looked busy conversing with a large bulk of a man who rode beside her. He wore his bright red hair down to his shoulders and a beard that consumed thick lips and appeared to perpetually smile, an odd occurrence for an otherwise fierce-looking warrior.

She smiled, assuming Anne was collecting useful information from the unsuspecting man, and turned around content that they would talk later. Her wide eyes widened even further when she caught sight of her husband bearing down on her.

The wind whipped his hair back away from his handsome face, plastered his pale yellow shirt to his muscled chest, and stung at his eyes until they shined bright blue like a shimmering lake.

He was truly a handsome man and, from the way he rode his horse, he appeared a skilled and, she had no doubt, a fearless warrior. He looked capable of doing what was ever necessary to see that his clan survived.

And he had.

He had deceived her.

He reined his horse in near to her with ease and confidence. "This weather chills you?"

She frowned, wondering over his query, and then realized that the man who had ridden off only moments before had gone to inform Ian of her shivers. The idea that she was being constantly observed irritated her and she made her annoyance known.

"This is the way it is to be?" She raised her voice and he raised a brow. "You have your men watch me like a hawk?"

"I have them protect you." His voice rose to match hers.

"From what?" she demanded. "Do you fear I will seek my escape?"

Ian gave an almost imperceptible nod and the men who surrounded her dispersed instantly. "Should I?" he asked, his tone having calmed, yet sounding much in command.

Her own temper cooled. Losing control would be futile. Discussing the matter would be beneficial and she had wisely learned that an intelligent mind could conquer many obstacles.

"While this situation is not of my choosing, it is a reality of my own actions and I will do as I must."

Ian could not hide his smile and he leaned forward on his horse. "You wound me, dear wife. I thought perhaps you were beginning to like me."

Her answer was curt. "You deceived me."

His smile faded. "Will you *never* forgive me?"

Forgiveness was preached regularly at the convent and Moira understood it well, though her heart may not always agree. "Never is a very long time and time has a way of healing even the most troublesome wounds."

His smile quickly returned. "You give me hope."

"I give you sound reason."

He laughed. "You give and you take in the same breath."

"I speak honestly."

Her words wounded him though he refused to display his reaction. He remained smiling, deciding that if honesty was what she wanted, honesty she would get. "You are proving to be a challenge, Moira. Do I accept your bold tongue or teach you to hold it?"

She was quick with her response. "There is only one way to stop my bold tongue."

He laughed heartily. "And you think that I would have trouble cutting it out?"

She smiled, impressed that he possessed a rapid wit. "You would need to catch me first."

"I have good, strong legs," he said with a firm pat to his thigh.

"And I am agile on my feet," she admitted, shaking her leather-clad foot out at him.

"We will have to test our skills one day."

"I am available whenever you wish."

He wished they could run together in the nearby meadows surrounding his castle but her condition prevented any such doing; though she looked fit and healthy, he could not take the chance.

She realized his concern and confronted it. "The babe does not curtail my activities and a good run would not disturb him or me."

"You will see to your care and his, or I will," he said firmly and more out of worry than demand.

She stared at him oddly and shook her head. "I am not accustomed to taking orders. You would do well to speak to me in a different tone."

He laughed once again. How could he not? She was not at all what he had expected from a woman who had been raised ten and seven years in a convent. And he wondered how she had gained such an audacious manner.

"And if I choose not to?" he asked, his laughter subsiding.

She shrugged. "Then I simply will not answer, discuss, or definitely not obey you."

He wanted to roll on the ground with laughter but he did not think that would win her favor. And while he did wish for them to share a comfortable relationship, he would not tolerate such blatant disobedience of his orders. The situation proved humorously difficult, but then he was always up to a challenge of one kind or another.

"Tell me," he said, his smile steady, "did your father tolerate your boldness?" He immediately regretted his words. Her confident expression faltered and sorrow filled her features.

"My father had little time for his daughter and made it known that when I was in his presence my silence was expected. Being young and dutiful, I obeyed his word."

Ian could almost feel the heaviness of her heart and could only imagine how difficult it was for a young girl trying uselessly to gain her father's attention and love. Even to the point of remaining silent and out of his way, if she thought that would please him. He did not like what he knew of Angus Maclean before and the more he learned about him the less he thought of him.

"It was the convent that gave me strength, courage, and confidence," she admitted with pride. "I was encouraged to learn, to question, and to discover."

Ian reined his horse in beside her and his intentions were clear, she was to follow alongside him so that they could continue their journey. And Ian could continue his questions. "I did not think that a convent encouraged personal pursuits. I assumed the nuns' purpose was strictly to serve the Lord."

"Ignorance cannot serve the Lord. And you forget that I never took the vows; therefore, my interests varied from those who were there to do the Lord's work."

"And what interested you the most?" he asked, finding himself more and more curious about her life at the convent. She was not like other women raised or educated in a convent. Those women were more compliant and willing to serve. Moira was not.

Moira wished she could speak freely with him and share all her acquired knowledge. Having watched his skills as a leader she realized he possessed an intelligence she admired. Even his deception, when she gave it thought, was rooted in clear reasoning.

Her answer was as it must be, regardless that she wished to speak more freely with him. She understood that was not possible. "Simply learning. I love to learn."

"It matters not what you learn?"

She thought for a moment and while she had her favorites she realized it was knowledge that was most important to her. "Any form of knowledge is a worthy pursuit."

"You are not what I expected in a wife."

"What did you expect in a wife?"

After Kathleen had died he had not honestly considered taking another wife for love. He had felt as if his heart had grown silent and was no longer interested in love. What love he had to share with a wife had died with Kathleen. He knew that one day he would marry again. It was his obligation. And that obligation had brought him to Moira.

He shrugged. "I had not given it thought."

"Any woman would do?"

Had he felt that way? Did he truly feel he would never love again? Was that why his decision to wed Moira had come with a sense of ease? It had allowed him to wed without feeling guilty. Without feeling he betrayed his love for Kathleen.

Moira answered her own question. "And I am *any* woman."

He smiled and slowly shook his head. "You are not *any* woman."

Moira stared directly at him. "Nay, that I am not and you will do well to remember it."

He could not forget it. He could not erase the events of the night he had tricked her into wedding him. Her shocked face haunted his memory and the look of disgust and hatred she had cast at him when she had been summoned to his and her father's side burned vividly in his mind.

Nay, she certainly was not just any woman. She was a woman he had hurt badly and though his intentions had been for the good of all she was the one person who had suffered considerably for it. How did he make her understand his decision? How did he make her realize that they could establish a worthwhile relationship? How did he get her to at least think favorably of him?

He had no time to ponder his query for Blair again summoned him and before he could ride off Moira requested that Anne be allowed to join her so that she would have a friendly face to converse with.

Ian agreed and Anne was soon by her side, an eager smile planted on her pretty face.

"Your smile must join mine as we talk," Anne advised, "or they will grow suspicious and wonder over our conversation."

"You have discovered pertinent information?" Moira asked, her voice eager and a smile beginning to spread across her face.

"Surprising information."

"Concerning?"

Anne lowered her voice. "The true reason your husband returned for you."

❧ seven

Moira forced her smile to remain firm. Her insides, how-ever, were responding to the anxious news with nervous quivers. "Tell me."

Anne casually glanced around to see if anyone watched them. The men who rode close by, though alert to their sur-roundings, paid them no particular attention. Their focus remained much broader than on two gossiping women.

She finally felt comfortable to speak and did so in a tone that was meant for their ears alone and with worried eyes fixed on Moira. "There is talk that your life is in dan-ger."

Moira's smile faltered briefly then grew broader, not wanting to bring attention to them. "Danger? Are you cer-tain?"

"I chatter endlessly with the men, going from question to question to question. By the time I get to the question I actually seek they are so caught up in the chatter they seem eager to answer. And two of the men were certainly eager to discuss the concern for your safety."

"Concern?"

Anne nodded with a smile. "Laird Ian of the clan Cameron made it known that his wife was to be watched and protected at all times and since the news of the babe the men have been ordered to be extra diligent."

"And the origin of this danger?"

"From what I can gather no one knows."

Moira attempted to make sense of it all. "Let me understand this. You are saying that the men have been told that I am in danger, but they do not know where this danger comes from or who is the threat?"

"Aye, some think it is a rival clan attempting to push the laird into warring. Others think it is merely gossip and means nothing, though none feel it should be ignored. You are after all their laird's wife and indeed should be protected, more so now that you carry his heir."

"So I am protected but no one knows from whom?"

Anne nodded, her smile remaining in place.

"And no one knows what danger I am in?"

"Nay, unless they do and none have spoken of it."

"You think this may be so?" Moira asked, attempting to make sense of it all.

Anne paused in thought. "It may be that the men are not being told the whole of it."

Moira's smile faded as she sighed. "I must know what is going on. I cannot protect myself from a danger I know nothing of, or even if it exists at all."

Anne agreed. "Aye, more information needs gathering."

Both their smiles were replaced by intent expressions as they discussed the pressing problem.

"My life held no special significance until the day that Ian appeared at the convent," Moira said intending to approach this problem like a mathematical equation that needed to be solved. Mathematics made sense to her. What was necessary for her now was to start at the beginning, and Ian was the beginning.

"Then you think the danger comes from your connection with him?" Anne asked.

"It would make the most sense. Before his appearance no one gave me thought."

"Then your marriage to him may be a strong factor in this danger," Anne said, her mind calculating the possibilities.

"But the child should have no factor in this," Moira added, her own mind calculating possibilities along with Anne. "Ian returned not knowing of my condition. His thought was solely on my safety."

"He must care some for you, to return."

Moira stared at Anne in surprise. "He protects what is his. And I am his wife."

Anne did not agree. "Nay, I think not. If he cared naught at all for you he would simply ignore the danger and let it be done with. Then he would be free to wed again once you were gone."

Moira gave her word thought, wondering if her husband had taken her from the safety of the convent for his own selfish reasons. He had deceived her before. Why not again?

Anne seemed to sense her misgivings. "He means you no harm."

Moira spoke her concern. "He deceived me before. How can I trust him?"

"You do not know him—"

Moira anxiously interrupted. "Precisely. I cannot trust someone I do not know."

"Then you must come to know him to learn if you may trust him. And to learn of his connection with this problem." Anne's advice sounded much too logical to Moira.

Logic was something Moira could not ignore. Through her studies and her solitude she had learned that when emotions ruled a situation a logical outcome was doubtful. And hearing of the clans and the monarchs and how they warred she knew emotions had started and driven many a battle, and waged many a war.

She herself knew it was wise for her to come to know her husband. She was after all to live the rest of her life with him. Did she really wish to remain wed to a stranger? She had already come to know some things about him.

"He was wed before me, you know," Moira said.

Anne nodded. "I have heard this. How did you know of this?"

"Ian told me."

"This is good." Anne's smile returned.

"Why say you this?" Moira's smile did not return.

"He does not hide it from you or allow you to hear it elsewhere. He speaks of it himself."

"He loved her. Her death hurt him badly." She understood his pain, remembering how badly her mother's death had hurt her.

Anne sympathized with her concern. "You think—and he thinks—he will never love again."

"Aye, I think as he does," Moira admitted softly. "He will never love again. He has silenced his heart."

"Nay, his heart but heals and in time he will love."

"Why think you this?" Moira asked curiously, knowing precious little of love and wishing to learn, though Anne was like her—a novice at love. Still, wise words could often be spoken from the mouth of a babe.

Anne responded easily, as if well aware of the answer. "I believe that once a person loves deeply and loses that love that he cannot help but search for it yet again."

"You think Ian looks for love?"

"Why would he not?" It seemed logical to Anne. "He shared a love that was strong and knows the capabilities of such a bonding love. Why would he not look to find love yet again?"

Anne's words made sense or perhaps Moira wished them to make sense. When Moira's mother died she never thought she would know such a motherly love again. And yet she had known the gentle caring love of Mother Superior. Was it because her mother had taught her such a love existed and was there if one just looked for it? And was willing to accept it? Did Ian not realize that his love for his wife had taught him the profound joy of love itself? Did he assume that once he loved he would never love again? Or had love taught him that anything was possible, that even when one lost a love one could love again.

"He needs time," Anne said. "And you need time."

"Time to know him?"

"Time to heal," Anne suggested. "You carry a bitterness in your heart toward him."

"I have the right. He deceived me, used me."

"Aye, he did all that, but at what price?"

Moira wrinkled a brow, not understanding.

"Wedding you was a sacrifice for him as it was for you."

Moira had never considered that he had made a sacrifice. But he had given no thought to wedding her. His only thought was to save lives and end a senseless battle. Should she not admire him for his difficult decision? That was a difficult if not impossible question to answer.

The logical part of her would have to agree with his choice, but the emotional part of her would vehemently disagree. How did she learn to balance or accept the two?

"You give me pause to think."

"You have taught me that thinking is critical to gaining knowledge."

Moira was pleased that Anne was such an apt student. "You learn well."

"I have an excellent teacher."

"You flatter me."

"I hope so," Anne said with a teasing smile.

"We will do well together."

"We have so far."

"We have much work to do," Moira said in a serious tone.

"Aye, there is much for me to uncover."

"Discover," Moira corrected.

Anne shook her head. "Nay, I think the information that we seek must be uncovered. Someone knows something and I think I know who I will learn it from."

"Who is that?"

"Blair," Anne said with a generous smile.

Moira caught the glow in Anne's eyes and smiled. "You favor this Blair."

"He interests me," Anne admitted, never being one to deny the truth.

"I think you interest him." Moira had watched the way Blair appeared more attentive whenever Anne was around. And he seemed to be around her often.

"I am bold and stubborn, as Mother Superior often reminded me. Not good attributes for a novice or wife. And since I cannot change my nature, I think it would be wise of me to realize that marriage is not in my future. Therefore, I feel that it is best for me to acquire as much knowledge as possible."

"Knowledge has power," Moira admitted.

"I see that with what you have learned," Anne spoke low. "I watched the way the convent prospered from your wisdom and guidance. I am amazed and filled with envy when I hear you speak fluently in Latin, French, and the Gaelics."

"Languages come easy to me. It seems I hear them and instantly understand them, but then you speak Latin well yourself."

"My father," Anne said with a loving smile. "He taught me. He was a common man who possessed a love of words. He told me that there was beauty in language if people would just listen more closely. He listened well at mass from a very young age and taught himself Latin. He shared his knowledge with me and encouraged me to learn all I could." She laughed softly. "Which I suppose is the reason why I talk much and seek answers to endless questions."

"I envy you such a loving and caring father. He left you with fond memories."

"Aye, that he did. There is not a day that goes by that I do not think of him or share with him a bit of knowledge I have acquired. He will always be in my heart."

"My father found me a nuisance and expected my silence whenever I was in his presence. Until finally he sent me away." Moira grew silent thinking of those lonely years after her mother died and she voiced a thought she had never shared with a soul. "I think I disappointed my father. I lacked the beauty and grace of my mother and he wanted nothing to do with me."

"At least he did right by you."

"Did right by me?" Moira sounded confused. "How would that be so?"

"He sent you to the convent, where you were loved by many and where you were able to gain courage, confidence, and knowledge far beyond the ordinary woman. He unknowingly gave you more than most fathers."

"I suppose I should be grateful." She did not feel grateful. While she had gained much from her years at the convent she had lost much as well. She had lost a family who she had thought loved her. When her father sent her away her heart had broken. He had not even bid her good-bye the day she left her home, nor had her brothers. A small group of clansmen brought her to the convent.

Her tears had been heavy when she watched the convent door close on the departing men and she had never felt so lost or unloved and so fearful. What would become of her?

"What is wrong?"

The startled demand snapped Moira out of her sorrowful musings and she looked up to stare at her husband's concerned expression that seemed to suddenly turn angry.

"You are crying. What is wrong?"

Moira placed a hand to her cheek and felt the tears she had not realized she had shed. She also noticed that she and Anne had come to a stop, which probably was the cause for attention.

With no answer forthcoming Ian turned to Anne. "What worries her?"

Anne answered in haste. "Women in her condition often shed tears for no reason."

He looked as though he pondered her explanation, then he asked of Moira, "You feel well?"

Moira wiped at her damp cheek, feeling foolish. "I am fine."

Ian drew his horse closer to Moira, and Anne wisely reined her mare away from them.

"Will you tell me what troubles you?"

His words were kind and he considerate, but she was not compelled to admit her foolish wanderings to him. "Nothing troubles me."

Slowly he reached out to stroke her cheek. "You do not trust me enough to confide in me, do you?"

He need not hear what he already knew to be true, so she avoided a definitive answer. "There is nothing for me to confide."

His hand drifted off her. "You avoid the question."

Since he insisted, she would tell, though she did not think he truly wished to hear her answer. "I do not trust you, but you know this, so why do you ask?"

His molten blue eyes tamed to a softer hue. "I understand your mistrust, but I thought you realized that if something troubled you or you felt unwell that you could come to me and I would help you. I want you to understand that I will be there for you no matter the problem." He smiled. "Even if it is a small one you think not worth mentioning, I wish you to tell me of it."

Moira hesitated to speak her mind, but he encouraged her.

"There," he said with excitement, "you wish to tell me something, yet hesitate. Tell me."

Truth was important to Moira so she spoke it. "You wish me to trust you and yet you deceived and abandoned me without a word exchanged between us only hours after pledging vows with me. How do you even dare ask me to trust you?"

It was a fair question and one he knew she would ask, but one he found difficult to answer. "I did what I thought best for all concerned."

"Now you avoid the truth," she accused and he raised a brow.

Perhaps he did, but then this was a private matter between husband and wife, not for the ears of others. "Another time we will discuss this."

His sounded as if he issued a decree that was to be obeyed at all costs and Moira discovered she did not at all like being dictated to. "There is no need for discussion, it matters not to me."

His temper flared, she could tell by the sudden change of color in his eyes. "What do you mean?"

"What I say, it matters not."

He struggled to contain his annoyance. "It matters not that you can trust me?"

"I know I cannot trust you."

"You have not given me a chance." He raised his voice and when heads turned his way he sent them all a scathing look that had their head snapping in a hasty retreat.

Moira kept her voice low though firm. "I owe you no chance."

He leaned forward. "What do you wish of this marriage, Moira?"

"What do you mean?"

"We will be wed until death parts us. Do you wish those years to be pleasant and caring between us? Or shall we remain in a constant battle and become bitter, not caring at all for each other?"

He made sense. They were committed to each other for life. What would she make of it?

"Think on my words Moira. The choice is yours."

He rode off and she understood that his departure meant he would give her time to decide. He was giving her a choice, though actually she was giving herself a choice. He could not demand she care for him or be pleasant to him. What truly did she want of this union?

Anne rode over to join her. "He is a handsome man and speaks with a charming tongue. If I had not seen him battle-worn that night at the convent I would not think such of him. The men talk of his fierce warrior skills and the fright he puts in his opponents when they lay eyes on him. They say he fears no man, but respects all and only when provoked does this fearless warrior rage within him."

"They tell tales," Moira said, though on occasion she thought she had seen a spark of that warrior within him.

"The men are all in agreement when it comes to their laird. I do not think there is one among them who would go up against him."

"You make him sound indestructible."

Anne nodded. "His men think he is."

"He is but a man."

"I would take a closer look if I were you," Anne advised.

"I have eyes, I can see."

"You refuse to see for he has hurt you. If you are to truly learn of his nature then you must open your eyes, no matter how it pains you to do so."

Mora smiled as she shook her head. "When did you become so wise?"

"While your eyes were closed," Anne said with a laugh.

Moira laughed along with her. "You think with these wide eyes of mine that I would see clearly. And I do now, for I see Blair heading our way."

Anne turned a pleasant smile on the man.

"Ian has ordered a brief stop so all may rest and refresh

themselves. A fire will be started so that you may warm yourselves."

"A sharp chill has filled the air," Anne said, looking heavenward at the gray sky.

"Aye, that it has and Ian wishes to reach the foot of the mountains before nightfall in case the weather should prove difficult."

"Then we will push hard after this rest?" Anne asked.

"Aye, that we will," Blair informed her. "So rest well."

He rode off and Anne turned immediately to Moira. "It may be wise if you rode in the cart the remainder of the day."

Moira gave it consideration but not for long. "I feel fine. I do not think the journey will be difficult for me, especially given this opportunity to rest."

"You will tell me if you grow weary or feel ill?"

"Stop worrying so much about me," Moira insisted. "I really am fine."

Anne lowered her voice. "You have fainted three times since you have gotten with child."

"No one needs know that and while I grow light-headed at times, I have not fainted in almost a week's time. Perhaps that has passed and I will experience it no more."

"Perhaps," Anne said but did not sound as if she agreed.

"I really feel well, I wish everyone would stop worrying about me."

"I will try though I cannot promise."

"At least you give me that and I am grateful," Moira said and lowered her voice as if imparting a secret. "There is something you can help me with."

Anne was eager to please. "Tell me."

"I am hungry almost all the time. The babe seems not to get enough nourishment. No matter when I eat, I find myself hungry a short time later."

"Yet you do not appear heavier," Anne said in surprise.

"A pound or two, I think, but nothing substantial," Moira admitted. "How I do not know for I was forever pestering Sister Mary at the convent for food in between daily meals."

"So you are hungry now?"

"Famished!"

"Then I will see to it that we have food that you can nibble on along our day's journey."

Moira sighed with relief. "Bless you."

Ian rode up to them, sitting his horse with confidence and smiling pleasantly. "Anything you ladies need?"

In unison Moira and Anne, their faces bright with smiles, answered, "Food."

❧ *eight*

The brief rest had fortified Moira. Her stomach was sub-
stantially satisfied and Anne had saved a couple of dried
apples for Moira should she become famished once again.

The skies had darkened considerably and the men could
be heard grumbling about the possibility of a heavy rain-
fall or snow. Ian pushed them hard intending to reach the
base of the hills before nightfall though it appeared night
might just fall early on this increasingly cold day.

Blair had delivered fur wraps to the two women for
added warmth and Ian found time to inquire as to his
wife's comfort throughout the journey.

Moira felt good. She was warm, her stomach was full,
and she shared good conversation with Anne as they traveled, discussing her many studies and deciding what Anne
would study first.

It was as the day wore on into an early evening that
Moira grew weary, her yawns following one after another.

Anne grew concerned. "You grow fatigued. We should
stop and move you to rest in the cart."

Moira objected adamantly. "Nay, I will not be the cause of us not reaching our destination on time. I am fine, weary but fine. The babe gives me no trouble, I am simply tired."

"A warning that you rest," Anne advised.

"When we stop for the night I will rest."

Anne said nothing but concern was evident in her worried expression.

Exhaustion crept over Moira with each step her horse took and she wondered herself if she was not being foolish.

Blair rode up to see if they needed anything and Moira was trying so hard to keep herself awake that she did not notice Anne lean over to whisper to him. He nodded and rode off at a gallop.

Ian appeared mere minutes later and addressed Anne. "She is being stubborn?"

"Aye, that she is," Anne admitted with no guilt.

Moira looked to Anne.

Anne spoke honestly. "You grow weary and need rest."

Moira sighed. "That I do, but I do not wish to impede our journey."

Ian rode up beside her and Blair appeared on her other side. Ian reached out and without the slightest difficulty lifted her off her horse onto his to rest comfortably across the front of him. Blair took charge of her horse.

Too tired to protest, she snuggled up against him and he wrapped the fur pelt more tightly around the both of them and drew her up more firmly to him.

"You will rest," he said adamantly.

"Aye, that I will," she agreed and placed her head on his hard chest. "I do feel fine, just tired. I would do nothing to harm our babe."

"I know," he whispered and held her tightly as her eyes drifted shut. And he did. He realized her sincere concern for their child and he realized it was the first time she spoke of the babe as *theirs* and that pleased him.

He could not say what the attraction was to her for she

was different from women he usually found appealing. She was nothing like his first wife, Kathleen. She had been a beauty who turned every man's head and captured every man's heart. She had been blessed with a sweet soul.

He could not say that about Moira. Moira was stubborn and bold with her words and possessed an intelligence he found surprising and intriguing. She was not a beauty but he found her attractive. She had the widest, most beguiling eyes he had ever seen and beneath the many layers of clothing she wore was a body that could tempt a man's soul.

He had intimately touched her but briefly and yet he could recall the exquisite feel of her and damned if he did not want to feel the soft silky touch of her again. He grew tight and hard at the thought. What was it about her that tormented his dreams and haunted his thoughts? He simply could not get her out of his mind. She lingered there and he could think of nothing but taking her to his bed and introducing her to the pleasures of intimacy.

He regretted their first union. It was fast and impersonal, a mere act to solidify their vows. He was certain she did not experience any satisfaction and that thought disturbed him.

He wanted her to know the joys of intimacy. He wanted her to become familiar with his touch. He wanted her to find pleasure in their coupling. He wanted her to want him.

Moira stirred in her sleep, snuggling closer against him. His arms remained firm around her and his instincts were to protect her with his life if necessary. She was after all his wife and she carried his child. It was his duty to see that she was safe.

Blair rode up beside him. "She is well?"

"Aye, she sleeps."

"She is unlike other women," Blair said on a whisper, as if not wanting to disturb her slumber.

Ian nodded and waited for Blair to say more.

"I have known willful women but they eventually relent

to a man when necessary. Moira seems capable of dealing with whatever hardships come her way. She is not only strong of will but strong of character."

"Which is why protection is needed."

Blair agreed. "But from whom? We have tried without success to determine who would benefit from her death or why anyone would deem her demise necessary. We have not come close to solving the problem."

"Do you think anyone knew of Moira being with child?" Ian asked.

"Have you asked her?" Blair queried.

"I have only thought of it."

"I could inquire of Anne and what she knows of the situation."

"Would she be forthcoming with information?"

Blair smiled. "She speaks her mind and then some."

"Good, then see what you can discover."

"You think the babe may be the reason she is in danger?"

Ian glanced down at Moira to see that she remained in a deep slumber. He did not want her to hear their discussion. "We need to find the reason if we are to find the culprit."

"I will spend time with Anne and see what I can discover," Blair said with a nod.

Ian grinned at his friend. "Is it too much of a chore for you to spend time with a pretty woman?"

Blair placed his hand on his heart and with a wide grin spoke. "I have pledged my loyalty to you and will do what is necessary to serve you well."

"Even if it means spending extra time with a charming woman?"

"I am up to the chore," Blair declared, his grin remaining firm.

Ian laughed. "I have no doubt you are, but remember, discover the information before you attempt to seduce her."

"How about seducing her to get the information?"

"I think you best take a closer look at Anne—she does not strike me as a woman who will be easily seduced."

"A skilled man can seduce any woman."

"I would not wager on that remark," Ian said with a laugh.

"Watch and learn," Blair said with confidence and rode off to prove his words.

Ian glanced down at Moira warm and safe in the protection of his arms.

Seduce.

He could slowly seduce his wife, little by little, day after day, until finally she willingly surrendered to him. He favored the thought. Seduction was always an appealing prospect. But a slow, purposeful one could prove challenging. And besides, he did wish to keep her close by his side while he determined the validity of this supposed danger.

She stirred against him, pressing her cheek firmly to his chest and releasing a gentle moan before she once again settled quietly in his arms.

His body responded instantly to her closeness and he gave a brief thought to how good it would feel to make love to her. Damn, but he wanted her.

Seduction.

He shook his head.

Trust.

She needed to trust him and attempting to seduce her would not help matters. He would win her trust, then think of seduction.

They reached the base of the hills before nightfall and Ian sent the men to search for secure shelter away from the impending storm. The sky had darkened considerably as the day wore on and foul weather seemed guaranteed.

Two caves were soon located; the smaller one was ample space for Moira and Anne to share and the two women were soon busy setting to work to start a fire and prepare their meal and their bedding for the evening.

The first crack of thunder startled both women.

" 'Tis glad I am that we are safely tucked away from the storm," Anne said, adding another piece of peat to the fire to keep the flames strong.

Moira joined her, having placed their rolled bedding to the side to later spread out near the fire. "The evening meal will be a light fare; the animals probably sought shelter early from this storm."

"Then we have Sister Mary to thank for our meal this evening, for she provided us with a good portion of bread and cheese for our journey."

Blair's sudden entrance surprised the two women. He stood with a handful of wood, water dripping from his hair, face, and garments. "A fire burns already?"

"We have seen to our own care for many years," Anne said as if this were common knowledge and he should understand.

He dropped the wood to the side and squatted down in front of the fire to warm his hands. "You have peat."

"I gathered it along the way, a logical choice since rain seemed promising and wet wood is impossible to light. As I mentioned, we have provided sufficiently for ourselves for many years."

Blair rubbed his cold hands together near the flames. "You need not worry about providing for yourselves any longer. You have the clan to provide for you and Ian sees that the clan does not go without. Food, shelter, protection, Ian sees that it is provided for all."

"So then his fields prosper and there is plenty for all?" Moira asked, helping Anne to unwrap the hunk of cheese and thick loaf of bread Sister Mary had wrapped for their journey.

Blair eyed the food appreciatively. "The fields do well enough and if necessary food is rationed."

Anne sliced thick pieces of cheese and bread. "We

never had to ration at the convent. The harvest was always bountiful."

"Always?" Blair asked, sounding doubtful.

Anne made herself clear. "Always. The harvest provided not only for the convent but for the less fortunate, with still enough to sell at market."

Blair furrowed his brow. "You must have had a bountiful harvest to provide for so many so abundantly. You never had a year where your crops failed to produce or produced less adequately than expected?"

Anne shook her head. "Never, our crops were well maintained."

"Even the best-maintained crops fail from time to time."

Anne was adamant. "Not ours. We saw to their care and tended the soil properly and our crops prospered."

Moira stood with a yawn after having finished several pieces of cheese. "Planting time, soil condition, crop location—all have a bearing on growth and production."

"How so?" Blair asked with interest and accepted the bread and cheese offered him.

Moira bent down to unfold their bedding. "Soil needs nourishment just as we do. If plants are continually placed in the same area year after year they do not prosper. A change of location benefits the soil and the seedlings. Timing is important as well. Too early finds production lacking, too late also creates less of a harvest. Planting time must be precise."

"You sound as if you know much about crop production," Blair said.

"It was necessary to convent life," Moira said candidly. "We produced a sufficient crop or we starved."

Moira kneeled to unroll the bedding and began spreading it out.

"What are you doing?" The snappish question startled everyone and Blair jumped to his feet at the sight of a soaked Ian.

"I brought wood for a fire but they had already seen to their own," Blair explained with a sense of guilt.

Ian shook his head, rainwater flying from the ends of his long dark hair. A shake of his body followed, excess water flying free, and he dropped the wet fur cloak that he wore to the ground before stepping toward the fire.

"I was not inquiring as to you, Blair, I wondered what my tired wife was doing on her hands and knees."

Moira answered without hesitation. "I am arranging mine and Anne's bedding for the night."

Ian squatted in front of the fire, eagerly accepting a large hunk of bread and cheese from Anne. "That palette does not appear large enough for a husband and wife."

Moira spoke up. "Should it be?"

Blair hid his smile behind a raised hand.

Anne openly grinned.

"Aye, it should be," Ian informed her. "You are my wife and I your husband. We sleep together."

"Why? I am already with child," Moira responded bluntly.

Blair stood as soon as he saw Ian's eyes glow bright green. "Anne, is there enough cheese to share with the men?"

"More than enough, Sister Mary is generous with her fine cheese," Anne said and gathered the large hunk up in its cloth wrapping and hurried to Blair's side.

They both made a hasty retreat, leaving the couple to battle alone.

"What difference does it make that you are already with child?" Ian finally asked of her.

Moira shrugged, having finished spreading out the fur and sitting in the middle of the comfortable bedding. "Why else does a husband sleep with his wife?" She answered her own question. "To get her with child so that she may give him an heir to carry on his name and see to his lands. Once she carries his babe, what need is there for sharing a bed?"

Ian walked around the fire and sat only a few inches away from her. "Some husbands enjoy sleeping with their wives."

"Do the wives?" Moira asked and in a way that made Ian realize her question was posed in a curious and serious manner. She once again answered her own query after giving it brief thought. "I suppose you would not know how other wives feel."

Ian grew curious. Moira had been raised in a convent and taught by celibate women. What had she learned? "Most wives in the clan sleep with their husbands."

"Out of necessity?"

Her question was asked with an intent interest. She was actually curious and Ian did not mind discussing the matter with her. It helped him to better understand his wife.

"In a way, sleeping space is limited, though—" He laughed. "Occasionally I find a man whose wife put him out of bed and he is sleeping alone."

Moira laughed and reached for a piece of bread, tearing off a large enough chunk to share with Ian. "And does he usually learn the lesson his wife is trying to teach him?"

Ian accepted the bread she held out to him. "I could name one or two that are still learning."

Her laughter sounded like a soft, sensuous melody that could tempt a man's soul. And damned but he wanted to tempt hers.

Instead he asked, "Why do you think that a husband only wishes to sleep with his wife to get her with child?"

"Mother Superior spoke to me of duty and honor to my family. She was charged with teaching me the skills and knowledge I would need to make a man a good wife. She spoke of intimacy as being necessary to conceive a child and no more. She advised me that I would receive no pleasure from the act and that I should consider it my duty to my husband and the church." Moira shook her head. "Marriage, it seems, has nothing to do with love, only duty, and once that duty is performed—" She shrugged. "Why then would a wife wish to remain in her husband's bed?"

"Not all marriages are loveless unions."

"Aye, I agree with you, but my father is the head of a mighty clan and as his daughter I have a duty to wed a man of his choosing—and why? To benefit him. It matters not how I feel or whether I love this man or not. I am to do my duty as his daughter."

She paused a moment as if weighing her words and then continued. "After years passed and it seemed unlikely that I would wed, I settled into a contented life. It seemed my father did not need me and in a strange way I was relieved I would not be made to wed a strange man that I would be answerable to. Then you arrived that fateful night, and I did what I thought was my duty. And to everyone's surprise I will give you a child. My duty is done to my husband and to the church. Therefore I need not share your bed."

Ian could not say what annoyed him about her refusing to share his bed. He only knew he was annoyed and that was enough for him to say, "Unless I as your husband deem otherwise."

Moira spoke her mind to Ian's surprise. "Then clarify for me, is it your bed you only wish me to share or do you speak of intimacy?"

"You speak bluntly."

"How else am I to find my answer?"

"Then answer me this," Ian said, intending to be blunt himself. "Did you find any pleasure with me?"

"The night we wed?" she asked, though she knew.

Ian nodded and knew himself her answer, though he waited to hear her words.

Moira answered quickly and with certainty. "Nay, I found no pleasure with you."

He knew he would hear her answer such, so why then did her words disturb him? He had had little time that night to make their first union a memorable one. He had never

taken a woman with haste or disregard. And he had not favored taking Moira as he did, but he had had no choice.

He intended to rectify that. "Then let me give you pleasure."

✿ nine

Moira stared at him perplexed. "Why?"

He was about to answer when she continued.

"You got what you wanted from me and my father. Why should I seek pleasure from a man who deceived me?" She did not sound angry, merely curious, as if she were attempting to solve a puzzle.

"We are husband and wife," he said, feeling that was explanation enough yet knowing it would never satisfy her.

Her next question shocked him. "Do you love me?"

He was speechless, which annoyed him and yet he could not answer her.

"Did you love your first wife?"

He answered without thought. "Aye, very much."

Surprisingly she smiled. "That is good. I am glad to hear that you knew love. We are stuck with each other. There is no love between us and since I have never experienced love I will never know what I have missed. But since it is necessary for us to live together, I would hope that we would at least live as good friends."

Ian spoke his mind for there was much on it. "My first wife, Kathleen, was my best friend. I could discuss anything with her. She was patient when I was not. She was tender when I was not. And she possessed compassion when I could not."

Moira nodded. "She balanced your life."

He smiled recalling all the times Kathleen had brought balance and sanity to his life. "Aye, she did do that."

"And you look for her qualities in another woman."

He supposed he did search for another Kathleen. His short marriage had been a good one and who would not want to have a marriage equal to or better than the previous one?

"I do not possess such qualities," Moira said without regret. "I am who I am and proud of my accomplishments. Unfortunately my qualities are not what men seek in a wife. I remained too long at the convent and became set in my ways and used to my independence. And I do not wish to change."

"You are telling me that I am to accept you as is or not at all?" Ian asked, not surprised by her audacious remark. He was beginning to understand that his wife spoke her mind with no ill will toward anyone. She was simply candid. And did not that come from her years of independence at the convent?

"I present my honesty to you, what more would you ask of me?"

Ian leaned toward her and gently ran his hand across her cheek. "I would ask that you accept my touch."

Moira did not recoil from his tenderness. She was tired and his gentle stroking was pleasing, but intimacy was a different matter. "I do not object if you touch me on occasion."

He leaned closer and brushed his lips over hers. "And a kiss?"

Her eyes had closed briefly when he kissed her and her lips had tingled, nothing more. She could endure a simple kiss. "On occasion I assume it would be appropriate and I have no objection."

He sat back away from her. "And sleeping together?" He nodded. "You are going to have to get accustomed to that for I wish to sleep with my wife."

"Whatever for?"

Her questions rarely sounded personal, rather they seemed to be asked out of an intense interest to learn new things. Another fact Ian was learning about his wife.

He posed his answer as a question. "Warmth? Friendship?"

She smiled and rubbed her arms. "Warmth I understand and since we are to share a life together it would be nice to be friends with my husband."

"Then we should work at it."

She hesitated and he understood her doubt. To be friends one must trust; without that trust there could be no enduring friendship. He and Blair possessed such a trust; each knowing the other would be there no matter what the circumstances.

She gave him the only answer she could. "I will try."

He said no more. He simply reached for a hunk of cheese and broke it in two, handing her a piece. She took it as if sealing a pact.

Blair and Anne ran into the cave out of the pouring rain.

"Trouble with the horses," Blair said, shaking rainwater from him.

"Rest well, wife," Ian said and deposited a hasty kiss on her lips before jumping to his feet. "I will return shortly."

He and Blair left the cave in haste.

Anne hurried to the fire to warm herself. "It is bitter out."

"Then perhaps we will see snow before morning," Moira said, addressing Anne while attempting to understand why her lips ached. The sensation felt similar to when she enjoyed a favorite flavor and wished for more. But she did not wish for more of Ian's kisses, or did she?

"I hope not. It will make traveling difficult." Anne rubbed her hands together near the flames. "Have you learned anything from Ian?"

Moira thought on her words. Had she learned anything? Certainly not concerning the reason for his return but she had learned that he expected more from her as a wife than she would have suspected. Did that give her reason to think that his return was not merely based on her being in danger? Could he have possibly returned for another reason?

A nonsensical thought, she told herself, and answered Anne. "Nothing concerning the presumed danger I am in."

"Do you think he will speak of it to you?"

"I think that will depend on if the danger actually manifests."

"I heard Blair post extra guards tonight."

"That could be due to the storm," Moira said.

"Possibly, or perhaps they fear something."

Moira shook her head. "Not in this weather. If someone was following us or intended an attack they are presently in the same situation we are and have sought shelter for the night."

"True enough," Anne agreed then shook her head. "Though they wait in readiness."

Moira stretched out on the fur bedding with a yawn. "They are warriors forever ready to defend."

Anne stretched out on her palette. "Aye, but I would like to know what they defend us from."

"In time we will find out," Moira said, another yawn following.

There was no response from Anne. She had drifted off to sleep and within seconds Moira joined her, slipping into a deep slumber.

Ian entered the cave much later. The fire looked as if it was about to die out and he added enough peat to keep the flames burning brightly. The storm continued to rage outside and Ian was not looking forward to travel on the morrow. Even if the storm abated the roads would remain in poor condition. It would be a tedious journey.

He removed his wet shirt but kept his plaid wrapped around himself. He squeezed the excess water from his hair and located a cloth in one of the traveling baskets and used it to dry his damp skin. He then joined Moira beneath the warm soft wool blanket she lay snuggled under.

He eased himself up against her back, draping his arm over her waist and pressing his face into the sweet scent of her long dark hair. He found it a comfort to wrap himself around her. Her body heat seeped through her clothes into him, chasing his chill away. And in no time he fell asleep.

Her whimpers and sudden movements woke him and he realized she was dreaming. She had turned and wrapped herself around him. Her arm lay across his chest, her leg over his, and her body was pressed tightly against him.

Her soft cries sounded like a wounded animal in need and he stroked her with a gentle hand and whispered soothing words to her. She calmed and pressed herself closer to him.

He wondered if he haunted her dreams and he held her tightly, hoping to chase away her fears even if he had to chase away himself.

The rain had ceased during the night but the torrential downpour had left the roads muddy and difficult to travel. Slow progress would be made for the day since the horses had to work twice as hard and complaints sounded early in the morning.

Ian and Blair were busy with problems the weather had presented them. Moira and Anne were left much on their own with only an occasional glance sent their way. The two women did not mind. They preferred being ignored, leaving them time to talk freely.

They were doing just that when a branch from one of the trees alongside the road cracked and fell, knocking the

man in front of them off his horse and sending him toppling to the ground, the tree landing with a solid thud on
top of him.

Moira and Anne brought their skittish horses under control and to a halt while the men behind them hurried to the
fallen man's side. Shouts filled the air and chaos reigned
momentarily until one man hurried off, presumably to get
Ian.

Moira looked to Anne. "I think they could use our aid."

She nodded and they both dismounted without help.

Moira hoisted the hem of her dress up between her legs
and tucked it in her belt. Anne did the same. They left their
fur wraps draped over their horses though they kept wool
wraps tucked snugly around themselves.

Two men were struggling to lift the large tree with little
success. Grunts and groans did not help and their efforts
only managed to cause the felled man more distress.

Moira studied the situation for a moment, taking in the
size of the fallen tree. "Leverage is required," she said to
Anne and pointed to a thick branch that lay off on the side
of the road.

Moira tapped one of the men on the shoulder. "Fetch
that branch." She waved her finger in its direction.

He snapped at her. "Can you not see I am busy?"

She snapped back, shaking a finger in his face. "You
wish him out from under? Then fetch that branch."

The man shook his head and mumbled, but did as she
had ordered.

He must have realized her intentions because when he
returned with it he hastily shoved it beneath the fallen tree.

"Not there," Moira yelled. "You will only cause him
more injury. There," she pointed to the opposite side, indi-
cating he should move his branch.

"I know what I am doing," he insisted, ready to press
down on the branch.

"Then you know that you will topple the tree further
down on him and most probably kill him."

"Listen not to her," the other man said and made ready to help him. "What does she know of such things?"

"I am wise enough to know that one of you needs to pull the man beneath out while the other one lifts the tree."

"He can get himself out; we are both needed to lift this branch," the one man said and an affirmative grunt was heard from the other man.

Moira shook her head. "He may be injured—though more than likely the mud cushioned his fall and prevented serious injury, in which case he could be solidly stuck in the mud."

The two men looked at her as if she were daft.

"With a tree this size falling on him he is probably dead," the larger man said and the second man agreed with another grunt.

"Nay, winded and startled by the accident but not dead," Moira said adamantly, "though with the time you two are taking to rescue him he just might succumb."

The larger man grew annoyed. "Stand aside, you know not of what you speak. This is for a man to decide."

Moira shook her head and motioned Anne to follow her. She climbed over the felled tree, scraping her hand on the rough bark but making it over with little difficulty.

"Can you help me pull him out when they lift?" she asked of Anne.

Anne was concerned. "This is not too strenuous of a task for you, being with child?"

"Nay, if we both pull and caution him to use his legs for further leverage we should have no difficulty retrieving him."

"What if he is . . . ?" Anne could not finish her question.

"I heard a groan. And the mud is thick, a good cushion for him to land on. I think he is fine, perhaps with a bruise and scratches, but no serious injuries thanks to the mud."

"Then we shall get him out," Anne said with confidence.

They heard the men on the opposite side grunt and

groan as they laid their weight on the branch and the felled tree began to lift. Moira and Anne bent down ready to do their part, and as the tree lifted up enough for them to see the man they both rushed forward.

He was well stuck in the mud as Moira predicted and Anne ordered him to push with his feet. The two women pulled and the fallen man pushed and it was a hasty rescue that found Moira and Anne falling on their backsides, but freeing the man.

"What the hell!"

The fallen tree suddenly dropped back down and all eyes turned to see a furious Ian jump off his horse and march straight for his wife.

"What the hell are you doing?" he demanded of her and before she could answer he swung around to glare at the two men. "And why did you two allow this?"

The big man attempted an explanation. "We tried to tell her to leave this to the men, but she would not listen."

Ian turned an accusing glare on his wife. "They told you to stay out of this?"

Moira glared back. "They did not know what they were doing."

"And you did?"

"Aye, that I did," she said with confidence and turned her attention to the rescued man. "You are well, I hope?— since no one has the sense to ask."

The man nodded. "Aye, if it were not for the mud I would not have survived." He paused a moment to catch his breath. "And if not for your insistence, those fools would have killed me. I heard what you told them but I had not the breath to speak. Thank you for saving me."

Ian walked up to his wife and reached his hand down to her. "Are you all right?"

She took his hand and with ease he brought her to her feet. "A bit winded but fine."

"The babe?" he asked, lowering his voice.

"I did nothing to harm our child."

"How can you be certain?"

Moira realized his concern though it was tinged with anger, which she could understand. "One can never be certain, but I am well and healthy and the small effort I put into helping that man would not damage the babe. He rests safe and strong inside of me."

Ian looked uncertain. "You will take no chances."

It sounded like an order to Moira but then his concern was for her and the child and she understood his fears.

"You will obey me on this," he demanded with a sternness that startled her.

Moira was not accustomed to being dictated to and while she wished to alleviate his fears she did not wish to offer him obedience.

"I will do what I know is right," she said, calmly and confidently.

He was about to run his hand through his hair in frustration when he noticed the blood on the palm of his hand. He grabbed her hand and turned it over to see her palm smeared with blood. "What is this?"

"Blood," she said as though it meant nothing.

"Your blood," he all but yelled, wiping roughly at her palm and causing her to wince.

He cursed softly beneath his breath. "I am sorry. I did not mean to cause you pain."

"Though tender, they are scratches that will heal, a minor price to pay for helping a man."

Ian held his tongue. He wanted to rant at her for being foolish but how did you accuse someone of foolishness when she helped to save a life? The only thing he could think of to say and that would alleviate his worries was, "You will ride in the cart the remainder of the day."

"I do not wish to. I prefer my horse."

"You will ride in the cart," he reiterated most strongly.

"I will ride my horse," Moira said calmly but with a firmness that had all eyes widening.

Anne walked up beside her to offer support.

"Blair," Ian shouted and the man advanced on Anne with a huge smile.

He scooped her up over his shoulder to her shock and protests and carried her to her horse.

"Anne rides alongside you the rest of the day," Ian ordered. "My wife will ride in the cart."

"I will not," Moira said defiantly.

"I say you will," Ian said, stepping forward until he was near on top of her.

Moira intended to have her way. She refused to follow his dictates and she intended to tell him so as soon as her head stopped spinning. She was merely reacting much too emotionally to the situation and once she calmed herself she was certain she would feel fine.

"Moira?" Ian watched her grow pale. "Moira, are you all right?"

She heard him clearly and wished to answer him but she simply could not find the strength or will to do so.

"Moira!"

He sounded as if in the distance and the light faded before her eyes and in an instant she realized she was about to faint and knew this would not go well for her.

❧ *ten*

Moira woke in Ian's arms and his first words to her were,
"Now you ride with me."

Her response was, "Good, a horse."

She heard laughter though it ended abruptly and she
could only assume one warning look from Ian had silenced
those around them.

"You are foolish," he scolded, lifting her up along with
him as he stood.

"I am hungry," she corrected.

He stopped briefly, his query short. "This is why you
fainted?"

"Aye," she admitted with a sigh. "I find that if I do not
keep my belly full the babe protests."

Ian kept walking. "Yet you look as though you have
gained not an ounce."

"A pound or two," she assured him.

"Should you not have gained more?"

"You worry needlessly. I am fine."

"You fainted," he reminded her.

"Due to hunger."

Hunger or not she had fainted and he did not like the feeling of utter helplessness he experienced when she fell into his arms. He did not know what to do and could do nothing. He had to wait for her to come to and for a moment he feared that she would not. He intended to keep a closer eye on his stubborn wife.

He was about to hoist her on his horse when she protested. "I am a mess with mud, please let me change garments before joining you."

Anne was close by and requested the same. "Aye, I would be more comfortable if allowed to change."

Ian nodded and motioned to the men who stood by awaiting orders. They were instructed to guard the area. Blair joined Ian and after the women had retrieved a change of clothing they walked with them to a thick growth of bushes that provided ample privacy.

Blair whispered to Ian so that the women would not hear him. "Is Moira all right?"

"She tells me so."

"Anne says she has fainted before and it is nothing to worry about," Blair said. "The babe being stubborn, so she says."

Ian heard his doubt. "You think not?"

Blair shrugged. "Who am I to say? I know little of a woman when she carries a child."

"Finish what is on your mind," Ian all but ordered.

"I do not recall any of the women in the clan fainting when with child and your Kathleen never did. Maybe there is something wrong and she keeps it from you."

"Why?"

"Because she is stubborn and foolish and refuses to obey her husband."

Ian smiled. "And you feel a woman should be compliant."

"In certain ways, aye," Blair said with a laugh.

"Then why are you attracted to Anne? She certainly is not compliant."

"Shhh," Blair said, turning to see if the women had heard Ian's remark, but their busy chatter told him they were deep in their own conversation.

"Well, do I get an answer?"

"I am thinking," Blair said as if trying to figure it out.

Ian laughed. "You have no idea, you only know that you wish to pursue that interest."

"Aye, that I do." His smile was wide and wicked.

"I think it is watchful eyes we will keep on the both of them."

"That will be no chore for me," Blair admitted.

"We shall see," Ian said, folding his arms over his chest. "Anne may prove to be a handful for you."

Blair shook his head and laughed. "You are challenging me just as you did when we were young. And you always lost the challenge when it came to a woman. There was none I could not charm."

Ian shrugged. "I needed no charm, my good looks were enough."

Blair laughed heartily over his remark. "Looks and a smooth tongue got you the women. They melted at your feet and still do."

"All but one." Ian's tone turned serious. Blair was right. Women had always been attracted to him and he had never had a problem finding a woman to share his bed. It was odd and perhaps a bit damaging to his male ego that Moira found no interest in him.

"She was raised in a convent," Blair said as if that explained all.

Ian knew better. His deception had left a bitter taste in her and while she accepted her fate she intended to deal with it in her own way. It was the one way she could retain her own pride and maintain her independence.

Moira and Anne stepped around from behind the thick bushes, Anne carrying their bundle of soiled clothes.

Ian reached out for his wife's hand and she took it without objection.

"I am fine," she said, assuming he would repeat his redundant query.

He made no comment and had no intention of inquiring to her condition. He simply wished to hold her hand. And he did not understand why himself, he only knew that the urge was too strong to deny.

He kept a firm grasp on her and asked, "Still hungry?"

"Even more hungry," she said with a laugh and her free hand went to cover her stomach. "I do not think he is ever satisfied."

"A demanding one is he," Ian said, a sense of pride filling him knowing his child nestled within her.

"Sounds like his father," Blair said from behind them, a chuckle following his remark.

"Me demanding?" Ian asked with mock surprise.

"I suppose you have no choice, being the laird of a clan," Moira said in defense of her husband. "A man who leads must make demands." She did not add her other thought.

Difficult decisions.

Had his decision to deceive her truly been a difficult one? Had he weighed all his options and determined there was no other possible way? If she could understand the thoughts that had determined his decision then perhaps she could find a way of coming to peace with it, for her own sake if for no other reason.

"Ian leads well and fairly," Blair said. "There is not a clansman who would not fight by his side."

Moira thought on Blair's words. Ian's clan had followed him to the convent and not one had made mention of his true identity. Every man there knew he was to wed his enemy's daughter and kept silent. They probably felt sorry for him, fate having dealt him the misery of an unwanted wife.

Had anyone felt sorry for her? Had anyone thought of

how Ian had manipulated her fate? She thought not. She was important yet unimportant in the scheme of things. She was but a discardable weapon that once used was no longer necessary.

She grew quiet with her haunting thoughts and spoke not a word.

Ian placed his hands around her waist when they stopped next to his horse, and asked, "Are you all right? You grow quiet."

She usually spoke her mind but her thoughts were much too private and troublesome to share with him. Instead she focused on what she thought he felt would be an easy matter to address. "I think of food."

"I think you avoid the real issue."

He waited, expecting an answer she did not wish to give. Honesty was her only choice. "I do not wish to speak of it now."

"The time will come when you must."

"Why?"

"It will forever stand between us if you do not."

He said no more. He nodded to Blair and mounted his horse. Blair lifted Moira up to Ian and with one strong arm he took hold of her and positioned her across the front of him. He placed a fur wrap around her to keep her warm and took hold of the reins.

Anne rushed up to the horse, a small cloth-wrapped bundle in her hands. "Cheese and apples."

Ian took it from her. "My thanks, Anne, and Blair will be your companion for the remainder of the day."

" 'Tis not necessary," Anne protested sweetly, not wanting Ian to know that she wished to talk with Blair and see what she could learn from him. "He must have more important matters to see to."

Blair stepped from around the other side of Ian's horse. "What more important matter could there be than spending time with a beautiful woman?"

Anne could not help but delight in his charming tongue.

And there was the fact that he considered her beautiful, though she was not foolish enough to believe she was the only woman he thought beautiful. She was a sensible young woman and remained interested in seeing what information she could extract from him.

Anne smiled. "How can I resist a man who possesses such a charming tongue?"

Blair grinned and shook his head. "For one raised in a convent you are outspoken."

"Which is the very reason Mother Superior suggested that I join Moira. She thought me not at all suited for convent life."

Blair walked up to her and offered her his arm; she took it. "And right she was."

"Now it is your turn to tell me of you."

The two walked off arm in arm and Moira knew that by nightfall Anne would have more information to share with her.

Ian directed his horse on the path, with Blair and Anne following behind and the other three men bringing up the rear and arguing over the tree incident. The man pinned by the felled tree kept insisting that the other two had no sense and that if it were not for Moira he would be dead.

The remainder of the troop waited a short distance ahead and as they approached the men joined them and they were all once again on their way.

Moira ate her fill of the cheese and apples, sharing a piece every now and again with her husband.

"I will see that you have a private stitching room in the keep since you mentioned that you enjoyed the weaving at the convent," he said, wanting her to anticipate a feeling of comfort in her new surroundings.

She was about to tell him that she was not interested in stitching itself but quickly thought better of it. If she could manage to secure a private room for herself then she could continue her studies.

"I would like that."

He was pleased that she thought favorably of his suggestion and that in time they would work well together. And given time she would accept him as her husband in all manners and terms. He was confident of it.

"I am curious," he said, recalling the fallen tree. "You handled the accident calmly and knowledgeably—however did you know the appropriate action to take?"

"Why would I not know?" She sounded as though the question were unnecessary.

"Did many trees fall on the sisters at the convent?"

"One does not need to experience an ordeal to prove oneself capable of handling it."

Ian smirked.

"You do not agree?"

"I think it depends on the situation." He continued to debate her opinion. "Take for instance a surprise attack."

Moira listened with interest. She so enjoyed an in-depth discussion on a challenging subject.

"Do you think you are capable of reacting sensibly to that?"

Moira was ready with her answer. "Definitely."

Ian raised a questioning brow, surprised she had not hesitated. "You would not be fearful?"

"Only a fool would not fear such a terrifying situation. A brave warrior knows that every time his sword is drawn he faces the possibility of death, and what fool would not fear death?"

Ian was impressed that she understood a warrior's plight. Most women never realized what a man faced when he entered battle. He remained silent to hear more.

"Though I would fear, I would also take action to defend myself."

"How?" he asked. "A woman is not capable of wielding a sword."

She paused a moment to contemplate the matter.

Ian watched her. She was intent in her thought, her expression serious and, to him, her features captivating. Her wide eyes brightened, she tugged at her bottom lip with her top teeth, and sometimes she gave a soft almost inaudible "mmm" while she thought. He found her utterly delightful. He did not think she could be coy if she tried. She was simply too blunt in her opinions. And then there was the feel of her.

With that he slipped his hand beneath the fur wrap to slide his arm around her waist and adjust her position on the saddle, a poor excuse to touch his own wife but one that was necessary. It was however not necessary for his arm to remain around her or for his hand to rest at her waist. And since she did not object, her concentration being on her response, he left it there.

Of course if he gave it thought himself, he could grow insulted, for she paid his action little heed and responded not at all to the personal gesture. Did that mean his touch did not at all affect her?

Finally Moira spoke. "I think my instincts would rise to the occasion and I would follow them without thought."

He grinned. "And what if your instincts told you to run?"

"I would do as they directed."

He leaned his face closer to hers. "What if I ordered you to run?"

She thought again, her teeth giving her bottom lip another tug. "I suppose it would be wise of me to follow your orders since you are a seasoned warrior and you understand the risk of a dangerous altercation."

"Good, then you are capable of following orders."

He teased with a charm that brought a smile to her face. "When I feel it wise."

"So you judge for yourself and then decide whether you will obey me?" He found her response humorous and almost laughed. "You think yourself wiser? More capable than me?"

"I trust my wisdom while I know not of your wisdom. If you prove wise I will not need to disobey you."

He laughed this time—he could not help himself. "Then you plan on disobeying me?"

"Only if I think your edict unwise."

"And you will determine this yourself?"

"Of course," she answered with a proud smile.

He could get angry, demand that she obey him, demand himself wise enough to lead a clan, but he decided he would have more fun with her by proving his wisdom. Besides, he at that moment much preferred to kiss her. And he did just that—he leaned down and captured her lips with his so quickly she could not protest or pull away from him.

She had little choice but to surrender to his kiss.

❧ *eleven*

His kiss coaxed and Moira found herself curious.

She relaxed and allowed him to pursue his intent, feeling completely in charge of the intimate exchange and knowing she could end it when she chose. At the moment she wanted to experience the results of his kiss. How did it make her feel? Did she like it? Would she like him to kiss her again? She hoped it would prove to be an interesting experiment.

Ian found her lips pliable enough and her body was certainly relaxed against him, but it was her sense of detachment that disturbed him, or perhaps injured his male pride. Did she not find his kiss exciting enough? Did it not tempt her innocent passion?

Hell and damnation, did it not affect her at all?

He slipped his mouth off hers and stared down at her.

She stared back and found his face fascinating. His blue eyes reminded her of a bright summer sky and she realized the intense color reflected the heat of an exceptionally hot summer day. His distinct features were a perfect symmetry of lines and angles as if arranged by an artistic mathematician producing a stunningly handsome face.

And being an inquisitive woman she raised her hand to his face and with her finger traced the many lines and angles that fascinated her as she said, "You are a work of art."

This wife of his was going to be a challenge to understand and he loved the thought. "Does this mean you think me handsome?"

"Aye, you are handsome," she admitted candidly.

"I am glad you are pleased with me."

"Oh, it matters not if I am pleased about your features; it is mere fact. You are a handsome man."

He shook his head and laughed. "So it matters not that my features are pleasing?"

She spoke her mind. "Do my plain features matter to you?"

It was his turn to slowly run his finger over her face. "Your face fascinates me."

His words surprised her, as did his tender touch. "Why? It is not a face that draws attention."

"Only a blind man would fail to recognize your alluring features."

She wished to believe his words, but she was not a foolish young woman in love. She was an intelligent woman of nine and twenty years who knew better than to fall prey to a charming tongue.

He playfully tapped her nose. "You do not believe what I say."

"I believe what I see and my reflection shows me a plain woman."

"Then you are blind."

"I see well enough," she argued. "And besides, you tell me this merely to please me."

He gently grabbed hold of her chin. "Aye, I wish to please my wife, but I also speak the truth to her."

Did he speak the truth? She did not know for sure and decided not to debate his word.

He smiled and whispered, "You have the most beautiful eyes."

A tingle rippled through her stomach and her hand rushed to rest there, only she connected with his strong, muscled forearm. She drew her hand back quickly.

"Nay, leave it rest where it settled. I like your touch on me."

Again the strange tingle attacked her stomach. Could his words have disturbed her? She placed her hand on his arm. What harm could it cause?

It took a moment for her to relax her touch upon him and when she did she found no strange feeling attacking her. She simply found the feel of him soothing. A good thought to keep in mind. Their marriage would not do well if she could not abide touching him or be averse to his innocent touch.

Intimate touch was a different matter, and why she even thought of it she could not say. She did not wish to be intimate with him. She found nothing about intimacy appealing. Then why had it been on her mind of late?

Curiosity.

She was merely curious, as was her nature—or was she?

"Do you often get lost in your thoughts?" Ian asked, interrupting her musing.

"Aye, often, and sometimes without realizing it. Does that upset you? My not being attentive."

"Would it matter?"

She thought a moment. "It can be inconsiderate at times and I do not do it intentionally. I would advise that you not take it personally."

He tapped at her nose again. "How can a husband not take an inattentive wife personally?"

"Is it necessary for a wife to be attentive at all times?"

"Is that not her duty?"

"I did not ask if it was her duty. I asked if it was necessary," she said, her look intent, as if the answer was important to her.

"It is not necessary for my wife to be attentive at *all* times. But there are times I would like her attention."

"And those times are?" she asked bluntly.

He was blunt on purpose. "When I am riding my horse with her and when I am riding her in bed."

"I will keep that in mind," she said with not the slightest bit of emotion, though a series of tingles attacked her tummy.

He, however, displayed his emotion. He brought his face close to hers and in a firm tone said, "I would definitely do that if I were you."

She noticed his eyes had fired to a brilliant green. He was angry with her and she wisely chose not to agitate him further. She remained silent. She did note though that when his temper flared he could intimidate. He seemed much more in command, more arrogant, more forceful. Not a person she would choose to confront.

A yawn chose to surface just as she was about to change the subject of their conversation.

"Tired?"

"Nay," she answered with haste.

He looked at her curiously. "You yawn but you are not tired?"

"The babe makes himself known."

"Then perhaps you should pay attention."

"He has a good and safe resting place, is well fed and well cared for; his needs are met and I will not submit to his demands. He will know that I am in charge and work accordingly with me."

"You expect this from a babe that has yet to be born?"

Her answer was a simple "Aye."

He shook his head. "You are unlike other women."

She knew that to be true and agreed. "Aye, I am."

He laughed. "You spare not the truth."

"Would you have me speak falsely?"

"I doubt you could."

She smiled, pleased by his words. "You begin to under-stand me."

"Not an easy process."

"I can be difficult."

He hugged her to him. "Nay, you are a challenge."

She looked into his eyes and they were a soft and ten-der blue. He spoke from his heart and that pleased her. But she wished to shift the conversation and she could think of no way to ease into what she wished to know so she asked, "Have you spoken recently with my father?"

If he was surprised by her query he did not show it. "Nay, we have nothing to discuss."

She continued, needing answers. "He does not know you came to the convent for me?"

"He has no need to know." His response sounded harsh.

"I am his daughter."

"You are *my wife.*"

"Will you tell him of our child?"

"He does not know?" Ian asked anxiously.

"No one knew except Mother Superior and Anne," Moira answered and recalled how she wished her secret could have remained confined to the convent.

"He will need to be informed of the impending birth of his grandchild."

"He will not be happy," Moira said confidently.

"Why say you this?"

"If I remember the marriage agreement correctly he will lose part of the Isle of Mull to his grandchild. Being he thought me barren, he thought he gave you nothing. And now?" She shrugged. "He has given you more than he wished to give."

Ian thought on her words. Could her father somehow have found out about the babe? Was he angry over that part of the marriage agreement he thought would never see fruition? Could he possibly care so little for his daughter that he would want her dead rather than part with his land?

The questions disturbed him though perhaps the answers would disturb him even more. Regardless, he
needed to find out.

Moira yawned again.

"You should rest."

He sounded as though he ordered her to, though she
chose to ignore it. "I am resting."

"It would seem the babe thinks otherwise."

She continued to ignore his concern for her and continued to discuss her father. "Angus Maclean is not an easy
man to contend with."

"I know this of him and I will deal with him. Do not
concern yourself."

"He is my father."

"I do not wish you to worry," Ian said adamantly.

"That cannot be helped."

"You are stubborn," he said, giving her a gentle hug.

"That is a fact," she answered and wondered why she
felt so content and safe in his arms.

"Tell me of your father," he said, thinking it would help
her to speak of him and help him to learn more about
Angus Maclean.

"I get my stubbornness from him," she admitted without reluctance. "His opinions and thoughts cannot be
swayed. When he is right, he is right and no one can make
him think otherwise."

"He will battle for his beliefs?"

"Without question."

"Perhaps he should question more and battle less."

Moira smiled. "A good suggestion but one I doubt he
would favor."

"He judges quickly."

"And is relentless in his judgments," Moira said softly.

Ian realized, more than she probably did, the hurt her
father had caused her. He himself had thought he considered enough the consequences of his decision, but had he?
His thought had been that one life could spare thousands.

He had not considered her life at all, merely that it was insignificant compared to thousands, but was that fair of him? If he'd known her then as he did now, could he have made the same decision?

No answer came to him, though he knew now her life meant much to him and in no way would he see her hurt or harmed.

"You are my wife now. No one, not even your father, has the right to judge you. You are under my protection."

She took the opportunity presented her. "Do I need protection?"

"Times are chaotic and unpredictable. A friend today can be your enemy tomorrow."

"Who then do you know you can trust?"

He answered quickly and with certainty. "You can trust me."

She spoke her piece. "How say you this after the way you deceived me?"

"Aye, I deceived you," he said, his eyes steady on her. "It was a necessary choice and one perhaps one day you will understand. But I am your husband now and with our exchange of vows came a commitment I take seriously and will honor."

"They were vows exchanged in deception. How can they be taken seriously or honored?"

"They were vows exchanged before God."

"They were lies before God."

He was indignant. "I did not lie before God. I exchanged vows willingly with you."

"Under false pretenses," she argued.

"Under necessary pretenses," he corrected.

"So say you."

He sighed with exasperation. "This gets us nowhere. One day perhaps you will come to understand my necessary decision; until then you have no choice but to abide by our vows."

"Perhaps one day you will understand the results of your necessary decision."

He stared at her for a moment. "The results I would say surprised all, and I can say I am pleased that you carry my child." He asked then a question that had been on his mind. "How did you feel when you discovered you carried my child?"

Her smile pleased him for he knew she had not been upset by her discovery and he waited impatiently to hear her say so.

Her hand went to her stomach. "At first I thought myself ill, retching so early in the morning without a bit of food in my stomach and then when I did eat I could not keep it down long."

"You were ill much?" he asked with concern.

"A couple of weeks, though it felt like months," she said with a laugh.

"You can laugh about this?"

"How could I not? I never thought that I would conceive a child." Her voice turned low. "My father made it quite clear that day that I was barren and therefore a useless wife. Everyone believed him—including myself. More the fool was I."

Ian said nothing for he himself had thought the same. She was too old to ever conceive a child and he had not even given it thought when he took her virginity. He felt as foolish as she did for he had allowed another's words to sway his thought.

"So when this terrible illness struck me, I never once thought possible that I was with child."

"When did you realize?" he asked, feeling guilty that she had gone through this alone. He was her husband and he should have been there for her and their child.

She smiled again. "I gave my illness thought. I had no fever and my sickness would come and go at the same time each day. Usually an illness grows worse; mine remained the same day after day. And then I realized an important fact."

He waited, wondering if she would feel comfortable speaking of it to him.

She seemed not at all reluctant to tell him. "I had not bled for a month and that is when I began to wonder. I then discussed it with Mother Superior and we both came to the same conclusion. I was with child."

"It did not disturb you?"

"Heavens no," she said on a laugh. "It actually delighted me. To think that something so wonderful and beautiful could be conceived of deception seemed a miracle. I was thrilled and I still am."

"You look forward to the birth?"

She laughed. "That I cannot say for I hear it is not a pleasant experience, but I think I will do well."

"I will be with you."

She stared at him strangely. "Not during the birth?"

"Aye, that I will," he insisted. "I will not have you suffer alone."

"What will you do?"

"I will hold your hand and offer you comfort."

"And if I do not want you there?"

He smiled. "You have no choice, wife. I intend to remain by your side and see you through this birth of ours."

"Husbands do not attend births."

"This husband does," he said adamantly.

"I have no say in this?"

"None," he said firmly. "I will be by your side, like it or not. I am the cause of your pain and I will suffer with you."

"You need not do this. Birth and pain are common enough. It is no fault of yours."

He took her face in his hand. "Hear me well, wife. I planted my seed in you and it found fertile ground. My child now nestles within you and I will see to your care and see that you do not suffer this ordeal alone. I will be by your side when your time comes."

"This is not necessary. I can manage the delivery on my own."

"It is necessary and I will have it no other way."

Her question was simple. "Why?"

He answered simply, "You are my wife."

After a moment of silence between them he leaned down and kissed her softly.

"I will always be there for you. Always."

❧ twelve

Moira was not permitted to help when camp was being set up for the night. She was to rest though she was not tired. Her mind was active and she longed for the solitude and challenge of her studies.

She was forever calculating numbers in her head or looking to make sense of the senseless. When questions were asked valuable knowledge was learned, but few if any asked sensible questions.

Over and over she had heard the men ask of Ian or Blair as to how long it was before they reached home. Moira had grown so tired of their asking that she asked of Ian certain questions that enabled her to calculate their arrival time. She would have shared it with the men but she doubted that they would have believed her so she spoke of it to Anne, who was pleased with the information and who of course did not doubt her ability.

Even now as she sat in silence watching the camp activity she could have suggested many ways that would have helped the men do some of their chores more efficiently, leaving free time for them to relax for the evening, which obviously many of them wished to do.

The journey was tedious and difficult at times. The chilling and often damp weather did not help and grumbles of complaint were often heard. She also had the feeling that Ian had slowed their pace due to her condition, which of course was not at all necessary.

She was accustomed to looking after herself and doing as she pleased. Sitting by and being idle was not to her liking. She was one to take charge and see that things got done. Her daily chores included making rounds of the convent and seeing that every part of the convent operated to its fullest capacity, leaving time of course for prayer and contemplation.

She could not and would not sit by and do nothing. She needed purpose in her life and she had found it in her studies. It was a lucky day when the stranger had shown up at the convent gates requesting nourishment and a place to rest. Mother Superior had gladly supplied him with both and when it was discovered he was ill he was offered sanctuary.

He was a monk who had chosen to wander and discover and he was a man of great knowledge. Some knowledge, he advised, was not meant to be shared. But he had shared it with Moira.

Moira shook her head, not at her own thoughts but at the way one of the men was attempting to start the campfire. The wood was stacked too closely together and he lacked sufficient kindling to set the flames, and worst of all he was impatient. Nothing got done correctly or efficiently if one was impatient.

She shook her head once again and held her hands out to the fire that she and Anne had set burning when they first set camp. They had the flames going in no time and Moira kept them so by adding just the right amount of wood when needed.

She had not realized the importance of knowledge until

she had begun to learn. She had thought that she had learned what was necessary and yet she had learned nothing; and though she had gained knowledge it was not enough. She ached to learn more.

A thought suddenly troubled her. Mother Superior was tolerant of her studies, even encouraged them, but what if Ian discovered her secret and thought differently? What if he ordered her to cease her studies? What then would she do?

It troubled her to think that someone could dictate her life. She had enjoyed her time alone and the independence that came with it. It was hard to even consider that much of what was basic to her was now gone.

Would she adapt to her new surroundings? She had come to realize that she would never expand her knowledge further if she remained in the convent, but then there was no thought that she would ever have the opportunity to leave. Now that she had that opportunity would she perceive it as such?

She smiled, content with the questions that filled her head and challenged her intelligence. And suddenly she felt the need to take action and put her knowledge to work. Besides, she could not tolerate sitting by and watching the man helplessly flounder in his attempts to start a fire.

Moira tossed her long braid over her back, slipped the fur wrap off her shoulders, and drew the green wool cloak she wore more tightly around her as she stood. She walked over to the impatient man and said, "The wood is too closely packed."

He was short and stocky, firm in muscle and thick in width. His dark red hair hung past his shoulders and his face was set in a perpetual frown. "I have started many a fire."

Moira nodded, not wanting to remark on how long it probably took him to get them started. "I am sure you have, but if you give space for the fire to breathe then you give birth to the flames."

He shook his head and grunted. "I know what I do."

She decided to be blunt, since she was certain he would pay no heed to her otherwise. "Obviously you do not or your fire would have been set by now."

He tossed the stick he held down at the flameless stack of wood. "You think you can do better?"

She answered with confidence. "Of course."

"Then do it," he challenged.

She looked to the stack of wood and then to the man. "If I do that then you will not learn. It would be better if you worked along with me."

"You think to teach me something I already know?" He sneered and grunted once again.

"Are we not always learning something?"

He looked at her as if he thought her mindless.

It did not bother her; she simply continued. "Perhaps one day you will be able to teach me something."

"A man can always teach a woman something," he boasted with a smile.

Moira smiled along with him, for his grin actually gave his face a tender touch and made her realize he was more bluster than not. "Can this woman teach a man something?"

He shrugged, feeling more at ease by her pleasant nature. "If you can."

"Let us see," she said and went down on bended knees to tend the wood. "What is your name?" she asked of him.

"John," he answered, bending down beside her.

"Let me show you what I think will work best." With that Moira went to work and John surprisingly enough paid attention.

In a few minutes the fire sparked to life and John and Moira were deep in conversation, he asking her questions without giving it a thought that she might know something more than him.

It was when she finally stood with John's help that a feeling of lightheadedness swept over her. She thought that perhaps she had stood too fast but John had helped her up slowly. When the feeling grew stronger she realized she was about to faint and the thought annoyed her. The babe picked the most inopportune time to make himself known.

She did not wish to alarm John, or anyone for that matter. If only she could return to her own blanket, but that was not likely.

She smiled at John and did the sensible thing. "Could you please get my husband? I am not feeling well."

Panic rushed over his face and with a sharp nod he hurried off.

She decided that if she took her time and walked toward her campfire perhaps she could rid herself of this faint. She at least had to try since standing there and waiting only seemed to make the dilemma worse.

She took cautious steps, her head fogging with each one.

"Moira!"

She heard her name as if from a distance but knew it came from behind her. She turned slowly to see her husband, Blair, and Anne rushing toward her. And to her surprise she reached out and called, "Ian!"

He raced toward her and caught her in his arms as she toppled forward. He scooped her up and carried her to their bedding. He placed her gently on the blankets and Anne immediately fell to bended knees beside her.

"She will come to shortly, do not worry," she advised the men. Even John had joined them and looked with concerned eyes upon her.

"How often does she do this?" Ian demanded, holding her hand tightly in his, his heart pounding and his mind full of fear.

"It is her condition, nothing more," Anne assured him.

"And this is normal?"

Blair answered. "I do not think so."

John agreed. "I would say the same."

Ian looked up at John. "What was she about when she informed you that she was not feeling well?"

John was reluctant to speak and hesitated.

Ian's eyes turned a sharp green. "I will have my answer now."

John obeyed his laird. "She was starting the fire."

"Starting the fire?" Blair asked as if not hearing him correctly.

"Aye," John admitted again with reluctance. "She was showing me how to start one faster and damned if she was not right."

"You do take time setting the flames to burn," Blair said as if his explanation made sense.

Ian glared at them both. "My wife, who carries my child, needs to help one of the clan start a campfire?"

John remained silent, as did Blair.

Moira groaned softly and all eyes turned on her.

It took a moment for her eyes to fully open and for her to gather her wits. When she finally did she looked to her husband and the worry she saw in his eyes caused her to say, "I am fine."

"You dropped in a dead faint and you are fine?" He raised his voice without realizing it.

"You are angry?" Moira grew upset.

Ian grew upset realizing he had upset her. "Nay." He softened his tone considerably. "Concerned for your well-being."

"Worry not, I am fine," she assured him and attempted to sit up.

He eased his hand beneath her back and assisted her in sitting up, his hand remaining on her lower back.

"You will do nothing but see to your care," he ordered as gently as possible though he wished to shout it at her.

"I am fine," she repeated, beginning to feel herself again. "There is no reason to treat me as though I were fragile."

"You carry my child," he reminded firmly.

"A natural condition."

Ian bit his tongue, about to remind her that she was not of the usual age for a woman bearing a child.

Moira waited. The look in his eyes told her that he was about to say something she did not care to hear.

Blair broke the silence thinking he was helping. "You should consider your age."

"And what do you mean by that?" Anne said, standing in a flash, her hands resting firmly on her hips.

Blair defended himself. "She is older and should take extra care."

Anne waved a finger in his face. "Moira knows what she does. She possesses more brains than the lot of you."

"She faints," Blair said as if it were Moira's fault.

"She carries a child," Anne reminded.

"And she is older than most women who bear children," Blair argued.

Anne's finger waved again. "Only a man would be stupid enough to speak such nonsense."

Blair's temper rose. "You call me stupid?"

"Are you deaf besides stupid?" she asked.

Blair looked ready to pounce on her when Ian yelled, "Enough! The lot of you go tend to your duties while I have a private word with my wife."

Anne looked to Moira and before a word was said Ian spoke.

"This is not a request, Anne."

Anne marched off in a huff, Blair on her heels. John had left when Ian first commanded them to do so. They were finally alone.

"You are certain you feel well?" Ian asked, sitting down beside her, his hand on her back slipping around her waist.

She placed a hand to his face, surprising him. "Listen well, husband, for I will not say this again and I have said it too often already. *I am fine.* Believe those words for they are the truth and never will you hear me say them again for it is not necessary."

He smiled. He wondered if it was more from the fact that her warm hand felt good against his cool skin, or was it her audacious manner? Did she really think she could command him not to ask of her how she felt?

"I will not stop asking," he informed her, his smile spreading wide.

Her smile joined his. "I did not tell you to stop asking. I but informed you that I shall not answer the query again."

He laughed, grabbed her hand at his face, and planted a firm kiss on her palm. "You are a challenge, wife."

"Good," she said, assuming the sensation in her tummy was due to her sudden hunger. "Challenges stimulate."

"That they do," he whispered and kissed her palm more gently.

A tingle raced through her rumbling stomach and she was not sure what caused the sensation. She only knew she had felt it often of late and it was usually when Ian touched her.

Ian heard the rumble and stated the obvious. "You are hungry."

"Much too much lately," she admitted. "I shall grow large soon enough if I continue this way."

"It matters not. You will eat and besides"—he paused, looking her over—"you have gained no noticeable weight."

Moira could disagree, having noticed of late that her stomach was rounding slightly, but then it was only noticeable when naked and she had no intention of being in any state of undress in front of him.

"The men have had a successful hunt and food is plentiful. You will enjoy yourself."

He sounded as if he ordered her to do so, but it mattered not for she was hungry and had every intention of enjoying every morsel. "Aye, that I will."

The remainder of the evening went well. Anne, understanding Moira's need to be useful, made Blair erect a cooking spit over their fire so that Moira could tend to their meal. Anne had gathered wild onions to roast and the two women found pleasure in working together.

As was usual Moira slipped beneath the blankets alone but sometime later Ian joined her. He always joined her, his arm draping over her waist and tugging her gently to his side. She could not say she objected for the heat from his body warmed her considerably and he was comfortable to rest against. She was growing accustomed to sleeping with him and accustomed to his touch, for his hand wandered gently over her at times during the night. Then there were his kisses. He would deliver them at the most unexpected times and catch her off guard. It was quite perplexing for she had not expected him to act so lovingly. And his touch was a loving and a caring one, which confused her all the more.

And then there were her own feelings, which surprised her. She was beginning to enjoy her time shared with him. He was an interesting man and took interest in her. They never lacked for a stimulating conversation and she favored that about him.

She yawned and snuggled closer against him.

His arm closed more tightly around her. "Warm enough?" he asked on a whisper.

A sigh confirmed her comfort.

"I will always keep you warm," he whispered and kissed the column of her neck not once but twice more.

A rush of tingles raced over her body and she shivered.

"A taste of what is to come," his murmur warned.

And she knew at that moment her husband wanted her and intended on having her.

The question was, did she want him?

❧ thirteen

"*Two days' time and we shall finally be home. I cannot wait*," Blair said, riding alongside Ian. "The weather grows cold and much too damp to journey. It is a warm fire and soft bed I look forward to."

"It is alert ears and eyes you will focus on," Ian corrected, his tone serious.

"You still think someone is out to harm your wife?"

"I cannot take a chance nor will I take a chance."

Blair nodded. "I understand your concern, but do you not think you should worry more of her health? She is either fainting or is ill and, while she eats well, her food often protests in her stomach."

Ian did not disagree, since Blair spoke the truth, though he had to admit, "Neither fainting nor ill stops her from doing as she pleases. She tends the fire, cooks the food, and instructs the men in their chores. You would think she would seek to rest but she ignores her yawns and continues on."

"She is stubborn."

"Without a doubt," Ian agreed.

"She will be a handful," Blair warned.

Ian laughed. "A perfect handful."

"She appeals to you?"

"You find that strange?" Ian asked curiously.

Blair shrugged. "She is different from Kathleen."

"Aye, that she is." Ian grew silent for a moment. "My Kathleen was a sweet one and always sought to please me. She stole my heart and it grew silent when she died. I do not think I will ever love another as I did her."

"Yet Moira appeals to you, why?"

Ian wondered himself and found it difficult to explain. "I cannot say why. She certainly is nothing like Kathleen. I do not think she will seek to please me though I find she pleases me in different ways. I find pleasure in speaking with her and her many questions interest me. She constantly searches for answers only to find more questions and is thrilled to discover them. She fascinates me."

"This is good since she will be your wife for the remainder of your days."

"I do not think I will mind, but then you seem to find a stubborn woman appealing," Ian teased. "You do not seem to mind keeping a watchful eye on Anne."

Blair grinned. "Aye, that I do not. She is a pleasure to look upon, quick-witted though fast to speak her mind. I am certain she is up to something."

"What makes you think this?"

"She talks and questions the men."

"About what?"

"Numerous things," Blair said. "She seems overly curious."

Ian rubbed his chin. "Do you think perhaps it is from being confined to the convent that these two ask endless questions?"

Both men looked at each other and shook their heads.

"You keep a closer eye on Anne and I will be more watchful of my wife." Ian glanced over his shoulder to see that Moira and Anne were only a few paces behind them and deep in conversation as usual. "They talk endlessly."

"Do you not wonder what it is they discuss?"

"Since we discuss them I suppose they could be discussing us."

"Aye," Blair agreed, "but what about us do they discuss?"

Ian gave his words thought.

"Perhaps it is best we do not know," Blair said.

Ian shook his head. "Nay, I think it is best that we do know. Only a fool would march unprepared into battle."

"We enter a battle, do we?" Blair asked eagerly. "This I look forward to."

"It will be a battle like none you have ever fought," Ian warned.

"All the more reason to be excited. A new adventure to experience."

"Women do not fight fair."

Blair laughed heartily. "Neither do men."

"I do not think we should underestimate our opponents."

"A wise suggestion and one I will remember well."

"Shall we converge on them in surprise and see what they are about?" Ian asked, his only armor a charming smile.

"A surprise attack. Perfect," Blair agreed, but before the two men could turn their horses their attention was diverted by a genuine surprise attack.

Shouting men rushed from behind bushes and fell from trees to converge on the unsuspecting group. Swords were fast drawn and metal clashed against metal, ringing loudly in the cold, crisp air.

Ian caught a quick glimpse of his wife and Anne attempting to escape the middle of the melee and he swung his sword swiftly and accurately, clearing himself a path to his wife.

Blair followed, driving off several unskilled but persistent warriors.

Ian's eyes took in the whole of the battle, a skill he had learned long ago from his father. He had taught him to focus and judge his opponents and surroundings in a swift glance and then proceed accordingly. His eyes told him the men were after his wife. Their attempts were concentrated on getting to her and while his own men did a good job of protecting Moira the opposing side was fast gaining ground.

He had to get to Moira within a minute or two, or she might be lost to him and that he could not accept. He had lost one wife through no fault of his; he would not lose another wife when he could protect her.

He descended on the converging men with his sword raised, his eyes blazing a raging green, and he released a bone-chilling yell that sent shivers through every person present.

Moira was busy keeping firm control of her horse and keeping herself from harm's way. Ian's men had built a wall of protection around her and Anne but she feared it would not last. And Moira could clearly discern that she was the central point of the attack. It seemed as if almost every man fought to advance on her. Could it be true? Could someone really want her dead?

Anne had gathered a cloth full of peat for the night's fire and began to use pieces as weapons, throwing large chunks at the men. Many of them were not fast enough or were too unsuspecting to deflect her aim and were hit about the head. One or two were knocked off their horses.

Moira attempted to ascertain with haste the options open to her and there were none. She and Anne were stuck and if the men did not hold the opponents firm she would soon find a sword descending on her.

It was as she arrived at that thought that she heard the ear-piercing yell. It shook body and soul and she watched as her husband descended in a fury down upon the melee.

His sword was swift and skillful, his aim sheer perfection, and his features that of a demon bent on revenge.

After three men fell easily to his sword, the others began to retreat, fearing the demonic man who looked about to breathe fire and smoke.

Moira herself wondered over this man. He was naught like her husband, the man who charmed with a pleasant word or smile. He was a man to fear and obey and to dare not offend. And she shivered at the thought that she did not know her husband at all.

In mere minutes he was beside her, lifting her with one firm arm around her waist to rest in front of him on his horse. His body pulsed with heat, his brow dripped sweat, and his sword dripped blood.

"Are you all right?" His arm tightened considerably around her.

She gave him a firm nod, fearful that her voice would tremble if she spoke.

Blair rode to Ian's side, quickly grabbing Anne off her horse and depositing her possessively in front of him. When she made to protest he ordered with a harsh firmness for her to be still. She did so but not without a pout.

The battle was soon quelled, with the remaining attackers scurrying off, dragging the wounded with them. A few of Ian's men followed after them to make certain they would not return.

Ian ordered the men to safer surroundings, which were found a short distance up the road. Wounds were seen to and damage was ascertained and not once would Ian release Moira from his grasp. He kept her seated on his horse in front of him while he issued orders. Only when he was certain that all was seen to did he direct his horse to halt; he dismounted then raised his hands to Moira's waist and plucked her easily off his horse.

He kept his hands on her waist and looked her over before asking, "All is well with you?"

"Aye, all is well," she assured him, noticing that his raging green eyes had calmed to a gentler blue though a spark of fury remained bright within them. He tempered his anger well. She decided to help ease his concerns. "Though . . ." she said, glancing up at him.

"What?" he asked anxiously.

She sighed. "I am hungry."

He laughed, strong and hard, and she could almost see his tension slip away. He hugged her to him and to her surprise he planted a firm kiss on her lips. And without thinking she kissed him back then rested her face to his chest and returned his hug most vigorously.

A shiver raced through her and he stroked her back. "It is over and you are safe."

She had not realized how frightened she had felt. The attack was so sudden that there was no time to think and little time to react. Ian's men had reacted instinctively, having faced battles often enough to react wisely. She had never faced a battle and hoped to never encounter one again.

She had felt helpless. She possessed not an ounce of defense against her opponents. She carried no weapon and knew how to use none, and that brought her to ask of Ian, "Will you teach me how to wield a sword?" Her wide eyes shined bright as she glanced up at him for an answer.

He thought to tell her that he was more than capable of protecting her, but he understood her feeling of total helplessness when all around her brandished a weapon and she did not, and he wished to appease her. "After the babe is born I will teach you."

She did not wish to wait but then she did not think she could convince him otherwise. "Promise?"

"Aye, I promise you, wife."

She smiled at him though it faded and her hand went to touch his cheek. "And you, husband, are you all right?"

Ian was stunned by the sincerity in her voice. She actually sounded as if she cared about him. And those large eyes of hers looked filled with concern. "I have participated in far worse battles. This was but a nuisance."

Relief swept over Moira. She could not say where it came from or why, and the thought stunned her. While she cared for the preciousness of human life and wished no harm on anyone, she realized her relief over her husband's well-being exceeded the common. And that thought remained firm on her mind though she directed her focus on more pressing matters. "Why attack us? We did nothing to provoke them nor do we look to be of wealth. It makes no sense."

Ian thought the same himself, and the way the men had converged on Moira and Anne led him to only one conclusion. They were after his wife. A conclusion he did not wish her to reach. "Who knows? A sorry lot who places no rhyme or reason to their actions."

"Everything has rhythm or reason if one but looks closely enough."

Why did he know she would disagree with him? Her curious nature; it was simply her way. "Perhaps hunger forced their attack?" he suggested, giving her a thought to dwell on.

She dismissed his notion instantly. "They did not look as if they starved."

She was obviously intent on finding answers and Ian was not certain how to dissuade her. To his relief Anne hurried up to them.

"Blair wishes to speak with you."

Ian nodded. "Stay with Moira."

"I will see to her."

Ian reluctantly released his wife. "Rest. I will return shortly."

He walked off but not before directing two of his men to stand guard over Moira and Anne.

Anne gathered a light fare for them and spread a blanket on the ground so that they could sit, eat, and rest after their unexpected ordeal. The two women sat close beside each other so that they could talk without their conversation being heard.

"This was a planned attack," Anne said.

"I agree, but on whom?"

"Their target was obvious."

"Me," Moira said without hesitation.

"It would seem so," Anne agreed.

"The question is why."

"Who could possibly want you dead?"

"We need to see who would benefit most from my death," Moira said with logic.

"Are you not frightened?" Anne asked, sounding worried.

"Nay, not at this moment. During the attack?" She nodded slowly. "I was terrified. Until—" She paused.

Anne waited.

Moira sighed softly. "Until I saw my husband descending on the attackers, his fury palpable, his intent certain, his skill extraordinary. He is a true warrior. All Highlanders are warriors. They fight for their land, their beliefs, and their freedom and sometimes I fear they fight for the sake of fighting alone. But Ian—" She paused again. "He fights to defend. This time, to defend *me.*"

"He is your husband."

"Aye, and obliged to defend me, but the look in his eyes . . ." She shook her head. "I do not know what I saw, I only know that when I looked upon him my fear faded and I knew I was safe."

Anne spoke her mind. "Then it is good to know you have nothing to fear from him."

"Nay, he means me no harm." She knew that and it relieved her to realize it.

"Then who?" Anne asked with frustration.

"That is for us to discover."

"And we begin with who would benefit from your death?"

"It would seem the most logical point," Moira said.

"Why would anyone wish me dead for naught? Someone, somewhere feels I pose a threat."

"I cannot think of how you would pose a threat to anyone."

"I agree. I have spent a good portion of my life in the convent."

"Then you married Ian," Anne reminded.

"Which changed everything." More than she even cared to admit. "It seems we cannot deny the fact that my problem started after my marriage so therefore this threat is somehow connected to my wedding Ian."

Anne thought a moment then lowered her voice. "What if someone discovered that the convent harbored the monk and that he taught you forbidden knowledge?"

"I had given that a brief thought."

"And?" Anne asked when Moira remained silent.

"How could anyone have known? You and Mother Superior are the only ones who truly know the depth of knowledge he taught me. And how could my learned knowledge harm anyone to the degree that someone would want me dead? Or benefit from it? It does not makes sense."

"Then it is not an area we need to give thought to."

"Nay, not at the moment, but it is one we will keep in mind."

"Then who do we look to first? Who would seem to be the most logical suspect?" Anne asked.

Moira did not hesitate. She answered, "My father."

❧ fourteen

"*Impressive,*" *Moira said to Anne. The two women stood* side by side in the great hall.

The room was not overly large though the fireplace was huge and heated the room with a generous warmth that was much appreciated after their long and chilling journey. Trestle tables filled the adequate space with room to spare and a long table, presumably for Ian, family, and special guests, ran across the back wall where it could sit in view of the entire hall.

There was a bustle of activity since their arrival only moments ago. An excitement filled the air over their return. Women had hurried to their lately absent men with eager smiles and outstretched arms. Hugs and kisses were exchanged and gaiety prevailed.

Anne sniffed the air. "The scent does not tempt as Sister Mary's did."

"The food probably lacks the herbs and spices that are common to us."

"We must do something about that. Eating bland food is

not to my liking," Anne said as if with a sour taste in her mouth.

"I agree. Become acquainted with the cook and let me know about her. We can proceed from there."

"A delicious scent," Blair said, sniffing the air with appreciation as he walked up behind them. "We will eat well this evening."

Ian entered the hall as Blair spoke and slapped his back as he passed him. "Hilda brews a feast for us as usual." He slipped his arm around Moira. "Come, I will show you to your quarters so that you may rest."

Moira was not tired. She felt active and did not at all wish to remain idle. "I would like to settle in, unpack my things, and you did promise me a stitching room."

"You are not tired?"

"Nay, I wish to see more of my new home," she said enthusiastically.

"Rest while I tend to some matters then I will show you through the keep." He took her hand and led the way.

She followed eagerly until he deposited her in a large bedchamber that she was certain was his. The bed was of sturdy wood, the mattress looked to be comfortable, and the bedcovering warm. A good-sized stone fireplace roared with a fine blaze. Various-sized chests sat around the room along with a small table and two chairs.

It was a nice room but it was his room.

"I will have your things brought here. Do as you wish with them, for you will share this room with me," Ian said and turned, silently waiting for her to protest.

It was not her intention. She knew there was no point in objecting and would not waste her time. She would seek to find a private room where she could retreat as often as she wished; perhaps after a while he would not miss her.

"And a stitching room?" she asked, eager to find space of her own.

He rested his hands on her waist, a slim, curving waist he barely remembered but wished to familiarize himself with again. "Tomorrow is time enough for you to find a room that will suit you. Settle here first."

"You are certain you wish me to share this room with you?" She had to ask. She could not understand why he wished her close. They shared no love. They were not even friends. Duty had brought them together. They were husband and wife.

But did that mean anything?

Ian saw the confusion in her eyes and while he could offer her no sensible explanation he could offer her reassurance in his own way. He leaned down and brushed his lips across hers. "Aye, I wish you to share my room."

A tingle raced over her and she shivered.

"Let me warm you," he whispered though he knew she was not cold. He hugged her to him and his lips went to her neck. He took delicate bites knowing how they would affect her. She shivered in his arms and he smiled to himself as he increased the sensuous nibbles.

He felt her body relax against him, heard a soft sigh escape her lips, and felt another shiver turn to a tremble. Damn but it felt good to have her respond to him, and damned if he was not responding himself. His hands ached to roam beneath her garments, to touch her intimately, to taste her, to enter her and bring her pleasure.

"I will not be that far removed from her," came the insistent voice before Anne burst through the door with Blair fast behind her.

"You will go where you are put," he warned her and stopped short when he caught sight of Ian, his wife in his arms.

Anne seemed to pay their intrusion no mind and walked up to Moira. "They place me on the lower floor far removed from you."

Moira shook her head gently, as if finding her senses, and stepped out of her husband's arms. "This will not do, Ian."

"You are right," he agreed. "It will not."

"Where else is she to go?" Blair protested. "I assume that she is to assist Moira so therefore her place is with the other women who see to the chores."

"Anne is my friend—nay, she is more like my sister," Moira said, indignant that anyone should think otherwise. "And as you treat me so shall you treat her."

"You are the laird's wife," Blair said as if she needed reminding.

Anne stepped closer to Moira as though Blair's statement was meant to separate them.

"Then I suggest you pay heed to my words," Moira said, her tone firm.

Blair looked to Ian. "Do I pay heed to her words?"

Ian crossed his arms over his chest and looked from one to the other. "My wife's word will be respected, though *my* word is the final one. Anne may be given quarters on the floor above, next to the room that I am certain will serve well as a stitching room, since I am sure they will spend much time there together. She will have chores like anyone else in the clan, but Moira will determine them."

Anne looked relieved, Blair annoyed.

"And," Ian emphasized in a tone that held the attention of all, "no one shall enter my bedchamber without first knocking and requesting entrance. Do I make myself clear?" He turned a stern glance on Anne.

"Aye, and I apologize for the intrusion. It will not happen again."

"Good," Ian said and turned to Blair, who was grinning. "And you?"

His grin faded. "I but followed her."

"Without thought?"

Blair nodded.

Ian grinned. "It is foolish to follow without looking where you go."

Moira was impressed by his wise words and his way of handling the situation. He was intelligent and she would need to remember that. He did not follow anyone, but he most certainly watched where he went and knew exactly where his steps took him.

Ian walked up to his wife. "I have matters to see to. I will have your things sent here so that you may settle in."

Their journey here had provided Moira with a deeper understanding of her husband. She now knew better how to deal with him and she intended to do so. "Would it be all right if Anne and I looked over the rooms above?"

"You are not tired? You feel well?"

She was tired of him repeatedly asking her but sought to ease his concerns so that she may have her way. "I feel not fatigue, only excitement at finally being here."

"Then do as you wish." He thought better of his words as soon as they were out of his mouth. "Go see the rooms."

Anne hid her smile.

Moira did not though she was wise enough to say, "Thank you."

Ian then smiled himself. "You are welcome, wife, and do not make me regret my words."

"However would I do that?" she asked on a soft laugh.

"You have your ways, which I am beginning to understand, so do remember that." Expecting no response, he turned and walked out, Blair close behind him.

"We will need to be careful in all we do. My husband has a watchful eye," Moira said, her smile broad. "Now let us look at the rooms above and see what we can do."

"You admire him," Anne commented, following Moira out the door.

Moira looked to see if anyone was about and when she was certain that they were alone, she spoke as they made their way to the narrow staircase down a narrow hall. "It takes courage to lead men and make decisions."

Anne voiced her opinion. "You grow fond of him."

Moira stopped abruptly and stared at Anne. "Do I?" She had not thought that she would ever find that possible after the way he deceived her. Yet she suddenly realized that she was rationalizing his decision in wedding her. Why? Did she wish his decision to make sense?

"I think you do. I noticed that you do not object when he touches you. And he touches you often. You seem to find comfort in his arms."

Moira continued climbing the steps, listening to Anne's every word.

"Do you enjoy his touch?"

Moira was surprised at her own quick response. "Aye, I do." She shook her head. "I think I do. I feel this strange tingle when he touches me. At first I thought it was the babe, but realized it had nothing to do with him at all. It was his father causing me the disturbance."

"The tingle pleases you?"

Moira smiled, stepping into the narrow hallway. "Since I do not object to it I suppose it does please me. But then I know little of men. There is where my knowledge is sadly lacking."

She and Anne entered the first door on their right. There were but two rooms on this floor and Moira hoped one was of sufficient size to accommodate her needs.

"Do you know of such things?" Moira asked, shaking her head at the small room.

Anne entered behind her. "Basic knowledge. I have never been kissed or touched by a man." Regret filled her voice though she paid it no heed. "This room is sufficient for my needs. It is bigger than the convent rooms, though not much. And I will spend little time here." She took a breath and asked, "How does it feel to be kissed?"

"I was curious and did not object when Ian attempted a kiss. And the results were interesting."

"But how did you *feel*?"

Moira thought a moment. How did she feel, truly feel? Had she concentrated so hard on determining results that she ignored what she wished to determine? And lately when Ian kissed her she found herself willing, sometimes eager.

She finally realized her answer. "Ian's kisses rob my senses."

Anne sighed. "How wonderful. Then you do grow fond of him."

"I suppose I do," Moira admitted with reluctance. "Though there is much for me to consider."

"The way he deceived you?"

"Aye, it haunts me and while at times I can rationalize his decision a part of me refuses to accept the hurt it caused me. I understand his choice. Many would die and I was but one. What other choice could he make?"

"It makes sense when you reason it."

"Aye, it does, that is why it is difficult for me to completely comprehend, for part of me feels he still had no right to do what he did. He made a choice for me without regard to me and that is what I must come to understand."

"And to understand this what must you do?"

"I must know him and know myself better so that I may reason sensibly."

Anne looked confused. "I do not think love is sensible. At least I remember my mother telling me so when I was very young."

"There is rhyme and reason to everything."

"Something tells me that love is different, though I know not why I say this."

"Are you fond of Blair?" Moira asked.

Anne smiled. "He can be a pest, a charmer, and delightful, sometimes all at once. I find him interesting. Am I fond of him?" She thought on it and spoke honestly. "I think I am fond of him."

"We will need to discuss more of love and see what we can determine."

"But we know little of it."

"Then we must find someone who knows more."

"Does not your husband know more? He was married," Anne said.

"True, he must know much of love, but do men and

women think differently of it? This we must determine. For now let us hope the other room is sufficient for our needs. We have work to do."

The two women crossed the hall to the other room and they both smiled upon entering.

"Perfect," Moira said with excitement.

It was a spacious room with two large windows and a fireplace that would heat the room well.

"This will hold much," Anne said with equal excitement.

"I agree. It is larger than the one at the convent, which means I can expand my studies. We will need to be discreet in bringing the many items we need up here, and we must keep this floor private. With your quarters up here it will make it easier. I doubt Ian will want to intrude on womanly endeavors."

"I noticed at the convent that there were times strange smells drifted from your room. Will we need to consider that here as well?"

"It is good you remind me of this. We will need to compensate for the strange smells. How I am not certain but we will think on it."

"If we spend much time up here many will expect us to produce much stitching," Anne said. "And since neither of us stitch well how will we explain we have nothing to show for our time?"

"We will make it known that we work on a large tapestry that will take months, perhaps years, to complete. After a while I do not think anyone will take notice, especially if we make certain not to let anyone know how much time we truly spend here."

Anne grew excited. "I am so glad I came with you."

"I am as well. It would be impossible for me to pursue my studies without help, but most of all it would be lonely not being able to share my interest with someone of equal enthusiasm."

"I wish to learn all you can teach me."

"And I wish to teach you. You forever ask questions and that is what makes a good student. After being introduced to the monk I began to ask him questions and never seemed to stop. He remarked later, after he had taught me for some time, that he knew I must learn, that I needed to learn. He told me that knowledge would give me something in life that would never be matched and that once gained I would forever search for more wisdom. He was right, for I seem to search endlessly for more answers."

"Do you find them?"

Moira shook her head and laughed. "I do not know, for I forever question. As do you."

"Then we will be forever searching. Do you think this is then a worthless endeavor? Not to find when one searches?"

"We find," Moira explained. "It is just that in finding we find other questions and that is how we expand our knowledge."

"So then if we find who wishes you harm we find other questions?"

"Aye, you understand. If we discover who, we discover why, we discover how, but each of those questions must be asked to be discovered."

"If ignored they do you harm," Anne said.

"Very good," Moira praised. "And we have learned something of this place already."

Anne scrunched her brow, thinking what it could be.

Moira laughed. "We learned that tonight's meal may not be to our liking."

Anne laughed along with her. "And all we had to do was sniff the air."

❧ *fifteen*

Anne combed Moira's long hair and spoke her mind. "The meal needs improvement."

Moira agreed after a yawn. "Aye, Hilda the cook needs to learn the benefits of herbs and spices."

"There was barely a taste to the meal and yet the men ate it as though its taste were divine. They have no palates. No concept of good food." Anne sounded disgusted.

"Do not judge harshly," Moira cautioned. "They do not know better."

Anne continued her chore, though combing Moira's hair was not a chore. It was a time for friends to share thoughts and opinions. Anne kneeled on the bed behind Moira, running the fine-toothed bone comb through her silky hair. "Do you say we are spoiled?"

Moira had to laugh. "Aye, we are. With the herbs we grew and the spices we bartered for, our food at the convent was exceptional."

"I did not know how exceptional until tonight." Anne giggled. "The meal had no taste to it."

"In time I predict it will improve," Moira said.

"I cannot wait."

Moira grew serious. "Nay, we cannot wait. We must begin putting together our room tomorrow. Most of my things are situated here and do not require my attention, so we will have time to concentrate on the upper floor. We will focus much on your room and creating a stitching room so no one knows what we are about."

Anne nodded. "I managed to move some of your personal things to the empty room and made random inquiries as to where I could find a few of the objects we require."

"You work fast," Moira said, pleased.

"I am eager to learn."

A noise outside the door brought them to an abrupt silence.

Ian entered a mere second later. "I intrude?"

Anne was wise enough to reply, "Nay, I am finished." And with a respectful nod to Ian and a knowing look to Moira took herself off.

"You enjoy her friendship?"

Moira stood, feeling the need to move off the bed. "Aye, we understand each other."

Ian untied his plaid and removed his linen shirt, tossing it on a nearby chest.

Moira at first thought to look away but then her inquisitive side took hold and she focused on his bare chest. It was impressive and appealing. Hard muscles and smooth skin and not a scar to be seen. It tempted the eye and the hand. He was meant to be touched, explored, and enjoyed and the thought disturbed her. Why would she ever think such a thing? Fool that she was, she actually wanted to touch him and that thought troubled her.

He was experienced enough to see her want in her eyes and he intended to take advantage of her own desires, fair or not. He had learned long ago that fairness was not always part of the game.

He stepped toward her.

She stepped back away from the bed, away from him, away from herself.

He looked her over slowly, lingering in the most intimate of places. She wore only a shift of soft white wool. The hem fell at her ankles, the sleeves at her wrists, and the neck dipped barely beneath her collarbone. Her long dark hair, shiny and straight, fell to her waist, and her wide eyes wore the look of a frightened animal caught in a snare.

He smiled, for he had caught her firm and hard and he had no intention of letting her go. She was his, plain and simple. His wife. His woman. His lover. And he intended to see that she remained all of those and more.

"You are comfortable in these quarters?" he asked though he knew the answer.

She was blunt. "You know I am not, why do you bother to ask?"

He smiled. "To hear your response."

"I would prefer my own chamber."

"Your place is beside me."

"Because you deem it such."

His eyes deepened blue. "Aye, that I do. You are my wife and shall share my bed."

"Whether I wish to or not?"

"You have a duty." He almost cringed at his own words. He did not wish her to share his bed out of duty. He wished her to want to sleep beside him.

"What you say is that I have no choice."

"There is always a choice. It is how you respond to that choice that makes the difference."

She thought on his words and understood the wisdom of them.

"Why not give us a chance, Moira?"

She paused to reason, but how did one make sense of emotions? He had hurt her with his deception and, while she attempted to understand it, part of her found forgiveness difficult.

"I trusted you," she said with honesty.

He stepped toward her and she made no move away from him. "I meant no harm."

"But you harmed nonetheless."

Her words hurt him for he realized the extent of the damage he had inflicted on her and regretted it. "It was not my intention."

"Intention or not it was done."

He came to his own defense. "I did what was necessary; perhaps one day you will understand this."

"Perhaps," she said. "Until that day perhaps you will understand why I keep my distance from you." She stepped away and yet could not understand why it hurt her to do so.

He let her go, wanting to reach out and stop her but preventing himself. *Time.* It would take time for her to accept him. Why then did he feel so impatient? He wanted her now, this very moment.

Moira walked to the bed and slipped beneath the covers, clinging to her side.

Ian stripped bare and climbed beneath the blankets. His first thought was to leave her be, give her time to acclimate to her surroundings, but a part of him wished to touch her, to be near her, to feel her warmth.

He moved up behind her, his body resting alongside hers, his hand slipping over her waist to stroke her stomach, his face resting near hers. "I do not wish to keep a distance from you."

His whispered breath tingled her flesh and try as she might she could not prevent the shiver that shook her body.

"You speak falsely, wife," he whispered, his hand drifting up to cup her breast. "You do not wish to keep me at a distance. You wish my touch."

Her voice trembled when she spoke. "I do not."

His fingers played with her nipple, squeezing, rolling, and pinching it to a fever pitch. "Then why do you respond to my touch?"

"I am foolish," she admitted.

He laughed and bit playfully at her neck. "Nay, you want me."

"I do not," she protested with a sigh while his fingers continued to torment her.

"I can prove it."

"You cannot."

His laughter was a soft breath against her neck that sent a shiver racing through her. "Do you challenge me?" His hand slipped down along her stomach and slowly inched to rest at the apex of her thighs.

How did she stop him, and did she want to? She called on her courage and spoke with strength though she fought her emotions. "I seek no challenge, I but wish you not to touch me."

"Then why can I feel the heat of you fill my hand?" he asked softly and pressed his palm against her.

She grew wet with the want of him and it startled her. How could she think one way of him and react another? She had found no pleasure in their first time together. It was fast, painful, and unfulfilling. Why would she ever wish to experience such a disappointment again? And yet . . . He had showed her kindness, his kisses had been tender, his innocent touches comforting. He had been gentle and understanding with her. Was this tender side of him real or was it too a deception?

"Why do you fight your feelings?" he asked, his hand cupping her intimately and making no attempt to move.

"There is no reason for intimacy between us."

"We are husband and wife," he said as though that explained all.

"That means naught."

"It means we have a duty to each other."

"We have discussed this before. I do not look on it as you do."

He applied pressure to his hand and his one finger delved a bit deeper between her legs. "Then you should look with clearer eyes."

She gasped slightly, the sensation his touch caused unfamiliar though pleasurable, a surprising reaction. "I do not know you."

"You know enough of me." His voice was firm and direct and accustomed to being obeyed.

She, however, was not accustomed to obeying. "Nay, I do not."

He rested his hand where it lay, his pressure light and titillating. "Then ask of me what you wish to know."

"Why do you touch me so?"

"I wish to."

"Why?" she persisted.

"I like the feel of you."

"Why?"

"You feel good to me. You make me feel good." He was surprised at his own response. He realized how very much he enjoyed touching her. He did not, however, realize how much touching her affected him. He had grown hard and he had done little to cause such a stimulating response. And yet he had responded without thought or reason.

Or was it desire? Did he actually desire his wife? He damned sure felt as if he did.

"Why do you ask why?" Ian asked of her.

"Why not?"

He laughed and nuzzled her neck. "There you go again asking why."

"Why is a relevant word."

"Why is that?"

She answered with reason. "How would we ever understand anything if we did not ask why?"

"Then ask me why."

"Why what?"

"Why I enjoy the taste of you," he said and nibbled along her neck.

"That is not relevant," she said, attempting to ignore the way her skin tingled. "The question is, why do you taste me?"

"I enjoy it," he answered. "Therefore I taste you and I would like to taste more of you." His hand returned to her breast. "Especially your nipples," he said with a tender squeeze. "They are so hard and they tempt my hunger."

Her breath caught in her dry throat and for a moment she feared she would not breathe. But she finally grasped a breath and breathed deeply. "Why do you do this?"

"There is that why again and I have told you why. I want to. I like the taste of you and I wish to taste more. Let me."

She almost surrendered to him. Why? She could not say and that was what stopped her. She needed a reason why, a good, solid reason why she should succumb to his charms. She had to understand, fully understand. It had to make sense. At the moment she could make no sense of it. So she could not surrender, though did she want to?

"You fight yourself," he whispered near her ear. "Why?"

Her answer was an honest one. "I do not understand."

"Is it necessary that you do?"

"For me it is."

"Then think on it," he advised. "Why do you feel as you do? Why does my touch excite you?"

"It does not—"

"Do not deny the obvious," he said brusquely.

"I must understand it," she insisted and attempted to move away from him. There was no room for retreat and he settled her more firmly in his arms.

"Surrender and you will understand."

"Would you surrender a battle?"

"This is not a battle."

"I feel at times it is," she said honestly.

"Why? I am not your enemy."

"Why then do I feel the need to protect myself." Her question surprised her and him.

"You need no protection against me. I mean you no

harm. I will not hurt you." He hugged her gently as if reaffirming his words.

The strength of his arms cautioned that he could easily cause her harm, but the gentleness with which he held her told her he had no inclination to do so. She was safe with him. Protected by him. He would let no one hurt her.

Why did she believe him? Why did she know he would allow no harm to come to her? Why did he feel the need to protect her?

Why did she always question? Why could she not accept his word?

Trust.

Did she truly trust him? Could she trust him?

He seemed to understand her silence and he wrapped her in his arms. "Go to sleep. I am by your side and that is where I will stay. You have no need to fear anyone." He grew quiet and then whispered in her ear. "Especially me."

✎ *sixteen*

Ian rubbed at the back of his neck as he examined the ledger in front of him. Blair sat beside him at the dais in the great hall, watching men carry a long narrow table up the narrow staircase, Anne directing their steps.

"She is up to something," Blair said with a steady eye on the young woman.

Ian grunted and with a quill pen scratched out a column of numbers to begin again.

"I keep a watchful eye on her. All she is about at the moment is furnishing her room and the stitching room." He rubbed at his chin. "Though I wonder why a table of that length would be needed in a stitching room."

"Damn," Ian muttered and inked out another column of numbers.

"My thoughts precisely," Blair said, his glance remaining on Anne, who sent him a smile every now and again as if acknowledging that she knew he watched her. "She thinks to outwit me."

"These numbers outwit me at every turn," Ian complained.

Blair seemed to pay his problem no mind; his attention was focused strictly on Anne. "Cauldrons. What would she be doing with cauldrons in a stitching room?"

"Hilda mentioned that Anne had spoken to her and mentioned that Moira enjoyed her own special herbal brew and so as not to give Hilda more work Anne suggested she could see to it herself if she had a cauldron or two."

"And she requires two cauldrons to satisfy her taste?"

Ian looked curiously toward Anne, who with a smile was instructing the men with the table and the cauldrons.

Blair lowered his voice. "You think they practice the black arts?"

Ian shook his head. "Two women who were raised a good portion of their life in a convent practicing the black arts?"

"Perhaps not," Blair relented. "But I still feel there is more to this stitching room."

"Then see for yourself."

Blair grinned. "You read my mind." He stood and called out, "Anne, let me help you." Her response surprised him.

"How generous of you. We can always use another pair of strong hands."

Ian looked about, expecting to see his wife lingering nearby, and when he caught no sight of her, he raised his voice. "Anne, my wife—where might she be?"

"With Hilda, getting acquainted."

He nodded, sighed, and returned to the column of stubborn numbers.

Moira found Hilda a staunch and strict woman possessing little congeniality. She was a short and rotund woman with a pretty face and beautiful blond hair that she kept braided and wrapped at the top of her head. Her staff was run tightly, everyone doing their jobs to Hilda's specific instructions. Moira was impressed with the spotless cooking area. Waste was swept up and cleared out immediately. No harsh or fetid orders lingered and garments were kept clean and fresh. Unfortunately the food tasted as sanitary as the cooking area appeared.

Moira also took count of the winter's food supply and while adequate it was improperly stored and would not last until harvest and replenishment. She also intended to inspect the kitchen garden for she had a feeling it was not as productive as it should be. Then there were the planting fields themselves, but in due time she would see to them.

Moira proceeded slowly in suggesting changes, knowing that Hilda was not the type to take kindly to intrusion in her domain. Several of the vegetables and meats had to be stored differently, but in time. Her most immediate need was to address the food itself. One day of bland food was all she could stomach.

"I have some herbs and spices we used at the convent with much success and I was wondering if you would care to give a few a try?"

Hilda looked at her skeptically. "Do you wish me to?"

Moira did not wish to make it an order but she did not think she had a choice, for Hilda seemed determined to keep complete control of her domain. "Aye, I wish you to and I think you will be surprised at the results."

"My food tastes good."

Moira forced a smile. "Your pork pie was memorable."

Hilda beamed. "Everyone enjoys my pork pie."

Moira recalled the tasteless dish and the too thick sauce and yet all who ate it, ate with a relish. "The herbs I have will only add to its appeal."

"It is enjoyable as it is," Hilda said stubbornly.

"I enjoy the flavor of these particular herbs and I thought that perhaps others would as well. You could of course add it just to mine and Anne's food if you wish."

"That I will do," Hilda agreed.

"Thank you," Moira said with a pleasant smile. "And tonight you will be serving . . . ?"

"Mutton stew."

Moira opened the leather pouch she carried and took several different dried leaves out. "Crunch these all together and add them to Anne's and my food, if you would?"

"As you say," Hilda said, eyeing the leaves with distaste.

"Thank you again," Moira said and left the kitchen, thoughtfully intending to pay daily visits and institute some necessary changes.

She came upon an exasperated Ian alone in the great hall. It was late afternoon, the noon meal complete and cleanup finished and everyone off to complete chores. Ian's chore seemed to be proving difficult for he rubbed the back of his neck and grumbled to himself.

He was attractive even in a contemplative state. His long dark hair hung over his shoulders and teased the sides of his face. His blue eyes concentrated heavily on his chore and his hand rubbed at his chin.

Coming upon him quietly she saw that he was attempting to add a column of numbers and from all the scratched-out columns it appeared he was having a difficult time of it.

She made her presence known with a slight cough so as not to startle him and he looked up at her approach, his frown turning to an instant smile. "It is good to see you, wife."

A smile tickled her face for she understood that his pleasure in her appearance meant he could ignore his chore. "You have missed me?"

"Aye," he said dramatically and leaned back in his seat. "I pine for you when you are not in my presence; my need for you is great." He held his hand out to her. "Come to me, wife, so that I may demonstrate my feelings."

"You are having trouble adding the column of numbers?" Moira asked as she approached him.

He shook his head, and Moira, more interested in the numbers than her husband, made the mistake of ignoring him, and glanced down at the numbers. His hand rushed out, grabbed her around the waist, and plopped her down on his lap.

He hugged her to him. "You keep yourself busy, I have not seen you—"

"But in a very short time," she reminded him. "I am accustomed to entertaining myself."

He grinned. "I would prefer that you let *me* entertain you."

The grin told her too much and of late she understood his desires much too much. It seemed that with each passing day he made his intentions clear. He wished for them to be intimate and she wished for more time. He did not force himself on her though he did touch her intimately, kiss her, nibble at her neck—and she did not stop him. She asked herself why. Did she enjoy his touch? Was she simply curious? Was she wishing for a young girl's dreams to come true?

Nonsense.

He was her husband out of necessity and he was attempting to make the most of it. She could not blame him for that. They were to spend a lifetime together and, as he reminded her, it would be easier for them both if they got along.

It would be much easier if they loved each other.

Her foolish thought startled her and she immediately focused on what was familiar and safe to her.

Numbers.

"What gives you trouble here?" she asked him, pointing to the column of numbers.

Ian was becoming familiar with her emotions. She retreated from any subject she did not feel comfortable with and intimacy was a subject she often avoided. But he was patient—at least, he was attempting patience. His desire to make love to his wife was growing stronger by the day. And it was his wife he wanted. He could if he so desired ease his frustration with any of the willing women. But he had no desire to do so; it was his wife who sparked his passion and it was his wife who would satisfy it.

He looked to the column of stubborn numbers, though it was his wife's slim waist and curving hips that caught his eye. She showed not a trace of carrying a child. Even when his hand drifted over her stomach at night when they were in bed together he felt nothing but a slight mound. Her breasts he had noticed were larger and her nipples more sensitive, but that was the only sign of her being with child.

She waited for his answer and he shook himself out of his deep musings. "They are a stubborn lot that will not add up in my favor."

"Numbers have a meaning all their own." She sounded like a teacher speaking with a stubborn student. "Respect them and you will understand them."

"You know numbers?" His voice held surprise.

She decided that the truth was her best ally. "I kept the ledgers at the convent."

Ian showed immediate interest. "Then perhaps you can help me." With his arm remaining firm around her waist they both leaned forward to glance down at the column of numbers. "These will not add correctly."

Moira looked them over in a glance, then picked up the pen and with ease and speed added the column. "This is your total, though something is not right."

"My feelings exactly."

Moira looked his ledger over, going back a few pages to understand his way of keeping records, and with her quick eye and mind she immediately took note of the problem. "Here it is," she pointed out to him. "You failed to carry this column of numbers over, causing your inaccurate total."

He was impressed and he let her know it. "You have an eye for numbers and that is not common in a woman."

"Numbers interest me." Moira decided that keeping all of her skills secret would not be wise and that if he understood her love of numbers then perhaps he would begin to understand her love of knowledge and the need to pursue it.

He nodded, studying the column she had added and reviewing the other pages where he had made an error. "This is not work to you then?"

"Nay," she said with a smile. "I find pleasure in calculating numbers."

He gave his idea brief thought and without reluctance asked, "Would it please you to keep the ledgers for the keep?"

Her wide eyes grew round with delight. "You mean this?"

"I do not say what I do not mean."

"You trust me?"

He kissed her soundly on the lips. "What must I do to make you understand that what I say I mean?"

She seemed lost for words.

"I find no pleasure in numbers and you do; therefore, it is wise of me to allow you to handle the ledgers. You may keep me well posted on such matters, but it will be strictly your domain."

"And you truly wish this of me?"

He kissed her again and laughed. "You have much to learn about me, wife."

"Moira," she corrected, wanting him to acknowledge her and who she was—not only his wife, but a woman of her own status.

"Moira," he repeated without hesitation and in sincere acknowledgment. "Your name sounds good on my lips."

"It is a harsh-sounding name."

"Nay," he objected. "It is no such thing. It is smooth and pleasant to speak."

She wondered if his words were true, but then, why did she doubt him? Would she forever think he deceived her? And was it fair for her to think such? The thought haunted her and she did not know what she would do with it.

"I know not where my father got my name." She did not even know why she mentioned this though she did recall her mother telling her that her father had insisted upon her being named Moira.

"You never asked your father?"

"He was not an easy man to speak with."

He heard the sadness in her voice and recalled with distaste the way her father had treated her the night they had wed. He seemed not at all to care about her. For some reason Ian wished to make up for all the years she had been so sadly neglected.

"You may speak to me anytime you wish and about anything you wish." He realized his voice was firm and a bit harsh and sought to soften it. "I want you to know that you may come to me no matter the reason. I will always be there to listen to you and share whatever troubles you."

Moira found herself speechless yet again. Ian had a way of startling her. When she thought she understood him she realized she did not understand him at all. He was a unique man. One minute he was a fierce warrior, another moment a gentle husband, and yet another a protector who would allow no harm to come to her.

"I thank you for that," she said softly and to her own surprise placed a tender kiss on his lips.

He thought to respond with a more fervent kiss and then thought better of it. She was placing her trust in him and sealing that trust with a kiss. He accepted the light pressure of her lips on his and when she pressed firmer against him and her lips sought more he relented slowly and patiently.

She was not certain what she was about or what to do; she only knew she wished to experience the taste of him.

His lips fed gently off hers, not demanding or expecting, simply accepting whatever she gave to him.

She pressed and brushed softly over his lips as if determining the flavor of him, and he did not object; he responded when appropriate and allowed her to explore at her leisure. She seemed to take pleasure in her innocent pursuit and sought his mouth most fervently.

"You taste good," she said as if surprised by her discovery.

"As do you," he said and tasted her softly, his lips brushing over hers confirming his opinion. "But I have tasted of you before this. What makes my taste so different?"

She looked puzzled as she attempted to determine an answer. Was it that she initiated the kiss this time? It was a kiss of gratitude, was it not? The questions churned in her head. Had she wanted to kiss him and found a reasonable excuse for doing so?

That thought truly disturbed her, and to prove it held no validity she decided another kiss was in order.

Her mouth descended on his with much more intent than she had expected and much more reaction than she had anticipated. Her hands cupped his face and she settled her mouth on his to enjoy.

He allowed her to explore, his arm resting comfortably around her waist and inching her ever so slightly closer and closer to him.

She moved with no objection, wanting to be nearer to him.

He waited patiently, as patiently as he could, and it was not until she groaned and her kiss became more demanding that he finally took command.

✂ *seventeen*

Ian pulled her close and took complete charge. He deep-
ened their kiss and had her responding like a woman in
dire need. Her groans resonated in his mouth, exciting him.
His hand ran up her back to stroke her softly then more
firmly, alternating between both, and she responded most
ardently.

That she was a novice was obvious but she was a most
apt pupil, eager and willing to learn, participate, and experience, or perhaps she just wanted him. The thought ignited
his already flaring passion and he delivered a kiss that sent
both their desires soaring.

"Damn," he whispered against her mouth and she
moaned.

She seemed not to be able to get enough of him and
then suddenly she pulled away from him as if struck with
a realization of her actions. She gazed at him strangely and
ran her fingers faintly over her swollen lips.

"It is permissible to enjoy your husband's kisses."

She did enjoy his kiss. Was she wrong for feeling such?

"Why do you question your feelings?" He moved his hands to rest at her waist, giving her the opportunity to leave his side if she chose to.

Feelings?

Was that not the question? What were her feelings? Did she respond out of love or mere desire? Love him? Desire him? Could either be possible? Or was she simply responding to his charm, his intention that they live as husband and wife?

She was not experienced enough to determine an answer or perhaps she feared the answer.

"No answer have you?" Ian teased with a smile and a playful poke to her side.

She looked at him curiously. "Nay, I find no answer forthcoming."

"Then do not question, simply let yourself feel." He squeezed her slim waist.

Could she? Could she let herself care for him? Could she drop her guard or would it bring her nothing but pain and suffering? But then if she did not try she would never know, would she?

"Give it thought," he suggested and gave her backside a gentle pat. "Now, about these numbers . . ."

He had dismissed the issue and left it in her hands. What would she do with it? She gave a brief almost unnoticeable shake of her head and turned her attention to a subject she was well versed in. Numbers.

They spent the next hour going over the keep's ledgers, with Moira explaining where he had erred and detailing a better way of keeping records. He listened carefully and said nothing until she finished.

"You will do well with the ledgers."

"Aye, I will," she said with a pleased smile. He had told her he wanted her to handle them and handle them she would. She would not ask him again if he meant his word, she would simply accept his word.

Fruit, bread, and cheese suddenly appeared on a platter

in front of them on the table, a series of giggles trailing off to the side from the young serving girls who had delivered the light fare.

Moira eagerly helped herself, reaching for a large chunk of cheese and warm bread. She munched with enthusiasm on the food and in between attempted a conversation. She actually munched more than she talked, though she had planned it so, hoping Ian would fill in the silence with vital information concerning her safety.

Instead he spoke with pride of his clan and all they had accomplished, and she had to agree. From her first sight of the keep and its surrounding lands it was obvious that the people had worked hard in building and planting so that sufficient food was produced and shelter was generous for all.

That first peek had also alerted her to an area or two that could produce more bountiful harvests and she was certain that with a few changes she could have the keep producing to its full potential. She wished she could institute a few changes immediately but that was not wise. She would need to take her time and slowly make changes that would benefit all.

A young man entered the great hall and with a respectful bob of his head to Ian he handed him a folded paper and left in haste.

Moira saw no fear in the eyes of the clan members for Ian. It was respect she saw and they treated him accordingly. Though to receive respect he had to have earned it, which made him a man of courage and conviction.

"My sister, Brianna, plans a visit here," he said with surprise and pleasure.

"She is like you?"

"How do you mean?"

"Charming and easy to converse with."

"You sound surprised that I should be so," he said, curious as to what she thought of him—besides her thinking him deceitful of course.

She seemed reluctant to answer.

"Speak your mind, Moira. I prefer truth between us." It was not an order though he issued it with a firmness that one paid heed to.

She took him at his word and spoke. "I have not been certain whether to trust your charm or not."

Ian understood her lack of trust in him and voiced her doubts more bluntly. "You wonder if my charm is not deceit."

"You read me well."

"Nay, a normal reaction after what has transpired between us, but as I have told you before, I wish to rectify or perhaps it would be better stated that I wish to heal what is between us."

He used words well for his deceit had wounded her deeply. What he had robbed her of that night he could never return to her and perhaps never heal, just as he had probably never truly healed from the loss of a wife he loved.

The thought was a strange one. Both their hearts had suffered a damaging hurt and both their hearts had grown silent not wishing to ever hear or feel again.

Was it not then easier for him to remain wed to someone he did not love?—for then love could not hurt him again.

And as for her—her tender heart trusted and was betrayed. How then could she remain with the man who hurt her heart?

"Give us time." How often would he ask this of her? How often would he see that painful look in her eyes? And why did that look tear so viciously at his heart?

Moira forced a smile and stood. "We have much time."

He accepted her vague surrender; he had no choice though he wished for more.

Time.

His friend and ally or was it his enemy?

Blair and Anne entered the hall laughing. The servant

girls returned to refill the pitchers with cider and a few
men entered from outside, a blustery wind following them
in.

Moira turned to leave, suddenly wishing time alone,
when she grew faint. Her hand went to her stomach and
her thought was, *Please not now, not in front of so many
strangers.*

She turned instinctively to her husband and called his
name, "Ian."

His name was a whisper on her pale lips. He was out of
his chair in a flash and he scooped her falling body up
tightly in his arms.

Anne ran to Moira's side.

"Something is wrong," Ian insisted, his protective embrace attempting to keep her from harm.

"Bring her upstairs where she may rest," Anne said, ignoring his worry and focusing on what was best for Moira.

"She should not be fainting so much," Blair insisted, his
sincere concern catching Anne's attention.

Anne and Blair followed Ian out of the hall while concerned faces looked on.

"Is there something she does not tell me, Anne?" Ian
asked, taking the steps with ease, his precious bundle no
burden.

Anne sought to reassure Ian and Blair, who looked anxious to hear her response. "The babe simply makes himself
known."

"She is months with child and has not even rounded
yet," Ian argued. "What will she suffer when her condition
becomes obvious?"

Anne could not honestly calm his fears for she was not
certain herself.

The three entered Ian's bedchamber in silence, each lost
in his or her own thoughts.

Moira's soft moan broke the heavy silence as Ian placed
her gently on the bed and sat down beside her.

Her long dark lashes fluttered and looked even darker to

Ian framed against her pale complexion. She possessed the most beautiful skin—soft to the touch with no blemishes or scars, just pure creamy skin that he loved to touch. And those eyes of hers were like none he had ever seen on a woman—wide, expressive, and passionate in all that she did.

Ian reached out and ran a gentle hand over her cheek, up along her temple, to brush her forehead and then stroke the top of her head, her silky hair feeling good to his touch. He loved the length of it; it ran down her back straight to her waist, not a curl or wave to it. She kept it mostly braided, though on occasion she had freed it, and he had seen how its shiny beauty had caught many an admiring eye.

Her eyes finally opened slowly after several failed attempts. "Ian?"

"I am here," he said softly, his hand reassuring her with a tender stroke to her cheek.

"Thank you for being there for me," she said, her eyes feeling weighted and not at all anxious to remain open.

"I will always be there for you, wife," he murmured and rested his hand against her cheek.

She turned her face into his hand as if seeking his touch. "I am tired."

"Rest, the babe wears you out."

Moira did not fight her heavy eyelids and, besides, his response had caught her attention. He was not blaming her for fainting; he actually acknowledged that the babe was responsible. This was an improvement. She smiled without realizing it and drifted off into a contented slumber.

"She is to do nothing that taxes her strength," Ian ordered, looking from Anne to Blair. "I will not see her suffer needlessly."

"She is strong," Anne said, knowing that Moira would not take kindly to having her activities curtailed.

"Strong-willed is more like it," Blair said.

Ian spoke up. "It matters not. She will do nothing strenuous. I have given her the ledgers to attend to."

"The ledgers? The keep's finances?" Blair asked, stunned.

"Moira is skilled in numbers," Anne said in Moira's defense.

"So I have learned," Ian said. "And they will take up a good amount of her time. A time spent sitting and resting all but her mind."

Anne remained silent, knowing the ledgers would take Moira no time at all—but then perhaps Ian would not object to his wife spending time stitching, another sitting and restful activity.

"She can rest while she stitches," Anne suggested.

Both men smiled.

"Aye," Ian said with an affirming nod. "I will see she is supplied with all that she needs."

"I can see to it," Anne said.

"I will help," Blair offered.

"Good, for there is much I need to sufficiently furnish the room," Anne said, thinking of how with Blair's help she would locate the necessary items to later move to the room.

"I will remain here for a while with my wife," Ian said, his hand remaining on hers.

"She is well and will sleep for an hour or two," Anne explained, though she doubted it made a difference to him. He looked immovable.

"I will stay." Ian was insistent.

Blair placed a hand to Anne's back and gave her a light shove.

She got the message and without saying another word left the room with Blair directly behind her, his hand remaining firm at her back.

Ian could not say exactly what it was about his wife that so intrigued him. She was not what he had expected for a woman raised in such a restricted atmosphere. She spoke her mind, did as she pleased, and pleased herself in manners which seemed of unlikely interest to a woman.

A thought suddenly occurred to him. Did she know something that could place her in danger?

He rubbed her hand and shook his head. "What could you have possibly learned at the convent that would place your life in danger?"

He thought with a frown. Could it have been something she heard? The convent must have gotten visits from time to time. But from whom, and was it anyone of consequence? Anyone who carried vital information?

It was a possibility he had not considered but one that was worth investigating. He could easily inquire as to her time at the convent for he had done so before. It would not be hard to discover whom she had met and from that he could determine if the person had any bearing on his present problem.

In the meantime he intended to discover more about her father. What he had learned so far about the man was that he did not seem to care at all for his daughter and that disturbed Ian. It was as if Moira was dumped at the convent and forgotten about.

Until that fateful night he showed up.

Her father certainly had thought about her then and came to her rescue, though it was his own rescue he was seeking. The one thought that nagged at Ian was that he had never determined how Angus Maclean had discovered his plan to marry his daughter. It was only when his small troop of clansmen was prepared to leave for the convent that Ian had discovered that Angus was fast on his trail.

He had trusted the delicate news to a few trustworthy men, at least he thought them so. Had someone betrayed him? And if so why? There were many unsettled questions that haunted him, but his most haunting fear was something he had no control over. And that fear gripped him every time Moira fainted.

He could protect her against someone who meant her

harm. He would defend her with his life, but he could not
protect her when it was time for her to deliver their child.
Then he was helpless and the thought tore at his strength
and at his heart.

He looked at her sleeping so soundly and so safely. Her
hand was tucked in his and she had not relinquished his
hold even in sleep. She had even turned to him when she
knew she would faint. She had sought his help without
hesitation. She was beginning, just beginning to trust him.

The idea that he had won a small portion of her trust
gave him hope that victory would be his. But he had
doubts. Moira could be stubborn, but then he was determined and was not one to allow anything or anyone to
stand in his way.

Had not his strength and determination been the driving
force that propelled him into making the decision to wed
Moira? Had he not known it was the only way?

He wanted to believe that it was, that he had considered
all options and that his choice had been the wisest.

Would he wed her again, now that he knew her?

The question persisted from time to time. He chose to
ignore it. The deed was done and could not be undone so
why torture himself with what could have been. It was
what was now that he had to face and contend with; he had
to accept his decision.

Would he wed her again?

Did he wish to answer it or ignore it?

Would he wed her again?

What difference did it really make?

Would he wed her again?

If he did not he would never have known Moira.

Would he wed her again?

"Aye, I would wed you again," he whispered and leaned
down to brush his lips lightly over hers. "I would, for I find
I want you in my life."

❧ eighteen

Hilda wiped Moira's damp brow with a wet cloth. "You will be fine."

Moira nodded slowly and closed her eyes, resting her head back against the wooden chair.

Hilda ordered the bucket removed from in front of Moira. "This time will pass."

Moira so wanted to believe that the contents of her breakfast would eventually remain in her stomach, but for the last two weeks it had insisted on coming up. "The babe does not favor the morning meal."

Hilda smiled. "Few of them do. It is a normal response when with child though it can be annoying and it does drain the energy from you."

Moira gave another nod, feeling just as Hilda said, drained. It had not taken long for her and Hilda to become friends. After the first evening, when Ian and Blair tasted her and Anne's seasoned dishes and commented most ardently on the delicious taste, Hilda sought her advice. Hilda then began to readily accept other suggestions Moira made and within the week the kitchen was not only producing more flavorful foods but was operating more efficiently, giving Hilda more free time.

Now the two women met each morning to discuss menus, preparation, and stock—and each morning Moira took ill. Until this morning she had been lucky enough to have only Hilda present and she immediately had seen to tending to her care. All in the keep knew of her condition and she knew that gossip had many thinking her too ill and frail to carry the child, but not so Hilda.

The woman simply kept a bucket nearby and wiped her brow through the ordeal and then cleaned up after her, all the time assuring her that this morning sickness was natural.

Unfortunately this morning two servant girls were present and Moira could hear them whispering as Hilda hurried them out of the kitchen. Ian would catch wind of the wagging tongues soon enough and search her out and insist that she rest.

She hated resting, especially as much as he wished her to rest. She liked keeping active, which she had managed to do this past week in spite of her husband's attentive eye.

Feeling much herself again, she and Hilda finished their conversation and decided on a few more changes to the work area. With a hug of gratitude to Hilda she left the kitchen and went in search of Anne. The sewing room was fast being completed and within the next few days she hoped to be able to have all she needed to begin her studies again.

Anne was doing an excellent job of securing the items she required and she had noticed that she and Blair were spending much time together, which probably was the reason for the continuous smile on Anne's pretty face.

She located Anne in the storage room. It was a rather large room that sat off the great hall and held a wealth of furnishings and odd objects. Many of the items in the room had been received through trade or confiscated from other clans after battle. Anne had put to work what many thought useless objects as well as the obvious useful objects she had found.

It was Anne's favorite place to spend time especially since the weather had grown harsh and most sought the warmth of their homes or the keep.

Moira threw the end of her blue shawl high over her shoulder so that it would lay snug to her neck and entered the chilled room. "Anne," she called out, having heard the young woman talking to herself somewhere amidst the plethora of furnishings and objects.

"Back here," Anne answered. "Follow the winding path past the chests."

Moira paid heed to her direction and in no time she joined Anne, who was busy removing several glass flasks from a chest.

"I thought these may be of use to us?"

Moira looked them over, studying the weight of the glass and its construction. "Aye, they may be, but we must be careful what we use them for."

Anne dusted her hands against each other, particles of dust floating around her. "There are such treasures here."

Moira smiled. Anne had pinned her hair up with a comb and donned a worn tunic and underdress. Dust and cobwebs clung to her clothes and blond hair and her cheeks were rosy from her strenuous but enjoyable labor.

"You are having fun," Moira said knowingly.

Anne nodded vigorously. "Aye, much fun. Our room will be well stocked with what we need and perhaps with what we do not need."

Both women laughed.

"Blair has been a help, I hear." Moira had seen herself how the two worked closely together—and then there was the keep gossip. Tongues were wagging about the two.

Anne blushed along with a wide smile. "He has been most helpful and he is a delight to talk with. He charms, though it is not his charm that I favor."

"I thought you favored him."

"I do," she admitted readily, "but I also keep alert to all he says and pose questions that will help me discover what he knows if anything about this supposed danger you are in. I have not forgotten my responsibilities."

"I do not think that you do and I am glad that you find his company pleasing."

"Whose company does she find pleasing?" Blair appeared from around a stack of chests, to the surprise of both women.

Moira wondered how much of their conversation he had heard but chose to assume he had heard only the latter portion, which she addressed. "Only Anne can answer that."

Blair turned to Anne. "So your answer is?"

Moira watched the two. Blair was not as tall as Ian and while he possessed good features that could catch a woman's eye it was more his charming nature that captivated the attention and probably won him favor with the women.

But it was the look the two settled on each other that interested Moira the most. There was an attraction and it was strong and Moira thought, though could not be certain, that it was packed with passion.

She would have to have a talk with Anne for neither of them was familiar with the ways of men. The act itself was basic and even being raised in a convent one learned the basics of mating from watching the animals. But men themselves were foreign and could be confusing creatures. They would talk and compare.

"I am waiting, and not patiently," Blair reminded, folding his arms across his chest.

"If I intended to answer you, do you not think I would have?" Anne asked candidly.

He laughed. "You do speak your mind, lass."

"Honesty is a virtue."

Blair walked up to her. "Then tell me who this man is whose company you find pleasing."

Moira decided to take her leave; their time was better spent alone.

Anne kept her eye on Blair but noticed Moira's departure and made no move to stop her.

Before she could answer Blair spoke, taking another step closer to her. "I find your company pleasing."

Anne tapped his hard chest. "I bet you have said that to many a young woman."

He shook his head slowly and whispered, "Nay, I have spent time with many women but have found none as pleasing as you."

Anne stood speechless in front of him.

He laughed softly. "I thought that might silence you." He lowered his mouth to hers and stole a quick kiss, then another and another and another until she finally threw her arms around his neck and clung to him.

Their kiss filled with a passion born of innocence and desire. Blair felt the tension in her slender body and the heat. He tasted her purity and her want and he knew that she did not understand these new, raging emotions. But he did and he took command.

He deepened their kiss, exploring her mouth, drinking in the exotic taste of her. He had kissed many a woman but none was as nourishing to his soul as Anne.

He moved his body against hers and she did not protest or back away in fear. She allowed him the closeness though made no move to press against him. He took his time with her, his hand stroking her back as he continued to feast on her mouth and she in turn enjoyed him.

As much as he wished for their kiss to go on he knew it was best to bring it to an end, for his body was becoming more heated than he expected and if he waited too long he would not want to stop himself. And he wondered if she would want to stop him, for her slim body was beginning to move suggestively though innocently against him.

He ended their kiss with reluctance and took a calming breath before saying, "I will have my answer now."

On a whisper she said, "You. I find your company pleasing."

"I am glad of this."

"Why?"

"Always curious," he said with a tender laugh.

"Aye, that I am; now will you answer me?"

"An easy answer," he said with a shrug. "I favor you and wish to know you better."

"Truly?"

"Honesty is a virtue," he reminded her.

"Aye, but is it one you possess?"

He laughed heartily. "You doubt my word, lass?"

"You seem an honest one, but—"

"But? You have doubts?"

She nodded. "You have a tongue that charms and—"

He was surprised by the reluctance he saw in her eyes. "You fear to say what you wish? This is not like you."

She lifted her chin and took a firm tone. "I cannot help but think that you took part in the deceit against Moira, and that leaves room for doubt."

"That is better. I prefer you speak your mind and I can understand why you feel as you do. And all I can do is attempt to explain. I can do no more."

Anne stepped back, crossing her arms over her chest. "I am listening."

Moira was asked three times how she was feeling before she reached her bedchamber. Ian had to have heard by now of her morning illness and was sure to be searching for her. She hoped to avoid him long enough to gather a few items she had packed in her chest and then sneak up to the stitching room where she could at least pretend to look as if she were doing nothing if he should find her. Perhaps then he would leave her alone and she would be able to accomplish some work.

She sighed when she noticed that the small chest she

needed was on the high chest in the room and that she was
not of sufficient height to retrieve it. She would need
something to stand on and no small stool would do.

Moira dropped her shawl on the bed and looked about
the room, spying a sturdy chest not far from the tall chest.
She went over to it and on examining it determined it was
sufficient for her needs.

She opened it and saw that it housed light articles such
as linens and bedcoverings. It would not be difficult or too
strenuous for her to move it on her own. With little effort
she managed to move the piece in front of the chest and
with a light step she climbed on top. She reached up and
grasped the edge of the small chest, knowing that too was
not burdensome and would be easy for her to take down.

Her fingers reached for the handle and she had just
grabbed hold when the door flew open and an angry shout
filled the room.

"Do not dare move!"

She froze, knowing it was the wisest choice.

Ian's hands were around her waist in an instant and she
was scooped up in his strong arms just as swiftly. His eyes
raged a fiery green. There was no doubt he was angry with
her.

He kept her in his arms and asked, "Are you a fool?"

She fought the urge to respond, thinking silence a better course of action.

Ian continued on. "I hear from near everyone I pass how
you were ill this morning soon after the meal and now I
find you climbing chests. You have no sense."

It was becoming more difficult to hold her tongue, but
she convinced herself it was a wise choice. He would calm
down soon. His tirade would not last long.

It had better not.

He paced in front of the fireplace, her weight no burden
to him. "You will hear me well this time, wife—"

That did it. "The whole keep can hear you," she said
with a raised voice.

He stopped and glared at her. "Then they will all know that you are not to lift a thing or do a thing—unless I command it."

"I think not," she announced with a calm sternness. "Now put me down."

"I think not." His forceful reply was not loud but was delivered with a strength that gave Moira pause.

It was a brief pause, though long for the likes of her independent nature. "It is not a request. I demand you put me down."

He paused to temper his anger—and he managed to, though his green eyes warned that it simmered beneath the surface. "Obey my command and I will put you down."

She crossed her arms over her chest and sent him a stubborn glare. "I will not be told what I can and cannot do."

"Aye, you most certainly will, wife!"

She opened her mouth but he spoke.

"And I will see to it that you do."

"Put . . . me . . . down!" Her voice rose with each word.

He smiled, not a wise reaction to her remark.

"You will not dictate to me." Why was she bothering to argue with him? A more sensible reaction would be to make him believe she acquiesced to his ridiculous demands and then keep her activities private.

It was his smile. It challenged her to defend herself, and how could she not?

"I will and I am."

"I have a right—"

"You have what right I give you."

Another unwise response that flared her temper. "I will do as I please, *husband.*"

He brought his face down close to hers. "You will do as I tell you, *wife.*"

"Put me down!" she demanded yet again.

"Or what?" he asked with a laugh.

Her temper mounted.

"There is naught you can do if I choose to keep you in my arms—"

The idea that she was powerless to defend herself infuriated her all the more and set her to serious thought.

"—And there is naught you can do but obey me."

She glared at him, his smile smug, his eyes turning from a fiery green to a gentler blue. He assumed he had won and his temper was abating. She had no recourse but to obey him and he would hold her in his arms until he chose to put her down.

Were there no options to force his hand?

What would cause him to think otherwise?

The idea came suddenly and, with haste and no forethought to her decision, she set it into action. She grabbed his face in her hands and kissed him soundly.

The shock of her unexpected action caught him off guard and for a moment he seemed too stunned to respond. Then he countered her attack.

He kissed her back and walked slowly toward the bed.

❧ nineteen

Ian stopped at the side of the bed and eased his lips off hers. "Now I will put you down, wife, and in a place I know I can keep you."

Moira grasped for his neck as he lowered them both to the bed. "This is not fair, Ian." And if it was not, then why did she wish to be here with him?

"Aye, it is," he replied on a laugh. "You started it."

"I but kissed you."

"And do you not know how your kisses make me feel?" he asked, stretching out beside her, his one leg resting intimately between hers and his arm draped over her waist.

She had not given her action proper thought. She had not taken time to consider the consequences. She had not . . .

"How do my kisses make you feel?" she asked him, all sensible thought slipping away from her.

He lowered his mouth near her ear and nibbled softly at her lobe before answering, "Your kisses make me want you."

"How could they?" she questioned. "I know not how to kiss."

"It comes naturally," he said and demonstrated by bringing his lips to rest on hers.

Her lips welcomed his and tender pecks and strokes soon turned heated, lips parted, and tongues mated; arms wrapped around each other and senses soared.

His hand drifted up to cup her breast; he teased her nipple with his fingers, and his leg moved between hers slowly and steadily.

"I want you," he whispered between kisses.

She drew damp and her need grew strong.

His hand moved to replace his leg, and he teased her until she pulsated against his hand and with each stroke he brought her closer and closer to complete surrender.

"Let go, Moira, let go and enjoy," he urged, feeling her body fight itself and understanding that part of her reluctance was her lack of trust in him. Which was why he wanted her to experience her own pleasure with no thought to anything else but her own emotions.

"Let go," he urged her again in a soft yet firm whisper. "Let me give you pleasure. You are safe with me."

"Am I?" she asked on a labored breath.

"Aye, wife, always you will be safe with me." She was vulnerable at that moment and the choice was his. Did he bring her to satisfaction or wait for her to decide?

The confused look in her eyes made his choice easy. He moved his hand over her and drove her past the peak of denial or refusal and brought her to her first climax.

She grasped tight hold of his shoulder, raised her hips up off the bed, pressing against his hand, and moaned loudly at the exquisite sensation that rushed her body.

His hand remained on her as she brought herself back to reality and he rained kisses over her face and whispered soft, reassuring words to her.

Her hands fell from his shoulders, her breath eased, the sensuous tingle abated, and her mind cleared.

She could think of no words to say to him and he said nothing. He simply kissed her gently about the face.

His touch felt heavenly, but then she had never thought any differently of it. Even their first time together he had been considerate and tender though rushed. She had felt nothing of what she had just experienced. It had been too brief and there had been pain and—

He tapped her nose lightly with his finger. "Where do you drift off to?"

"My mind forever drifts," she said, not actually giving him an answer.

He did not insist. He had a feeling he knew her thoughts; and some memories, for now, were better not spoken of.

She decided to be direct since that was her way. "That felt good."

"I like giving you pleasure."

Moira was not certain how to respond, and he eased her worry by placing a finger to her lips, requesting her silence.

"I care for you, Moira, which is why I worry about you so much. I do not like to see you faint or take ill or take chances that could cause you harm. I may shout and rant and demand you obey, but I want to keep you safe. Even from yourself," he said with a laugh.

He spoke the truth; this she knew without a doubt. "Could we compromise?"

"No surrender?" he teased.

"Nay, I have done that once already." Her tone was serious. "This time I must stand firm."

He knew she spoke of their wedding night and she had surrendered. She had surrendered everything to him, even her trust. He kept his voice light. "Tell me of your terms."

A smile crept over her face, as she felt victorious but did not wish to openly gloat. "I promise you that I will rest when I am tired and that I will take no unnecessary chances."

He stated his terms. "You will rest at least once a day, tired or not, and no unnecessary chances means climbing, lifting, moving, or exerting yourself in any way."

"I can lift small items—" She did not bother to finish since Ian was busy shaking his head.

"You will lift nothing." He was adamant.

"A stitching needle?" she asked, eagerly.

Ian thought this a fine time to convince her that her stitching room was a good and safe place for her to pass her time. "Stitching is something I feel would be a safe and healthy chore, and I would not be offended if you spent a good amount of your time at it."

Moira agreed enthusiastically. "That would suit me."

"There we agree on something. And I will see that your room is kept in full supply with all that you need." It was a way to make certain she remained put as well as satisfied.

"That is generous of you. Anne and I have been discussing the possibility of working on a tapestry."

A tapestry would take time. Ian thought this a perfect solution to the problem and encouraged her. "We do not have many tapestries in the keep. Another would do well." He would not have to worry so much about her for she would be safely tucked away with needle and thread. What harm could come from her stitching?

"We have reached a compromise then?" she asked, pleased with getting exactly what she wanted.

"Aye, we have," he agreed, much relieved that all was settled and in his favor.

"I think I will see how the room is coming along. Anne has been working hard on it."

She sounded eager and Ian was happy that she was pleased and that he would know her whereabouts. "Go and take your time, but remember you will rest sometime today."

"Aye," she said, excited. She pressed a kiss to his lips, lingering just a bit, and then hopped off the bed and rushed toward the door. She stopped and turned a breathtaking smile on him. "I am glad you like my kisses, husband." Then she was out the door before he could respond.

Ian laughed, lying back on the bed, his arms pillowing his head. "I like much more than your kisses, wife, and you will learn that soon enough."

Moira rushed up the steps with a smile. She felt delighted, exhilarated, thrilled, and she did not understand why. What was the reason for her delightful emotions? And did it matter that she understood? Should she not simply enjoy?

At the moment reason seemed unimportant and she entered the stitching room to be greeted by an equally delighted Anne.

They were soon seated on a thick fur hide in front of a roaring fire, drinking an herbal brew specially prepared by Moira.

"I am glad we are no longer at the convent," Anne said. "Life is much more interesting here."

"Very interesting," Moira agreed. "And there is still much for us to learn yet."

"I am learning fast." Anne's smile grew wider.

"Tell me."

Anne looked to see that the door was closed and that no one could hear them. "Blair kissed me."

Moira was eager to hear her news. "You enjoyed this kiss?"

Anne sighed. "Aye, I enjoyed it very much and would not mind him kissing me again."

Moira grew quiet in thought.

"What do you think about?"

"Ian has kissed me many times and I suddenly realize that I enjoy his kisses."

"This troubles you?"

She grew quiet again and Anne waited. "It is not only his kisses. He seems to truly be concerned with my safety and well-being. And . . ." She paused in thought again as if uncertain whether to speak her mind. But Anne was her friend and she needed to talk with someone she could trust. "He is patient and considerate of me when it comes to intimacy."

"Perhaps he loves you."

Moira looked at Anne, expecting to see a smile or hear her laugh in jest, but she was serious. "He could never love me."

"Why?"

Mora looked puzzled.

Anne waited for an answer.

Moira struggled for one.

Anne finally answered herself. "There is no reason he could not love you. You are a woman and he is a man, is that not all that is needed?"

"Do you think Blair loves you?"

Anne grinned. "He told me that he favors me and if he thinks to get any of my favors then I better hear the word *love* and he better mean it."

Moira laughed though it faded. "Do you really think Ian could love me?" She felt foolish asking but she felt more foolish believing that he possibly could love her. There was no need for him to love her. They were husband and wife and would remain so whether they loved each other or not.

Anne was direct. "I see the way he worries over you, the gentle way he touches you, the way his eyes light when you enter a room. These signs show he cares."

"Cares but not loves." Moira sounded disappointed.

"Do you love Ian?"

Moira stared in utter confusion at Anne.

"If you wonder if he can love you then you must wonder if you can love him. Love begins with someone—perhaps it is you."

Moira voiced her doubts. "How can I love a man who deceived me?"

"Blair spoke of this to me."

Moira was eager to hear. "What did he say?"

"I will tell you his words, but I must tell you that I believe Blair to be an honest man."

Her words warned Moira that she might not care for what she was about to hear.

"Blair explained that your father raided a clan village that was under Ian's protection. Ian warned him to leave or face the force of his clan. Your father adamantly refused and Ian attacked. Your father called for more men and the battle raged past reason. Many men lost their lives, more clans joined the melee, and there seemed to be no end in sight. Your father's intention was to sweep across the Glencoe and devour all in his path."

Moira made no comment; she listened.

"No amount of negotiations worked. Your father was determined to have his way. It was as if he were mad with power. Blair insists that the fighting would have continued if Ian had not made the decision to wed you and bring the destruction to an end. He said that he had never seen the amount of blood spilled the way Angus Maclean spilled it. Blair says that Angus is a ruthless man and cares naught for anyone."

"He loved my mother. I sometimes think that when she died his soul died with her."

"I suppose love can damage as well as heal."

"I know not about love and only recently have had to give it thought. There is no rhyme or reason to it."

"I do not think it is meant to be understood," Anne said. "I think it is merely to be felt and experienced. To reason love would lose the meaning."

"But reason and meaning are important if we are ever to understand and gain knowledge," Moira insisted.

"True enough," Anne agreed. "But love needs no reasoning, it simply is. And when you find and accept it, I think then is when you comprehend it."

Moira smiled and reached out to pat Anne's arm. "You

will do well in your studies and I look forward to working with you."

Anne was pleased with the praise. "Let me show you what I have done with the room so far."

Anne pointed out how she had fashioned the chests and tables so that at first glance the room appeared to be a stitching room, but when things were moved and changed around, the room became a place of bubbling potions and interesting mixtures. Ledgers were stacked away in a wooden chest beneath a writing desk.

"I convinced Blair that a writing desk would be perfect here, for you were skilled in letters and would enjoy sending word to Mother Superior from time to time, and of course that would keep you busy. He had the desk carried right up here."

"You are a gem," Moira said, pleased with all that Anne had accomplished. "I could have never done all of this on my own. I do appreciate your hard work."

Anne giggled. "Hard work? Never. I love every minute of hunting for furnishings and odd pieces for this room. It is an adventure. The drying rack for herbs I got by convincing Blair that it was perfect for holding the yarn. Which it can be, in between the herbs of course, and then no one will be the wiser."

"I told Ian that we wished to start a tapestry and he seemed pleased. He knows that a tapestry takes time and the more time I spend here the less he feels he will have to worry."

"It works out perfectly and we should have few disturbances since I will see to getting anything we need, and I think with you having befriended Hilda that she would be only too willing to supply us with any strange materials and make no comment about it."

"In time. For now, you can gather what we need with no one being the wiser."

The two women went on to discuss their most pressing needs and how Anne could secure the items. And it was several hours later that Ian entered the room and reminded Moira of her rest period.

He was pleased to see her sitting on the fur relaxing in conversation and he was pleased when she made no protest that she rest. But then, she had agreed to. He was pleased when he assisted her down the stairs to their bedchamber and tucked her into bed for a nap.

He was not pleased that he had to leave when he wanted simply to crawl in bed beside her and hold her close.

"Ian," she called out to him as he neared the door.

He turned.

She seemed hesitant. "Are you busy?"

He walked slowly back to the bed. "Nay, a few things to see to, that is all. Why do you ask?"

She rubbed at her arms, which lay above the bedcovering. "They are not important things?"

He knew that she could not be cold for he had made certain to stoke the fire and heat the room for her, so her arm rubbing was a nervous gesture. "They can wait. What is it you wish?"

She sighed softly then took a breath as if drawing on her courage. "I thought you would stay with me awhile."

He reached the bed and leaned over her, tapping playfully at her nose. "Only if I can join you in bed."

She smiled and pulled the cover back in invitation.

He discarded his boots, pulled off his tunic, and climbed beneath the soft wool bedcovering. He positioned himself directly behind her and drew her body back against his, his hand going to rest comfortably and protectively on her stomach.

"It is months by now and you barely show signs of rounding."

She snuggled against him and with only her underdress on she was able to feel the full length and strength of him. And it certainly impressed. "The babe will grow in his own good time."

His hand moved to her breast. "You grow here."

She had not expected him to notice.

"They fill with milk and your nipples are extra sensitive to my touch." He proved his words by brushing a finger over her one nipple. It instantly hardened and tingled, sending a shiver racing through her.

He lowered his lips to her neck. "See, I am right." He teased her neck with nibbles.

"You do not play fair," she said on a yawn.

"Why is that?" he asked, realizing she was growing sleepy.

"You know where to touch me so that I respond. I know not that of you." She yawned again.

"Then explore and find out," he whispered in her ear.

A challenge. Would she accept?

He waited for her answer.

She yawned. "Tonight, husband, I touch you."

❧ twenty

Moira was deep in discussion with Anne, both women having finished their evening meal and still sitting beside each other at the table.

Ian sat beside Moira, and Blair was beside him. There was room for six at the dais but no one else had joined them this evening. A few men occupied a nearby table but many of the tables were empty, most having finished their meal and returned to their homes. It was a cold winter night and a roaring fire and warm bed, not to mention a companion to share it with, was where most wanted to be.

Including Ian.

"You seem impatient this evening," Blair smiled then asked, "Or is it anticipation?"

Ian glared at him and Blair just laughed.

"Come, let me show you."

The two men heard Anne's eager remark and looked to see her standing.

"I had one of the men move it to the room early this evening," she continued on as Moira stood.

Ian looked about to remark then shut his mouth and dropped back against his chair.

Blair grinned and Anne caught it as she passed by the two men.

Moira thought nothing of following her without a word to her husband.

"She is accustomed to her own way," Blair said, attempting to ease his friend's disappointment.

"Aye, but when married, husbands and wives should consider the other."

"Give her time."

"I have, but I grow—"

Blair finished for him with a laugh: "needy."

Ian had to smile. "Aye, I grow very needy." His need had grown steadily since his wife had told him earlier that tonight she would touch him. He had been looking forward to her touch and the time they would spend together and he had hoped that they would finally make love.

"Moira was raised most of her life in a convent. I doubt she understands the ways of a man."

"I tell myself this and understand. . . . And other times?" He shook his head. "I have no patience for it."

Blair offered his help. "I could go interfere and see that Anne is kept occupied."

For a brief moment Ian thought to agree, then thought better of it. "I want her to come to me because she wants to."

"I do not know about that," Blair said with a smirk. "You know women when they get together. They never stop talking and time is simply lost to them."

Ian groaned and shook his head again.

Anne and Moira stopped by the stairs.

"Something is going on," Anne said. "Blair gave Ian the strangest grin just a moment ago."

Moira did not want to draw the men's attention so she kept her eyes on the stairs. "What think you about this look?"

"I cannot be certain but I think Blair teases Ian. For what reason, I could not say."

Moira gave it thought and it suddenly struck her. Was Ian actually looking forward to her touch? She had given it thought since she woke from her nap but she thought that perhaps he was simply satisfying her curiosity. Was she not looking at this clearly enough? Could he really desire her, want to be with her?

"What is it?" Anne asked, seeing the perplexed look cross Moira's face.

"I do not know enough about a man to understand my husband."

"Then ask him," Anne said.

"Ask him?" Moira looked stunned. "How can I ask him such personal questions?"

"He is your husband, why can you not ask him? And you always ask questions—that is how you learn. Did you not teach me this?"

Moira nodded.

"If questions are difficult for you then experiment."

Moira smiled. "That was what I was to do this evening."

Anne giggled. "Then you should be going upstairs with your husband—and experimenting."

"Aye, that I should."

"Will you discuss the results with me?" Anne looked eager for an answer.

"Perhaps you should do your own experimenting with Blair this night."

Anne beamed with excitement. "An excellent idea, and since my teacher has told me to experiment, I would not want to disappoint her."

"Now how do I get Ian upstairs?"

Anne shrugged. "Be honest with him."

"Tell him I wish to experiment on him?"

Anne whispered, "I think a different choice of words might work better and bring startling results."

"I would like to touch him."

"Good choice of words," Anne said.

Moira sat down on one of the steps.

Giving no thought to her action, Anne turned and called out, "Ian, your wife needs you." She then turned back to Moira and winked.

Blair followed on Ian's heels and when Ian went down on bended knees to speak to his wife, Anne grabbed Blair by the arm, gave him a wink, and the two smiled and drifted off together.

"What troubles you?" Ian asked anxiously.

Moira took a calming breath, for her heart raced and her tummy tingled. She was nervous and did not wish to show it. "I wish to go to our bedchamber."

She need say no more. Ian had her up in his arms in no time and walked up the steps asking, "You do not feel well?"

"I feel fine," she assured him, resting her head on his chest and draping her arms around his neck. He smelled so very good. It was a scent of wood smoke and fresh earth and all man and it simply intoxicated the senses.

He stopped for a moment when they reached the top.

"I wish to talk," she said before he could say anything.

"Talk," he repeated, sounding disappointed.

She raised a finger to his lips. "And touch. I wish to touch."

Ian hurried his steps to their bedchamber, kicking the door shut behind him and fastening the bolt.

She smiled at his actions and commented, "Now no one will disturb us."

He would kill anyone who disturbed them and the outrageous thought brought a smile to his lips. He stood her next to the bed and neither one of them moved or spoke. They simply stared at each other.

Ian broke the silence. "It is better if there is nothing between us if you wish to touch."

She was not certain if he meant for her to disrobe or for him, for she was the one who would be touching.

He sensed her doubt and his hand went to caress her neck. "I wish to touch as well and I wish you naked to my touch."

She swallowed the sudden lump in her throat. Naked? Could she actually stand naked in front of him? She would be vulnerable then, completely vulnerable, and the last time she was, he had taken advantage of her.

His hand continued to stroke. "I will not hurt you. Trust me."

She was honest with him. "I wish to trust you but—"

"You must start somewhere, Moira, why not here and now?" He stepped back and began to undress.

Moira stood frozen, unsure what to do. Unsure if she could trust. Unsure of herself.

Ian discarded his boots, pulled his shirt off, and then slowly unfastened his plaid wrap and dropped it to the floor.

Moira reasoned that it was best to keep her eyes on his face, but reason fast disappeared as her curiosity got the better of her and her glance began to drift. He was certainly a fine-looking man and powerfully built from top to bottom and definitely in between. No extra weight marred his perfect form. His muscles were firm and plentiful and he was quite ready for mating.

He approached her. "Can I help you?" He reached out slowly and untied the loose cloth belt at her waist, giving her ample time to object. When she did not, he continued. He tossed the belt aside and hoisted her tunic over her head, leaving her in her underdress. He leaned down and with a lift to each leg he rid her of her sandals.

He stood then and with his hands on her last garment he looked at her, waiting again to see if she objected.

Moira briefly thought to stop him, very briefly. She wanted to experience this moment with him. She wanted to know more about intimacy between a man and woman and she would never know if she never tried. She made no move to stop him.

Ian read her clearly and with a gentle touch he shed almost all that stood between them as he cast off the last of her clothing.

He lifted her then and lowered her to the bed, lying down beside her. He ran a tender and exploring hand over her. "You have a beautiful body."

"You truly think this?"

He leaned down and gave her a quick kiss. "Aye, I truly do. And I love touching every inch of you."

His words gave her confidence and she admonished herself for needing it, but she doubted her abilities as a woman. She did not even know what womanly abilities she possessed, but she was about to find out.

She reached out and ran her hand slowly over his hard muscled chest and a sense of pleasure sped through her. "I like the feel of you."

"Touch me as much as you like. I like when you touch me."

"You do?"

He ran his lips across hers. "Aye, I do. Very much I do."

She felt it important to tell him, "This is new to me and I am not sure how—"

He stopped her with a gentle finger to her lips. "There is no how. Do as you like. Do what pleases you. Simply let your hand wander, wherever it wishes to go."

"You do not mind?"

He smiled. "A man likes when a woman touches him."

She got daring. "Does a man like when a woman touches him in certain places?"

His laugh was gentle. "You forever ask questions."

"Do you find that one too difficult to answer?"

And challenge, he thought. She forever challenged. "Nay, it is not too difficult to answer. Do you wish to know where I want you to touch me?"

She nodded, feeling a bit nervous.

He took hold of her hand. "Let me show you."

She nodded her approval since he waited for her response.

He moved her hand slowly down along his stomach and though there was a slight tremor to her hand he did not stop until he rested her hand on the hard length of him. He released her hand and half expected her to pull away.

She did not and he waited.

He felt warm, smooth, and thick, and without forethought she began to explore him. She liked the way he felt like velvet to her touch and when she reached down to cup him she found that his groan brought her pleasure. She continued to touch and explore and thrill in the feel of him. She allowed her fingers to run out over his thighs and then back over him and when she playfully squeezed him hard and felt him pulsate against her, her breath caught with excitement.

She went on, resting her head on his chest so that she could study her movements and results and of course his moans and groans could be heard much better with her ear to his chest. She ran her foot up his leg and leaned her body close to his without any thought to her actions or the consequences.

Ian finally forced himself to speak. "You must stop."

She looked up at him, bewildered and disappointed. "Why? I enjoy it. And you enjoy it too."

"Too much I enjoy it," he said through heavy breaths.

"I do not understand." She looked to him for an explanation.

"There are consequences from your touch. Do you not feel them?"

She gave it thought and then realized that her body was experiencing the same exquisite feelings it had earlier in the day when Ian had touched her and brought her such pleasure.

She smiled at him. "I am giving you pleasure."

"Much pleasure and I want much more."

She realized the full extent of his meaning. "You wish to join with me."

"Aye, wife, I wish to join with you."

"You will not force me."

"I will not force you," he assured her. "I want this joining between us to be a willing one and a desirous one. I want you. You feel how much I want you. The choice is now yours."

"If I say nay?"

He groaned. "I will suffer the torments of hell." He regretted the words for he wondered if perhaps she did not want him to suffer in return for what he had done to her, but if so he had the feeling she would be honest with him and make it known.

She gave no thought to his suffering, only his pleasure, for she realized that in his pleasure was hers as well. "I wish to join with you too."

"Truly?" he asked with a smile, cupping her face in his hand.

Her smile was joyous. "Truly, I do. I think it is time for us to do so. We are husband and wife."

"But do you want me? *Me,* Moira, *me?*"

Was he reminding her of who he was? Was he reminding her of his deceit? Was he reminding her of what had passed between them on their wedding night? The questions flashed through her head in mere seconds and in mere seconds she disregarded them.

She could not say why, nor did she wish to reason her choice. She only knew she wanted him—wanted him badly—and no memories, no deceit, nor regrets would stop her.

This was her choice and she made it freely.

"I want you, Ian. Lord, how I want you."

❧ twenty-one

Ian kissed her mouth gently, then her chin, her cheeks, and down along her neck.

Time.

He intended to take his time with her. He wanted to make up for their first hasty encounter. She deserved to experience lovemaking at its best. And besides, he wanted so very badly to make love to her. Lately he could think of little else and his thoughts had startled him. He had wanted Kathleen but not with the urgency he wanted Moira and it baffled him. He had not thought he would love again after Kathleen and yet Moira affected him in ways no woman ever had and that he could not make sense of.

And at the moment he was not interested in reason. He was interested in making love to his wife.

His hand moved to cup her breast and his mouth descended on her nipple; his tongue rolled across the hard orb before his lips closed over it. He took his time tasting her, lingering in her sweetness and transferring his attention to her other breast when she began to squirm beneath him.

Her sensual cries were soft as if she feared making a sound. He smiled to himself for he intended to make her moan quite loudly. While his tongue continued to torment her, his hand drifted down her body exploring her curves and silky smooth skin.

He stopped his hand for a moment, for the feel and taste of her was exciting him beyond reason. He felt like a young boy unable to control himself, his desire was so strong.

With a quick deep breath and a flick of his tongue over her nipple, he continued. His hand settled between her legs and she made no protest, she welcomed him. His touch was a gentle probing and it was not long before her hips moved in a steady rhythm against his hand and when his finger finally entered her she cried out loudly.

It was then he lowered his mouth on her and her hips lifted and he slid his hands beneath her bottom and drew her more closely to his eager mouth. He would taste her climax and then begin again and again and again.

Moira grasped the sheet tightly in her hands as her husband's tongue pleased her in ways she never thought possible and would probably think sinful if she could reason rationally. But she was not rational nor did she wish to be. She wanted to feel, just feel the crazy and delightful and tormentingly pleasurable sensations that raced through her body and turned her completely mindless.

There was no sound, thought, or reason, just complete abandonment to emotion, and it felt exquisite. She knew she was close to fulfillment; it built inside her like a coiling snake ready to attack and then writhe in satisfaction.

She moaned and then cried out his name. She grasped the linen bedding so tightly her knuckles turned pure white and when he squeezed her backside and drove deeper into her she completely lost all sanity and toppled over into total abandonment.

She climaxed in a flurry of shattering lights and sounds, her cries echoing in the bedchamber. Her hands grew limp and the bedsheets fell from her grasp and she relaxed as tingle after tingle subsided into a pleasing warmth.

Ian crawled over her, stroking his body along hers, and she sighed with pleasure.

She lay with her eyes closed, looking content and satisfied, so he was surprised when she said, "I was to touch you."

"You still can," he whispered and kissed her lips gently before laying alongside her.

She opened her eyes and turned to her side, her hand resting on his chest. "I like how you make me feel."

"I like that you tell me."

"Am I not supposed to?"

He smiled. "You do what pleases you."

"You do what pleases you?"

"I do what pleases *you and me.*"

"So what pleases me should please you?"

He gave her nose his usual playful tap. "Aye, it should."

"If it does not, you will tell me?"

He nodded. "As long as you do the same with me."

"Oh, but all you have done pleases me," she said eagerly. "You have done nothing to me that I object to."

"I am glad that my lovemaking satisfies you."

She looked at him with wide, serious eyes. "I wish to pleasure you. It does not seem fair that one should experience more pleasure than the other. This lovemaking must be mutual."

"I do not wish you to pleasure me out of fairness, I prefer you to pleasure me out of desire."

She looked at him strangely. "I know not much about sex but I think I am learning enough to realize that unless the act is mutual, pleasure is not derived from it. I suppose each partner could receive satisfaction without pleasure, but I do not think it would be the same."

"It is not and I do prefer the pleasure."

She smiled and ran her hand slowly down his stomach. "And I can do what I wish to pleasure you?"

Ian surrendered completely. "I am all yours."

"Mine to touch," she whispered running her hand over the hard, swollen length of him. She then cast him an odd look and seemed to hesitate as if she wished to speak but was not certain if she should.

"Tell me, wife," he said with a gentle stroke of his hand to her cheek. "I do not want you to fear asking me anything."

She took him at his word. "Am I permitted to taste you?"

His blood raced and his heart pounded wildly. "Aye, wife, that you are."

She smiled as if having received a gift. "I know not how to proceed, but you will be patient?"

"Aye, I will," he agreed though wondered exactly how long his patience would hold.

Moira found herself growing excited at the thought that she was now the one to bring him to pleasure. She was in control, or so she thought, for when her mouth descended on him she realized that her actions fueled her own desires and as his pleasure grew so did hers.

She started out gently exploring him with her tongue but it was not long before she become bold and began to taste him. Then she took him full into her mouth and Ian thought he would burst with the pleasure she brought him.

His patience grew thin fast and he reached down, scooped her off him and onto her back, and covered her with the length of him. "I need you now."

"And I you," she admitted anxiously.

He wasted not another moment. He entered her slowly so that she could accept the swelling size of him, but she was impatient herself and lifted her hips to welcome him.

She was wet with the want of him and he throbbed with the want of her and in one driving thrust he entered her.

She cried out and grasped at his arms and he moaned with the exquisite feel of her.

Sanity was lost and they set a rhythm that brought them both to an explosive climax and sent their cries echoing throughout the bedchamber.

Ian collapsed on top of her and, realizing his weight, he quickly rolled off to her side.

Moira's breath was labored but she rolled to her side so that she lay pressed against the heat of her husband. She knew not why she needed to feel him, she just did, and she surrendered to that need without thought.

He moved his arm to wrap around her and they lay in silent contentment.

Moira wished to talk with him. Numerous questions filled her head while her eyes grew heavy. She would rest a moment and then they would talk. He would answer her, she was sure of it, for he had told her she was not to fear discussing anything with him.

They would talk, she wanted to; she would just rest her eyes.

Ian realized that she was asleep. Her breathing had grown calm and steady and her body relaxed completely against him.

He managed to grasp the edge of the blanket and pull it over them.

This was a good night and one he had not expected, but one he was grateful for and while there were still wounds to mend between them this joining would bring them closer and help heal the wounds.

He drifted into a contented sleep, his wife safely tucked in his arms.

"This food is delicious," Blair said for the third time, sopping up the sauce from the pork pie with an eager urgency. "Have you noticed how tasty the food has become since your wife made her presence known in the kitchen?"

Ian nodded, busy himself eating the flavorful food.

"Have you noticed too that the keep seems to run more efficiently since Moira's arrival two months ago?"

Ian nodded again. He had taken note of the changes. They were subtle at first, such as furniture being moved from one place to another. He had assumed it entertained his wife to rearrange things but then he noticed that the changes had made a difference in the daily running of the keep. Things ran more efficiently and the servants complained less.

The keep even began to look better. There was a fresh scent in the air; the hearths kept steady flames, keeping the rooms at a comfortable temperature, and everything seemed cleaner.

"I heard tell that your wife was examining the seeds for spring planting and asking about the fields. It will not be long before we ready them for planting, six to eight weeks at the most," Blair said, taking the last bite of his pork pie.

"You must admit the planting beds at the convent produced in abundance, so I would say Moira knows about planting and any help that she can give us for our crops to be bountiful is gratefully accepted."

"I agree, a bountiful harvest benefits all, but how did she learn so much, about so much?"

Ian shrugged as if the question were obvious or not important. "She had time at the convent to plant, cook, and sew. She learned over the years."

"And the ledgers? She works with numbers faster and more accurately than anyone I have ever seen."

"She does seem to have a way with numbers, perhaps it is natural. Have you talked of this with Anne?"

Blair grinned.

Ian shook his head and smiled. "You have been doing other than talking with Anne?"

"I found a way to silence her many questions," Blair said with a satisfied grin.

"And if I should tell you it is no longer necessary for you to spend time with her?" Ian kept a firm smile.

"It would matter not to me for I find myself seeking her out more often than not and I find myself wanting more than a few stolen kisses."

"Could you be falling in love?"

Blair shook his head. "I never thought it possible. I loved the ladies too much to settle for just one, but Anne?" He shook his head again. "She is different. She tempts my heart, she does. And for one so small she has much strength—which she needs, since she so often speaks her mind."

Ian laughed. "You would think that two women raised in a convent would be docile and agreeable."

"Anne and Moira have no concept of those words," Blair said on a laugh. "They are both strong-willed and sharp-eyed. Anne has a way of asking questions and getting answers without the person realizing he is giving away a secret."

Ian grew serious. "Do you think she searches for something in particular?"

"I have wondered if she realized that there is a threat to Moira's life."

"Has she spoken of it to you?"

"Nay," Blair said, "but the questions she asks lead me to believe she suspects something. She has made mention several times as to how well the keep is guarded. She believes that it would be just as difficult for someone to escape the keep as to enter it."

"She is perceptive."

"She is very aware of her surroundings and all that goes on around her."

"Perhaps she will learn something about this mysterious threat before we do." Ian sounded annoyed. "Since our return all has been quiet, so I can only assume that the threat is from an outside influence. I am reluctant to talk with Moira about her father. I feel it will upset her."

"Then maybe we should look to him as being the problem."

"I have given that thought. The babe will inherit a good portion of his land. I remember how he laughingly offered me the arrangement. He never thought his daughter would give birth to a child and assumed he gave me nothing. He thought I was a fool for marrying her and told me to consider myself lucky that Moira would live out her days in the convent so that I may live my days as I wished."

"Did he not care for his daughter?"

"It does not appear so and I see the hurt in my wife's eyes when he is mentioned. If the threat does come from him then he will forever regret his actions for I will kill him without remorse."

"But how do we determine if he is the threat?"

"That is what troubles me. With the source of the threat coming from outside the clan there is naught I can do but wait until the culprit chooses to strike again. Then I must make certain we capture whoever makes the attempt so that we may discover who he leads us to."

"Patience is not a warrior's virtue."

"It should be," Ian said. "If a warrior possessed patience he would suffer little defeat."

"You possess enough patience for the whole clan," Blair praised.

"Aye," Ian agreed with a smile. "That is why I am laird."

"Hurry! Hurry!" A young servant girl cried out as she ran into the hall. "Moira has fainted."

Ian and Blair bolted from their chairs and followed the young girl. They almost collided with Anne, who had also been summoned and was running directly behind the servant girl who had delivered the news to her.

They all entered the cooking area to find Hilda helping Moira to sit up. She was sprawled on the floor a short distance from the fireplace.

"A faint, that is all." Hilda was assuring her with a comforting hand to her back.

Anne hastily fetched a clean damp cloth to pat gently at Moira's pale face.

Ian, with a worried look on his face, walked over to his wife and went down on bended knees beside her.

Moira gave him no chance to speak. "I was just about to take my nap."

"And this floor is more comfortable than our bed?"

She smiled and spoke low. "Nay, our bed offers me comforts I can get nowhere else."

It was Ian's turn to smile and he did. "You must be well—your mind and tongue are sharp."

"It was but a simple faint," she assured him.

"Your simple faints occur much too often."

Moira reached out to him to help her stand. "Tell your son this, since he is the one being obstinate."

Ian slipped his arm around her waist and hoisted her up with ease, keeping a firm hold on her. "He learns well from his mother."

"Nay, I will not take his stubbornness, he will do as I tell him."

"He does not seem to be listening," Ian remarked, his smile widening.

Moira was glad to see that he was not as upset as he usually got when she fainted, and it had been a couple of weeks since her last faint.

Raised voices and shouts from the hall caught all their attention and an older servant woman hurried in to announce, "Brianna has arrived."

✖ *twenty-two*

Ian had his sister up in his arms in an instant. They had all hurried to the great hall, Moira's faint being ignored and she being grateful for the interruption. As soon as Brianna caught sight of her brother she ran to him and he welcomed her with open arms.

"She is beautiful," Anne whispered to Moira as they stood together to the side and watched the joyous pair.

Moira nodded, finding herself speechless. The young woman was stunning. She had the most beautiful dark hair that Moira had ever seen. It was not black and not brown but a rich darkness that defied description and it fell over her shoulders in a riot of curls and waves. Her face was angelic; there was no other way to describe it. She possessed the beauty of an angel; her features were soft, her complexion a creamy pale, and her eyes a brilliant blue. She had full breasts, a tiny waist, and curving hips and she stood five foot three inches or four but no more. And her smile could light a room it was so captivating.

"I have missed you, brother," Brianna said before planting a big kiss on his lips.

Ian hugged her fiercely to him. "And I you, little one."

She laughed and it sounded like a pretty melody. "I am little no more."

"You will always be my little sister and I will always protect you."

"She has me for that now, Ian."

Moira watched with interest the man who approached Ian. They joined in a hug and a friendly slap on the back. He was handsome, too handsome. His good looks stole the senses and allowed him to hide his true nature. Moira did not get a good feeling from him and she would make certain to keep a watchful eye on him. And he did not at all match the beauty and caring that Brianna projected. She wondered over the two.

"That she does, Arran, but she is my sister and always under my protection."

Moira thought the two men to be in a contest of wills. Who was the stronger was obvious, her husband naturally. He possessed a strength that one could see and feel and one he easily demonstrated. Arran possessed no such strength, mere arrogance, and for some odd reason she felt him more a coward than a courageous man. Again she wondered how he and Brianna ever joined in marriage.

"We are all under your protection," Arran said with a smile.

Moira did not like the man, especially his smile. There was something false about it, though she did like Brianna. She seemed sincere and trusting, much like her brother.

Trusting?

Did she really trust Ian?

"I want you to meet someone very special to me," Ian said to his sister. "My wife."

Special?

The word rang in Moira's head.

Ian held his hand out to her and Moira immediately went to him and grasped his hand firmly.

Brianna squealed with delight. "I have a sister!"

Moira was not prepared for the young girl throwing herself against her and Ian laughed, standing behind his wife and keeping the pair from toppling over.

"I am so happy to meet you and so happy that Ian has found love." Brianna beamed with joy.

Moira thought to correct her about love but thought better of it when she caught the look on her husband's face. He seemed to ask of her patience and understanding and she decided to give it.

"And," Ian said with a grin that could shed light on the darkest of places, "I am to be a father."

Brianna cried out and flung herself once again into her brother's arms. "How wonderful! I will be an aunt and I will spoil him senseless."

Moira grinned at the two. That they cared and loved each other was obvious and it was wonderful to see siblings who actually loved beyond reason.

Brianna turned her attention to Moira. Without thought or permission she threw her arms around her and hugged her tightly. "I am thrilled for you and if I can help in any way, please let me know."

Moira spoke honestly. "Having you here so that we may come to know one another is a good start."

Brianna grinned. "Aye, a very good start. And when do we expect the bairn?"

"June sometime," Moira said.

Brianna looked her over. "You hide your condition well."

Ian was thinking the same. Moira had barely gained an ounce since arriving at the keep and he wondered over it.

"My mother showed little when she carried her babes so I suppose I follow after her."

Ian did not like her words since her mother had died birthing a babe, but he kept his worries to himself. He instead asked of his sister, "And when will you and Arran make me an uncle?"

Moira caught the brief flash of sorrow that crossed Brianna's face though her husband did not notice it.

"In time," Brianna answered with a lightness that she certainly did not feel. "For now I will have a nephew to spoil."

"Then you plan to stay for a while?" Ian asked hopefully.

"As long as you will have us," Arran answered.

"I miss my sister and wish her to extend her visit as long as she wishes," Ian informed him and then turned to Brianna. "You will stay until we grow tired of each other."

Brianna laughed softly. "We never grew tired of each other. We always found something to entertain us or some trouble to get into." She turned to Blair. "And of course we always dragged Blair along with us."

Blair laughed and went to her, giving her a huge hug. "It is good to have you home with us."

"It is good to be home."

Ian realized for the first time since his sister's arrival that she sounded relieved to be here with her clan and he wondered if something troubled her.

Moira stepped in. "Do you require rest or nourishment?"

"A light fare would serve well right now," Brianna said.

Arran stepped up behind his wife, placing a firm hand to her shoulder. "Perhaps rest would be best first."

It disturbed Moira that the man should ignore his wife's wish for food and expect her to follow his dictate, so she came to her sister-in-law's rescue. "I would be pleased if Brianna joined me since I was about to take some nourishment myself."

Ian eyed her skeptically since he knew that she was about to take a much-needed nap. He decided that perhaps it would be good for the two women to spend time together. He did not, however, wish his wife exerting herself especially since she had recently fainted.

Ian settled the matter. "I will have Hilda send a light fare to my solar; you may both relax there."

Arran kissed his wife's cheek. "Do as your brother says."

Moira raised a brow and Ian took advantage of the moment. He walked over to Moira and placed his arm around her. "Aye, do as your husband says, wife."

Moira paused in thought and then with a smile said, "I prefer to take our fare in the bedchamber. Have Hilda send it there. Brianna, please join my friend Anne and me. I am sure there is much for us to talk about." With that she stepped away from her husband and held her arm out to Brianna.

Brianna was surprised by her sister-in-law's independent response and hesitated to take her arm.

Moira did not care for the smug look on Arran's face; it was as if he gloated over his wife's obedience. She was, however, pleased that Ian did not interfere and knew then that his remark was intended to tease her. At that moment she appreciated his charming humor.

She cast a sickening sweet smile on Arran and slipped her arm around Brianna's. "You will love Hilda's fruit tarts."

"Aye," Ian agreed eagerly. "Hilda's fruit tarts are delicious."

Brianna looked confused and Moira could only assume that she had tasted Hilda's food before and found it lacking. "Try one," she suggested. "And decide for yourself." With that said Moira guided the young woman from the room, with Anne following on her other side.

"Come, Arran," Ian said, "join Blair and me in a drink."

The three men took seats at the dais and Blair filled three tankards with ale.

"Your wife is persistent," Arran said, sounding disapproving.

Ian made it clear how he felt about his wife. "She is strong of character and I admire and respect her strength."

Arran immediately sought to correct his remark. "I meant no disrespect."

"I did not take it as such," he assured him. "But let us talk of how things go with you. Has there been any trouble in your area?"

After Arran had married Brianna, Ian had placed him in charge of a small village with a small keep to the south. It was Cameron land but set at a far enough distance that for safety reasons Ian had had the keep built near the village for protection. Arran saw to keeping that protection intact.

"Minor difficulties but none that cannot be quelled with little effort."

His confident arrogance warned Ian to beware. Often that attitude could be detrimental to a leader. "Do these minor difficulties involve other clans?"

"A minor clan of no consequence," Arran said as if dismissing the issue.

Blair raised a brow and eyed Ian over his tankard.

Arran seemed not to want to waste his breath over it. "It has been seen to."

Ian was insistent and with curt words made it known. "Tell me, I wish to know."

Arran obeyed his laird though reluctantly. "A small, inconsequential clan sought to join with the Camerons. They could provide little benefit to us and I rejected their offer. They caused a few minor problems that have since been solved."

"This clan sought Cameron protection?" Ian kept firm hold on his annoyance.

"They were a small lot, more farmers than fighters. They could give us nothing in return."

"If farmers they must know about farming," Blair commented.

"We have no need of more farmers," Arran said, sounding irritated that he needed to explain. "The Camerons are a fierce fighting clan and welcomes those who can fight strongly by our side."

"Food is needed to feed these fierce fighters you speak of," Ian said, attempting to make Arran understand his mistake. "Farmers are as beneficial to the clan as warriors. When you return, see that you extend a most cordial invitation for them to join with us and see that they are well treated."

Arran did not seem at all pleased but did not protest, he simply nodded and took a hefty swallow of ale.

"Have you heard anything of the Macleans?" Ian asked.

Arran was instantly alert. "Do they trouble us again?"

Ian realized that Arran loved to war. The senseless deaths and destruction that came with it seemed to excite him. He rivaled in the battles and even small skirmishes. He had spoken of the power that the Camerons would amass when they defeated the Macleans. But not once did the loss of lives disturb him. He simply saw it as a necessity of battle.

"Nay, I have heard nothing. I thought perhaps on your way here you might have heard news."

"They seem quiet enough." Arran sounded disappointed. He poured himself more ale. "I was thinking that perhaps it would be wise to build a larger keep. The village grows around us and more protection will soon be necessary."

"We shall see," Ian said. "Did you bring your ledgers with you?"

Arran nodded. "Aye, I have them for you to see."

Ian had no intention of telling him that it would be his wife who looked the ledgers over. He was gaining an appreciation for his wife's talent. She kept the ledgers running smoothly and made improvements in the running of the keep.

"Tell me of your last harvest," Ian said and settled back in the chair to listen.

●　　●　　●

The small table in the bedchamber was spread with a fine assortment of delicious treats. Once Brianna took her first taste she could not stop tasting.

"Hilda's cooking skills certainly have improved," Brianna said between bites of the delicious honey bread spread liberally with a honey butter.

"She has done well," Moira said and poured them each a cup of chamomile tea.

"Tell me of your marriage to my brother," Brianna asked eagerly. "I always hoped that he would find love again." She bit at her lower lip as if she had just let a secret spill out and wished to take it back.

"It is all right," Moira assured her. "I know of Ian's first wife, Kathleen."

Brianna spoke with a sadness that showed. "Her death hurt him badly and I thought he would forever suffer and never allow himself to love again."

Anne listened along with Moira, both women having similar thoughts. What would they learn that would prove useful?

Brianna continued, "So I am glad to see that he allows himself to love again."

Moira did not wish to appear dishonest. "Our vows were exchanged out of necessity."

Brianna looked disappointed. "You wed each other out of necessity?"

"It could not be helped." Moira did not wish to dwell on the marriage and it was Ian, not her, who should speak of this to his sister. "And there is the babe." Moira placed a hand to her stomach and felt the slight rounding. Others might think it strange she gained barely a few pounds, but she felt the difference in her body and of late a strong movement and she knew the babe to be alive and well.

"I am so thrilled," Brianna said. "Everything goes well? The babe does not make you ill?"

Moira laughed. "The babe has upset the whole keep."

"Aye," Anne agreed. "He has a mind of his own and makes himself known when it pleases him."

Moira explained; Brianna looked too confused to speak. "I have my fair share of morning illness, but it is the fainting bouts that have disturbed everyone."

"You faint often?"

Anne answered with a smile. "Too much for the likes of your brother."

Brianna sounded concerned. "Aye, he would worry."

Moira sought to appease her worries. "There is no need for him or you to worry. I feel fine and I am fine. I eat well. Sleep well. And nap daily."

Brianna grinned. "Which my brother makes certain of."

"You know him well."

Brianna's grin turned to a fond smile. "My brother has been good to me and I love him dearly."

"Then it is good that you have come home for a visit," Moira said and watched the young woman's beautiful smile fade.

"You do not mind if we stay a while? I do not wish to interfere with you and Ian."

"Nonsense," Moira assured her. "You may stay as long as you wish. I welcome your presence. It would be nice to have you here for the birth."

Brianna grew excited. "You wish me to stay for the birth?"

Anne added her opinion. "It would be good to have you join me in birthing the babe."

Moira agreed. "Aye, I would much prefer to have women with me whom I have come to know and care about, and you are my sister now." Moira could not say why but she felt Brianna needed to know that they could have a close relationship, that they could talk and even share secrets.

Brianna appeared tearful. "I have always wanted a sister or a close friend."

"Now you have both," Anne said and reached out to give her hand a warm squeeze.

Brianna returned the gesture. "I shall ask my husband if we can remain here for the birth."

"Why?" Moira asked without thinking and then thought better of her question. "Forgive me, but I keep forgetting that wives usually seek their husbands' permission for such matters. My life at the convent was vastly different than married life."

"Was not the convent strict with rules and obedience?" Brianna asked curiously.

Anne laughed. "Moira had a way of making her own rules."

"And you did not?" Moira asked with a teasing glint in her eye.

"Stories," Brianna said with a delightful clap of her hands. "You must tell me some. I fear my life has been dreadfully boring and I wish to hear at least of someone else's excitement."

"We can trust you to keep a confidence?" Moira asked, feeling the young woman trustworthy.

"Aye," Brianna whispered. "I will speak of this to no one."

Moira smiled and whispered her response, "Especially your brother."

Brianna giggled. "I will finally know something he does not."

"You never kept a secret from him?" Moira asked, surprised.

"He always found out."

"Always?" Anne asked. "How did he do that?"

"I wish I knew," Brianna said. "He seems to have a way of discovering things. I sometimes think Blair is his eyes and ears when necessary."

Anne grew suspicious. "You mean Blair spied on you?"

"I think he did," Brianna said, "though I probably chattered away all my secrets, the few I had, since Blair can be a charmer."

Anne leaned over the table. "We will teach you how to keep secrets and how to discover them."

"Aye, that would be delightful," Brianna said like a young pupil eager to learn.

Moira took charge. "Now for your first lesson and we will begin by making a discovery."

✿ twenty-three

Moira's nap usually turned into a rendezvous with her husband; that was why she was not at all surprised to feel him climb beneath the bedcovers and snuggle beside her just as she was dozing off.

A heavy rain fell outside and thunder could be heard moving in from the distance, so a warm bed, a roaring fire, along with a warm body, were most welcomed, and Moira did welcome her husband's presence. He had become a constant in her life, like the orderly way of life at the convent, something she could count on. And lately she had counted on him often.

She especially counted on him joining her during her naps. She enjoyed intimacy with him and each time they made love she discovered more and more about herself and about him.

Today, however, she was tired. She realized that after a faint she experienced some fatigue and with the excitement of Brianna's arrival and the delay in her nap, she felt more tired than normal.

She yawned as her husband's hand came to rest on her breast.

"You are tired," Ian said, snuggling closer to her. She napped with only her underdress on and slept at night naked beside him. Her nakedness had evolved naturally. They would make love and she would fall asleep shortly afterward. Soon she did not bother to wear any garment to bed, which quite pleased him since he wore not a stitch of clothing to sleep in.

"Aye, I am," she admitted with a sigh.

He heard the disappointment in her voice and teased her neck with playful nibbles. "Too tired to play with me, are you?"

"I wish I were not."

Ian liked that his wife did not deny that she enjoyed intimacy with him. She let him know when she desired him and that she wished to learn what pleased him, for pleasing each other, she had discovered, made making love more pleasurable.

"Want me, do you?" He whispered kisses along her cheek.

"Aye, that I do."

It always startled him when she admitted that she wanted him. He had thought it would take time for them to become comfortable with intimacy but that was not so. Making love with her felt natural and so very comfortable. What he found even stranger was that he realized he enjoyed making love more with Moira than he had with Kathleen. He had never thought he would ever feel that way. He had known women after Kathleen died but they were meaningless encounters meant to satisfy his lusty masculine need.

With Moira he had discovered something different. Something he did not quite understand. And stranger still he was beginning to wonder if that something different had anything to do with love. He could not say why he thought himself possibly in love with his wife, but if he were honest he would admit the thought was always there in the back of his mind.

He pressed his cheek to hers. "Sleep, we will play later."

"Stay with me?" she asked, her words sounding drowsy and her hand clutching his where it lay at her breast.

"I will be right here."

Though he spoke low he spoke with a firm sureness that quelled her worries and had her body relaxing against his.

He continued to kiss along her cheek and up along her temple until he rested his face in her dark hair. He loved the scent of her. Her hair always smelled sweet and her body smelled fresh, like the meadows after a hard spring rain.

"I like your sister," she said, her voice barely a whisper.

"I am glad."

"She will stay to help birth your son."

Ian smiled at his wife's command. "If you wish."

"I do."

"Then she shall remain," he assured her with a hug.

She sighed contentedly. "I like you here beside me."

"And I will be staying beside you."

He barely heard the words she spoke. "Until you want me no more."

Her breathing grew soft and steady and he knew her to be asleep, but her words disturbed him. Did she think that one day he would discard her?

Angus Maclean.

Her father had discarded her. Did she fear that one day it would happen again though this time it would be her husband that discarded her? She had thought her father loved her and yet he sent her away. She wed a man who abandoned her on their wedding day only to change his mind and return for her.

He had fought a hard battle that day with himself. He had thought to bring her back to his home, but her father had convinced him that she was content at the convent.

She was set in her ways and by taking her away from all that was familiar to her Ian would certainly cause her pain. And had she not suffered enough? And besides, what good would she do him? She was too old and barren to be a dutiful wife.

Ian had not wished to provoke further battles and he thought then that perhaps her father was right. Perhaps he would cause her more harm than good. So he decided once again what he thought best for her.

He had been wrong and it hurt him to admit it. He should have discussed it with her. He should have given her the choice to leave or stay. She had the right to make at least that choice for herself.

It was not long after he left that he realized his mistake and decided to return for her. His plans had been set for the trip to the convent when he heard news of a possible threat to her life. Either way, his intentions were to return for her.

He had found that he could not get his wife off his mind. Theirs was a brief encounter, and yet . . .

He shook his head as he always did when the thought haunted his mind. How did he make sense of it? He would sit and daydream of her. At times he would think he could feel his hands on her slim waist and taste her sweet lips.

It was crazy the way he had dwelled on her.

And it was crazy that he still did. He felt the need to know where she was at all times. Of course he tried to convince himself that it was her protection that caused such concern. But he knew it was his own desire that fostered such a need.

Or was it love?

Love.

Did he dare think he could love again?

She turned in his arms, snuggling her face against his chest.

He rested his cheek to her head and kept his arms firm around her. Something warned him that he had the answer he searched for; he only need accept it.

• • •

Anne was busy searching through the storage room and Blair was busy watching her. He sat in one of the high-backed, velvet-seated chairs that Anne thought would suit the dais well. In time she would manage to have them moved but for now she was searching for a small chest she had remembered seeing had a lock and key. It would be perfect for Moira's research papers.

The stitching room was complete but there were always changes that could benefit their studies and Anne made certain to make them.

"What think you of Brianna?" Blair asked, lifting his feet to rest on a flat chest.

"She is good and caring, though I cannot say the same for her husband."

Blair could always count on Anne speaking her mind. It made for good conversation. "You do not like him?"

Anne halted her search to glare through the rungs of a chair back at Blair. "You sound surprised."

"He has a way with the ladies. There is not a head he does not turn."

"He did not turn mine," she said and returned to her foraging.

Blair smiled, relieved to hear that a handsome face did not catch her fancy. Her next remark startled him.

"Besides, you are much handsomer than he."

He was speechless and when he found his tongue it made no sense. "Yo—you—ah, think—"

Anne's laughter forced his silence. "Never been told you are handsome?"

Blair regained control of his senseless tongue and startled her with his remark. "Never when it mattered."

It was Anne's turn to be speechless though it was brief and she did not trip over her response. "My words matter to you?"

He stood and started walking toward her.

Anne was always impressed with the size of him;

though he stood a head shorter than Ian, he was solid in muscle and firm in strength. And his smile could delight the most disgruntled person. Then of course there was the way he made her feel when near. Her heart raced, she grew warm and tingled all over, and her lips ached, constantly ached for him to kiss her.

He stepped around the chair she peeked at him through and stopped in front of her. "Your words matter much to me."

"Why?"

He smiled and reached out to cup her face in his hands. "This is why."

He kissed her and it was no soft kiss. It was packed with an urgent passion that ignited her own. Arms flew around each other, bodies collided, and nothing existed but the two of them.

Anne came to her senses after his hand became familiar with her breast and she began to feel things that she knew would lead her to trouble. She pulled back away from him.

"I am not a woman who gives easily of herself."

Blair took a deep breath to calm his desires. "I did not think you did."

"I feel strongly for you, Blair, but I have my honor and my commitment to my faith to consider."

He laughed and shook his head. "Then I guess I will have to marry you, lass, for there is no way I am not going to have you. I love you."

Anne's calm response did not match the thrill that raced through her. "You are sure of this?"

He grabbed her around the waist and swung her up and back down to plant a solid kiss on her lips. "Aye, lass, I am sure. I have never known that such a tiny woman could possess such a mountain of strength. I want you as my wife and I will have you as my wife."

"Only if I agree," she said with a poke to his hard chest.

"You will agree." He sounded arrogant.

She gave him another poke. "And what makes you think this?"

He rubbed his nose to hers. "You love me, lass, and you know it."

Anne sighed and threw her arms around his neck. "Aye, Blair, I cannot deny it. I love you. Fool that I am."

"Fool you say?"

"Aye, I am a fool for loving a handsome man with a charming tongue."

He hugged her to him and settled his mouth on hers for another kiss. "My tongue will charm only you, lass."

"Promise?"

"Aye, that I promise."

They kissed, sealing their love.

"I forbid it!"

Blair and Anne snapped apart, startled by the angry voice. It took them a moment to realize that the command was not meant for them. They remained quiet and listened to the voices of the two people who stood directly outside the room by the door that looked to be closed but stood slightly ajar.

"I will not repeat myself, Brianna," Arran said with mounting anger.

Brianna spoke with a hesitant fear. "Moira wishes me to remain here for the birth."

"I care naught for Moira's wishes. You are my wife and will obey me."

"I would like to stay," Brianna said with a bit of courage.

Arran grabbed his wife's thin wrist. "Nay, you will not."

"You are hurting me," Brianna said, near to tears from the tight grip he had on her.

"Then obey me so you need not suffer."

Blair was at the door, swinging it open, before Anne realized that he moved.

"Everything all right, Brianna?" he asked, sending Arran a heated look that challenged.

Arran immediately released his wife's wrist.

"Everything is fine, Blair, truly it is."

The unshed tears in her eyes told him otherwise, but womanly tears were something he had always had trouble handling.

Anne stepped in, for which he was grateful. "I could use some help, Brianna. Blair is needed elsewhere. Would you help me?"

Brianna sounded relieved. "Aye, I will help you."

Arran looked about to object but Blair's angry eyes warned him to hold his tongue.

"I will see you at the evening meal," Arran said and stormed off.

Blair looked to Brianna and she forced a smile. "He is upset. I should have waited to speak with him."

Blair simply nodded, knowing it was best to say nothing to her. It was her brother he would speak to. And besides, he was certain Anne would have something to say to her. He was leaving her in good hands and that made him feel a little better. "I will see you ladies later."

Anne sent him off with a generous smile and took Brianna by the arm to disappear into the storage room behind a closed door.

Moira rounded the corner at that moment. "Blair, have you seen Anne?"

"She is in her favorite room." He pointed to the closed door. "Brianna is with her."

The sound of his voice told her something was wrong. "I will join them."

"That is a good idea," he urged and rushed over to open the door for her.

Moira thanked him with a smile and a nod and waited as he shut the door behind her. "Anne," she called out.

"In the back by the chairs with red velvet seats."

Moira made her way around the piles of furnishings to

join the two women, who were seated in chairs that looked fit for a king.

"You still have not convinced Ian to move these favorite chairs of yours to the dais?" Moira took the empty seat to the opposite side of Brianna. She could see that the young woman was upset, but would wait on her word.

"He will agree soon, I am sure of it."

"I do not know, Anne," Brianna said. "I remember these chairs being here when I was young. Ian never liked them."

"But they are comfortable," she insisted.

"I agree," Brianna said, "but Ian is used to his hard wooden chair and does not wish to change."

"Sometimes change is necessary," Moira said. "Have some of the men move these chairs to the dais for this evening's meal."

Brianna grew upset. "My brother will grow angry."

"Nay, he will not," Moira said with confidence. "He may comment, but he will not grow angry."

"You should seek his permission first."

Moira laughed. "He would think I was ill if I did that."

Brianna shook her head and fought the tears that threatened to spill. "You are right. My brother only grows angry when necessary and that is seldom."

Moira decided she could no longer hold her tongue. She reached her hand out to Brianna. "What is wrong?"

Brianna was about to speak when the door banged open and an angry shout summoned her, "Brianna, I need to speak with you now."

"I must go." She sounded fearful and for a moment Moira almost stopped her but thought better of it. "We will talk."

"Now, Brianna!"

Brianna sent the two women a hasty smile and hurried to her husband.

"She needs help," Anne said.

"Aye, she does," Moira agreed. "And we will make certain she gets it."

❧ twenty-four

*Moira was busy at the work area she and Anne had fash-*ioned out of a long narrow table. She was planting seeds in a small tray, seeds that she had propagated in hopes of producing a sweeter onion. Last year the batch she had grown were tasty though not exactly what she had expected. This year she was hoping for a sweeter batch.

She had also gathered a sample of the soil from the planting field, intending to test it and see if it was rich enough to nourish the seeds this year or if it required a boost. Her work pleased her for it involved improving life not just for one but for many.

She rubbed at her back, which ached from sitting on the high stool that allowed her easy access to the tabletop. In the last two weeks since Ian's sister arrived she had rounded slightly, though no one took notice and she had not fainted. Her morning illness had subsided though her naptime had increased. She was feeling quite well, especially when she kept herself busy in the stitching room, and Ian certainly did not object to her time spent there.

Her morning time was usually spent on Ian's ledgers and as of late she had been spending a good portion of the time on the ledgers Arran had brought with him. Ian's accounts were running smoothly and everything going accordingly. She had dealt with a few of the merchants who stopped by the keep, especially after negotiating a good price with one on merchandise. Ian could not believe the bargain she struck with the man and told her that buying for the keep was now her domain if she wished. She immediately accepted the chore; it was one she had thoroughly enjoyed while at the convent.

She did not, however, enjoy going over Arran's ledgers. Something did not add up right. Amounts were crossed out, prices changed, numbers not calculated properly. She did not know how the man could run his keep with such horrendous record keeping. She intended to talk privately with Ian about it but not before she made some sense of the incoherent mess.

Life had settled into a pleasant routine at the keep. And while there were moments she missed the solitude of the convent, there were times she was happy that she was here with Ian. They were becoming better acquainted in ways she would never have expected. She had not thought to be intimate with him ever again and yet she discovered that intimacy was an important part of a marriage. And a part she found pleasurable.

Now if there was only love—Moira shook her head.

She wondered about love lately, especially when she watched Brianna and Arran. He was attentive and charming to his wife in front of everyone, yet when they were alone he was demanding and insensitive, and oddly enough Brianna seemed to think nothing of it. He was her husband and she was to follow his dictates. And she insisted that Arran loved her deeply. She often told Moira and Anne that Arran had insisted that she would find no one who would love her as much as he loved her. He had convinced her that their love was pure and whole and perfect. The more she listened to Brianna the more curious Moira became about love.

Anne, however, seemed the opposite of Brianna. Blair had said they would marry and, while Anne was joyous, she was not in a hurry to marry Blair. She enjoyed her independence too much to hurry into a binding wedding agreement. When Blair understood and accepted her ways, then she would marry him.

Blair assured her she could do as she wished after they wed. He liked her spirited nature and had no intention of restraining it. Anne wanted to be certain; a logical choice to Moira but one that seemed foreign to many in the clan, though Brianna encouraged Anne to take her time and do as she wished.

Anne hurried into the room drenched. "It storms."

Moira smiled. "You set the buckets?"

Anne looked pleased with herself. "Aye, that I did and it will be a good rain count we get."

"Rain count?" a voice asked from outside the door before Brianna appeared and stared wide-eyed at the— "Stitching room?"

It had not been easy keeping Brianna from the room. She was a fine one with a needle and thread and was anxious to join them. It took many excuses to keep her away, but now . . .

Moira shrugged. "It is better you know. I am tired of trying to keep our secret from you and, besides, you are trustworthy."

Brianna glanced at Anne as she walked past her into the room. "You best rid yourself of those wet clothes or you will find yourself ill."

"I was about to do just that," Anne said and gave a peek out the door to check for any other surprise visitors before shutting the door and latching it.

"What is all this about?" Brianna looked about the room with interest as she walked over to Moira.

"I study the properties of animals, plants, and metals," Moira said.

"You are an alchemist?" Brianna looked startled.

Moira smiled. "In a way I suppose I am, though *educator* sounds a better choice of words. We live in a time when men are beginning to study things that were once ignored and thought unimportant or they thought was God's domain. God gave us intelligence and I think he meant for us to use it to our benefit."

"Women as well as men?" Brianna asked.

"Especially women," Anne answered, slipping out of her wet garments and rubbing herself dry before reaching for a soft green wool underdress hanging on a metal wall peg.

"Women possess an innate sense of nature and nature holds many of the answers to improving our lives," Moira explained. "Take for instance cycles. Everything follows cycles: the stars, the moon, the seasons, and even women's bodies."

Brianna sat on the stool beside Moira. "And there is a connection?"

"A birth, a growth, a shedding away to begin again, a continuous cycle," Moira explained. "A constant turning, an evolution of things."

"Where did you learn this?" Brianna asked curiously and with a bit of envy.

"That is not important," Moira insisted. "What is important is that I learn."

Brianna was hesitant but forced herself to ask, "Can I learn?" She added with haste, "I will tell no one."

Anne approached them, tying a green braided cloth belt around her small waist. "We will have a school going before you know it."

"Moira teaches you?"

Anne nodded. "And glad I am that she does. It is so interesting to learn the growing cycle of a plant or the workings of an animal. The metal properties are difficult for me to understand but in time and with study I am certain I will learn."

"My brother would find this fascinating," Brianna said, taking in all she could with a slow glance.

"I was not certain how he would feel and therefore I chose to keep my work secret. Some who remain ignorant of the strides made in knowledge continue to call certain things the 'work of the devil.'"

"More fools they," Brianna said while closely examining the seeds Moira had laid out in front of her on a wooden tray.

Moira sensed that her brother would respond in a similar fashion, but until she was certain she would proceed with caution. "I will teach what I can while you are here; I only ask that you tell no one. That means you can say nothing to your husband."

Brianna nodded. "I am a fool where he is concerned."

"Aye, you are," Anne said bluntly.

"I was young and thought myself in love." She spoke with a sadness that could be seen on her lovely face. "He told me of his love for me and how he would always care for me and take care of me. I believed him."

"Why would you not?" Moira asked. "He is handsome and charming and appears caring."

"Appearances can be false, especially to a young girl so blindly in love. I have come to see that his true wish was to join the Cameron clan and his true love was power and money, but by the time I realized his true nature I was well wed to him."

"Have you spoken of this to your brother?" Moira asked. "He would help you."

"There is naught he can do. I am soundly wed and wed I shall remain."

"Perhaps your brother can see to it that you spend more time here with us. I will need help once the babe is born."

"You have Anne, and all in the keep will be eager to help you," Brianna said, wishing otherwise.

"Anne cannot do it all and everyone in the keep has their chores to tend to. I could use extra help." Moira was insistent.

Brianna smiled. "How I wish I could return here to live. It would be wonderful to be with you and Anne, and helping with the babe. At least I would be where I know I was wanted and loved."

Moira felt her sadness for she had experienced it once herself and she had feared she would experience it again when Ian had taken her away from the convent. Not so, though, and as the days passed, Ian and this place were beginning to feel more and more like home to her.

She offered Brianna empathy. "I know how it feels to feel unwanted."

Her words startled Moira. "My brother wants and loves you. Any fool can see that."

Anne smiled and nodded as though in agreement.

Moira was stunned but managed to respond. "You are here but two weeks and you tell me that you think your brother loves me?"

"I know my brother loves you."

Anne added her opinion. "You can see it in his eyes when he looks at her."

"And his touch," Brianna said with a sigh. "He touches her with such tenderness and longing that it tugs at the heart."

"He professes no such love to me," Moira insisted, thinking both women crazy.

"He does not know he loves you yet," Brianna said confidently.

Moira now knew she was definitely crazy.

"Let me clarify," Brianna said. "He does not admit to himself he loves you. Once he does you will hear him speak from his heart."

Moira shook her head.

"You can deny it if you like just as you deny your love for him."

That remark left Moira speechless. "You can speak your own mind; this is good," Anne praised Brianna.

"I once spoke my mind often," Brianna said proudly. "My marriage to Arran robbed that of me."

"Well, you certainly have not lost it entirely," Moira said, finding a strong voice of her own. "Though you have lost your mind."

"I think not," Brianna said most confidently.

"I agree with her," Anne said and set about to heat the cider in the pitcher on the table.

Moira thought she could find herself no more stunned. She was wrong. Anne's words completely shocked her. "Why have you not spoken of this to me?"

"It was yours to discover," she replied as though the answer was simple.

"What makes you both think this?" Moira asked, needing to hear their reasoning, sound or not.

Brianna answered first. "In my short time here I have noticed how you look at my brother. It is a longing I see in your eyes and one you have yet to understand. You seek him out often, you talk closely with him and then"—she giggled—"there is how you both hurry from the hall at night arm in arm. Then there are the times you both disagree; they tell me the most."

"You do not make sense," Moira said, annoyed at hearing the truth. She did look at him with a sense of longing lately and her own emotions had begun to disturb her. There still, however, was the fact that he had deceived her. But that was between Ian and her and she would not bring Brianna into it.

"I make perfect sense. It is just that you both are stubborn and refuse to see the obvious or perhaps you fear it."

"Fear what?" Moira snapped.

"Love," Brianna said, calmly. "When love has disappointed or hurt, you can fear ever experiencing love again for you do not wish to suffer the pain."

"I have never loved before," Moira insisted, though knew in a way that Brianna's words rang true.

"Aye, we all have loved," Brianna said. "Think on it and you will understand my words."

Anne handed each a mug of hot cider.

"You know much for one so young," Moira said, as the three women took their drinks and walked to sit comfortably on the warm fur rug in front of the fire.

"I am two and twenty, not so young."

"I am nine and twenty, not so young," Moira said, waiting for the usual response. She did not get it.

"I would think you my age, but age has little bearing on character."

Moira was fast growing fond of Brianna. "I am glad you are my sister now."

Brianna grinned. "And it is glad I am to have you as a sister." She turned to Anne. "And you, Anne, as a friend."

"I think we will all do well together," Anne said, raising her mug in a toast.

The other two joined in, raising their mugs.

"To secrets, knowledge, and lifelong friendships," Anne said.

They clinked mugs and drank.

"So tell me of love," Moira said, looking to each woman.

Brianna shook her head. "Nay, you tell us."

The three women laughed and began to chatter endlessly.

It was time for the evening meal when the women finished chatting and making plans. Plans that would help solve each of their concerns.

They took themselves off to freshen and change for the evening meal.

Moira had much to consider. With no other threats to her life, and life at the keep seeming tranquil, her mind did not linger much on any danger she may be in, though she and Anne would continue to gather and sort pertinent information.

At the moment her most pressing matter concerned her feelings for her husband. When her feelings had begun to change she could not say. But somewhere along the way she had begun to see a different man from the one who had deceived her. But had she truly ever known that man? The night he arrived at the convent long haunted her memory. She often thought back to his words; he had never once told her of her father's death or her brothers'. He merely suggested and she foolishly allowed the suggestion to take root.

But then if she were honest she would admit that by marrying Ian she had thought she would please her father even after death, and that thought had robbed her of sound judgment. She had wanted to believe that her father needed her and had asked for her help with his last dying breath. In the end he had sought her help, her love to save the clan. A young girl's—she shook her head—nay, an older woman's foolishness.

Brianna was right. She had loved once and that love had hurt. And though a love for a husband was a different kind of love, it was still painful when not returned. And Ian had hurt her with his deceit so how could she trust him not to hurt her again? And why? Why did he leave her at the convent after they wed? That was the one question that she needed an answer to.

Then of course she had to ask herself why she had chosen to be intimate with him when she had promised herself she would not.

In all honesty his touch soothed and comforted her and she had tried to understand why. While she had seen a strong, courageous, warrior side to him, he was always gentle with her though firm in his intentions. He made clear what he wished from her and made certain she realized he would have his way. But he gave her time and in that time he allowed her to come to know him.

He was a good man.

He was a strong man.

He was a man of courage.

He was her husband.

She sighed at the thought, her hand going to her stomach. She stroked the small mound lovingly and thought how lucky she was to be carrying his babe.

He had promised her that they would share a good life together.

Did he mean it?

Did she truly want him to mean it?

Did she want him to love her?

Did she want to love him?

"Moira, hurry, we are hungry and the food smells scrumptious," Brianna called from outside her door.

Moira was grateful for the interruption. She had lingered far too much on her thoughts lately. Action proved more beneficial. She hurried, tossing off her green tunic and replacing it with a dark red wool one that blended well with her dark green underdress. Her long hair was braided, the dark strands remaining neatly in place.

She rushed out the door. Anne and Brianna were already at the top of the steps and catching sight of her they took flight.

"Catch up," Anne teased, "or we will eat your share."

Moira laughed and raced to the top of the stairs, catching their hasty flight down the curving staircase. She was about to take a step when she heard her husband's voice.

"In a hurry, are you?"

She smiled, knowing she would see his face in mere seconds, and took a step so that she could hurry to greet him.

She felt someone push her from behind and she tumbled forward.

❧ *twenty-five*

Ian rounded the curve, eager to see his wife, and watched in horror as she tumbled toward him. She took action before he did, though they both responded with instinctive speed, she to protect the babe and he to protect them both.

Her arms flew out along the narrow stairwell and she pressed them as hard as she could against the rough stone, feeling the scraping of her skin as the force of her actions began to halt the speed of her fall, giving her time to regain her footing and time for her husband to reach her.

She fell with relief into his strong arms, her heart beating wildly and she feeling very close to tears.

"What happened?" Brianna asked anxiously as she and Anne came up behind Ian.

Moira could not speak. Her face was buried in her husband's chest, her arms wrapped tightly around his neck and her body pressed firmly to his.

Ian held her as if he never intended to let her go, his own heart beating like crazy. "She fell."

"I was pushed," Moira said loudly and clearly and without thought.

"What?" Three voices rang out the same question.

Ian held her more tightly. "You felt someone push you?"

"Aye, that I did. I felt a firm hand to my back just as I placed my foot on the first step."

"Did you see anyone, Ian?" Brianna asked.

"Nay, I turned the curve of the stairs and she was already tumbling forward."

"Let us get her to the bedchamber," Brianna suggested.

Moira regained her composure and her courage. "Nay, I am hungry."

Ian laughed and hugged her to him. "Then you are well, wife."

"Aye, and hungry," she repeated.

He released her slowly, running his hand down her arm, and she cried out in pain. He turned her arm gently and saw that the arm of her wool underdress was torn and, beneath it, her skin was scraped and bleeding.

"Anne, she requires tending," Ian said, scooping his wife up in his arms. "Brianna, will you please see to it that a meal is brought up to our bedchamber for us?"

"Aye, I will see right to it and will return to help Anne."

"This is not—"

He cut Moira off. "It is necessary."

She rested her head on his chest, realizing that she did not feel as strong as she had thought and that perhaps for the babe's sake she should rest.

Her sigh told him that she would not argue the point and he was relieved. He was also angry, very angry; that his wife should be unsafe in her own home infuriated him and he intended to do something about it immediately.

Anne hurried to fetch a bowl of water and a cloth while Ian saw to placing his wife on the bed and arranging pillows behind her back so that she could sit up comfortably.

"You will need to get out of these clothes," Ian said and

turned to Anne. "Get her a soft tunic. It is better that she wears nothing that will irritate her arms."

Anne turned her back and kept her eyes averted, giving Moira privacy while Ian helped his wife shed her garments. Anne placed the tunic on the edge of the bed. "There is a salve I have that will help with the healing. I will get it."

Ian was grateful for a few moments alone with his wife. "You do feel well?" He dropped the tunic over her head, noticing that her stomach was rounded more than usual and he smiled. Their babe was growing.

Moira was honest as he tucked the covers around her waist and sat down beside her. "A bit startled and upset."

"That is understandable." He reached for the bowl of water on the nearby chest and set it on the small stool near the bed. He soaked the cloth and rinsed it and then began to gently cleanse her wounds. "Did you see anyone?"

"Nay," she said, shaking her head though looking doubtful of her own words.

"What troubles you?"

She winced when the cloth touched the raw scrapes and he softened his touch. "When I recall the incident, for some reason I think that a moment or two before I was shoved I thought I heard a heavy breath, but I cannot be certain." She shook her head. "I cannot understand why someone would do such a thing. Why would someone wish to hurt me?"

Blair entered the room along with Brianna.

"What happened?" he asked anxiously rushing toward the bed. When he saw her wounded arms his eyes darkened with anger.

"Someone pushed her while she stood at the top of the steps," Ian explained. "I want a guard with her at all times."

"I want no guard," Moira said adamantly. She would never be able to spend time with her studies. She would be a prisoner.

"I need not ask your permission," Ian said firmly. "You will do as I direct."

"I do not want a guard," she repeated, raising her voice.

Ian raised his own. "It matters not what you want. It matters what is best for you."

"I decide what is best for me."

"Nay, wife, I decide what is best for you and it is a guard you will have."

Moira was ready to battle.

Ian was not and pressed a finger to her lips. "Listen to me, Moira."

His voice was firm yet gentle in his request and she remained silent.

"I do not wish anything to happen to you and the babe and the fact that someone attempted to hurt you in your own home does not sit well with me. It is my duty to keep you safe and that is what I will do, no matter what it takes for me to do that. And presently a guard would suit this situation well."

"I will feel a prisoner," she complained.

"You have your freedom. I am not restricting your movement only who you move about with."

"Anne can remain by my side or Brianna," she pleaded. "I do not need a guard all the time, not when they are with me." The thought that she would never have a moment alone troubled her. Her time alone was important to her. It gave her time to think, to reason, to make sound decisions and she would not relinquish it so easily.

"They can offer you no protection," Ian said.

"Their presence offers me protection," Moira insisted.

Anne had returned and stood behind Blair and Brianna, listening. The concern was clear on all their faces.

"I do not know that for certain," Ian argued.

Moira did not relent; she intended to have time to herself. "At least allow me private time in my stitching room."

Ian held his tongue while he gave it thought. He wanted to refuse her immediately, not out of stubbornness but concern. He did, however, understand her need for her own time. He had come to realize how important it was to her and he did not wish to deprive her of it. Nonetheless, he did intend to see her protected.

"I will post a guard outside your stitching room."

Her first thought was to object. She did not want a guard so close to her place of study, but Ian appeared adamant and she decided it was wise to accept his compromise. "Thank you, I appreciate you allowing me my time."

Ian had come to know his wife well and he leaned close to her and gave her nose a playful tap. "Promise me you will give the guards no trouble."

She had to smile for the thought had crossed her mind. He understood her well and she wished to ease his mind. "I promise."

"Good, now I will leave Anne and Brianna to finish tending your wounds while I speak with Blair. I will return and we will share the evening meal here together."

Her smile grew. "I would like that."

"Aye, so would I." He gave her a gentle kiss and left her side.

Ian and Blair walked directly to the spot where Moira had fallen. They stopped and looked about.

"Someone could have easily hid in the shadows, especially if Moira was in a rush and paid her surroundings no heed," Blair said.

Ian nodded and studied the area in silence. The idea that someone had waited in hiding for Moira made him furious. "Who in the keep would have the audacity to do this?"

"I was wondering the same myself."

"Have you heard anything about the Macleans?"

"I heard that they were not on the Isle of Mull," Blair said.

"I have wondered if they could have hired someone to carry out a dirty deed for them."

"We have had merchants stop at the keep and a few

travelers who have rested here, but I cannot say I have seen any strangers in the keep."

"He would not want you to see him," Ian said. "He would hide in the shadows. That is, if it is her father who is responsible for this."

"Who else could it be? I doubt Angus Maclean would want your child to inherit any part of his lands. He is a selfish man."

"All had been quiet," Ian said. "I was beginning to believe that perhaps what I heard was wrong and Moira's life was not in danger. Now I worry and I am angry, for it has been brought into my home."

"The clan will guard her well and you know it."

Ian looked to his friend. "Aye, but what if it is one of the clan?"

"We have not put enough effort into finding the culprit who wishes you dead," Anne said while tending to Moira's arm.

"What?" Brianna asked, startled. "Someone wishes you dead?"

"We think this is so, but we are not certain," Moira said, wincing as Anne applied the salve to her clean wounds.

"We were attacked on our way here and the attackers seemed more interested in Moira than anyone else," Anne explained, trying to make her touch light so as not to hurt her.

"What does my brother do about this?"

"We do not know," Moira said. "He has not spoken of it to me or Anne. We learned of it on our own and have chosen to investigate without anyone's knowledge."

"Only we have not investigated enough," Anne said, wrapping Moira's arms in a gossamer cloth that would help shield and heal the wounds.

"Settling into our new home has taken much of our

time," Moira said, "though it is no excuse. We should have paid closer attention to the possibility of a threat."

"Threat?" Brianna repeated with a firm shake of her head. "Danger is what you are in. And I cannot believe that my brother has failed to tell you of this."

"He thinks he protects me."

"Protects with ignorance," Brianna argued. "You should be told so that you could be more diligent of those around you."

"He does not wish me to worry."

Brianna was about to continue arguing when she suddenly smiled. "You defend my brother."

Anne laughed softly while she cleaned up after herself.

Moira made ready to protest. Defend Ian? First, he needed no defending and she of all people would probably be the last—

She stopped suddenly at the thought. She would not be the last to defend her husband. She would in all likelihood be the first. When had this happened? When had he become important enough to her that she wished to protect him?

Moira spoke up. "Aye, I defend your brother and gladly. He is a good man."

"Aye, that he is," Brianna agreed. "A good man to love."

Love. Moira had given it more and more thought lately, but she was not ready to admit to anyone that she could love Ian Cameron. It was something she had to understand and deal with before she admitted it to anyone. And when she did choose to admit it, it would be to Ian.

When she did?

Was it only a matter of time? Were her feelings so strong that she instinctively knew she loved him but refused to admit it to herself? Or did she feel she should not love him? Did she fear that she would be hurt if she loved him?

She said no more and was glad she held her tongue for

Blair and Ian returned, with a rushed Arran following in behind them.

"I have just heard," Arran said, concerned. "I was out looking over the fields and when I returned the keep was talking of nothing else but Moira's accident. She is well?" He looked to Ian.

Ian nodded. "She is well and will rest in bed for the remainder of the evening."

A servant entered with their supper and Anne saw to helping the young woman with the large platter. Bowls and trenchers were placed on the small table Ian had signaled Blair to move by the bed.

Blair walked over to Anne and slipped his arm around her waist. "Supper waits us, come eat and talk with me." On a whisper he added, "I have missed you."

She smiled and looked to Moira. "Do you need anything else?"

"Nay, I am fine. Go and enjoy yourself."

The two women exchanged knowing grins and then Blair and Anne eagerly left the room.

Brianna walked over to her husband. "Come, Arran, let us have supper."

Arran spoke to his wife like an impatient parent to a child. "You go. I am sure that Ian has things to discuss with me."

"There is naught for us to discuss," Ian told him. "And I wish time alone with my wife."

Though Arran seemed disappointed he slipped his arm around his wife. "Come then, we will join Blair and Anne at the dais."

"Rest well," Brianna said to Moira.

"If you need me," Arran said, and added no more, knowing those words were enough.

Ian nodded his appreciation and after the door closed he turned to his wife.

"Hungry?"

"Aye," she said softly.

Ian moved off the bed, but Moira's hand grabbed his and he looked down at her in question.

"It is not food I want to satisfy me." Nay, she needed more than mere food to nourish her. She needed his touch, his love. "It is you I want."

Ian looked stunned for a moment and then he smiled and sat down on the bed, his hand going to stroke her face. "You truly want me."

She sighed and moved her face against his gentle touch. "Aye, I want you, Ian."

He felt the need to say something to apologize for the past and make promises for the future and yet he could not find sufficient words to express himself. His struggle was obvious on his handsome face.

Moira pressed a gentle finger to his lips. "I do not wish to talk. I only wish to love."

Her words touched his heart and he kissed her finger. "Your arms?"

"They are sore, but I will be careful."

He shook his head slowly. "Nay, you will place your arms above your head and leave them there. I will do the pleasuring."

Moira pouted. "But I enjoy touching you."

He kissed her lips. "Another time you may touch me as much as you wish. Now, sweet wife, I touch you."

❧ *twenty-six*

Ian stood and stripped himself of his garments with Moira watching.

"Have you no shame, wife, staring at me with such hunger?" he teased.

Moira laughed gently. "I like watching you disrobe."

He leaned over her and kissed her soundly. "And I like disrobing *you.*" He reached beneath the bedcovers and pulled her tunic up and over her head, being careful not to hurt her arms. He then discarded several pillows so that she was resting comfortably on one and he made certain that her arms were stretched above her head.

"Keep them there," he told her and sealed his edict with a kiss.

"It will be hard," she said, her body feeling a need for his. "I want so much to touch you."

"Another time, I promise."

She was beginning to realize that his promises were his word and that he would not go back on them. "Another time then," she whispered and welcomed his lips as they settled over hers.

Theirs started as a gentle joining. A tender touch, a sweet kiss, but it was not what Moira wanted. After the accident she felt a strong sense of life and being alive and she needed to experience the fullness of making love.

Ian felt her need, her anxiousness for more, and he felt his own need to reaffirm that she was well, alive, and in his arms.

Their kiss turned demanding and it was near impossible for Moira to keep her arms above her head, but when she made an attempt to move them Ian warned her.

"Do not dare, or I will tie you down."

She knew he would not do that to her, that he but threatened out of concern, so she kept her arms above her head with great difficulty.

His mouth descended on her nipples and feasted like a man long starved. His tongue suckled, his teeth nipped, and she was completely lost to the passionate emotions racing through her body and she surrendered eagerly to his touch.

His hands explored and demanded that she respond and she did. He touched with an urgency she found equaled her own and no matter where his hands stroked or caressed she responded, her body writhing with the want of him.

She moaned her pleasure and every now and then he caught her moan in his mouth and fed it with a kiss.

He kneeled between her legs, lifting them against his hard chest, and entered her easily. She sighed with the feel of him and relished the exquisite sensations that rippled through her heated body as he moved inside her. He took his time and set a steady rhythm that she matched, but it soon was not enough. He increased the tempo and their bodies worked in unison to a melody that intoxicated.

Moira could not think. Her breathing was rapid, her heart raced, and her blood heated to a fire that consumed her. She cried out her need to him, pleaded with him, and demanded that he not stop, that he continue, until she screamed out his name and tightened herself around him.

He burst in a forceful climax as soon as she clamped down around him and his own cries joined hers. He collapsed over her though kept his full weight off her and together they rested until their breathing calmed and the ripples of pleasure faded.

He moved off her to lie beside her.

And it was not long before she announced, "I am hungry."

"For food this time?" he asked with a laugh.

"Aye, and lots of it."

She looked so serious that he had to laugh harder and she poked him in the ribs and this time smiled. "I am your wife and heavy with child and it is your duty to take care of me."

He splayed his hand over the small mound of her stomach. "You call this heavy with child?"

"He grows," she said adamantly, "though he will not if his father refuses to feed his mother."

He leaned down and kissed her stomach. "It is a demanding mother you have."

"It is a good mother he has for she sees that he is properly nourished."

Ian kissed her mouth. "You are a good mother and it is glad I am that you carry my child." He stood and walked to the chest at the foot of the bed and retrieved a black robe.

His words pleased her but so did the sight of him. She loved his long lustrous brown hair that resembled the colors of the rich earth and flaming fire, and his long side braids were fun to tug at on occasion. His handsome features always caught the eye and held it, but it was his body lately that most captured her attention. He carried his solid frame with confidence and every muscle and limb moved in graceful orchestration.

She suddenly felt inadequate, he possessing such perfection and she . . .

She shook her head and reached for her tunic, anxious to cover her nakedness.

He reached her as she fumbled with the garment, taking it from her hands and watching as she grabbed and held the bedcovers over her breasts.

"Why do you hide from me?"

His question startled her though it was asked with a gentle concern. She was ready to lie and the idea that she would be dishonest upset her and brought the truth to her lips. "I suddenly felt uncomfortable being naked in front of you."

"Why?" Again he asked with a gentle concern.

"You possess a perfection seldom seen and—"

He did not allow her to finish. "If you wish to see perfection you only need look at yourself."

She laughed. "Now you tease me."

"Nay, wife, I speak the truth." He traced his finger along her face. "You possess a rare beauty and a remarkable intelligence . . . and your body?" His grin needed no explanation though he gave it. "Your body is the most exquisite I have ever seen or touched."

Was he being honest with her or only attempting to ease her concern? She thought not to ask and then thought, why not? She wanted to know. "You truly mean what you say?"

"You doubt my word?" He sounded hurt.

She remained silent, her eyes on his, waiting.

He kissed her softly. "I speak from my heart and my heart does not lie."

She slipped her arms around his neck. "Then I shall trust your heart." She kissed him as if sealing her word.

Her words touched him and gave him hope. If she could trust his heart there was hope for them.

"Now for food," he announced joyously and rubbed his hands together.

They ate, laughed, made love again, and then, wrapped

in each other's arms, fell asleep, their thoughts similar.
They were both happy to be exactly where they were—together.

Ian and Blair rode the land and watched the clan eagerly
tend the planted fields. The weather was warm with barely
a chill in the air. It was well into spring and summer would
soon be on them. Everything blossomed, including his
wife though she continued to gain little weight, a fact that
disturbed him.

"It has been three weeks since the accident and nothing
more has happened," Blair said as they slowed their pace.
"Do you think we have frightened the culprit into hiding?"

"I have wondered," Ian said with concern. "I thought by
now he might attempt another try. It is frustrating for I can
make no sense of it. The only one who would benefit from
Moira's demise would be her father. He would lose part of
his precious land. I know he can be ruthless, but ruthless
enough to kill his daughter?"

"A question that has yet to be answered and until it is
you do wish for the guards to continue around your wife,
do you not?"

"Aye, I want her protected at all times."

"It is not difficult," Blair said. "She spends much time
in her stitching room."

"As do Anne and Brianna. It is good she enjoys stitching and that she is not alone. How goes it with you and
Anne?"

He grinned then laughed. "That woman has the strength
of twenty. She persists in making me wait and I grow
steadily impatient."

"Marry her."

"I wish to but she keeps telling me that she wants to be
certain that I accept her as she is, which I do, but then I
wonder if there is something she does not tell me."

"What is it that she does not tell you?"

Blair rubbed his chin. "I do not know, but I sense she harbors a secret."

"One that you worry about?"

"Nay, I do not feel it is some deep, dark secret, but perhaps one she feels that I may not be able to accept."

"Ask as many questions as she does and you may find the answer," Ian said with a smile.

"She fires my mind and body and she keeps me wondering for I never know what she is up to."

"Then let us go find out for I have a desire to see my wife."

The two men rode off at a hastened pace.

A cauldron bubbled over the hearth flames, a variety of healthy seedlings grew directly in the warm sun that shined brightly through the narrow window, and soil and rocks of all sizes were spread across the top of the narrow table.

Moira was in the midst of her studies and enjoying every moment of it. She had finished the ledgers early in the day and had questions to ask of Ian concerning Arran's ledgers but that could wait. She was excited over the results of a new soil mixture she had used on her seedlings. They were hardy and healthy as were the ones growing outdoors in the field.

She rubbed at her back, which always managed to ache her, but which she had managed to ignore. Her fainting spells had stopped and morning illness was a thing of the distant past. The babe had made himself known and was active, moving around inside frequently, to her and Ian's delight.

The first time he had felt the babe his hand had been resting on her stomach. She was about to nap and as was Ian's way he would join her to talk and sometimes to make love. The babe had decided to give her a hefty kick and Ian felt it. He was thrilled, though afterward he would barely leave her alone. His hand was forever going to rest on her stomach.

She smiled recalling the day and thought about what he had once said to her, that they would have a good life together, she, him, and the babe. She was beginning to believe him.

She heard the door creak open. "Anne, more seedlings are ready for planting."

When no answer came she turned and there in the doorway stood her husband.

She knew not what to do so she simply smiled.

Ian shut the door and stared in wonder. He glanced slowly around the entire room and shook his head in disbelief. "What is all this?"

Moira slid off the high stool and her smile grew and it was with pride she said, "My room of knowledge."

He took his time, seeing so much that he did not understand but so much that interested him. He finally stopped in front of her. "Explain."

"Where do I start?" She rubbed at her back.

He gently pushed her hand aside and rubbed her back. "At the beginning."

"That would be the convent."

"Tell me," he said anxiously.

She had known this time would come when he would discover her secret. She had wondered over what she would do. How much would she tell him, or how much would she trust him enough to tell him? She had gained more time than she had thought. He had been good about allowing her private time, which was why he had never bothered her when she was in her stitching room—until now.

She could choose not to tell him all, but she realized that her secret was safe with him, that she could trust him, so she chose to tell him everything.

"A monk arrived at the convent one day. He was very ill, his sight was failing, and he had not many years left to his life. He feared dying alone but worse than that he had told Mother Superior that he feared all his acquired knowledge would die with him and he felt that would be a horrendous sin. He asked for shelter at the convent and in return he would teach one of the nuns his knowledge. He promised that what she learned would help the convent grow and prosper. It was due to my quick mind and never-ending curiosity that Mother Superior chose me as the monk's apprentice."

"Come, let us sit," Ian suggested. "This sounds like a long story."

They sat in opposite chairs near the window, the warm sunlight falling across Moira's feet.

Moira continued her story.

"We began with mathematics, simple equations that soon turned to more intricate ones until he was showing me equations that began to resemble a language, which it is in a way. Mathematics help me in all that I do."

She pointed to the soil mixture. "With mathematics I can determine measurements of various material that I add to that mixture. I keep records and record results and work until I have an improved product. The same with the clay mixture; I was able to produce a stronger pottery though of a finer texture that makes it more appealing."

"This is amazing. Tell me more."

Moira was relieved at his interest and inquiry. She went on to speak of the monk and of all the things he had taught her and how he told her she must continue her studies, always learning, always gaining more knowledge.

"You will teach me," Ian said as if it were already decided.

"You wish to learn?" Moira sounded surprised.

He stood and turned in a full circle then extended his hands. "Why not? Look at all this. There is so much to learn."

"Aye, much," she agreed excitedly. Her husband actually had an interest in learning and in her work. "I will teach you all you wish to know."

"Everything." He laughed and threw his hands up in the air. "Teach me all you know and then we can learn more." He hurried back to his seat beside her. "My father sent me to study at St. Andrews and I enjoyed it but it was not enough. I wanted to learn more but it was necessary for me to return home."

"Now you may continue your studies." She smiled.

He went down on bended knees in front of her. "Why did you not tell me?"

"I was not certain how you would react, and Philip, the monk who taught me, warned me that my acquired knowledge could place me in danger."

"Danger?"

She took a deep breath. "Philip studied with men who worked strictly for King James IV but they worked as alchemists. They were attempting to turn metal—"

"—into gold," Ian finished.

"Philip told me that the men looked to make riches, when riches could be found in knowledge, and that knowledge must be shared for the benefit of all mankind."

The door flew open and Blair, with Anne struggling to keep him from entering, burst into the room. Blair looked around the room, shaking his head.

Anne looked to Moira, shaking her head, then stopped when she saw Ian.

"I will ask about all this later," Blair said. "Right now you need to know that Angus Maclean and his sons have just entered the village."

❧ twenty-seven

Moira sat beside her husband at the dais, her hand in his as her father and brothers made a boisterous entrance into the great hall. She was grateful for the supportive squeeze her husband gave her hand.

Angus Maclean was a large, angry-looking man with wrinkles and scars as evidence of his misery and many battles. His two sons, Boyd and Aidan, stood equal to his height and both were thick of muscle. Angus's long hair flamed red as did Boyd's, but Aidan's hair was a deep red and he had always, since young, entwined leather strips in his side braids. And while both brothers possessed fine features, it was Aidan whose looks caught every woman's eye.

The three impressive men stopped in front of the dais.

"I heard you took my daughter from the convent," Angus said, his voice deep, harsh, and accusing.

"I took *my wife* from the convent to bring her home," Ian corrected.

Angus laughed. "Did you miss her?"

"That I did," Ian said with a sharp firmness that had Angus raising a brow.

"You are a fool. What can she do for you?"

Ian was angry. The man had not even acknowledged his daughter's presence. He spoke of her as if she did not matter. Ian released his wife's hand and stood tall and confident. "No man calls me a fool, especially in my own home."

Blair stood up beside him and all the men in the great hall got to their feet.

Angus had no choice but to be sensible though he did not retract his words. "A fool in love then you must be."

Ian smiled and did not hesitate to respond. "That I will admit to."

The tension in the hall broke as laughter echoed the room.

Moira was not laughing. Were her husband's words spoken to prevent an altercation or did he mean what he said? Could he really love her?

"Why did you come here, Angus?" Ian asked as a table was cleared and moved in front of the dais for the guests to sit.

"I heard you took my daughter from the convent and I wanted to make certain she was safe." He grabbed for the tankard of ale a young serving girl poured for him.

Ian returned to his seat and took his wife's hand. It trembled in his and he squeezed it gently. "She is safe, as you can see."

"And will remain so?"

"What do you accuse me of, Angus?" Ian asked calmly.

Angus's words startled everyone. "I heard my daughter was in danger. I wanted to make sure that danger was not you."

Ian's eyes grew bright green though his voice remained calm. "I protect what is mine, Angus, and Moira is mine. I protect her"—he paused and leaned forward in his seat—"and my babe that she carries."

Angus spit out a mouthful of ale. "She is with child?"

His stunned response let Ian see that the man had had no previous knowledge of the news. If so then there would be no reason to think that Angus was a threat to his daughter. If not from him then from whom?

"Is it true?" Angus asked, turning his attention to his daughter.

"Aye, I carry Ian's child," Moira said, her chin high.

His face grew red. "You can do nothing right."

Moira smiled and spoke calmly. "Aye, I can and I did."

"Will you not congratulate us?" Ian asked, his own smile strong and his fingers firmly entwined with his wife's.

There was a moment of silence then . . .

"Congratulations."

Heads turned toward Aidan.

The young man stood and with a broad smile he rushed to his sister's side, his arms flung wide. Moira slipped her hand from her husband's and rushed into her brother's arms.

She had helped take care of Aidan after her mother had died giving him birth. She was young, barely seven years, but he was her brother and she felt compelled to care for the tiny bundle. They had been close and she had been devastated when he had cried in her arms when he had learned she would leave him.

"I am happy for you, Moira, and I have missed you."

Moira looked into his dark eyes and saw that he spoke the truth. "And I have missed you."

He reluctantly let her go and went to Ian, who had stood as soon as his wife had. He held out his hand and Ian gave it a firm shake.

"I am happy for you both," Aidan said.

"Thank you."

Boyd followed his brother's actions, to their father's surprise.

Moira could barely get her arms around her brother's

wide chest. Boyd was only four years younger than she and they had gotten into much mischief together. They hugged and though no words were exchanged she could tell he felt as Aidan did and it pleased her that her brothers cared.

Boyd shook hands with Ian and by then Angus had no choice but to do the same, but it was a reluctant hug he gave his daughter and a sharp handshake he shared with Ian.

"You will stay and visit?" Ian asked of Angus.

"Aye, there are things I wish to discuss with you." Angus sounded annoyed.

"Sit and eat, we shall talk tomorrow," Ian said.

His "aye" sounded more like a grunt but Ian ignored it and the meal went without incident and within the hour laughter and shouts filled the room, most being well into their cups and enjoying themselves.

Ian made no excuse for taking his wife from the hall early. He felt they needed to talk especially with the unexpected arrival of her father.

Moira and he entered their bedchamber hand in hand.

She broke away from him and went to stand by the window. It was spring and the days were warm, the nights cool, and the sky bright with hundreds of stars. "When did you intend to tell me that my life was in danger?"

He followed her and slipped an arm around her waist. "When I was ready."

"Did I not have the right to know?"

"I did not want you to worry." He ran a hand over her rounded tummy. She had grown some though she continued to remain small and he continued to worry. "Especially when I discovered you carried my child."

She looked into his dark eyes and asked, "Is that why you returned for me? To protect me?"

Now was the time for honesty and he spoke the truth. "I returned for you because I wanted to. I wanted you to be my wife."

She looked doubtful and reluctantly asked the one question that had haunted her. "Then why did you leave me that night we wed? Why did you not speak a word to me? Why did you walk away from me?"

He heard the hurt in her voice. "I did not think I had the right."

"I was your wife and you rejected me." Her hurt went deep.

"You did not wish to be my wife. I thought I did what was best for you."

"By wedding me and leaving me behind?" She fought the tears brimming in her eyes.

He had fought hard with himself that day. She was his wife and his to protect and take care of and yet . . . "Your father told me that you were content at the convent and I had upset your life enough. I did not think it was fair to take you from all that you knew."

She looked incredulous. "Was not that my choice? You had given me none—would it not have been fair to at least allow me to decide my fate?"

"You were angry." He thought his words explained all.

She did not. "Aye, I was angry, but what of it?"

"When angry one cannot make a wise decision."

"So you made the decision for me."

"Would your anger have allowed you to make a wise choice?" he asked softly.

Her anger cooled as she gave his words thought. Her anger went beyond reason that night. She was furious with everyone. She had even snapped repeatedly at Anne when she had come to offer comfort. Would her choice have been wise?

If she were completely honest with herself she would have to answer nay. She would not have made a wise choice. Her decision would have been based on her anger and it would not have served her well. Had he done her a favor by giving her time and had he intended then to return for her at a later date?

"That night you left had you planned on returning for me at a later date?"

He would not lie to her. "I was not certain of my own intentions."

She waited, not judging him; she wanted to hear all he had to say.

"You were on my mind much that day I left the convent and continued to haunt my thoughts every day for the weeks to follow. I was not certain what caused this for I did not truly know you and yet . . ." He shrugged. "In some odd way I felt I knew you well. You lingered in the privacy of my mind and no matter what I did I could not get you to leave nor did I want you to."

"And that is why you returned for me, or was it because you suspected my life to be in danger?"

"I had already made plans to return for you when I learned of a possible threat to your life. I had no substantial facts to prove such was the case, only rumor, but rumor or not I could not take the chance. Besides, I was already prepared to return for you."

She wanted to clearly understand his reason for returning. She wanted to hear him admit that he purposely returned for her, to bring her to his home and make her his wife. "Then you returned why?"

He was no fool. He knew what she needed to hear and he knew what he needed to say. Had to say for it was necessary. "I returned for you. I wanted you to be my wife in every way. I wanted us to have a life together."

Again she asked, "Why?"

He answered without hesitating. "Because you were forever in my mind and I needed to know."

She rested a hand on his chest and felt the rapid thumping of his heart. "Know what?"

"Know why I could not stop thinking of you," he said softly.

"And do you now know?" Her words were spoken quietly, almost at a whisper, almost as if she feared asking or feared more the answer.

"Aye, I do." He leaned down and kissed her gently.

"Tell me," she said between kisses.

He kissed her one more time and whispered, "I love you."

Her breath caught and her heart felt as if it skipped a beat.

He continued, "That night when you stood before me with such courage and strength remained imprinted on my mind. You did what was necessary, as did I, to save many without thought to yourself. You were unselfish and I have met few women who possess such a quality. And though I felt your fear and uncertainty when you willingly submitted to me, I also felt your bravery. You left an indelible mark on me and I knew that you were a woman I wished to have remain by my side."

"And this love for me? When did this come about?"

He smiled. "I cannot say for sure, perhaps it was there from the very first time we met or perhaps it developed along the way. I do not know its origin nor do I care. I only know that I do love you and will continue to love you for all the days to come."

Love.

She could not believe he spoke of love to her. She wished him to, had hoped though doubted it of him—or had she doubted that she would ever find love? She smiled for it did not matter. He loved her and that was what mattered. And what mattered even more was that she loved him.

"I thought you deceitful," she said with honesty and a generous smile.

"I was," he admitted freely.

"But it was a necessary deceit. I understand that now."

"Truly you do?"

She nodded. "I have come to know the man you are and how much you care. You would not have made such a difficult decision without giving it much consideration. A chieftain must make difficult choices for the good of his clan and surrender his own needs for the needs of others. You gave of yourself for your clan as I felt I gave of myself for my clan. You did what you felt was right as did I. We both surrendered ourselves for others and in so doing received the greatest gift of all—love."

He stared at her though a smile grew on his handsome face. "What are you telling me, wife?"

"I am telling you, husband, that you sneaked into my heart when I was not looking and stole it from me. My heart belongs to you, as does my love. I love you, Ian Cameron."

For a moment he looked stunned though his smile remained firm. "I thought it would take years for you to come to that realization."

She laughed. "Oh, you knew of my love for you before I did?"

"Aye, I did," he insisted. "It was obvious."

"Was it, now? And how so?"

His hand stroked her stomach. "You carry my child with pride and you cannot do that if you do not love the man who seeded your womb. I know that from the first time you discovered that you carried my child you were happy and never once hated the babe or me for the circumstances of his conception. Your love began then and grew, for you truly are a unique woman and it is proud that I am to call you wife."

Her tears fell and she threw her arms around his neck. "I love you and you are right. The day I realized that I carried your child I loved him and never once felt hatred toward you. I was happy that you left me with such a generous gift especially when that night had held such bitter memories."

He eased her gently away from him, holding her arms firmly. "I want to change that night. I want to show you what would have transpired if we had had time. I want to make love to you as if for the first time and that is the memory I want you to forever hold in your heart and mind."

Her tears continued to fall, running down her cheeks and spilling onto her tunic. "I would like that."

He scooped her up in his arms and carried her to the bed. "You will forever remember tonight, this I promise you."

She smiled. "As will you."

He laughed softly. "You are a virgin and know nothing of making love."

"I am a woman and I learn fast."

His laughter grew. "I would not expect such a debate our first night together."

"Then you underestimate your new wife, husband," she said with a playful tap to his nose.

"I will remember this."

"See that you do." Her command was haughty.

He placed her on her feet, his hands going to her waist to untie her belt. "And you, sweet wife, underestimate your new husband."

"How so?" She was already sensitive to his touch and found her voice quivering.

"You think I have taught you all there is to making love."

She shivered at the mere thought. "There is more?"

"Much more," he whispered.

"You will show me," she said almost too eagerly.

His hands reached down to yank off her tunic and then made ready to rid her of her underdress. "Aye, wife, I will show you."

He had her naked in seconds, and himself, then he scooped her up and together he lowered them to the bed.

❧ twenty-eight

Ian rained kisses over his wife's face until he settled on her lips though not before telling her, "You are so beautiful."

"I like when you tell me that for now I believe you."

"Believe me, wife," he said sternly, "for it is the truth I speak. You are beautiful."

"And you are handsome."

"This I know."

She laughed gently and poked him in the ribs. "And I will be the only one you hear that from."

"Aye, wife, for I want to hear it only from you."

His words tugged at her heart and she settled a kiss on him that sparked their already heated passion.

And what was to be a soft and slow mating turned quickly to a heated coupling.

They both demanded from each other. Their hands touching, their lips seeking intimate places where pleasure was brought to new heights and cries of delight filled the air.

He suckled at her breasts until she was certain he would

draw milk from her and she did not care, for the pleasure he brought her was undeniably exquisite and torturous and oh-so-delightful that she did not want him to ever stop.

His hands worked their magic, his fingers finding the spots that forced endless cries from her and brought her endless pleasure. And when she grew completely mindless he rained kisses down her body and with his tongue brought her to an explosive climax that had her screaming his name.

He then moved up and over her and with a smile whispered, "Let us start again."

Before she could recover he entered her and moved in a rhythm that intoxicated her once again. She could not think, she could only respond, and she climaxed over and over again until finally they climaxed one last time together.

"You will remember this night always," he whispered, his hands braced at the sides of her head and his muscled arms easily holding him up over her.

She calmed her rapid breathing enough to say, "Aye, I will."

He brushed a kiss across her swollen lips. "Aye, you will, for we are not finished. We have only begun."

The night faded to morning and just before dawn peeked on the horizon the two lovers fell into a contented sleep wrapped in each other's arms.

"More visitors?" Ian said hearing noise at the hall doors. He then looked down at the chair he sat in at the dais, shook his head, and then glanced along the row of matching red velvet-seated chairs that somehow had replaced the wooden ones he favored. He looked to his wife for an explanation.

"Anne," Moira said, looking up from a column of numbers she was calculating. "We need to talk about these ledgers, Ian." She sounded concerned.

"Something is wrong?"

"Something does not add up," she said with a shake of her head.

Commotion at the great hall doors interrupted any further discussion on the subject, though Ian made a mental note to talk with her later, not only about the ledgers but about the chairs.

"Soon there will be no room in this keep. Your father and brothers have been here a week and show no signs of leaving, and while I enjoy having my sister here, her husband annoys me."

"I do not think Arran cares for my family."

"Nay, he does not and the tension is felt." It concerned Ian that there were so many people at the keep who did not actually belong there. He had placed more guards around his wife, without her knowledge of course. He made certain they kept their distance but kept close enough to protect her if necessary. He intended to take no chances with his wife's life. And since he did not know who posed the threat to her he decided that they all would be watched.

"Let us see who now visits," he said and reached for his wife's hand as the great hall doors swung open.

"Bishop Roderick," Moira said beneath her breath though Ian caught her words.

"You are familiar with the bishop?" Ian asked.

"He visited the convent from time to time. He wished to see how we managed to survive without coins from the church. We did so well that Mother Superior declined the small stipend that the church granted most abbeys. She felt it was best spent on the needy."

"Does he know of the monk and your acquired knowledge?"

"Nay, not that I am aware of. Mother Superior felt that it was best kept to ourselves."

He nodded but made note to discover for himself just how much the bishop knew.

Bishop Roderick was a tall, slim man with a long face

that rarely wore a smile. He was solemn in nature and often listened more than he spoke. Moira had had a few interesting though limited conversations with him and she realized he was a man of great knowledge. She had often wished she could speak in depth with him, but that was not possible.

He approached the dais slowly and out of respect for the man's station Ian stood along with his wife.

"Welcome to our home, Bishop Roderick," Ian said with a warm smile.

The bishop nodded. "Thank you for your gracious welcome. It would not be an imposition if I requested shelter for a few days?"

A few days?

Ian wondered how many were a few, but did not bother to ask. He certainly could not refuse a high-ranking member of the clergy. "By all means, Bishop Roderick, you are welcome to stay as long as you would like."

"I do not intend to impose indefinitely. A week at the most."

A week was not bad; Ian could live with that.

"Moira," the bishop said with a warm smile that surprised her. "It is good to see you again. I had heard you married and left the convent. And please sit, I can see that you are with child, a most pleasing sight."

Ian sat along with his wife. "Can I offer you refreshments, Bishop?"

He sighed softly. "A place to rest my weary body would be appreciated. It has been a tiring journey."

Ian signaled a servant girl.

"I look forward to sharing the evening meal with you both." And with a polite nod of his head the bishop followed the servant girl from the hall.

"I wonder what brings him here?" Moira asked.

"I wondered the same myself."

"Now tell me of these ledgers," Ian said, dismissing the

bishop's visit until later and curious as to what his wife had found.

"Moira!" her brother Aidan shouted across the hall. "Come take a walk with me in the sunshine."

Moira looked to her husband and he could see in her eyes that she wished to go. It had been ages since she spent time with her brother and since his arrival they had had little time alone. Aidan obviously was making an attempt to reacquaint himself with his sister.

"Go and enjoy yourself. We will talk later."

Moira jumped out of her chair and gave her husband a sound kiss and a fast thank-you before hurrying to her brother's side.

Aidan grabbed her hand and together they fled the hall like two children bent on an adventure.

Ian almost called after her to be careful, but he knew his men would watch out for her so he held his tongue.

Arran entered the hall in a rush. "The border clan skirmishes near the keep."

Ian did not grow excited. The border clans often made their presence known and then negotiated terms. He had never felt they wished to war, only to show their strength at times and make harmless demands.

"See to their demands," Ian ordered without concern.

Arran grew agitated. "We always relent. It is time to take a stand and show them we will take no more from them."

"You wish to war too easily," Ian said with patience.

"And you do not war enough," Arran snapped back. "You relent too much to these clans."

"It has been this way for many years and I will not war with a peaceful clan."

"Peaceful?" Arran raised his voice. "They make demands."

"Harmless demands," Ian said firmly and stood bracing his hands on the table.

Arran shook his head. "You gave me that keep to protect and you prevent me from protecting it."

"Arran," Brianna called out, running into the hall. "It is a beautiful day—walk with me."

Arran turned on her in a rage. "Can you not see that I am in an important discussion with your brother, you foolish woman?"

Brianna came to an abrupt halt, a look of fear crossing her face.

Ian vaulted over the dais and came to stand face to face with Arran. "Do not raise your voice to my sister."

Arran looked ready to explode. His face was a bright red and his lips were tightly pursed. He seemed to be attempting to control himself and Ian gave him the time though remained in an imposing stance before him.

Through gritted teeth and with a controlled timbre Arran said, "She is *my wife.*"

"Aye," Ian said, emphasizing the word so hard that the veins in his neck bulged. "But she is *my sister* and you are in *my home* and I am the laird of this clan, making *my word* final."

Arran immediately relented. "Forgive me. I was worried about the keep and the growing problem with the border clans."

"There is no growing problem," Ian said sternly. "It can be settled as it has always been settled, with little conflict and much negotiating. See to it."

"Aye, I will see to it," Arran assured him and turned to his wife. "I am sorry, Brianna. I should not have raised my voice to you."

Ian noticed that Arran's apology made his sister look more fearful than relieved.

"Come," Arran said and held his hand out to her. "We will take that walk."

Brianna reluctantly took his hand and with a forced smile to her brother the couple walked out of the hall.

Ian was shaking his head when Blair entered the hall shaking his own head.

"What is wrong?" Blair asked.

"I should ask the same of you," Ian answered.

Blair poured himself ale from the tankard on the table then filled one for Ian. "Anne is a stubborn lass. I kiss her, touch her, and—" He shook his head again.

"Wed her and be done with it." He sounded as if he ordered it.

"Tell her that. I have asked her to wed me until I am tired of hearing myself ask."

"What is it she wishes from you?"

Blair shrugged. "I do not know though I have told her she spends too much time in that stitching room or whatever it is. It is strange in there and I worry what she learns."

"That is your problem," Ian said. "You always did fear learning."

"I was not good at it."

"You would not even try," Ian insisted with a laugh. "Tell Anne you wish for her to share her interests and then listen to her. You may be surprised at what you learn."

Blair frowned.

"Do you love Anne?" Ian asked.

"Aye, that I do and I want to wed her," Blair said adamantly.

"Then put your fears aside and do what I tell you."

Blair grinned. "Is that an order from my laird?"

"Does it need to be?"

Blair downed the last of his ale and once again shook his head. "Nay, I need no order from you to help me wed. The friendly and wise advice is enough."

Ian laughed. "See you learn quickly."

"Have I a choice?" It was Blair's turn to laugh.

"Not if you wish to wed Anne."

"Then I go find her and begin my lessons." He slammed the tankard on the table. "But it will be lessons she will be learning soon enough when we wed and I take her to bed, for it is there I know with certainty that I am more learned than she."

Ian laughed harder. "Be careful what you boast of."

"I boast with confidence," Blair said loudly as he walked out of the hall. "Much confidence."

Ian shook his head and walked around the dais to sit and relax in the quiet. Life had been good this last week, ever since Moira and he had admitted their love for each other, and he intended to see that it remained that way.

Having a keep full of visitors did not help but then there was much that needed to be settled. He had not yet spoken with Angus Maclean and he was most eager to do so. He also wished to speak with his sister for he felt something troubled her. And now there was Bishop Roderick to contend with and above all there was his wife's safety to consider.

While no other attempt had been made on her life he remained fearful that the danger had not passed and that the culprit but waited for a convenient time to strike again. He intended to make certain when that happened the fellow would be caught and he would have his answers.

Moira seemed to be doing well, no more fainting spells, and she saw to taking her daily naps, which he enjoyed along with her though he rarely napped. After making love to her he would hold her until she fell asleep and then leave her to rest.

He leaned back in his chair and smiled. He was content, life was good—except for this chair, which he intended to see removed and his old one returned.

"Aye," he said with a satisfied sigh, "life is good."

A woman raced into the hall shouting, "Hurry, Moira has taken a fall!"

❧ twenty-nine

Ian ran out of the keep following the frantic woman. His thoughts were on his wife and her safety. Had someone tried to harm her? But then her brother was with her and would protect her, but what if her brother wished her harm? His thoughts raced as fast in his head as his feet raced to the spot in the meadow where a group of people stood circled.

His heart beat wildly and his most anxious thought was that he did not wish to live without Moira. She had become a necessity in his life. He loved having her wake in his arms. He was eager to have conversations with her for they were always stimulating. He loved learning from her, her patience being remarkable and her ability to communicate her knowledge exceptional. And then there were the times they made love.

He had loved his first wife, Kathleen, very much, but he loved Moira with a depth he never knew existed but was awfully glad he found. He loved her with his heart and soul and wanted her part of his life, needed her part of his life; she was his life.

Ian pushed his way through the crowd though when they saw it was he they moved out of his way.

Aidan held his felled sister in his arms; his alarmed look frightened Ian and he dropped to his knees beside them.

"How did she fall?" Ian demanded as he reached to take his wife in his arms.

Aidan relinquished his sister reluctantly and shook his head. "One minute we were dancing in circles, our hands raised in the sky as we did when we were young, and then she simply collapsed."

"She fainted," Ian said, sounding relieved, and glanced down at his wife. She looked so lifeless that it frightened him.

Aidan sounded worried. "I do not think she fainted. She collapsed so suddenly, as if struck."

Ian grew alarmed and cradled his wife in his one arm as his other hand felt the back of her head and when his fingers felt a warm wet spot, his heart skipped a beat. He brought his hand out from beneath her head to see his fingers covered with blood.

Anne and Blair raced into the circle at that moment and Anne stared in horror at Ian's bloody hand.

She dropped to her knees beside him. "Lift her gently so that I may see the wound," she ordered him as if in charge.

Ian obeyed without thought. He lifted Moira gently to rest upon his chest.

Anne carefully pushed Moira's dark hair aside. Her straight, waist-length hair was usually braided but not today. Today she had simply tied it back with a white ribbon that had come loose in the fall.

Anne probed her scalp slowly and with a tender touch. When she finally located the wound she gave it a thorough look and sighed as if relieved. "It is a minor abrasion."

At that moment Moira began to wake, stirring in her husband's arms.

Blair dispersed the crowd, informing them that Moira was well. He then looked to Ian. "I will question the men."

Ian nodded, his bright green eyes the only sign of his anger. "I want answers."

"Aye," Blair said and walked off.

Ian turned to Aidan. "We will talk. Remember what you can of the time you spent with your sister."

"Ian?" Moira whispered.

"Aye, I am here and you are safe," he said, soothing her with his confident response.

"We must get her to the bedchamber so that I may tend the wound," Anne said, standing.

Ian nodded and without difficulty rose with his wife in his arms.

She moaned. "My head hurts."

"You have suffered a wound. Anne will tend to you as soon as I get you to our bedchamber."

Moira kept her head rested on her husband's chest and Ian took careful and slow steps to the keep.

"You feel well? The babe is all right?" He could not help but ask he was so worried about her.

"The babe kicks and fusses as is his way," she said on a sigh as if it tired her to speak. "My head pounds."

Her effort to reassure him worried him even more. "Rest, do not speak."

She as usual paid him no heed. "What happened?"

He was relieved that she was her willful self and answered, "I should be asking that of you."

She wrinkled her brow in thought and he grew alarmed.

"Do not trouble yourself. We will speak of this later."

"Nay," she insisted. "I want to remember." She became alarmed. "Aidan—he is well?"

Ian entered the keep and took slow steps up the winding staircase. "Aye, Aidan is fine. He told me that you both were playing as you did when you were children."

He was pleased to see her smile.

"We spun in circles with our arms extended to the heavens. We would pretend that we evoked the power of the old gods." She took a deep breath and moaned from the discomfort.

"I will have you in our bedchamber shortly."

"I am comfortable in your arms," she assured him and softly added, "I feel safe with you."

"You are safe with me and from this moment on you will not leave my side."

Even in her pain she understood that he was adamant in his declaration and she did not bother to argue with him. There was time for that later.

"I am glad you do not argue with me." He entered the bedchamber.

"It is pointless."

He smiled. "You know me well."

"Very well, husband," she said. "But then I think you know me just as well."

He stopped next to the bed and glared at her. "Aye, wife, that I do and you will be staying by my side. I will see to it."

She smiled though winced from the pain.

"No more talking. Anne and I will tend you."

She seemed surprised. "Anne can see to me."

He shook his head. "I will help her. I want to make certain you are all right."

"I am fine."

"You are stubborn."

"Aye, I am my usual self, which makes me fine."

"I will determine that," he insisted, keeping her in his arms.

"I know if I am fine or not. I do not need someone else telling me so."

"I will tell you," he said adamantly.

"I decide for myself." Moira was just as adamant.

"*I* will decide," Anne said in a shout, startling them

both. "Now place her on the bed so I may examine the wound more thoroughly and then cleanse it."

Ian did as instructed, though his smug grin warned Moira he would have his way.

*Arran paced nervously in front of the dais, his wife stand-*ing silently to the side.

"I tell you that her father and brothers are up to something. They mean her harm and your brother is a fool for not listening to me."

Brianna looked worried and sounded so. "I wish to go see if I may be of help to Moira."

"Nay," Arran snapped. "I have already forbid you to do so. You have spent far too much time with Moira and Anne and have neglected your duties to me."

His words had their desired effect. Brianna felt chastened and guilty, as he often made her feel. Only this time there was cause for it, for she actually had neglected her husband of late. She had made certain to keep herself from his presence. She had spent a good deal of time with Moira in the stitching room learning all she could and she had discovered she liked her growing knowledge.

She had begun to look at life differently and even considered possibilities she had never explored before.

Arran interrupted her thoughts. "We will not be remaining here. There is trouble with the border clans and I must see to it."

"The skirmishes have already been settled peaceably." She did not wish to leave and the idea of it upset her.

"You are as foolish as your brother." His face turned red with rage.

Brianna slowly took a step back away from him. She hoped it was the first step in many away from him. "My brother leads wisely."

"You know nothing," he said with a dismissive wave.

"You are good for nothing. You are worthless in bed for you cannot even bear me a child."

His insult hurt, but then his cruelty had become commonplace soon after their marriage. And the bedchamber had become a place Brianna soon grew to dread. Her husband was far from a gentle lover. He made demands and expected those demands to be met with no regard to her feelings.

Love was not what she thought it to be and she wondered if it even existed at all. Though seeing Moira and Ian together gave her hope. Against all the odds they had fallen in love and that love could clearly be seen in their eyes and the way they treated each other.

Arran grabbed hold of her arm. "You do not pay attention to me."

"You are hurting me," she said and knew better than to fight him. Her resistance only brought her more pain.

"Then pay heed and do as a good wife should."

Loud, boisterous voices near to entering the hall caused Arran to release his wife. "The Macleans, they will prove trouble."

Brianna had paid little attention to the Macleans. Angus kept much to himself while the brothers made their presence known within the clan, talking and making friends with many. The sons, Brianna had realized, were far different from their father.

Angus entered the hall with an angry voice that demanded, "Where is Ian?"

Arran immediately became defensive. "What do you wish of him?"

Angus used his bulk to intimidate, walking up to Arran with his chest extended. "It concerns you not. It is the laird I wish to speak with."

Arran stood firm knowing he had the protection of his clan. "Ian is seeing to his wife. It is me you will speak to."

Angus snickered. "You have little say in this clan and I will not waste a breath on you."

Arran's face glowed red. "How dare you insult me! Take your sons and leave. You are no longer welcome here."

Brianna grew alarmed and placed a hand to her husband's arm. "Arran—"

Before she could utter another word Arran gave her a shove. "Quiet, woman."

She stumbled and righted herself just as Blair entered the hall.

"What goes on here?" he demanded and went to Brianna's side.

"This fool thinks he can insult me," Arran said, sounding more confident with Blair present.

Blair looked to Angus whose face raged red and whose hand went to rest on the hilt of his sword.

"This fool will have you soon tasting his blade."

"Enough!" Blair shouted and slipped his arm around a trembling Brianna.

Aidan stepped up behind his father and whispered near his ear. His father dropped his hand off his sword.

"Brianna," Blair said, "Anne could use your help."

She nodded and without looking to her husband for his approval she ran from the room.

He then addressed the angry men. "Both of you will hold your tongues until Ian is able to join us."

Angus protested. "I do not care about this fool. I want to know about my daughter."

"Since when did you care about her?" Arran asked caustically.

Angus grew angrier. "She is a Maclean and we protect what is ours."

"Unless of course she poses a threat to your lands," Arran said with a smirk.

Blair stepped in front of Angus when he moved toward Arran.

"Spit out what you mean," Angus demanded.

Arran obliged him. "All know that Moira's life has been

threatened and all know that a life is threatened when death benefits someone. You benefit from her and the child's death for then you do not forfeit Maclean land."

Angus turned furious and not only Aidan, but Boyd stepped up to his father's side to demonstrate his support.

"How dare you suggest that I would do my own daughter harm," Angus shouted, his fist raised and ready for battle.

Arran agitated him even more. "You care naught for your daughter. You have barely spoken two words to her since your arrival."

"She is *my daughter.* I protect her."

"Her own brother could not even protect her today," Arran remarked snidely.

"He was a coward who attempted to harm my sister," Aidan said. "If he was a man of courage he would have made himself known. She but played in the field meaning harm to no one."

"But you took her out where someone could cause her harm," Arran said. "Was that protecting her, leaving her vulnerable, when you knew someone threatened her?"

Boyd stepped forward, the width and bulk of him intimidating any man.

Arran wisely took a step back.

"You go too far," Boyd said with an angry firmness. "We care deeply for our sister and would let nothing happen to her."

"But you did let something happen," Arran said, his grin smug. "You let your enemy wed her."

The three Macleans were about to charge forward when a shout halted them.

"Enough!" Ian stepped from the staircase into the great hall. "There will be no bloodshed in my home."

"He insults us," Angus shouted back.

Ian approached them with slow confident steps. That he was a man in charge and a man of courage was obvious and a stillness settled in the air that was not there before.

"I care naught for this bickering," Ian said, coming to stand between the warring men. "I care for my wife's safety."

"Which I was addressing," Arran said with pride.

"You accuse her family," Aidan said with an angry tremble.

Arran showed more courage with Ian present. "With good reason."

"Enough!" Ian shouted once again and looked to Angus. "Do you wish your daughter harm?"

Arran turned livid. "You expect him to speak the truth?"

"You call me a lair?" Angus said, moving forward.

Ian blocked his path with a firm arm and raised a finger to Arran. "Not another word from you."

Arran glared with angry eyes at Ian but clamped his mouth shut.

"Answer me," Ian demanded of Angus. "Do you wish your daughter harm?"

Angus turned solemn. "Nay, I never wished my daughter harm. I made an arrangement with you upon your marriage to my daughter, and while I did not wish for the union, I will keep my word. The land will go to my grandchild."

"Regardless of whether the child is male or female, as we agreed."

"Aye," Angus confirmed. "Male or female the land will belong to the child."

Aidan and Boyd smiled at their father's words and so did Ian and Blair. Arran was the only one who remained angry.

"Is Moira all right?" Aidan asked with concern.

"A wound to the back of the head," Ian explained, "and I wonder over its cause."

"I saw nothing," Aidan said, shaking his head. "I have thought and thought on it and pictured Moira twirling in circles, though I twirled as well—as we did as children."

"Evoking the gods," Ian said.

Aidan smiled. "She told you."

"She was happy sharing childhood memories with you."

"And I with her. I have missed my sister."

Ian could tell he was concerned. "Go and visit with her. She was asking of you."

"She was worried about me?" Aidan asked, surprised.

"Aye, she wanted to make certain you were well."

Aidan looked uncertain, as if he were choosing his sister over his father.

Surprisingly, his father settled the matter. "Go to your sister and make certain she is well."

Aidan nodded and did not wait; he rushed from the room. Boyd remained steadfastly by his father's side.

Ian turned to Arran. "I instructed you to see to the border problem. Have you done so?"

Arran looked annoyed. "I will see to it."

"Now," he ordered firmly.

Arran left the hall in a huff.

Blair understood that Ian wished to speak with Angus alone. "Boyd, come and let me show you the improvement made to our arrows. They fly a more accurate course and hit a more accurate target."

Boyd was interested. "This I would like to see."

"And wait until I tell you who helped design the arrow," Blair said with a friendly slap to Boyd's back as they walked out of the hall.

Ian looked to Angus, his eyes a dark green. "I will have the truth now from you, Angus Maclean."

❧ *thirty*

The two men stood facing each other in silence.

Ian waited on Angus's word for he wanted to hear from his mouth the truth for his visit here and once and for all he wanted to make certain that his wife had nothing to fear from her father. And if for the slightest moment Ian thought otherwise Angus Maclean would not live to take another breath.

Angus grew surly, his own temper flaring. "I spoke the truth to you."

"I think not." Ian was adamant. "I grow impatient waiting."

Angus crossed his thick muscled arms over his chest. "I owe you no explanation."

Ian stood firm. "You owe me respect in my home."

It was an understanding among the clans and one that was greatly respected and adhered to.

Angus gave a sharp nod that meant he would comply but not like it. "I came to see after my daughter."

Ian was blunt. "You thought I would do her harm?"

"You wed her for selfish reasons and while I still think her a fool, she is my daughter and deserves my protection."

"And when you heard her life may be in danger you assumed I was the danger?"

"Who else would she be in danger from?" Angus asked. "She is several years older than you and I thought barren. Why would you ever wish for her to remain your wife?"

"I pledged a vow," Ian said as if insulted. "A holy vow that I take seriously. She is my wife and will be treated with the respect due her." Ian shook his head. "But even so, the reason Moira remains my wife is because I love her and I will have it no other way."

Angus shook his head. "It is foolish to love. It brings nothing but pain."

"I know the pain that love can bring, but I also know the joy and I would trade neither the pain nor the joy, for love is too wondrous to miss."

"I remember nothing but the pain," Angus said with sorrow.

Ian placed a hand on the man's shoulder. "Then remember the joy, for only if you remember the joy can you love again."

Angus remained silent, his brow heavy with thought.

Ian removed his hand and poured them each a tankard of ale. "Tell me how you learned that Moira was in danger."

Angus gladly accepted the drink. "I am not certain the source of the information. It was simply brought to my attention one day and while I thought it nothing but idle gossip, knowing Moira was safe at the convent, I kept my ears open. Then I heard that you had returned for her and planned on taking her from the convent. I grew concerned thinking perhaps she was in danger from you. And though I still thought of her as foolish, she was mine to protect."

"She is mine to protect," Ian corrected.

"I see now that she is, but then if she is not in danger from you or from me, who threatens her?"

Ian shook his head slowly. "I have yet to find out. I can find no reason for such a threat."

"Who would benefit from her death?"

"You, if you do not wish to honor the marriage agreement," Ian answered honestly.

"I did not know Moira was with child, and I keep my word whether I like it or not. There must be someone else who would benefit if she died."

"I can think of none."

"Then the only other reason would be that she knows something she should not."

"I have thought of that," Ian said, "but she resided at the convent where her life was sheltered. What could she know?" His own words came back to haunt him. She knew much. The monk had taught her things that Ian found difficult to grasp. But who would be threatened by such knowledge?

"This is a puzzle that needs solving," Angus said and they both took seats at the nearby table to discuss it.

Brianna gathered the soiled linens in a bundle. "I will get a soothing brew for you after I leave these to be cleaned."

Moira sat in bed with her head resting back against several pillows. "Thank you for your help, Brianna. It is much appreciated."

"I was glad to give it and glad I am to have you for a sister." Brianna quickly left the room with unshed tears in her eyes.

"She needs to be away from that husband of hers," Moira said to Anne. "I do not trust him."

"He is a mean one though hides it with a false charm." Anne fussed with the bedcovers, making certain Moira was comfortable.

Moira stopped her with a hand to her arm. "Tell me what you think caused my accident."

"I knew you would ask me this so I studied the wound

as I tended it. I was not certain at first but after carefully viewing the wound I realized it was the mark of an arrow. A badly aimed arrow, thank the Lord."

"So it was intentional."

"Aye, that it was."

Moira moved her hand off Anne and closed her eyes. Her sigh weighed heavily with concern. "I cannot understand this. I have thought over and over who would mean me harm and can find no reasonable explanation for it. Have you learned anything?"

"Only that Ian is as frustrated as you over this. He can make no sense of it and that alarms him for he does not know who to protect you from."

"And the attacks are random and far between as if someone patiently waits to accomplish his deed." Moira opened her eyes.

"The last two were closer; perhaps he grows impatient."

"Or perhaps time runs out."

"Time runs out for what?" Anne asked.

"I do not know." Moira moved to shake her head but immediately stopped and shut her eyes briefly against the pain. "It throbs," she explained when she saw the look of concern on Anne's face.

"It will for a while. We must keep careful watch on it and you."

"I feel fine and the babe is his usual active self. I think all will be well with me and him."

"You will rest in bed for a few days."

Moira protested, "It is not necessary."

"Aye, it is," Ian said, already in the room and closing the door behind him. He walked over, sat gently on the bed beside her, and slipped his hand over hers.

Anne made a discreet exit.

Moira decided not to argue and, besides, she did not wish to take any chances with her birthing time drawing near. "As you wish, husband."

Ian grinned. "I have never heard you say these words to me, but I do like hearing them."

Moira smiled softly, making certain to hold her throbbing head still. "Then enjoy them for they are not words you will hear frequently."

Ian laughed and leaned down to tenderly kiss her lips. "Now I know you are well for you are your stubborn self."

Moira's smile faded and she placed a gentle hand on his arm. "I am well because you are here with me and I feel safe."

He kissed her cheek. "You will always be safe with me. That is why you will not be leaving my side."

Her smile returned. "You cannot spend every minute of the day with me."

"Aye, I can, though Blair will share the time with me."

"Ian—"

"Do not bother to argue. Your words fall on deaf ears."

"But—" Her second attempt to protest was cut short by words that touched her heart.

"I love you, Moira. I never expected to love this strongly again and I thank the Lord for you. You are a precious gift that I will cherish forever."

Tears welled in her eyes and she fought them, but lost. They trickled slowly down her cheeks one after the other.

Ian wiped them away with his finger. "My love makes you cry?"

"Nay," she said with a quiver. "I never thought I would love and I never thought I would love you as deeply as I do."

He kissed her gently. "I never meant to hurt you, Moira."

She laughed softly. "And you never meant to love me."

He laughed softly. "Aye, you are right. I wed you out of duty, but I love you of my own accord. And I will never stop loving you."

"There was a time I would not have believed your words," she said on a sigh. "But now I do not doubt them for I know you to be a man of honor and courage and a man I will love forever."

They kissed gently, lingering in their tender union, and when they stopped, her words made him laugh.

"I am hungry."

"Then I will see that you are fed."

She smiled. "You are a good husband. I will keep you."

He looked at her with loving eyes. "I am glad of your decision."

"Aye, it is my decision and one I make freely."

"Then it is a good, solid union we will share."

They kissed again, lingering a little longer and their cheeks coming to rest against each other in perfect contentment.

It was not until two days later that Moira met once again with Bishop Roderick. He sat next to her on the dais for the evening meal. It was her first time out of bed since the accident and if she had not insisted on her freedom she still would be stuck in her bedchamber. She was feeling well and wished to be up and about. There were things for her to discover.

"I am glad to see that you are well," the bishop remarked in his solemn, sonorous voice.

"Thank you, I do feel fine."

"I remember how busy you always were at the convent. It seemed that the sisters depended much on you."

"We all worked well together."

"You are being humble, my child. Mother Superior confided in me how invaluable you were to the convent."

Confided?

Exactly what had Mother Superior confided to the bishop?

"She commented on your spirit and enthusiasm and how contagious it was and how it inspired others to work hard."

Moira felt relieved though she remained on alert. For some reason she felt the need to guard herself, or perhaps guard her knowledge. "I did no more or less than others."

"Mother Superior tells me you were of quick wit and could work out problems easily. A definite asset for the convent."

Moira chose to remain silent and learn, for obviously the bishop had something on his mind.

"The convent does remarkably well. I cannot believe it is so self-sufficient; few if any of them are."

"Hard work can produce a bounty for all to reap," Moira said.

The bishop slowly nodded his head. "Unlike some, who dabble in alchemy, hoping to create wealth without work."

Moira turned silent. Odd that he should mention alchemy. The monk had spoken of it to her in secret. She had never shared the knowledge he imparted with anyone though she studied it from time to time. She had not agreed with the equations and thought the process lacked a missing piece. It was not an area she wished to pursue. The results, she felt, would only benefit the wealthy and would do little good for the poor. Whereas her work would benefit all.

The concept was, however, avidly pursued, especially if one understood the equations and the process. She suddenly realized the importance of that information and wondered. Could that knowledge have a bearing on why her life was in danger?

But why then would someone want her dead? Would that person not prefer to gain from her knowledge?

"Alchemy is an interesting idea though not likely," Ian said, joining their conversation.

"I agree," the bishop said, "though many would tend to disagree—our late king, for one of them. He had several monks and an abbot working specifically on alchemy."

"The king thought knowledge was important, especially the expansion of knowledge," Ian said.

The bishop thought otherwise. "Some knowledge is better left unlearned."

Moira added her opinion. "Knowledge is better when it is understood. Once understood then it can be determined if it is better left unlearned."

"You speak wisely," the bishop said. "You have taught *yourself* well."

Moira grew uncomfortable with his words. What did he know that she did not? And did she have need to worry?

She purposely yawned. "I must excuse myself for I grow tired."

Ian looked at her with concern.

She eased his worry. "Please do not rush your visit with the bishop. Anne will see to my needs."

Ian immediately knew she purposely took her leave. But was it for herself or for him to learn more from the bishop—a thought that had been on his mind.

"Rest well, I will see you later," he said.

She stopped by his chair to kiss his cheek and whisper, "Listen well, husband."

He smiled and gave her long braid a tug. "I always do, wife."

Anne stood and waited for her.

Brianna moved to stand, thinking to join them, but her husband grabbed her arm and forced her to remain seated.

Moira caught his possessive action and stopped by Brianna's chair. "I would be pleased if you would join me. There is a matter I wish to discuss with you."

Ian cast a look at Arran waiting for him to deny his wife's request.

Arran removed his hand and with a charming smile said, "Go and enjoy your time with the women."

Brianna did not hesitate. She jumped from her chair and raced to Moira's side.

The three women left the room together.

They immediately went to the stitching room and sat comfortably on the thick fur rug before the fire. Anne saw to brewing them hot cider and it was with a pleasant sigh of relief for being off on their own that Moira began the conversation.

"I do not think Bishop Roderick's visit is a coincidence. I think he has come for a reason."

"I thought the same myself," Anne said. "He has asked questions that are simple yet intrusive in their own way."

"You know him well?" Brianna asked.

"Nay," Moira said, shaking her head, "though I think he knows me well."

"You think he knows of your studies?" Anne asked.

"He made mention of alchemy," Moira said on a whisper.

"You know nothing of that," Anne said in defense of her.

Moira stared with wide eyes at both women. "Ah, but I do."

❧ *thirty-one*

Anne and Brianna looked alarmed.

Moira explained. "It was the last of what the monk taught me and he told me I was to keep the secret. But there is no secret, for those who professed its success spoke falsely. Is it possible?" She shrugged. "If studied enough perhaps, but presently the equations do not make sense or the method."

"You have tried this?" Brianna asked with disbelief.

"Nay—once I looked over the equations, I told the monk it would not work. He smiled at me and told me that someday he was certain that I would discover how to make it work. I never pursued it after that."

Anne looked concerned. "Do you think the bishop knows and wishes you harm?"

"Why would he wish her harm?" Brianna asked. "If she truly did know how to turn metal to gold would he not want her to perform such a feat for the church?"

Anne lowered her voice. "He may think she works with the devil to produce such magic."

The realization of such an idea horrified Brianna and her eyes grew round with fear. "Then it certainly could be the bishop who wishes you harm."

"A thought," Moira said, "and one that needs further study."

"I will find out all I can," Anne volunteered.

"As will I," Brianna added. "One of us is bound to learn something."

Moira thought differently. "The bishop chooses his words wisely and listens even more closely."

"You mean he guards secrets well," Anne said.

Moira nodded. "I remember when he and Mother Superior would talk. He remained quiet and attentive, and he learned much."

Anne grinned. "I have a way of doing much the same."

Moira laughed. "That you do, so you will be the one working magic."

"Arran says that I talk too much and do not listen enough," Brianna said. "Perhaps I should learn from you, Anne."

Anne could not hold her tongue. "You need to learn to speak up and teach that husband of yours to treat you with respect." She instantly regretted her harsh words when she watched as tears pooled in Brianna's eyes.

Moira slipped an arm around Brianna. "Anne has a way of speaking her mind."

"She is right," Brianna said sadly. "I foolishly fell for his false charm. I believed all he told me and I was blind to the things I did see but chose to ignore. Arran must always have his way. He comes first in all he chooses to do and his edicts are final. He cares naught for my feelings or opinions. He expects to be obeyed at all times"—she paused to take a heavy breath—"especially in bed."

Moira and Anne realized that she needed to talk. She had kept so much locked away and now that the door was open she needed to set her emotions free.

"I had thought that he loved me, but I learned fast

enough that Arran loves no one but himself. He does what pleases him and wants what pleases him. If he thinks I have not pleased him he makes a point of telling me. And he has repeatedly told me that I do not please him in bed and of course I am a failure as a woman for I cannot conceive a child."

She wiped at the tears that began to fall. "And I wish he would stop trying to get me with child. I cannot stand his touch any longer."

"You must speak to your brother," Moira said.

Brianna shook her head adamantly. "Nay, I am wed and there is nothing he can do about it. And Arran would only make me suffer if I confided in my brother."

"Arran does not need to know," Moira said. "But your brother does need to know how you feel. He worries over you and wishes you to be happy."

Brianna managed to smile. "He always worried over me. He always made certain I was protected, as did Blair. I thought Arran was just like them. I was wrong." She turned to Anne. "You are lucky to have a man like Blair love you."

Anne smiled. "I am beginning to realize just how lucky I am. Blair has made an effort to ask me about my studies. At first he did not seem interested and that concerned me for I could never wed someone who objected to my penchant for learning. Now, though, he has taken interest in my work and asks me endless questions. I think we will wed very soon."

"This is good news," Moira said. "We shall have a large celebration."

Brianna grew excited. "Aye, we shall make it special."

The women were soon deep into discussing wedding preparations and it was not until some time later that the three drifted off to their respective bedchambers. A guard followed Moira's footsteps.

Moira found her husband pacing the floor in front of the bed.

"I was about to come after you," Ian said with a smile

and walked up to his wife and took her into his arms. He kissed her softly and pressed his cheek to hers. "I have missed you."

"We have not been out of sight for very long."

"Long enough for me to miss you." He kissed her again, a little more slowly and intently.

She sighed and melted against him. "Tell me what you and the bishop discussed."

He kissed along her cheek and down her neck then up again. "I do not wish to discuss the bishop now. We can talk of him later."

"I am curious."

He rubbed his body to hers. "I want you."

His words sent a tingle racing through her and her question suddenly seemed less important. Though she found a much more pertinent question to ask him. "Why do I always want you?"

He laughed with a gentle confidence. "Because I am so desirable."

She giggled softly and rested her head on his chest. "You think that, do you?"

"I know that," he whispered and pressed his cheek to the top of her head.

She slipped her arms around his waist and pressed her body to his. "You are right."

"I love when you agree with me," he said on a laugh. "Which is not often."

Her tone was serious. "It matters not what else we agree on as long as we agree on our love for each other."

With one finger he lifted her chin. "You woke my silent heart and taught me to love again and it is glad I am for it and glad I am that your own silent heart woke with mine."

Her brown eyes grew teary. "Mine was an empty heart and you filled it."

He kissed her lips softly, then her cheeks and then her eyes and when a tear fell he kissed it away. "And I will keep it full for all of our days."

He scooped her up into his arms and carried her to the bed.

"It is a gentle loving we will share tonight, wife."

"Long and slow too?" she asked enthusiastically.

He grinned. "'Tis glad I am you enjoy the marriage bed."

It was her turn to grin. "Aye, that I do, husband."

"Good," he said, lowering them both down on the bed. "Then let us both enjoy a night of long, lazy loving."

Ian sat beside his wife at the narrow table in the stitching room, staring at the column of numbers in the ledger.

Moira tapped at the column. "It does not make sense. The column of numbers on the previous pages does not allow for this calculation. And the listing of harvest and livestock does not match production equations." She shook her head. "The ledger makes no sense though at first glance it would seem to. Do you go over Arran's ledger regularly?"

"Not as I should," he admitted. "I assumed I could trust him. He is Brianna's husband and I thought a dependable and trustworthy man."

Moira was blunt. "Brianna is not happy with him."

His response did not surprise her. Her husband was astute and not much got past him except for numbers in ledgers. "I know this. I can see the worry and unhappiness in her eyes."

"Can we do something for her?" Moira said with concern. With Ian being such a caring and loving husband she could not comprehend being wed to a man who cared naught but for his own selfish needs.

"I must speak with Brianna first and then if she agrees I thought of speaking to Bishop Roderick about the situation and seeing what could be done."

Moira smiled, pleased with her husband's plans, but then, she did not expect anything less from him. He cared deeply for his sister and she did not for once doubt that he would allow her to go on being unhappy.

Ian returned to the matter of the ledger, needing more specific answers. "What think you of all this?" He pointed to the columns of numbers.

"I think Arran needs to be made answerable for this quandary."

"So he does not tell me the truth?"

"If you need ask that question then you already have your answer," Moira said.

Ian smiled. "You have a quick wit about you, wife."

"I speak my mind—" She paused for a moment. "And I speak the truth."

"Whether I like to hear it or not," Ian said with a gentle poke to her nose.

"The truth hurts but a moment, lies hurt forever."

"You have a wisdom about you that I admire and respect."

Moira's smile broadened. "That is a compliment that warms my heart."

Ian moved closer and trailed slow kisses over her neck to her ear. "I can warm all of you if you wish."

"Not fair," she whispered. "I have work to do and you know that I cannot resist when you tempt me."

He laughed. "I know—that is why I tempt you."

She turned her head to capture his lips with a kiss when she grew dizzy and grabbed onto his arm.

"What is it?" he asked anxiously, watching her turn pale.

She was too disoriented to answer and Ian did not hesitate to gently take her up into his arms and cradle her protectively against him.

She was relieved when the dizziness passed. "The babe makes himself known much too often of late."

Ian's concern showed in his blue eyes. They reflected a concern that touched Moira's heart.

"I am fine," she said. Although she had promised that she would not utter those words again, she could not help but try to relieve his worry.

Anne and Blair entered the room in a flourish at that moment with exciting news.

"We wed in two months' time," Blair announced, though his smile turned to worry when he saw the way Ian protectively cradled his wife.

"What is wrong?" Anne asked as she hurried over to the couple

Blair followed her, his brow creased in concern.

"She felt faint," Ian explained.

"I am fine," Moira repeated once again, feeling as though she forever uttered those words.

Blair voiced his strong opinion. "She is too old to birth a babe."

"You are a fool," Anne snapped at him.

"She has been ill since the start," Blair argued.

Anne defended her friend. "She is with child and suffers no differently than other women."

Ian listened to the two argue over his wife. His own fear mirrored Blair's. He worried over her health and the safe delivery of their child. Yet he also could not help but realize that his wife possessed a vitality that many lacked. There was a vibrancy about her that even the young could not match. Perhaps it had to do with her uncommon knowledge, her thirst for discovery that set her apart.

He looked at his wife and saw that her face had regained its usual color and that she seemed well and rather content tucked in his arms.

"I am well," Moira reassured them all.

"She should be made to rest," Blair said more from concern than anything else.

Anne took umbrage at his remark. "She rests when necessary. She would do nothing to harm the child."

"Then she should stay abed," Blair said adamantly.

"Is that what you would expect from me when with child?" Anne asked.

Blair wisely thought before he responded. "I would trust you to do what was necessary."

Anne smiled and walked over to him, slipping her arms around his neck. "That is why I love you. You truly understand me."

He hugged her to him.

"And you must understand that Moira instinctively knows what is best for her babe," Anne said. "She would do nothing to harm the child. She would surrender herself before hurting the babe."

Anne's words alarmed Ian. While he longed for a child, he did not wish Moira to sacrifice herself. Life without her would be unbearable. She had become necessary to his life. He enjoyed studying with her in her stitching room. He enjoyed conversing with her on a variety of topics. He cherished the intimacy he shared with her. He loved her much too much to live life without her.

"You are well!" Ian sounded as if he were decreeing her healthy.

"I keep telling you so," Moira said, annoyed having to repeat herself.

"I want nothing to happen to you," he said as if confirming his edict.

"What do you fear, Ian?" Moira finally asked, realizing it was time he faced his unspoken fears.

Anne, realizing this was a moment they should share alone, tugged at Blair's arm and reluctantly forced him to leave the room.

Once the door closed Ian spoke freely. "I do not want to lose you."

"You will not," she assured him.

"I do not know this for certain." His hold on her grew tighter as if reasserting his claim on her.

"I am not Kathleen," Moira said firmly.

Ian shut his eyes for a moment recalling his first wife and realizing that there was a vast difference between them. "Aye, that you are not."

Moira raised a gentle hand to his face and stroked his

cheek and along his chin. "Then know that I am strong and will deliver you a healthy child."

Ian had his doubts and voiced them. "You have been ill and have fainted too many times for me to count. And you barely look as though you carry a child." He had not admitted his fears to anyone. Moira had barely rounded with child. She carried small and looked almost not to be with child though her breasts grew large with milk.

Moira attempted to ease his concerns. "My mother barely showed when she carried each child."

Ian remembered that her mother died birthing Aidan and reminded her. "Your mother did not survive the birth of your brother."

She tugged at the braid in his hair. "You worry that I will follow my mother."

"Aye, I do," Ian said, his hold on her even firmer.

She realized he physically tried to keep a firm grip on her, preventing any harm from befalling her and hoping to keep her safe from her own delivery.

Moira attempted to ease his worry. "I will deliver this babe with ease—and any that follow."

Ian raised a brow. "You think to have more children?"

"Why would I not?"

He eyed her strangely.

She laughed. "You think me too old?"

He suddenly worried. He knew he could not keep himself from her. He was much too attracted to her and after the babe was born he would bide his time but soon enough desire her. She could very well conceive another child. What then?

He voiced his fear again. "I do not want to lose you. I love you."

She playfully tapped at his nose. "I am strong and fit and will bear you many children."

Doubt marred his expression.

She whispered words she had once thought she never would. "Trust me, for I trust you."

❧ thirty-two

Ian found he could not get her words out of his head. A week had passed since he last heard them but they were as strong in his head as the day she spoke them. And they meant much to him. He not only had her love now, he had her trust. He was truly blessed.

Moira's brothers had insisted on helping to protect their sister. So between Blair, Aidan, and Boyd, and of course Ian, Moira found herself vigilantly guarded. Ian understood that his wife was none too pleased with the constant guard but that could not be helped. He would not take the chance of anything happening to her. Her time was drawing near and he worried enough over a safe delivery.

She had continued to carry small, her stomach rounding but not to a common size. He wondered if the babe had grown sufficiently or if he would be too puny to survive on his own. Moira seemed strong and healthy and she possessed a strong will. He hoped that strong will would see her through to a successful birth.

At the moment he waited in the great hall for Arran. He

intended to speak to him concerning the ledgers. Blair and Anne were with Moira, Anne having found a chest in the storage room that she insisted held interesting items that might be of help to their studies.

Ian for the moment felt his wife to be in good hands and he relaxed in the red velvet-seated chair at the dais, allowing himself for a moment to wonder about his old wooden chair and how he intended to hunt its whereabouts down and see to its immediate return.

Blair walked through the maze of furnishings and objects in the storage room making certain to remain close to Moira's side. He did not think danger would find her here but he would take no chances.

"The chest is all the way in the back of the room," Anne said as she led the way. "I discovered it beneath an old worn rug. It contains charts, maps, and books that are foreign to my eyes, but I thought that you might make sense of them."

"I am eager to see them," Moira said, following behind her.

"Be careful what you lean on," Blair warned as he kept close to Moira. "Some of these pieces are not stacked well."

Moira soothed a stray hair back away from her face and into her long braid as she took cautious steps. "We should see to cleaning up this room one day, Anne."

Blair laughed. "Anne sees to that every day. She comes here and makes a rich find, as she describes it to me, and finds a place for it in the keep. Soon she will have the room empty and the keep full."

"And the keep will look better for it," Anne declared.

Moira felt herself suddenly grow tired. She was doing that of late and she assumed it was due to the approach of the babe's birth. Perhaps she needed extra rest so as to be strong for the ordeal of delivery. Whatever the reason, she paid it heed and made certain to rest when needed.

"I wish to rest a moment."

Anne and Blair showed immediate concern.

"You do not feel well?" Blair asked, moving several items off a heavy wooden chair so that Moira could sit.

"A bit weary," she answered and sat down with a sigh of relief.

"Should I get Ian?" Anne asked.

"Nay, do not disturb him. A short rest is all I require." Moira released a soft sigh of relief as she closed her eyes and rested her head back.

Blair nodded to Anne who quietly made her way out of the room.

Blair sat down on a small sturdy crate and eyed his surroundings. There were chests stacked precariously on top of one another: baskets piled high, rugs thrown over items, and heavy metal candlesticks resting upon each other. It was not a safe place and he suddenly felt the urge to move her to safer surroundings.

He stood and walked toward her. "Moira—"

She opened her eyes at the sound of her name and at that moment the tower of chests behind her toppled forward.

Blair lunged but a large chest tumbled toward him and his quick reactions prevented him from suffering serious harm, but stopped him from reaching Moira in time.

The chests tumbled down one after another and in the chaos he could not see Moira. When the chests finally finished falling Moira was buried completely beneath them.

Blair cried out at the top of his lungs. A cry that was saved for battle and one he knew would bring every able-bodied man running. He did not wait for help. He began to dig away at the fallen chests, frantically calling out Moira's name.

Ian rushed into the room with Anne close behind him. Blair spoke before Ian could. "Moira is buried beneath," he said, throwing chests off to the side and hearing a few splinter as they hit the stone wall with force.

"Moira!" Ian called to her loudly as he dug at the many chests.

Arran appeared, as did Aidan and Boyd, and soon there were many hands digging at the chests and the added debris that had followed.

"Moira!" Ian yelled again and this time he heard a muffled moan. He prayed with all his heart that she was all right. He could not lose her; he could not. He loved her much too much.

"Ian!" Moira called out with difficulty.

"I am here, hold on," he said and yelled to the men to work faster and they did.

It took only a few moments for all the chests to be cleared away and all caught their breath at the sight of Moira's toppled chair with her crumpled beneath it.

Blair tore at the splintered arms of the chair as Ian made his way over the few surrounding chests to get to his wife. He went down on his knees and reached beneath the chair.

"Moira, are you all right?"

She took a deep breath and spoke slowly, her hand reaching to grasp his. "I think I am."

Ian managed to carefully slip his wife out from beneath the broken chair and into his arms. He cradled her gently against him, his glance racing over her to see how badly she was hurt. He could see no bumps or bruises and his hand immediately moved to run over her rounded tummy.

"The babe?" he asked anxiously.

Moira had calmed herself and was regaining her composure when the babe decided to answer for himself. He gave his mother a swift kick that his father felt.

Ian looked concerned.

Moira calmed his worry. "He but lets us know he is fine."

"You are certain?"

Moira squeezed her husband's hand. "I am certain, Ian."

"And you? Do you have any pain? Does anything feel broken?"

She smiled and then laughed. "The only thing broken is that chair you favor. It toppled over as the chests descended down on me and protected me with its strong stiff back."

"I knew there was a reason I favored that chair." He stood slowly, keeping his wife tucked safely in his arms, and turned his attention to Blair. "Meet me in the solar."

Blair nodded, understanding exactly what Ian wished of him.

Ian remained by his wife's side in their bedchamber while Anne tended her, making certain that she had not suffered serious harm. He kissed her gently, ordered her to rest, and placed three guards outside her door. Then he took his leave as his sister rushed into the room and almost collided with him.

"Slow down, she is fine," Ian said with a smile that confirmed his own relief.

He closed the door behind him as Brianna rushed to the bed.

"I truly am fine," Moira said when she saw the look of concern that Brianna wore.

Brianna nodded. "I know. Tongues wag endlessly throughout the keep about your accident, though none believe it an accident."

Anne looked startled.

But it was Moira who spoke. "They think it another attempt on my life?"

"That is the talk and extra guards have been posted throughout the entire keep." Brianna took a deep breath before she continued, as if needing to fortify herself. "And I have learned startling news." She lowered her voice and gave a quick glance to the door to make certain it was closed.

Anne drew closer to her.

"I was in Bishop Roderick's chamber making certain his care had been properly seen to when I spied his journal on the desk. No one lurked about and my curiosity got the best of me so I glanced through a few of the pages."

Both women remained silent, wishing to hear it all.

"I am so glad my father had me learn Latin for I read the pages with ease. I found nothing of interest until I closed the book and a single page fell out." Brianna looked bewildered. "It was Bishop Roderick who made it known to Ian that Moira's life could possibly be in danger."

Moira felt the babe stir and placed a comforting hand on her stomach.

"You are in pain?" Anne asked anxiously.

"Nay, the babe is extra active, that is all, and I am weary. I must tell Ian of this news, though I cannot understand any of it. Why would my life be in danger from the church? And is it? It does not makes sense. I must talk with Ian. Tonight after the evening meal I will discuss all I know and suspect with him. Perhaps then we will find a solution."

"Rest now," Anne ordered, like a concerned mother.

And Moira did just that. She fell fast asleep, content that her husband kept close watch over her.

Ian paced the floor in his solar. It was a small room with a minimum of furnishings and a place he did not spend much time in. He preferred the company of many to just himself and he now preferred the company of his wife and found the bedchamber a preferable place to be with her.

"This was no accident," he said to Blair, who agreed with a nod. "There is someone in the keep who wishes my wife harm and I want him found."

"I was thinking about that," Blair said. "It must be someone in the keep, for the guards have been diligent and have allowed no strangers entrance."

"I thought the same myself," Ian said with a frustrated rake of his fingers through his hair. "But who in the keep would be so devious as to want Moira dead?"

"If we could find an answer to that question we would solve our problem."

Ian continued his pacing, his thoughts keeping pace with his strides. "Moira possesses knowledge that could bring her harm." He shook his head. "I do not think that is the concern here. Why? I cannot say."

"Your instincts have never failed you before."

"That is true and it would be wise for me to follow them now."

Blair agreed with a simple nod.

"Something tells me that if I reasoned this more clearly I would find my answer."

"You feel you miss something?"

"Something obvious," Ian said and stopped his pacing. "It is as if it stares me in the face and yet I fail to see it."

"So the obvious becomes the most hidden."

"It would seem that way, though what is obvious cannot be that well hidden. It must actually be in plain sight. So why can I not see it?"

"It is too close to you."

Ian thought on his remark. Could it be that simple? Could he be blinded by its nearness? He would give it thought.

"Make certain extra guards are posted where my wife spends most of her time and then make certain guards are posted where they cannot be detected. I want them to watch all that goes on in the keep. And make certain that you use only our most trusted men."

"You expect another attempt?"

"This last attempt seemed rushed, not at all planned, which leads me to believe time is of the essence to him."

"The babe?" Blair questioned. "Could it have something to do with the birth of the babe?"

"I have thought the same and wondered over it. And I

still wonder over who would benefit the most if Moira were to die. That question forever haunts me."

"You would not benefit."

"Nay, I would not," Ian agreed. "I would suffer and hurt and know that life would not be worth living."

"You love her."

"You sound as if this is something you have known," Ian said, surprised.

Blair laughed. "I knew when you made it clear that we were to return to the convent for your wife that you had feelings for her."

"Feelings I had yet to explore."

"Feelings nonetheless and feelings you could not ignore."

Ian smiled. "She captured my interest."

"She captured your heart."

Ian turned bright green eyes on him that quickly softened to a gentle blue. "You know too much."

"I know you, my friend," Blair said kindly. "And it was glad I was to see that you finally allowed yourself to love again. When you lost Kathleen I thought you would forever keep your heart locked away. It took an older woman with sharp wit to make you realize that you could love again. And I must say that I admire and respect her; she truly is a woman worth loving."

Ian grabbed his friend and hugged him tightly. "I know now why you are my best friend. You speak from your heart."

"All Scots do. We can speak no other way. We feel too deeply and care much too much for family and friends."

They gripped forearms.

"You are my brother, Blair," Ian said, "and forever will be."

"Aye, that I am and I will always watch out for you and yours."

"As will I for you."

Blair nodded. "Then we find this man and see that he gets what he deserves."

Ian grinned. "Aye, that we do."

*The evening meal went well. The food was flavored to per-*fection and all ate with gusto. Tongues wagged about the "accident." Ale flowed freely and many a voice was raised in song. It was as if they celebrated life, the continuous cycle of birth, growth, and passing until birth was sought again.

Moira sat beside her husband, who gripped her hand through the entire meal. She did not mind, she felt safe being physically connected with him. He would allow no harm to come to her for when he had entered her room after her nap he had informed her that he would remain by her side until this problem was solved. He would in essence be her shadow.

She had kissed him and told him how much she loved him and they had lain together snuggling against each other and feeling the power of their love.

The pain was low and dull in her back and she paid it no heed. When it came again she gave it thought but for a moment and then dismissed it as a nuisance. When the pain struck stronger she began to give it credence and realized that her accident just may have brought on an earlier delivery.

She said nothing, waiting to see if what she suspected was true.

She chattered with those around her and gave her husband's hand a squeeze every now and then and he in turn gave her a smile.

So the night went on until finally Moira turned to Ian and said, "The babe is ready to be born."

✿ thirty-three

"Now? The babe comes now?" Ian asked with disbelief.

Moira nodded with a smile. "Aye, he waits no longer."

"But it is not his time yet."

"The babe chooses his time." Moira bent forward in her chair and rubbed at the pain that centered in her lower back.

Ian, finally realizing his wife was ready to give birth, stood and shouted, "Anne!"

Anne sat only two chairs away so his shout drew everyone's attention.

"The babe is ready to be born," Ian said, announcing it to the entire room.

Shouts of cheer filled the air and Anne and Brianna hurried to Moira's side, shoving Ian out of their way.

Ian would not have it. He intended to remain by her side no matter the protests. He gently moved his sister and Anne out of his way and snatched his wife from the chair up into his arms.

He had her upstairs in their bedchamber in minutes,

with Anne and Brianna busy readying the room for the birth.

Ian helped his wife change into a linen tunic and then he sat himself down beside her on the bed, keeping hold of her hand.

"There is no need for you to remain here," Moira said patiently. "My pain is much too far apart for the birth to be soon. It will be some hours before the babe makes his entrance into this world."

"I stay by your side." He was adamant and his eyes glowed a bright green, which meant there was no arguing with him.

"You will stay out of our way." Anne was just as adamant.

"I take orders from no one," Ian warned.

Brianna attempted to calm the tense debate. "No one gives you orders."

Anne was her usual blunt self. "Nay, I give you orders, Ian Cameron, and it is best you listen to them. I will not have you interfering with the birth. It is Moira who I worry of now and no one else. So take your Scottish temper and—"

"Enough!"

Everyone turned wide eyes on Brianna.

"Moira does not need to hear you two bickering, and if you do not stop I will see that you are both removed from this room and I will tend to her myself. And I mean it," Brianna said with a shake of her finger at them both.

Ian smiled. "You sound as you did when we were young, strong and confident. It is good to have you back, sister."

Brianna placed her hands on her hips and lifted a defiant chin, though a smile peeked through. "You paid me little heed then, but you will heed me now, brother."

Ian looked from his sister to Anne. "I will follow your instructions, but I will not leave her side no matter what either of you say. I want her safe, and with me by her side I know she will be."

Anne and Brianna nodded, both women having similar thoughts. They felt he would tire of sitting by and doing nothing and once the pain turned difficult he would probably take his leave.

Moira thought differently. Ian would not desert her; she knew this from her heart. She trusted him and the thought filled her with pure joy. She had come to respect and love her husband and understand him. He was a man of integrity. He did what was necessary, what would benefit his clan, not only him. He understood love for it was unselfish and given with no thought to what it would return.

She gripped his hand. "I love you."

He smiled and his blue eyes softened. "And I you, wife." He leaned down and brushed his lips over hers. "Just as we made this child together, we will bring him into this world together."

She was about to give him a kiss when a pain shot across her stomach and she moaned.

Ian moaned along with her and Anne and Brianna laughed softly.

An hour passed slowly with little pain for Moira and she understood that she was in for a long night. Ian kept a steady flow of conversation with her, keeping her mind occupied. Anne and Brianna fussed over her and made certain that everything that was needed was there and waiting.

A furious knock sounded at the door and it burst open. Blair stomped into the room. "There is trouble with the border clans. Arran speaks with a messenger now."

Concern flashed across Brianna's face and she looked immediately to her brother.

Ian stood though his hand remained locked with Moira's.

"I am sorry," Blair said, "but you best come and speak with Arran and settle this before it turns difficult."

Moira made it easy for her husband. "Go, Ian, I am fine. It will be hours before the babe arrives."

He leaned down and kissed her. "I will not be long."

"I am not going anywhere."

"I will return soon," Ian said and walked to Blair, his sister following him.

"I must know what goes on," Brianna said with worry.

Ian nodded and with his arm around his sister the three left the room.

Anne looked to Moira. "You should rest while you can. They will return soon enough and keep you busy once again."

Moira sat forward and rubbed at her aching back. "The pain remains low and annoying."

"Give it time. It will become more than annoying."

Another knock interrupted their conversation and Anne went to answer it when the door remained closed.

Bishop Roderick stood on the other side and Anne respectfully bowed her head. "Please come in, Bishop Roderick."

"I do not disturb Moira, do I? I but wish to pray with her for a moment."

Though the pain annoyed Moira, she retained her senses and her curiosity. She bowed her head and recited the prayers along with the bishop and Anne. When he finished Moira took the opportunity to question him.

"Please sit a moment, Bishop, I wish to talk with you."

Anne moved a chair closer to the bed and the bishop sat.

"I wish to know why you sent Ian a message insinuating that my life may be in danger."

His eyes betrayed his surprise though he remained silent.

"It matters not how I know of this. What matters is what you know," Moira said firmly.

The bishop nodded slowly, as if agreeing with her, and then he began to explain. "Many years ago the abbeys had been alerted to a monk who had been schooled in the art of alchemy leaving one of the abbeys and going off on his own. There was concern that his secret knowledge, if passed along, could prove critical for many. I was instructed to locate him, but he proved to be elusive. Finally after many years of searching I tracked him to your convent at Loch Lomond. And since the convent flourished, I assumed that the monk had taught someone there his knowledge."

"You learned that it was me the monk had instructed," Moira said.

"Mother Superior advised me of the situation when I made it known to her that I knew of the monk's presence. I must admit that I feared for your safety."

"Which is why you advised Ian of possible danger?"

The bishop nodded. "There are many men who would want your knowledge for their own benefit. I knew Ian would protect you for he is an honorable man. I arranged a simple altercation along your journey home to make the threat plausible."

Moira shook her head. "It does not make sense. If men wished my knowledge they would not wish me dead. The attack we experienced on the road was not a simple one. Those men wanted me dead."

"Nonsense," the bishop argued. "A fright was all they were to give you."

"You and Mother Superior were the only ones who knew of my knowledge?"

"I took no chances. If I had spoken of it to anyone I would have been inviting danger, so I chose silence and swore Mother Superior to it as well."

"Then what threat could there be to me if no one knew?" A pain startled her and her hand went to rest on her stomach.

"I will leave you to rest," the bishop said, standing, and after a brief blessing he took his leave.

"None of this makes sense," Anne said with a shake of her head.

Moira rested back on the pillows and began to add all she knew in neat columns in her head. The idea that her knowledge would cause her harm was a plausible threat, but not a sensible one. Her death would prove useless, her knowledge dying with her. Her father, while an angry man, meant her no harm and his word meant much to him. So he would honor the marriage agreement whether he liked it or not.

She rubbed her tummy and continued to calculate in her head.

The question that continued to haunt her returned.

Who would benefit from her death?

A sudden thought hit her. What if she was not the main object of the threat? She had assumed she was, but what if she was like a column of numbers, where it was necessary for one to be added to another in order to determine the value?

What was the value?

"Are you all right?" Anne asked.

She nodded, too deep in thought to answer.

Anne continued talking. "You think Arran would have settled this problem with the border clans by now. Brianna told me there have been skirmishes for years and they were always settled peaceably. But it seems Arran feels these farmer clans are not worthy of the clan Cameron's protection. Ian and Arran have continued to dispute this since his arrival."

Moira shook her head. "The missing piece. Why did I not realize?"

"Realize what?" Anne asked, excited, knowing that Moira must have reached a conclusion about something important.

Moira threw the linen sheet off and swung her legs off the bed. "I was not meant to add but subtract. Help me, I must speak with Ian."

Anne looked startled. "You cannot mean to go down to the hall now?"

"Get me a plaid to wrap around myself," Moira said and stood slowly, her hand going to rest on her back.

"Ian will be furious," Anne said with worry and not doing as Moira asked.

"A plaid, please, Anne, or I will look for one myself."

"You are serious about this?"

"Aye, it is imperative that I speak with Ian now."

Anne shook her head but did as Moira asked, though she protested. "You should remain abed."

"My delivery time is not near. The babe takes his time, giving me time to speak with Ian."

"Ian will return soon and you can speak with him then." Anne attempted to convince her while she retrieved a plaid and helped wrap it around Moira.

"I cannot wait," Moira insisted and headed for the door with Anne close behind her.

Chaos reigned in the great hall. It seemed everyone was speaking at once and most seemed in disagreement. Ian, Blair, and Arran were cloistered together in private discussion, standing in a close huddle in front of the dais.

The chaotic noise came to an abrupt halt when Moira entered the hall.

Ian was stunned to see his wife.

Moira thought nothing of her actions; she was anxious to talk with her husband. She walked straight toward him until a birthing pain grabbed her hard and fast and she almost stumbled to her knees.

Ian rushed to her side, his arm going around her and her body resting against the strength of him.

"What are you doing here?" he demanded, unable to believe his own eyes. "I left you safely tucked in bed."

"I need to speak with you."

"I have little time, Moira," he said with reluctance. "I do not wish to but I must go and settle the problem with the border clan. It grows troublesome and I do not wish senseless bloodshed."

"I thought Arran was to settle this," Moira said and cast a suspicious glance at Arran.

He seemed alarmed by her accusing eyes and took a step toward his wife, who stood a few feet away from him, rubbing her hands in a nervous gesture.

"It did not settle as easily as he had thought it would. Now as laird I must go see to it. I want no blood spilled."

"There may be no choice," Arran said. "The clan makes unfair demands."

"We should take a sizeable troop of clansmen with us," Blair suggested.

"Blair goes with you?" Moira asked, seeing all the pieces of the mysterious puzzle falling into place.

"Do not worry," Ian said, thinking her concerned. "You will be safe."

"You will not be here, how would that make me safe?"

"I do not wish to leave you. I have no choice," he said, upset that he could not remain there with her.

Surprisingly, another pain tore into her and if it were not for Ian's strong arms she would have collapsed. Her pains had leaped in frequency and she realized that she might just deliver the babe sooner than possible.

"You cannot go," she said with labored breath, the pain subsiding but having stolen a bit of her strength.

His duty to his clan and to his wife tore at his emotions.

"I need you, Ian," Moira said and rested her head on his chest.

This was not at all like his wife. She was independent, full of courage, and willful. Why suddenly did she feel so needy?

"You must go, Ian," Arran said firmly. "This problem will turn disastrous if you do not."

"Will it now?" Moira asked, raising her head from her husband's chest and taking a confident step away from him. "Why is that?"

Arran grew annoyed. "The problem should have been dealt with more harshly, then the border clans would not dare cause problems." He calmed his tone. "You need not concern yourself with your safety. You will be well protected here and will deliver a fine babe."

"Aye, that I will and I will deliver my babe with my husband by my side."

"Your husband is needed elsewhere," Arran said, once again annoyed.

Ian wished time alone with his wife so he could determine what she was about. Something disturbed her, of that he was sure. He extended his hand to her. "Come, you need to rest."

Moira took his hand and slipped back into the comfort of his embrace. "Tell me, who will protect me while you are away?"

"Arran has agreed to remain here and look after you," Ian said, hoping to ease her concern.

Moira laughed, to everyone's surprise, a good, hardy laugh. "How convenient that the man who wishes me dead offers to protect me."

✖ *thirty-four*

"Why say you this?" Ian asked, taking his wife's remark seriously.

"This is ridiculous," Arran protested. "She accuses harshly for no other reason than to make certain her husband remains by her side for the birthing. She is selfish and weak-willed—"

"Enough!" Ian ordered with a shout. "You will not speak of my wife that way."

Arran clamped his lips tightly shut to keep his anger from spilling forth.

Moira rubbed at her lower back, the pain having intensified more rapidly than she had expected.

"Tell me why you accuse Arran of this, Moira," Ian said more calmly and brushed her hand aside to rub her back for her.

The room remained silent and anxious to hear her words and she spoke them with confidence.

"I could not understand why anyone would want me dead. The most logical explanation would be that someone would benefit from it. But who would benefit? My father agreed to a marriage contract and would abide by it, for he is a man of his word."

"Aye, that I am," Angus Maclean boasted proudly.

Moira looked to her husband. "My husband loves me and would never do me any harm."

"Aye, that I do love you," Ian said proudly.

Moira then looked to Bishop Roderick. "And the bishop knew that there was potential danger due to information I possessed and he felt I needed protecting. Therefore, he sent word to Ian of a possible threat to my life and he staged an altercation on the journey here to substantiate his claim. But the altercation proved more menacing than he ordered, but why? And how did my father learn of this threat and why did my father really go to war with the Camerons?"

Angus answered that question. "The Camerons attacked us."

Ian objected. "I ordered no such attack."

"Aye, you did," Angus insisted. "I had no fight with you. You attacked a clan under my protection and left me no choice."

Moira halted any further debate. "Someone obviously manipulated both clans. The question is why." She paused when a pain tore across her abdomen and she leaned back against her husband.

He took her weight and wrapped a supportive arm around her. "You need the comfort of our bed."

"I need to finish this, for it is important."

He did not argue, for while he worried over her he wished to hear what she had to say and if it proved necessary he would simply scoop her up and carry her to their bedchamber.

Moira continued. "Again the question surfaced, who would benefit. That is when I realized that my death would benefit no one; but my death, the babe's death, and Ian's death would certainly benefit Arran."

All eyes turned to him.

"She speaks foolishly because of the birthing pains," Arran said. "Her words are utter nonsense."

"Are they?" Moira challenged. "This problem with the border clan could have been settled easily. But I think perhaps that you have made an agreement with them to help you in your plan. You hunger for power and wealth, which are the very reasons you wed Brianna. You saw potential in the clan Cameron. After all, if Ian were gone who better to lead the clan than his sister's husband? You had hoped to do away with us all on our return trip home and how lucky you must have felt when your attackers discovered Bishop Roderick's attackers and your group bid them to join."

"This is nonsense, I tell you," Arran insisted indignantly.

"Is it?" Brianna asked quite calmly. "You have never really loved me, have you, Arran?"

"Do not be ridiculous."

Brianna grew teary and turned to her brother. "What Moira says makes sense, for Arran cares for naught but himself."

Arran approached his wife, shaking his head. "Nonsense, Brianna. You are distraught because Moira is older and can bear a child and you cannot." He looked to Ian. "Your sister is barren and cannot accept the fact that she cannot give me a child."

Tears spilled down Brianna's cheeks. "You are selfish, unloving, and I am a fool for ever thinking otherwise."

Moira grew angry over Brianna's hurt and lashed out at Arran. "Why this trouble now with the border clan, Arran? Could it be that when Ian rode off to defend his land, you would dispose of his wife and child while the border clan saw to Ian's demise? Of course that would leave only Brianna, and as her husband you would rule the clan Cameron, quiet the skirmish, and by chance join forces with the border clan? Did you also intend to attack the Macleans?"

Angus shouted several foul words at Arran and his two sons rose behind him, ready to battle. Blair and a few other men stepped forward to prevent an altercation, and with everyone screaming accusations, chaos quickly reigned.

In the middle of the melee Arran drew a knife from his belt, grabbed his wife, and pressed the blade to her throat.

"I will kill her if anyone attempts to stop us," he warned.

Ian gave orders to let them pass and Arran wasted no time; he held firm to his wife and fled the hall.

"Blair," Ian shouted, "organize two groups of men, one to see to the border clan problem and one to go after Arran and return my sister safely to me. I intend to remain here and see to my wife's safety and to the safe delivery of our child."

"I will see to Brianna's safe return," Blair said.

"I have no doubt that you will."

Angus stepped forward. "My sons and I will join you, Blair."

Blair looked to Ian for approval.

"I will not have my sister harmed in any way," Ian said, his heated eyes resting directly on Angus.

"We will see to her safe return. I give you my word," Angus said and offered him his hand.

Ian took it and both men knew a truce had been struck.

Angus cast a glance to his daughter. "Do me proud and deliver your husband a fine son."

Moira held her chin high. "I have always done the clan Maclean proud." And at that moment her water broke and she gave a shout.

Ian had her up in his arms in an instant and Anne, after giving Blair a quick kiss and ordering him to return unharmed to her, followed close behind Ian as he carried his wife to their bedchamber.

Ian prepared for a long night and a difficult birth. Moira

was older and she was certain to have problems. He intended to remain by her side throughout the whole ordeal and do whatever was necessary to help or comfort her.

Anne quickly shooed him aside while she tended to Moira, settling her comfortably in the bed and preparing clean linens around her.

Ian rolled up the sleeves of his shirt. "Tell me what to do."

"Sit and wait," Anne said and continued to scurry about.

Moira held her hand out to him. He took it and sat down on the bed beside her.

"I feel helpless," he admitted.

Moira smiled. "You do not need to be here. Anne can see to everything."

He shook his head adamantly. "I cannot leave you. I will do whatever I can even if I just sit here with you."

"Do not look so fearful," Moira said, attempting to alleviate his concerns. She understood how worried he was; he had after all lost his first wife in childbirth and that thought probably weighed heavily on his mind. And then there was her age. She knew that concerned him, for few women her age gave birth.

A pain ripped through her and she clutched at his hand. He offered her tender and reassuring words and Anne gave him a damp cloth to wipe her brow when the pain had passed.

Ian knew the fear of battle but watching his wife suffer pain after pain was worse than any battle he had ever fought. He thought that any moment he might lose her and he could not imagine life without her.

"The babe intends a hasty entrance," Moira said after a pain subsided, though it was followed quickly by another more potent one.

Ian looked to Anne. "Can this be so? I thought birthing takes time."

Anne shook her head. "The babe decides the birthing time and your babe is impatient or demanding."

It wasn't long after and with little effort and ease that Moira delivered a fine son who quickly demonstrated how healthy he was by releasing a strong, demanding cry.

Ian looked with a mixture of joy, relief, pride, and love at his squalling son and at that moment he realized how truly blessed he was.

The evening grew late and, after seeing to Moira, Anne retired to her room to rest, insisting sleep would elude her until Blair returned safely. She did, however, intend to spend her sleepless time praying for his and Brianna's safe return.

Ian lay stretched out on the bed beside his wife, their son cradled in her arms sleeping comfortably between them.

"You wish a certain name be given to him?" Moira asked with a yawn.

"I thought to name him Duncan after my father," Ian said, unable to keep his eyes off the babe. "He has my father's mighty fists, but he rarely swung them. He relied more on his wisdom."

"Then Duncan is a good name for our son and a good way to honor your father."

Ian kissed her cheek. "I am lucky to have you for a wife."

"Aye, you are," she said with a laugh and yawned again.

"You are tired and should sleep." He ran a gentle hand over her cheeks and faintly brushed his finger over her lips. "You delivered our son much easier than I had thought you would."

Her laugh had faded to a soft smile. "The birth was not as difficult as I expected, but then he was a persistent one and did much of the work."

"Thank you for our son," he said and kissed her lips gently.

She laughed again. "You were the one who started it all and glad I am for it."

"Truly?" he asked with concern.

Her laughter died and she placed a tender hand to her husband's cheek. "Look at him, Ian. He could not have been conceived of lies or deceit—only love could have created someone as wonderful as him."

He kissed the palm of her hand. "I will love you forever."

This time she giggled. "Then we best be careful for with that much love we will be bound to have many children."

Ian placed a protective arm around his wife and son and together they fell into a peaceful slumber.

He was wakened near dawn. Blair had returned with his sister and he immediately went to her bedchamber to see how she fared.

Brianna sat on the edge of the bed crying. Her long hair was tangled with bits of leaves stuck here and there. Dirt and sweat marred her fair complexion and her underdress was ripped at the sleeve. She not only looked disheveled, she felt it.

Ian immediately went to her and sat down beside her, taking her into his arms.

"I am such a fool," she sobbed, pressing her face to his white shirt.

"You are no fool, Brianna," he assured her.

"I thought he loved me."

Her sobs tore at his heart.

"How could I be so wrong?"

He wished Moira were here. She would know what to say to her. Ian was not certain how to comfort her so he finally said what he felt. "I know not how to answer your question, but I do know that Arran is not worth you wasting tears over. He was selfish and deserves no more of your emotions."

Brianna sniffed and wiped at her tear-stained cheeks.

"It will take time to heal from this, but you will and all will be well."

She raised her head. "I hear you have a son and I a nephew."

He smiled proudly. "Aye, and we named him after Father."

"Can I see him?"

"He sleeps, along with Moira."

"I will be quiet," she said softly.

Ian knew it was important for her to see the babe, to see that life continued on, no matter the circumstances. "Do not wake them."

Brianna stood. "I promise. I will be very quiet." She tugged at his hand impatiently, as she had done when they were children and she was eager. "Hurry, I cannot wait to see him."

The babe's cries could be heard as they descended the stairs and with a wide smile Brianna ran into her brother's bedchamber to meet her new nephew.

Blair rounded the corner, Anne by his side. She quickly went in the room to see if Moira needed help, leaving the two men time to talk alone.

"Tell me what you know," Ian said, walking a short distance from the open bedchamber door. He wanted no one to hear their words.

Blair seemed reluctant to speak.

"Tell me," Ian ordered firmly.

"Arran dumped her along the road, shoving her off his horse as if he cared naught for what happened to her. She was lucky she was not seriously injured and lucky no one else came along before we found her."

Ian's eyes flared bright green. "You did not find him?"

"He evaded us and I did not wish to prolong Brianna's ordeal. I left a few men to see if they could pick up his trail or discover what they could."

"I want him, Blair," Ian said, holding back his temper. "He has much to answer for and it is a fitting punishment he deserves."

"His deception has hurt many."

"He will be the one who hurts."

Blair knew then that Ian would hunt the man until his dying day.

"It is a joyous day and we should think of Arran no more," Blair said. "It is time to celebrate the birth of your son."

Ian grinned like a proud new father.

"Congratulations. Anne tells me that he is a fine, healthy babe."

"That he is."

"Where is my grandson?" Angus Maclean shouted, walking up the stairs.

Ian shook his head.

"He is your father-in-law," Blair said with a wide grin.

Angus came into sight, his two sons following eagerly behind him.

"Moira is all right?" Aidan asked.

Ian appreciated the man's concern. Out of the three he cared the most for his sister. "Aye, she is fine."

"My grandson?" Angus asked again and impatiently.

His grandson made his presence known at that moment, crying out like a mighty warrior and causing the five men to smile.

"Come and meet Duncan Cameron," Ian said and led them into the room.

Angus shoved past everyone and walked up to the bed.

Moira lay against several pillows looking more beautiful than Ian had ever seen her. She was radiant, her face flushed with color, her eyes sparkling, and her smile magical.

Angus glanced down at the squalling babe in her arms. His arms swung, his face was bright red, and he screamed until Moira settled him down with a soothing pat to his bottom and a gentle rocking of her arms.

"You did well, daughter," Angus said curtly.

"That I did, Father," she said with confidence.

Aidan made his way around his father to lean down and touch the babe's tiny fingers. Boyd moved to the opposite side of the bed and stared in awe at the little fellow. Blair joined Anne near the bottom of the bed and slipped a firm arm around her waist.

And Ian went to his sister, who fought to control the pool of tears forming heavily in her eyes.

Angus gave the babe one more look then turned and walked to the door.

Aidan and Boyd moved in closer to get a better look at their nephew.

All eyes turned to Angus when he called out, "Moira!"

She stared directly at him, her chin high.

"You are as beautiful as your mother," Angus said and left the room.

Moira looked to her husband and smiled.

✿ thirty-five

The great hall was quiet after the morning meal, most being outside tending to their chores or enjoying the beautiful summer day. Calm and order had finally been restored to the keep within the last six weeks and due to the excitement many guests had remained longer than planned and were just taking their leave.

Moira left Anne to watch over her sleeping son and joined her husband and Bishop Roderick, who was leaving within the hour.

She approached them with a smile though her vibrant eyes settled on her husband. He looked tempting to her. He wore his usual pale yellow linen shirt and his wrapped plaid lay snug over his chest. His long dark hair shined with a silkiness that made her want to reach out and touch it, and his moist lips were simply much too appealing.

She sighed with the familiar want of him, which had grown strong in the last few days. And she refused to deny how much she wanted her husband. She ached for the intimacy that had been absent since the birth of their son and, feeling herself fully recovered, she intended to satisfy that want this evening.

Her smile grew along with her determination.

Ian was pleased to see her happy and he opened his arms in welcome.

She settled into his embrace and she turned his simple kiss into an invitation.

He seemed a bit startled at first, then grinned when their lips parted and whispered, "Tonight, wife."

"Without a doubt, husband," she said with a tap to his chest.

The bishop gave a discreet cough to remind them of his presence.

They stepped apart, their grins remaining.

"It was good to have you here, Bishop," Ian said.

"I am glad to have been here and pleased that I could offer your son baptism," the bishop said. "Before I go I would like to ask you a few questions, Moira."

Ian took his wife's hand and his action reaffirmed that he would always protect her, even against the church.

"What would you like to know, Bishop?" Moira said, confidently and with an appreciative squeeze of her husband's hand.

"The convent prospers far beyond any other and I must admit I have wondered over it." He paused, took a deep breath, and with reluctance asked, "Have you learned the secret of turning metal into gold?"

Moira answered without hesitation. "Knowledge, and hard work, is the secret, Bishop. I learned how to assist crops in growing to their full potential and I crossed certain seeds to produce hardier varieties of plants. I created new dyes for the wool and made improvements to the pottery clay, and of course the new dyes helped create more colorful pieces that soon were in demand because they were unique."

Moira continued to outline the many improvements she had instituted in the convent, and at the keep as well, until finally Bishop Roderick raised his hand and she stopped talking.

"You are a remarkable woman, Moira, and I wish to ask a favor of you, and your husband of course."

She nodded and looked to Ian.

"I cannot agree until I hear the favor," Ian said.

"Of course," the bishop said. "I would like to apprentice a monk or two to Moira so that she may teach them her knowledge."

Moira was startled.

Ian answered. "That is up to Moira, though I will not have my and my son's time robbed from us for her to teach."

Moira soothed his concern. "You and Duncan will always come first to me."

"Then do as you wish," he told her.

Moira grinned. "One monk, Bishop, will I have time for."

The bishop thanked them for their hospitality and took his leave.

Ian and Moira waved to him from the steps of the keep.

"Your father and brothers leave next," Ian said with relief.

"I will miss Aidan," Moira said.

"And I you." Aidan stepped from behind her and they hugged.

Boyd and Angus were a few steps behind him and Boyd gave her a hug as well. Angus simply walked past her and mounted his waiting horse.

"You will bring that fine son of yours to Mull for a visit. He has good lungs and strong fists, he will do the clan Maclean proud."

"In time, Father, I will visit," Moira said, making it known the decision would be hers.

Angus shook his head at Ian. "You will have your hands full with her, but know this. If you hurt her, I will hurt you." He then turned to Moira. "You do your namesake

proud. When you were born I knew you would be strong
and courageous so I named you after a woman who was
just as courageous and who I loved dearly. I named you
after my mother and you do her proud."

Tears threatened Moira's eyes but she held them back
and acknowledged her father with a brief nod. Her heart,
however, swelled with joy.

Aidan and Boyd smiled as they rode off with their father.

Moira smiled as well for her father's words let her
know that he loved her.

"Let us walk in the sunshine," Ian suggested with a hug
and Moira agreed with an eager nod.

They had taken but a few steps when they heard their
son's cries.

Ian pulled his wife to him. "Will I ever get you alone
again?"

Moira had no time to reassure him. Anne appeared at
the keep door with Duncan.

"He is hungry."

"He is always hungry," Ian said with a laugh.

Moira took her son from Anne and they all returned to
the great hall.

Moira settled in a comfortable chair to feed her son and
Ian sat beside her to keep her company.

Blair rushed into the hall, looked about, and hurried
over to Ian.

Ian saw the concern on his face. "What is it?"

"Arran has eluded our men again and this time we can
find no trace of him. His trail turns cold and we know not
where to look."

Ian accepted the news though he did not like it. "We
keep extra guards posted and you and I shall discuss this in
more detail later."

Blair nodded, knowing this was not finished. It had only
begun.

Anne walked over to Blair with a tankard of ale and he

in turn handed it to Ian. He then swung Anne up into his arms.

"It is you I want, lassie." He then kissed her soundly and she turned bright red.

"This wedding best be soon," Ian demanded with a smile.

Blair lowered Anne to the ground but kept a firm hand on hers. "Will you give us your blessings on our forthcoming marriage, Ian, laird of the clan Cameron?"

Ian stood and looked to them both. "May God and the heavens watch over you both and may you know much happiness all yours days together."

Blair and he clasped firm hands. Moira and Anne kissed cheeks.

"I have missed good news?" Brianna asked, hurrying into the hall with a smile that had been absent far too long from her pretty face.

"You must tell her now, Ian," Moira whispered. "It is not fair to keep this from her."

Ian realized his wife advised him wisely but if he could he would keep the news from her, for he knew her smile would fade once again.

Anne chatted away to Brianna about Ian blessing their marriage and how there was much to do and how her help would be appreciated, until finally Ian spoke.

"Brianna, I need to speak with you."

Silence instantly filled the hall and Brianna nodded, her smile already fading.

Brother and sister walked out of the great hall into the bright sunshine. They walked quietly beside each other, their destination known to both though not a word was exchanged. There was a small stream that ran behind the keep and a secluded spot where Ian and she had often gone when young. It was their secret spot and it was there they would share secrets or troublesome news.

It was there Ian had told her of their father's death and

it was there Brianna had held him while he cried for his wife, Kathleen.

They sat on the soft cushion of green foliage that covered the surrounding area like a rich carpet.

Brianna demonstrated her courage. "Do not spare me, Ian, tell me what you must."

It was with deep regret that Ian spoke. "Arran has eluded all our attempts to find him. We do not know where he is nor do we have a fresh trail to follow. He has disappeared."

Brianna nodded, a sadness to her eyes that tore at Ian's heart. "I do not love him, Ian, and I do not care what happens to him. Is that terrible of me?"

Ian slipped a comforting arm around her. "Nay, it is not. He treated you badly and you have a right to feel as you do. I only wish I could have brought this ordeal to a definitive end for you. This way you would be free to find happiness and wed."

Brianna laughed as her tears fell. "I never wish to wed again."

"Nonsense," Ian argued. "You will find a good, handsome man who will treat you right."

Brianna shook her head adamantly. "A good man, aye, a handsome man, nay. If I am lucky enough to find a true love it will be to an ugly man."

"Then I will find you the ugliest man in all of Scotland," Ian said and hugged his sister tightly. "Until that day you will remain here with me and Moira."

Brianna turned a sad smile on him, her eyes wet with tears, and brother and sister sat in silence, holding each other, as they had many times before.

Duncan slept after drinking himself full. The keep itself was silent, it being late in the night, and Moira and Ian were finally alone.

They lay in bed snuggled together as if they could not get close enough.

"I wish to give you a gift for you have presented me with a fine son, and I wish you to decide what that gift shall be."

Moira thought a moment, only a moment, then she smiled and slipped her arms around her husband's neck. "There is something I want."

"Anything."

"You must promise me."

Ian grabbed her around the waist and brought her up tightly against him. "I give you my word, wife." He kissed her then as if sealing a pact.

"I want you, Ian Cameron. I want you as often as I can get you for I love you with all my heart and soul."

He felt his own heart swell with love and knew that his heart was silent no more. It beat with a deep love for a special woman.

He kissed her then and gave her what she wanted. He gave of himself. He gave her his love.